# THE
# KILLING EDGE

# HEATHER GRAHAM

# THE
# KILLING EDGE

MIRA®

ISBN-13: 978-0-7783-2771-4

THE KILLING EDGE

Copyright © 2010 by Heather Graham Pozzessere.

www.MIRABooks.com

**Printed in U.S.A.**

First Printing: April 2010
10 9 8 7 6 5 4 3 2 1

For family and friends in south Florida
who make me glad that Miami has always been home,
especially Graham, Franci and DJ Davant
and my brand-new little nephew Noah Edward Davant!

And for Victoria Sophia, Alicia and Bobby Rosello—
and Anthony Robert Rosello!

# PROLOGUE

Silver.

It was the color of the night, of the light of the full moon seeping in through the open drapes in the living room.

As he entered carefully, mentally calculating the floor plan of the house, he marveled at the brightness of the night.

He stopped and stood over a sleeping young man, then hunkered down and studied the boy's face. So young, bathed in a buttermilk glow, the silver of the night muted, warm and gentle.

He placed a powerful gloved hand over the young man's mouth, then slit his throat, his sharply honed knife moving as smoothly through flesh as the fastest Donzi speeding through a calm sea. It wasn't half as easy as it appeared in movies to slash a throat. Even with a knife as sharp as his, it took effort. And talent.

He had the strength, and he had the talent.

The boy made a slight gurgling sound, but that was it. Two feet away, crashed out on the floor, a young woman slept with her hands curled around a throw pillow. She hadn't heard a thing.

He stepped closer to her.

His overwhelming impression as he stood there was of gold, the color of her hair.

He dispatched her to a more glorious world with swift, cold calculation, then paused to take a good look at her face. He held still for a split second, then told himself to move on. He had not yet achieved his objective. Of course, he wasn't working alone, but still....

He couldn't trust anyone else not to screw things up. Not to mention that *he* was the one with a mission.

He paused again, going dead still. Silence. The house was filled with silence. It was time to make his point before finishing the mission. He dipped his gloved finger in the dead girl's blood, then walked over to the wall, writing quickly so he could finish while the blood was still wet and glistening. There was still so much to be done.

A cloud slid over the moon, bringing pitch darkness in its wake, a blackness that ruled for a few breaths of time.

Black.

How apropos.

Because black was the color of his soul.

★ ★ ★

Red.

Dark, rich crimson.

The color spilled, deep and thick, over the white marble flooring.

At first, hidden beneath the king-size bed in the master bedroom, Chloe Marin was aware only of the richness of the color.

She was so frozen with terror that she couldn't comprehend the meaning behind the flow, only the fact that it was red.

Time had no meaning, either. She didn't know if she had wakened just a few seconds ago, or if a dozen minutes had ticked away. She'd heard something, some sound, as she slept in the beachfront mansion, and though it was enough to wake her up, it hadn't scared her in the least. After all, the housekeeper was sleeping somewhere on the property, as were the two live-in maids, and there were at least twenty young people scattered around the house, ranging in age from sixteen to twenty-one.

David Grant, a big, burly football star, had passed out on the sofa downstairs, she knew. And Kit Ames, his girlfriend, had claimed the floor nearby. Even if it meant sleeping on the floor, Kit wouldn't go far from David. She protected her turf with more ferocity than most of the players demonstrated on the field.

But then something, something too elusive to identify, had alerted her, as if her every sense had been attuned to the night. She'd sensed movement somewhere in the house.

Not the natural movement of those who belonged, those who had been invited in. It was subtle, as if she had heard the slithering of a snake moving through distant grass.

She was sharing a room with two of the other girls, and at first both of them had appeared to be sleeping peacefully. But then she'd realized something was wrong, though she couldn't explain how she'd known it. She'd tried to wake Jen Petersen, but Jen had been so deeply asleep that she hadn't responded to her urgent whispers. She'd had more success with Victoria Preston, who'd just begun to rouse, when she had seen the man enter the room. He'd been all in black, wearing what looked like a black dive suit, including a tight hood that covered everything but his eyes and mouth. He hadn't seen her or Victoria but had gone straight to Jen and stared down at her for a moment. Then, before Chloe could move, he struck.

She tried not to scream and clamped a hand over Victoria's mouth. Jen's bed was close to the door, so to get away they had to make it to the bathroom connecting their room to the bedroom next door. Amazed by how quickly her mind was working in the midst of panic, she grabbed Victoria's arm and dragged her into the bathroom, slamming the door behind them.

Victoria started screaming then, and Chloe shoved her out into the hall. As Chloe started to follow, someone closed the door from the outside, leaving her no choice but to retreat to the other bedroom.

There was more than one stranger in the house, she realized.

More than one killer.

The bedroom door started to open as someone began dragging a body in. A big body.

Chloe quickly plunged under the bed.

The full moon suddenly burst through the clouds, spilling oyster-shell white light across the room through the gaps in the drapes.

That was when she saw red.

Crimson. Spilling across the floor.

Dripping from above her. From a body on the bed.

She tried not to scream and waited, listening. They were barely discernible, but she could hear footsteps. She stared into the room from her hiding place and saw that the killer wore clear plastic freezer bags over his feet. And his dive skin, appropriate for the balmy waters of Florida and the Caribbean, was sold by the thousands in the area.

Two killers, one in this room and one next door. Or were there more? Had Victoria made it down the stairs?

She watched his feet moving stealthily across the floor and into the bathroom.

He would find her there beneath the bed. He was bound to.

Knowing she had no choice, she rolled out from beneath the bed, and carefully, silently, on bare feet, hurried to the door to the hallway. She looked out and saw no one, so she slipped out, hoping to find someone else alive, hoping to find something with which to save herself.

Nothing. No one. She raced along the hall to the stairway. Ochre light filled the living room at the foot of the grand stairway.

Red spilled out across the marble there, too.

Red spelled a message on the wall.

*Death to defilers!*

There was a picture in red, as well....

A strangely shaped hand drawn in blood.

She sensed movement behind her and turned to look. Brad Angsley, Victoria's college-age cousin, was staggering out from one of the other bedrooms, holding his head. She rushed toward him.

"He's right behind us!" he cried

"Move!" she insisted, and helped him stagger down the stairs. As they reached the great entry with its double doors, she dared a quick look back.

Someone was coming after them, another man in black, with some kind of knapsack or canvas bag over his shoulder.

Which killer was he?

Were there more ahead? What would happen when she opened the door? Would another killer be waiting there?

She had no choice but to find out. She struggled briefly with the lock, then threw open the doors and raced out, with Brad clinging to her shoulder. They made it down the long gravel path to the driveway and had almost lost themselves amidst the collection of BMWs, Audis and beat-up cars that belonged to the average kids who had made their way here.

Behind them, closing in on them, she could hear pounding footsteps.

They turned together, and she could see the knife gleaming in the moonlight, the blade dripping blood.

She leaned Brad against a car and grabbed a statue of Poseidon. It was heavy, but she barely noticed its weight as she wrenched it from the ground and swung it with both arms.

She caught their pursuer on the side of the head. He staggered back, and she let out a scream that seemed to last forever, until she realized that Brad had broken into the car, setting off its alarm.

Lights suddenly blazed, illuminating the driveway. Chloe saw Victoria stagger from the trees bordering the drive, holding tight to Jared Walker, who appeared to be unharmed, though his face was ashen.

Victoria was waving a cell phone as she yelled, "Hang on! Help is coming!"

Thank God for technology, Chloe thought.

The lights were coming from the cop cars that were swarming onto the property.

Chloe stared at her attacker, praying that he would fall, that he wouldn't come after them again before the cops could take aim and fire.

The man stared back at her, his mask torn where the statue had caught it, and she felt as if she was staring into the face of pure evil.

Her heart stopped, and she prayed.

But he didn't come closer; instead, he took one look at the approaching cops, then turned and ran.

As if on cue, the moon slipped behind a cloud, and the killer was lost in the deep shadows beside the house.

Cops and paramedics began rushing onto the property.

Someone took Brad; someone else grabbed Chloe, and she opened her mouth to scream.

"It's all right," a man's voice assured her, and she found herself staring at a policeman. "You're hurt. You need help."

"I'm not hurt," she said, then lifted her hands and realized that they were bathed in blood.

Crimson with blood.

Red-shot darkness descended on her, and she slipped into oblivion.

It was over, and yet not over.

In the days and months that followed, she saw them all again. Her friends, with their good traits and their bad, who never had a chance to mature and become good people or selfish assholes.

They haunted her dreams.

She saw them dead, where they had lain on the floor in spreading pools of red.

Yes, she saw them in her dreams. Or were they dreams? She would simply open her eyes to see them there, surrounding her bed, looking at her.

Asking her for help. *Begging* her for help.

"How can I help you...? Tell me," she asked aloud more than once.

But they never answered.

Of course not. They weren't real. They were symptoms of her own psychological stress and trauma.

They were dreams. Bad dreams. Nightmares.

And in the therapy that followed, she was convinced at last that she didn't see them, that they were symptoms of survivor's guilt that haunted her heart and soul, and that only time could ever begin to heal such a wound.

Finally, like mist, silver and gray, they slipped away, and she learned to live.

# ONE

---

*Ten years later*

The old Branoff mansion on the beach was exquisite. Built at the dawn of the area's first age of sophistication, it was over eighty years old and elegant in the Mediterranean-slash-Spanish style of the mid-1920s. It wasn't far from a similar house where, not so many years before, Gianni Versace had been gunned down, and tourists often passed on their way to gawk at the murder scene, establishing their right to say they had been there.

The less notorious mansion, now the local HQ and informal models' dorm for the famed Bryson Agency, sat on an acre of land, with a formidable front lawn, now alight in a rainbow of colors. The gardens and walks were elegant, and the ornate iron gates that controlled access past the ten-foot stone wall that surrounded the villa weren't locked this evening. But access still wasn't easy. The beautiful people were entering tonight for the latest agency party. Mainly beautiful women. The kind of women who, if they didn't already personify absolute perfection, could be airbrushed to get there.

Only the beautiful made it past the guards with the guest list, only the most elegant.

And, of course, those with the most money. This was, after all, the ritzy area of Miami Beach.

As he walked to the gates, displaying his invitation and fake ID to the tuxedoed men on duty, Luke knew he fell into the "rich" category—at least for the evening. Thanks to the fact that he spent the majority of his life in cutoffs and T-shirts, his few ensembles with designer labels were in excellent repair. And thanks, he commended himself dryly, to his tall-but-not-too-tall, just-right build, he was able to disappear into any crowd full of said labels. Despite the age of the clothing, it—and he—fit right in. He wasn't a cop, but he was undercover. He had to fit in.

He didn't usually wear sunglasses at night. But with this crowd, he had surmised that he might look more as if he belonged by wearing them than not. He hadn't been mistaken. Even the guards at the gates checking IDs and invitations were wearing shades. Though in the colorful but soft light bathing the place, he was surprised that they could read anything.

Maybe they didn't read. Maybe they just *knew.* Or perhaps the rumor circulating among the less fortunate was true and exquisite beauty got you in, with or without an invitation.

He noticed that the guards were only scrutinizing the IDs of the "regular" people, and then only if they didn't recognize and approve of the labels being worn.

He thanked the two burly men at the gate who stepped aside after eyeing him carefully. He had the height to match them, but he'd never been built like a bulldog, though he worked out enough each day to keep up the muscle he needed. He supposed, however, that for this evening, his appearance of being tall and lean worked well, and it made the clothes fit better, anyway.

Once across the lawn, as he neared the house, he noticed a bevy of beauties on the porch. They were sipping cocktails and posing. Perched on the railing, seated at the edge of a chair, legs folded just so, elegant and certainly provocative. They weren't being overt about anything—these girls weren't looking for careers as porn stars. They were shooting for the big leagues, for uberstardom. Swimsuit issues and the covers of fashion magazines.

They must have seen instantly that, though his features were attractive, he wasn't young, and he was far from model perfect. In their world, that meant he was money.

He was welcomed with a cascade of hellos and smiles, a few of them more obvious than the rest. He smiled in return and made sure to look like a businessman with a personal interest in the modeling business. The Bryson Agency, with offices not only across the country but around the world, was one of the most reputable in the business, known for creating some of the most highly paid celebrity models of the century, women far above the sleazy sex-for-a-swimsuit-spread trade-offs that were common at the low end of the profession, though he suspected some girls would certainly be more willing than others to engage in a little extracurricular activity to achieve the goal of stardom.

But that was different, of course. Or was it?

But as to the agency being legitimate…

It was so aboveboard, in fact, that only her family and friends had even looked twice at the agency when a girl had disappeared on a shoot. Bryson hired beautiful girls and offered them the world; the disappearance of one would-be model was not enough to keep the star-seekers away. Two months ago, Colleen Rodriguez—a typical young Miami woman whose Cuban and Irish-American genes had combined to create a green-eyed, raven-haired beauty—had disappeared while on a shoot for the agency in the Keys. Both the Monroe County and Miami-Dade authorities had been mystified, and the case remained open, with some believing the girl had been the victim of foul play, while others believed that though she had been seeing a man named Mark Johnston, she was young and impressionable—and ambitious—and might have run off with someone who could offer her a bigger career and the promise of big money. Alive and well or dead and gone, Colleen had been over twenty-one when she had taken the job and sailed off to the shoot on the privately owned island. With no body and no evidence of foul play, she was officially classed as a missing person, and her case remained open.

Luke didn't think she'd left of her own volition, though. Her best friend, Rene Gonzalez, was listed through the agency, as well. Rene was avoiding her parents, certain that their overprotective instincts in the wake of Colleen's disappearance were going to cost her a career, so whether she really believed it or not, she was insisting that Colleen had disappeared on purpose. And so he was here, suddenly an up-and-coming designer, to find a way to speak with Rene and see what she knew that could help him discover the truth about Colleen.

"Hi there." A lissome blonde uncrossed long legs and stood as she saw him coming, then offered him a perfectly manicured hand. "I'm Lena Marconi. And you're...?"

Luke produced a card. "Jack Smith, Mermaid Designs," he said. "A pleasure to meet you."

"Mermaid Designs?" Lena asked, her gray eyes smoldering. "Beach clothing?"

"Exactly, women's beach clothing," Luke said. "Bikinis, tankinis—'inis' of all kinds."

"How wonderful," Lena gushed.

A dark-haired woman rose with a fluidity that might have been spellbinding if it hadn't been so practiced. "A bathing-suit designer! How perfect. They're just starting to plan the next agency swimsuit calendar, you know," she said as she offered an elegant hand. "Maddy Trent, late of Amarillo, Texas, and quite fond of South Beach. A pleasure to meet you, Mr. Smith."

"Likewise," he assured her.

There were two more women sitting on the porch, both blondes. The first, very light, with huge blue eyes and a look of friendly amusement about her, rose. "Hi there, Mr.

Smith. I'm Victoria Preston. Please, come in. I'll introduce you to Myra—Myra Allen, the head of the Miami office—and see that you get something to drink."

The fourth woman, seated on a gently swinging wicker love seat, didn't move, though she looked at him assessingly. There was a touch of red in the smooth fall of blond hair that curled around her shoulders. Her eyes were green, lime-green, almost like a cat's eyes. She continued to survey him thoughtfully, without speaking. Strange—she didn't look as if she was trying to appear cool and aloof; she was just more interested in studying him than introducing herself.

Interesting.

"Chloe?" Victoria Preston said quietly.

"Oh, of course." The woman with the sunset-streaked blond hair rose. She was tall, five-nine, maybe, hard to tell. She was wearing sandals with small, weirdly shaped heels, probably the newest thing. She wasn't the most classically beautiful of the four—that title would have gone to Victoria—but she *was* the most intriguing. It was her eyes. They were light colored, but also large and well set, and just slightly tilted, giving her a look of mystery. She had a wide smile and full lips, perfect white teeth. A necessity, he imagined, in her business. She wasn't quite as thin as the others; she looked more like an athlete or a runner.

She offered him a hand at last. "Chloe…Marin," she said.

It was a strange hesitation, as if she didn't really want to identify herself. The first name came easily, the surname not so much. Maybe it was a model's equivalent of a pen name because she had a tongue twister of a last name with twenty syllables or six consonants in a row. Awkward to say. Schwartzenkopfelmeyer or Xenoskayanovich or something.

Or maybe, instinctively, she just didn't trust him.

"Chloe, nice to meet you," he said.

"You're a designer?" she said.

He nodded.

The ghost of a smile played over her lips, and skepticism touched her eyes.

"Chloe, let's introduce Mr. Smith to Myra," Victoria urged.

"Oh, look who's coming!" Maddy drawled. "It's Vincente!"

"Vincente…who?" Lena asked.

"Vincente. Just Vincente," Maddy said. "There was just a huge article on him in *GQ!*"

Luke tried not laugh out loud; he had just become dog chow as far as Maddy from Amarillo was concerned.

"Come on in, Mr. Smith," Victoria told him, and led the way. Chloe followed them.

The house was even more elegant inside than out. They had barely stepped into the travertine entryway before a uniformed server was there to offer him champagne from a silver tray. He accepted a glass with thanks, noticing that the women didn't follow suit.

Maybe it was the expensive stuff, reserved for clients and the other guests.

They kept going, to a living room with mile-high ceilings, a curving white staircase and white marble flooring covered with expensive rugs. The house boasted a huge fireplace and mantel, though he was sure the fireplace hadn't been used in decades.

Three pairs of French doors led to a massive patio with a pool and adjacent hot tub. They stepped out and headed for a tiki bar set up at the south end of the pool, weaving past small groups of extravagantly dressed people on their way.

"That's Myra," Victoria said, pointing out a woman to the left of the bar. She was speaking with two women who appeared to be in their early forties, attractive in simple black dresses, short black hair and medium black heels. "She's talking to the women from Rostini. You've heard of the label?"

Not before today, when he had crammed on the fashion industry. "Rostini," he said, nodding. He felt Chloe watching him, and sensed that she was suspicious. *Of what?*

"They make a lovely couple. When you think that they met at college and have lasted longer than a lot of marriages…They're *the* name in cocktail dresses, if you ask me," he added.

Myra looked up from her conversation just then and saw the three of them drawing near. He'd met the woman once before, to set up his invitation for the evening, but he kept his gaze bland, as if he'd never seen her before.

She smiled, and waved them over, her own expression a match for his. He might only have met her once, but he found her fascinating. Myra Allen had once been a super-model herself, until shooting a commercial on the beach had left her with a scarred cheek. She had accepted an administrative job with Bryson Agency while she convalesced, and she had also accepted a nice settlement from the client's insurance company. Rather than accept plastic surgery or rely on makeup and go back to work in modeling, she had risen swiftly in the company and now managed one of their most lucrative locations, the Miami Beach mansion.

She was still a beautiful woman. Tall, slim and capable of turning on a warm smile.

"Mr. Smith," she said. "You've made it. I'm delighted."

She extended a hand, and he stepped forward to take it, wondering, from the way she presented it, if he was supposed to kiss her fingers. No, a Frenchman certainly would, but he was an expat Brit living and working in the U.S.

He shook her hand.

She smoothed back a lock of sable brown hair cut at a sophisticated angle. "Mr. Smith, Josie Rowan and Isabel Santini. I'm sure you know they—"

"Are Rostini, of course," he said, smiling at the women.

After that, Myra took over, leading him back into the living room, introducing him to various people in the business.

Jesse and Ralph Donovan, a young couple who designed evening wear together. Bob—or Bobby—Oscar, flamboyant and arrogant, but hardly someone who seemed liable to seduce a young woman into disappearing. Cindy Klein, dramatic and conceited, but a powerful player with one of the biggest labels in the world.

Harry Lee was there, too—a big shot with the Bryson group. He was a man of about sixty, slim, articulate and impeccably dressed. Another man, nondescript—small, slim and wearing large black-rimmed glasses—seemed to be his assistant, completely at his beck and call. Not unexpectedly, a veritable flock of women also surrounded him.

Harry Lee seemed to take Luke at face value and was glad to welcome him to the party. "Nothing like Miami Beach. Each of our offices does a swimsuit calendar, but this one is, arguably, the most important. Miami is known for— frankly—hot bodies. Beach bodies. Of course, too many women walk around in suits too small to hold a teacup Yorkie." He paused to shudder. "But the beautiful bodies are here, as well, and naturally we take full advantage of that. Myra tells me you'll be shooting your first catalogue in tandem with our calendar shoot. So, welcome. As you're about to see firsthand, Bryson will always be known for the most spectacular and most talented models. Nothing will ever change that fact."

Luke politely agreed with him, then moved on.

To the young women.

To the "most spectacular and most talented models."

He couldn't help recognizing Lacy Taylor, the wholesome beauty who had graced the covers of at least a dozen major magazines. She was pleasant but vague, and he was sorry to realize that she was high, as well as more than a little drunk, which was when he noticed the small, mousy brunette following her everywhere, making certain she didn't crash into a table or drown in the pool. Lena Marconi, energetic and sweet, reappeared and granted him a few minutes when she wasn't chasing down Vincente. Lena seemed to have the energy to cover all the bases— and in her mind he might just be the next hot thing, which made him a base worth covering. Then there was Jeanne LaRue—a *professional* name, he was certain—who was tall, slim, angular and, he assumed, ultrachic, but she was also hard-edged, the opposite of the naturally stunning Lacy, who didn't have to work to draw as much attention as she could possibly desire. Lacy was like a golden-retriever puppy; Jeanne was like a pit bull. There were plenty of other models in attendance, but he saw no sign of Rene Gonzalez.

He managed not to embarrass himself in conversation, because everyone else seemed happy to do most of the talking. As long as he nodded appreciatively now and then, and agreed with whatever other people said, they seemed to like him.

He still managed to find out a few things, though; he just had to be careful with his questioning. He asked Myra first about Rene, learning that oh, yes, certainly, she would be along at some point.

Jeanne LaRue was uninterested in the subject when he sat down beside her at the bar. She knew Rene, but in her opinion the girl was gawky, and she had no experience, so if he was planning on doing a beach shoot, he wouldn't be getting much for his money by hiring Rene. "Victoria knows her stuff. She would be good. And Lacy, of course. As long as you can keep her sober, though she has done some exquisite doped-out shots for that new perfume, Dream. And naturally you'll want me. I'm the best. Especially in a bathing suit."

He frowned. "What about that other girl? Colleen Rodriguez? For a couple of weeks, her disappearance was all over the news, and then people seemed to forget all about her."

Jeanne wrinkled her nose. "Because the little twit obviously fell in love and decided to hightail it."

"Odd. If you fall in love, don't you announce it to the world?"

Jeanne was clearly getting bored with so much conversation about another woman. "Maybe it's some kind of a publicity stunt. You know, some kind of scam. I hope they put her in jail when they find her—she nearly ruined everything."

"Oh? Aren't you worried about her? Was—isn't she a friend?"

"Sure—we're all friends. But she behaved like a selfish brat. We were all on the island, shooting an ad, and everyone was happy—then she just up and disappeared. *With* her purse and passport, I'd like to point out."

"But she didn't take all her things?"

Jeanne waved a hand in the air. "I don't know what she did and didn't take. I didn't room with her. I don't room with anyone. It's in my contract. You could talk to Lacy. They roomed together. That Colleen, she was clever. Lacy is the golden girl, and Colleen knew that and hung around her, looked out for her. If anyone knows anything, it's Lacy. Of course, Lacy is tweaked half the time, so if Colleen walked by her on the way out and told her where she was going, Lacy might not have noticed."

He made a mental note to talk to Lacy about Colleen Rodriguez, preferably when she was sober. But tonight he needed to find Rene.

Jeanne was going on about her competition again, though. "I don't know about Chloe Marin. She's best for something a bit sporty. She does have those unusual eyes, though. And great breasts—which, from what I understand, are all hers.

Personally, I think a little silicone helps the puppies stay right up where they're supposed to be. And I've yet to meet a man who objects, and most seem to prefer it. What do you have to say to that, Mr. Smith? I'm right, aren't I?"

She was fishing for a compliment, he realized, leaning closer and actually coming on to him.

He lowered his head, trying not to smile and betray his amusement. She no doubt expected him to take her up on her not-so-subtle offer. There was a time in his life when he would have, those days of his youth when he was eager and raw, thrilled by the prospect of shagging just about anything that moved. But those days were long in the past. It wasn't that his life had come to fruition with a deep relationship. In fact, his deepest relationship had ended bitterly. He didn't know what he wanted yet, but he knew it wasn't what Jeanne LaRue was offering.

No sharp edges, no daggers, no bartering. Not in the bedroom.

As he considered his response carefully, he was jolted—literally—by the arrival of someone at his side.

"Oh, I'm so sorry. I didn't mean to push you out of your seat."

He turned, saved from having to make a reply by the arrival of the all-natural assets in question.

Chloe Marin had come up on the other side of him, and he couldn't have been more surprised by the effect she had on him, her eyes wide and intent, the soft and ethereal scent of her perfume sweeping over him. She was different from the others. He had an impression of the world's most sinuous and elegant cat. It wasn't overt, and yet she had an amazingly sensual allure.

She continued to stare at him with those cool jaguar eyes, and he realized he was being studied.

She accepted two beers from the bartender and slid one in front of him, then leaned close to ask softly, "Do you need rescuing?"

"Well…"

"It's not a complex question. You may not want to be rescued. If that's the case, I'll slip away and let you enjoy Jeanne's…company. If not…"

"I'll slip away with you, if I may," he returned, his own voice low.

She didn't smile flirtatiously. She hadn't been flirting, had simply noticed his plight and given him a chance to escape if he wanted to.

She spoke more loudly. "Mr. Smith, Victoria's cousin Brad has arrived. I mentioned him to you earlier."

He turned to Jeanne. "If you'll excuse me, Miss LaRue. Miss Marin has pointed out someone I need to meet."

"It's Brad," Chloe explained. "He's going to need to rent transportation for his catalogue shoot."

"He should just hop on a company boat," Jeanne said.

"He'll want his own transportation. Anyway, the more boats, the more fun," Chloe said.

Jeanne frowned, as if wondering what experience Chloe was drawing on to support that statement, but Chloe didn't wait for the other woman to continue the conversation, just slipped an arm through his and steered him away. "Brad owns a fleet of rental boats. And if you're going to be going back and forth to the island while we shoot, you'll be glad to have your own transportation."

She was friendly, helpful, and yet she was also aloof. There was a contradiction somewhere in Chloe Marin that aroused his suspicions.

"Is Rene Gonzalez going to be part of the calendar shoot?" he asked.

She glanced over at him sharply. "Rene? I'm not sure."

"I would have expected her to be here tonight."

"Really? And what do you know about Rene Gonzalez?"

"I've heard that she's very exotic looking, perfect for what I want for my catalogue," he said.

"She *is* lovely," Chloe said, and offered nothing more.

At the far end of the pool, they found Victoria standing with two men, both of them late twenties or early thirties, dressed in the appropriate Miami-chic attire, handsome jacket, open-neck shirt, no tie, creased slacks, everything with a designer label. One was a sandy-haired man with a short, spiked-and-gelled cut, and the other was darker, his hair a thick fall that slashed across his forehead. They might have been a pair of rockers on their way up.

"Mr. Smith, you've met Victoria, and I'd like you to meet Jared Walker and Brad Angsley. Brad is Victoria's cousin," she added, nodding toward the dark-haired man.

"Nice to meet you," Luke said. "Call me Jack, please," he added.

"Jack's one of the up-and-coming designers here tonight," Chloe explained. "He wants to do a catalogue shoot for his new line while we're shooting the swimsuit calendar down in the Keys. And I've told him that it's simply no fun being out on an island if you don't have a boat. A nice little cabin cruiser. And who but you to hook him up?" she asked Brad.

"It's what I do," Brad told him, smiling with boyish charm.

Luke was startled when Victoria shivered. "That island— we shouldn't be going back out to that island."

Jared slipped an arm around her shoulders. There was sincere affection in both his eyes and his tone as he said, "Victoria, there's nothing evil about the island."

"It's where Colleen disappeared," Chloe said flatly. She was addressing Jared, but she nodded toward Luke. "Mr. Smith—Jack—is a new client for the agency. We should be hyping the shoot, not scaring him off."

Brad smiled at Luke. "She's right. And you'll love the place. It's the agency's own little piece of pristine heaven. Not to mention that it's three miles from Islamorada, which you must have heard of. It's the sportfishing capital of the Keys, for sure, maybe the world."

"Still, it's true. It *is* where Colleen suddenly went missing," Chloe said. Push-pull. She had said they shouldn't frighten him, yet here she was focusing on the other woman's disappearance. Clearly she didn't want to let the conversation drop, and she kept glancing at him, which definitely struck him as strange.

"I did hear about that," Luke said. "Are they sure nothing happened to her? I mean, why would she just disappear?"

Jared shook his head. "Who knows? Models tend to be emotional and just plain crazy."

"Hey!" Victoria elbowed him.

"Most models. *Some* models," Jared said. "Not you, Vickie. You're totally sane."

"But, honestly," Brad said, lowering his voice, though with the conversations going on around them and the pulsing music playing in the background, it was unlikely anyone could hear them. "Tell me that Jeanne LaRue isn't a bit on the wacko side."

"She's...blunt, that's all," Victoria said.

Jared snorted. "She'd walk over her own mother in spike heels if it would get her where she wants to go."

"But she's honest about it," Chloe said. "I like that. What's that saying? Something about the enemy I can see being less dangerous than the friend I trust?"

"Yeah, something like that," Brad agreed. He slipped a hand into his jacket pocket and produced a card for Luke. "While I'm thinking about it. We'll get you set up for the shoot. Lots of people fly in, but you're not even talking fifty miles, and a boat gives you a lot more control over your schedule. You know anything about boats?"

"Actually, I do," Luke assured him.

Brad nodded. "Then it will be up to you whether you want a captain to come along or not. Depends what you'll find more relaxing."

"Are you associated with the agency?" Luke asked him.

Brad laughed. "No, not really. But I'm Vick's cousin, kind of like her big brother, so I watch out for her."

"And Chloe," Victoria said.

Brad blinked. "And Chloe. Of course."

"We've all known each other a long time," Jared said.

"So you're all from the area?" Luke asked.

"Born and bred," Jared assured him, and grinned. "I have no association with the agency at all, though. I just tag along because we're all friends, and the girls set me up now and then. I wouldn't mind doing some modeling, though." He lowered his voice. "This is actually a big night for me. First time I've actually met Myra Allen."

"Myra likes working from the mansion or, if she even goes along to a shoot, her hotel room. She's not into the great outdoors," Brad said.

"She's a legend, though, and it's really cool to finally meet her," Jared said.

"Sounds like somebody's got a crush," Victoria teased.

"My only crush is on you. Myra Allen is on a pedestal, to be—worshipped from afar," Jared assured her.

He was speaking casually, but Luke had seen the way he looked at Victoria, how his eyes softened when he spoke to her, even jokingly. He was in love. Maybe he'd been pining away for years. Victoria might set him up on dates with some of the other models, and he might go, but it meant nothing. He was in love with her.

"Besides," Jared said, his eyes steely as he spoke, "I don't buy it that Colleen Rodriguez just up and left. I think something happened to her, so if you girls are going out there, then I'm going, too."

From the corner of his eye, Luke saw through to the living room and got a fleeting glimpse of someone slipping through on their way to the stairs.

"What do you think—Jack?" Victoria asked.

"Pardon?" he said, distracted. He needed to get away, get upstairs and see what was going on.

He turned to make his excuses and noticed that Chloe wasn't standing there any longer.

Luke excused himself quickly, saying he was on a search for the loo—a term that made them all smile—and quickly headed inside. He moved carefully through the crowd and up the stairs.

The place was huge—he wasn't sure how many rooms were up here, but he had a sudden and inexplicable feeling that Rene Gonzalez was in one of them.

He opened the door to a large master suite. No one, though it looked as if someone was living there. He saw pictures on the dresser, and chanced a quick look. The images were of Myra—when she had been young and incredibly perfect.

He left that room and tried the next. There was a bag at the foot of the bed, and the luggage tag said Jeanne LaRue. So she was making the mansion home, too, at least for now.

A third room turned out to be Lacy's. Teddy bears adorned the bed.

He moved more quickly. The next room was occupied, as well, but it seemed that whoever was staying there was keeping the space impersonal.

As he glanced around, though, he saw movement. The sheer drapes over the doors that led out to the balcony were shifting. He hurried over and discovered a sturdy wooden trellis that could easily be reached by climbing over the balustrade.

And someone—a woman—was running across the side lawn, on the other side of the trees that lined the pool. She was headed toward the back of the property. Luke had studied the plans and knew the wall went all the way around, unbroken except for a second gate that could be opened for easy beach access.

The gate shouldn't be open tonight, but that didn't mean someone *couldn't* open it. And he didn't see any guards there.

He was certain now that the racing figure was Rene Gonzalez, alerted by the fact that her thick dark hair trailed behind her in the wind as she ran.

Would she make it to the beach? Or would she find herself trapped? And was she running from him? Had she heard he was looking for her, or was she fleeing whoever had engineered the disappearance of Colleen Rodriguez?

He quickly crawled over the railing and started down the trellis.

Then he heard someone clear their throat and looked up.

Chloe Marin was standing at the railing, staring at him with sharp suspicion.

"I'd heard you were looking for the bathroom, Mr. Smith. You really don't have to climb down from the balcony and make use of the beach as a 'loo,' as you call it—I'm assuming that's the story you're going to give me?" she asked sweetly.

Rene Gonzalez was slipping away.

"Nothing like the great outdoors," he said, then swiftly climbed down a few feet, praying the trellis would hold, jumped to the ground and took off in pursuit of Rene Gonzalez.

# TWO

---

Damn the man.

She wasn't dressed to go swinging from balconies and leaping to the ground.

But the man who called himself Jack Smith had been beyond suspicious even before he'd climbed down from the balcony and followed Rene toward the beach—a feat that put her in a position where she longed to call in the police. But at the moment, what would be the point? He had an invitation to be here, though he'd certainly been a rude guest, looking into bedrooms, not to mention leaping off a balcony. Still, Victoria had told her that two years ago Bjorn Bradikoff, famed for his jeweled sandals, had streaked down the beach in nothing but a pair of his trademark sandals, proving their elegance, whether matched with cocktail finery, casual attire or nothing at all.

Compared to that, exiting via balcony wouldn't even begin to get a man arrested.

Swearing, she tossed off her borrowed designer heels and swung a leg over the balcony railing, carefully maneuvering herself to the trellis. She crawled down the latticework, amazed that none of the slender slats had broken. Just as she thanked her lucky stars, she grasped at a piece of wood that split in her hands, and tumbled down the last six feet, landing hard in a patch of mixed dirt and sand, but avoiding the sharp-toothed needles of the bougainvillea that grew in a riot of color around the house.

Swearing more vociferously, she got to her feet, dusted herself off and followed in the direction the other two had taken.

As she tore around the trees, she felt a twinge of guilt; her uncle would be furious with her for going in unprepared pursuit of a man who might be dangerous, might even be armed.

But she didn't think so. At least, she was pretty sure he wasn't armed, though he might well be dangerous. Certainly in her observations of the agency, he was the first truly suspicious character she had seen. Then again, it could be hard to tell sometimes. Eccentricities could hide all kinds of stains on the human soul, and it was often difficult to tell the truth from illusion.

The man had an educated, British accent. Or was it feigned? Probably not. It was slight, as if he'd been away from his homeland for many years.

The back gates were open. There was one guard on duty,

but he was flirting with someone Chloe didn't know, a slim young woman with long blazing red hair. She was wearing a strapless tube gown and doing it very well. If Chloe was right in her assumption that the other woman wasn't on the guest list, then apparently the guard wasn't above allowing uninvited guests into the party, at least if they met his own personal requirements.

She herself was now covered in dirt, sand and bits of bracken, and her hair was undoubtedly in a wild tangle. She should ask the guard if he'd seen anyone exit, but she doubted he had seen anyone but the flirty redhead.

She tore out to the beach. Neither the guard nor the redhead spared her a glance. So much for security.

She ran south down the beach, following a trail of foot-steps in the sand that led from the mansion. She wasn't afraid; she could see late-night wanderers as she ran. Remodeled deco hotels, which had once been cheap housing for down-on-their-luck locals, now gleamed proudly in the night, lit in bright colors that drew the eye. The gentle sound of the surf made a pleasant background, and the breeze was almost dainty, carrying in a cooling note from the water.

How far could they have made it so quickly?

Chloe stopped running. They could have gone anywhere. Their footprints had gotten mingled with all those left over from the day.

She caught her breath as she looked around. They could have gone in a half-dozen different directions. Not only were their footprints impossible to distinguish anymore, she had passed at least five hotels, restaurants and clubs as she ran, and the pair could have ducked into any one of them. Not to mention that a block ahead, the hotels and restaurants shifted, and were all on the other side of the street, providing another range of possible hiding places.

What if this man had something to do with Colleen Rodriguez's disappearance? Was Rene in danger now, too?

She closed her eyes, fighting a wave of panic.

Every once in a while, hitting so briefly that no one else even noticed, it came. That sensation of absolute terror. A memory of the colors of death that had bathed the world in red and black that night ten years ago.

This had nothing to do with the past, she told herself. Nothing at all.

She fought the panic, and as quickly as it had come, it was gone. Fighting back had become her way of coping on a day-to-day basis with what had happened a decade before. Her uncle had told her that she could curl up and hide for the rest of her life, or she could learn to live again.

She had chosen to live. And she had taken classes in every form of defensive—and even offensive—fighting that she could. She had also become a crack shot.

She could even string a crossbow.

But all the training in the world couldn't help if you couldn't find the person you were trying to protect.

It was time to go back. To admit defeat. To live to fight another day.

Except that this was what she was fighting for. To discover the truth about the Bryson Agency and the disappearance of a young woman who'd had everything to live for.

She turned around to head back and was stunned to find herself staring at Jack Smith.

"Where's Rene?" she asked, immediately going on the offensive.

"You tell me. And thanks for confirming that that *was* Rene. At least we know she's alive at the moment, and presumably well."

Chloe frowned, watching him. "What is your concern with Rene?"

He shrugged.

He was an interesting man, she decided. Tall and lean, but with broad shoulders and hard-muscled arms, and an abdomen that was probably like steel. And his eyes. They seemed to cut right through her. His face had too much of a hard, rugged edge to be termed handsome, but somehow the conglomeration of all his features made him more attractive than any of the perfect models back at the party. He was undeniably compelling. She was extremely suspicious of him, and yet…being close to him seemed to make the night warmer. She had the sense that touching him now would be like trying to hold on to an electric shock. He'd been courteous when they'd been introduced before…but there was something in his eyes. Something hard. And it made him all the more suspicious—and, somehow, physically appealing.

"She'll make a great swimsuit model," he said.

"So great that you were wandering around upstairs—hunting her down?" Chloe demanded.

"You have to break a few rules to get ahead in this world," he told her. "So, your turn. Why were you chasing me?"

"Because you were chasing Rene."

"Why wasn't Rene at the party when she *was* at the house?" he demanded. "You girls are tight—I assume. Or are you?"

She was a fake, of course.

But the others were the real thing.

"I don't know," Chloe said. "Maybe she was afraid that some strange new designer would be looking for her. Some guy who'd gone a little off the deep end, enough to chase her down a trellis and all along the beach."

He grinned at that. She was surprised to see how that grin made him…even more appealing and…flat-out sexy.

Dangerously so? she wondered. After all, some of the most heinous killers in history had exuded a deadly charm.

"All's fair in the fashion industry, or so I understand," he said.

As they stood there, frozen in an odd face-off, someone suddenly emerged from the low foliage that separated the sand from the street.

It was Rene, and she jetted off like a rabbit in alarm.

Jack immediately lost interest in their conversation and turned to go after Rene.

Chloe's own response was impulsive—and protective. She flew across the sand after him and leaped onto his back. To her amazement, he managed to remain upright and sling her around so that she fell to the sand. He started to run again, and she caught his ankle. Still, he didn't fall, not until she twisted around in a mixed–martial arts movement that brought him down at last.

She didn't need to win; she just needed to buy enough time for Rene to disappear somewhere. She didn't know what was going on, but designers did not chase down models, whether all was fair in fashion or not.

Chloe jumped back to her feet—it was her turn to run.

But apparently he knew he'd lost Rene and had decided to maintain whatever connection he had with her instead. This time *he* caught *her* ankle, and she plunged back to the sand. Before she knew it, he was straddling her, pinning her wrists. He wasn't really trying to hurt her, though. His hold was easy, and he was keeping his full weight off her.

"All right, time for an honest conversation," he said. He spoke like a man accustomed to being in command, and she resented it. But she was also acutely aware of the way his thighs cradled her body as he held her down. Warmth spread through her, and she was appalled by the way she found herself wondering what he would be like if he cared about a woman....

She gritted her teeth. They were engaged in a physical battle, she could be in danger, and he could be a monster. What the hell was wrong with her?

The man couldn't be a monster. Every instinct she had was sure of it.

She told herself not to be an idiot. An untold number of dead women had no doubt told themselves the same thing.

No. There would be no conversation, and no letting him maintain that edge of authority. Her wrists might be pinned, but her legs were free, and she could tell that he wasn't prepared for her to fight back. She twisted and slammed her knees up at the same time. To her delight, she did take him by surprise, throwing him off to the side.

But he was quick to rebound. He caught her before she

could rise. She tried a feint to the left, but he was ready, so she became a flurry of motion. He swore, trying to contain her flying arms and legs, but she got in one good whack to his chin; she heard the *thunk* and his grunt of pain.

But he didn't give up. She might be a vicious terrier, but it seemed she had come across a rottweiler.

And he was still trying to restrain her, not knock her out. She had definitely hurt him, but he was just fighting for control—and he was winning.

"Hey, hey, hey! What the hell is going on?"

Chloe knew the voice, and she sighed with relief.

Lieutenant Anthony Stuckey, metro police. Stuckey never had to leave a desk these days unless he wanted to, but he was an old-time cop, and—he wanted to. He was friends with her uncle Leo, and friends with her. He had encouraged her to pursue her interest in art after her sketches had helped solve her own case, and he had encouraged her to use her artistic talent to help the police, though he also spent plenty of time warning her that she *wasn't* a cop herself.

"Tony! Help!" she cried.

"Officer," Jack Smith said.

He rose, as calmly as if they'd just been lying there soaking up the moonlight, not fighting like a couple of rival gang members.

When she started to scramble to her feet, he offered her a hand, but she slapped it away.

"This man was trying to attack one of the models at the Bryson party," she informed Stuckey.

"This young woman is mistaken. I didn't attack anyone. As I'm sure you know, Lieutenant Stuckey."

Chloe's jaw dropped, and she snapped it shut quickly. This man knew Stuckey!

She stared at the lieutenant. He was built as powerfully as a bull and didn't have much of a neck. He kept his snow-white hair cropped close to his skull, and his eyes were a clear sky blue that were incapable of mirroring anything but the truth.

And in his eyes she saw that it was true. He and this man knew one another.

Stuckey looked at her. "I gather there's been a misunderstanding of some sort," he said.

She kept her jaw clamped tight, beginning to feel belligerent. Stuckey had found Jack all but beating her to a pulp, and now he was excusing the man?

"What are you doing out here?" he asked her.

"I was at the party," Chloe said. "As you know."

Stuckey's bushy brows drew together. "Yes, why did you leave the party?"

"Because this man was chasing Rene."

"Chloe, we've talked about situations like this," Stuckey said.

Yes, they had talked about it. Often. He was one of her best friends—or so she had thought until just now. She had even promised that she would never let her "sniffing around" lead her into danger—such as leaving a crowded area to take risks alone—but... She dropped that uncomfortable topic for one that could feed her anger.

Since when was Stuckey buddy-buddy with the local fashionistas?

Which simply proved the truth of what she'd already been sure of. Jack Smith was no designer. So who—and what—the hell was he?

"Let's take this inside somewhere," Stuckey said—and it was not a suggestion.

Chloe realized that a small crowd had begun to gather around them. Stuckey took her by the arm and started toward the street and his car. It was a good thing he was a cop, she mused. Parking on South Beach at night was a near impossibility.

She was aware that Jack Smith was following them, and she wasn't pleased. If she'd truly been a terrier, the hackles on her back would have risen.

"Where are we going?" she asked Stuckey.

"Somewhere private," he said. "We can duck into Jimmy Ray's—it's too late for the teenagers to be hanging out, too early for the club crowd to be looking for a snack on the way home. We can find a booth."

"I don't have shoes," she said.

"You can wear my flip-flops."

They stopped at his car. Here on the sidewalk, the night was alive. Bands from a dozen clubs vied for dominance. People were everywhere, some in a hurry, some just soaking in the neon lights and the music.

Cars moved past at a snail's pace.

Stuckey opened the passenger door and grabbed a large pair of flip-flops. She slipped them on. It looked as if she was wearing shoes intended for Frankenstein's monster.

"They'll do," Stuckey told her curtly.

So far, Jack Smith—a name she was growing more and more certain wasn't the one he'd been born with—hadn't uttered a word. He gazed at Chloe as she took her first step, trying to keep the shoes on. His eyes were silver, and they had an edge. Everything about the man had an edge, from the angles of his face to the tone of his voice, and that edge seemed to demand respect. There was something about him. She didn't like him. She was attracted to him, but she didn't like him. And that was that.

No matter what Stuckey might have to say, she didn't trust the man.

They made it across the street and down the crowded walk to the ivied opening that led down a narrow alley to Jimmy Ray's.

Jimmy Ray had been born and bred on South Beach. He liked to talk about the old days, and he knew what he was talking about, too, because he had to be somewhere in his eighties. But he still worked every day, and he served the best pizza on the beach. He also had the best bar, and the lowest prices on mixed drinks. There was never a DJ there blasting dance music, though he brought in an acoustic guitarist now and then, someone with a mellow voice. People went to Jimmy Ray's to talk, because he knew there was no talking when you had to compete with blasting speakers.

As Stuckey had predicted, the place was relatively quiet.

"Hey, Jimmy Ray!" he called as they entered.

Jimmy Ray, bald as a buzzard and equally intimidating, looked up from behind the counter. "Hey, Stuckey. Chloe."

He didn't greet Jack. Chloe was glad.

Stuckey had the good sense to usher her into a booth, then follow her in to sit beside her, blocking any escape. Jack Smith sat down across from them.

Stuckey rubbed his hand over the crisp white hair on his head. "All right," he began, then stopped. Jimmy Ray had sent his waitress, Katia, over to them, her order pad in hand. "Coffee for me," he said. "And...ah, hell, I'm here. A Mighty Meat pizza."

"Chloe?" Katia asked. She was a very pretty girl, an immigrant from Ukraine, and had only been there for five years. In that time, she had learned English with only the trace of an accent.

Chloe smiled at her. "Iced tea, please."

She was disturbed when Katia turned to the newcomer and smiled—familiarly. "And what would you like, Luke?"

She'd been right about one thing, Chloe thought with satisfaction. He wasn't Jack Smith.

"Coffee, thanks, Katia," he said.

Katia went away, and Stuckey turned to Chloe. "Seems as if we ought to start from the beginning. Chloe, this is Luke Cane. Luke, Chloe Marin."

"Luke," she said sweetly, staring at him.

"Miss Marin," he returned.

"Chloe Marin," Stuckey said, frowning, as if he wondered if he had remembered to mention her first name. "Chloe, Luke is investigating the disappearance of Colleen Rodriguez and looking into what's going on with Rene Gonzalez."

She stared across the table, frowning.

"But nothing's happened to Rene—until he chased her away tonight," she said, staring accusingly at Luke.

"Her parents have been worried," Stuckey explained. "The last few times they called the mansion, Myra told them that Rene wasn't there, and she didn't know where she was or when she'd be back. And after what happened to Colleen on an agency shoot…"

"But…she…oh," Chloe said.

"Oh what?" Stuckey asked.

Chloe shook her head. "I don't know the whole story. But I think she's kind of hiding from her father. He's Cuban, very macho, very old school. He doesn't want her modeling. It's not what nice girls do, you know? But she's over twenty-one, and it's what she wants to do."

"I'd still like to talk to her," Luke said.

Katia brought their drinks, then discreetly slipped away.

"Why?" Chloe demanded suspiciously.

"Because of Colleen Rodriguez."

She stiffened. She had infiltrated the agency herself because of Colleen Rodriguez.

"Why are you trying to talk to Rene specifically?" she asked, pretending she didn't know.

"They were best friends," Luke said.

Damn. He knew his stuff. She frowned.

"So I gather you two know each other well," Luke said, looking from her to Stuckey as he changed the subject.

Stuckey sighed. Explaining their friendship was always difficult.

Luke sat back, one arm stretched along the seat. His eyes

hadn't lost a shred of hard silver suspicion as he stared at her. "Are you a licensed P.I.?" he asked her.

She was irritated to feel her cheeks grow red. "No. Are you?"

He nodded.

"I'd like to see your license," she said, making no secret of her own suspicion.

He arched a brow and produced his wallet, opening it before handing it over. She stared at the insert, then glared back at him. "That's a fishing license."

He shrugged, not about to comply any further.

"He's the real deal," Stuckey said quietly, obviously getting irritated himself.

"Well, you might have said something," she said, staring accusingly at Luke.

"Just what do you do, Miss Marin?" he asked. "Since you're not a model."

She had never said she was, but even so, she resented his implication that she wasn't—something—enough to be a model.

"I'm a psychologist and an artist," she said.

"Oh. I see." The words were polite—and cutting.

"A sketch artist," Stuckey put in for her. "Chloe has been of tremendous help to the department as a sketch artist. And as a psychologist, she's helped lots of survivors—of crime, abuse, you name it—learn to cope again."

"So you were there to sketch…models?" he asked. His tone made her teeth grate.

She decided to let Stuckey take that one.

"There's still a lot of concern regarding Colleen Rodriguez's disappearance. Victoria is with the Bryson Agency, and Chloe and Victoria are friends, so it was easy enough to arrange to plant Chloe there. She's trying to see if she can discover anything in a casual way, working out of the mansion. And except for tonight, you're being careful—right?" he said sternly, staring at her.

"I see," Luke said, though his expression conveyed that he obviously didn't. "Degrees in psychology—and…art?—make you qualified to investigate a woman's disappearance and possible murder?"

"Tony told you, I know Victoria, so it's easy for me to fit in. If anyone can learn anything about what goes on inside the agency, it's me." She stopped speaking. She had met Colleen, casually, and had liked her very much. This was personal for her. And she *was* the best person for the job. She and Vickie had been best friends ever since the event that had shattered their lives, along with Brad's and Jared's. Even the fact that they all traveled for both work and pleasure, and might not see each other for months at a time, didn't change anything. When they were home, they were thick as thieves.

She thought about telling Luke that her uncle had handled more criminal investigations than he would see in ten lifetimes, and that Uncle Leo valued her opinion and had actually asked her to keep an eye out and tell him anything she learned.

But she didn't have a chance to respond further before Stuckey's cell phone rang. He listened for a moment, grinned, then turned to Chloe. "Yes, she's here. I'll tell her." He hung up and said, "That was Victoria. When she couldn't get you and the guard said he'd seen you heading for the beach, she figured I might have seen you."

"Has she seen Rene?" Luke asked.

"She won't show up again tonight. Not after someone chased her," Chloe said, looking at him accusingly.

"Where will she go?" Luke asked her.

*Even if I knew, I wouldn't be telling you,* Chloe thought. She still didn't feel comfortable with his explanation, even if Stuckey had bought it.

"Luke, maybe you want to explain why the Gonzalezes are so concerned about their daughter," Stuckey suggested.

Did he *want* to explain? she wondered. Certainly not to her. She could see that. But she could also see that he respected both Stuckey's position and Stuckey himself, and because of that he would fill her in.

"Did you know that Colleen and Rene were *longtime* best friends?" he asked. "Since childhood. And their parents were friends, too."

Chloe was silent. She didn't think Victoria or any of the other models knew that. The girls had probably downplayed the strength of their friendship, afraid that it might hurt their individual chances of getting work if the powers that be thought they were unwilling to work separately or that jealousy would lead to trouble in the house.

"Octavio Gonzalez, Rene's father, came to me after they couldn't get hold of their daughter," Luke explained. "She wouldn't even answer her cell. They're worried that whatever happened to Colleen Rodriguez was happening to her, too—that maybe someone was targeting her, forming a relationship with her so he could lure her away, presumably to kill her. The thing is, Colleen was over twenty-one, and her purse and passport were gone, which makes it look like she took off on her own. The authorities found nothing that suggested foul play. But Colleen's parents are sure their daughter would never have just taken off without letting them know. So now Octavio is going crazy. The man is sure that something happened to Colleen, and he's afraid his daughter is about to meet the same fate. The agency is no help—but then, they don't have to be. Rene is twenty-two. They don't have to force her to talk to her parents if she doesn't want to. Even so, Octavio is convinced that the agency is dirty."

"I don't think so. I really don't," Chloe told him.

He leaned forward. "Is that because you've been doing some work for them? Or because your friend Victoria is such a success there?"

She would have stood up and gotten right in his face—if Stuckey hadn't been blocking her in. He had no right to accuse her that way.

She clamped down hard on her teeth, realizing that she was going on the defensive, when she herself had been there to spy on whatever was going on. Colleen had been like a beautiful puppy, full of life and energy and eager anticipation. She had loved Miami and loved her parents and friends. There had been no reason for her to just up and disappear. Chloe hadn't needed to hear that from Luke Cane, or whoever he really was.

Chloe lowered her eyes, dismayed with herself. His name was Luke Cane—Stuckey had told her so. He was a legitimate private investigator—even if he had shown her a fishing license. They had definitely gotten off on the wrong foot, but it had been a long night, and she wasn't sure that she wanted it to go on any longer.

"I'll do what I can to get Rene to speak with you," she said. "Tony, if you'll excuse me, I need to get back to the mansion. Vickie is probably ready to go home."

Luke reached across the table and touched her arm. She started, looking at his hand. It was large, with long fingers— maybe he should have been a guitarist or a pianist. His nails were clipped short, and they were clean. His palm felt callused; she imagined that when he wasn't investigating someone, he indulged in some kind of manual labor. Building things, maybe. They were very masculine hands. She gritted her teeth again, wondering why his touch could send rivulets of fire streaking through her when she was absolutely convinced that she didn't like the man.

She looked up and found him staring into her eyes. "Victoria doesn't live at the mansion?" he asked.

Chloe shook her head. "She lives about a mile away from me. We're in the Grove. She stays at the mansion sometimes, especially if she has to get up early for a shoot. But she does more than model. She also substitute teaches at a magnet school for the performing arts, so she prefers living at home."

"But she has a room at the mansion, right?" he persisted.

"Yes. Look, if your main interest is Rene, I can try to make her call her parents, but I can't guarantee I'll succeed.

And you're not going to change her mind. She believes she can make it. Her father may love her, but he's smothered her, and she's over twenty-one and this is America. It's her decision to make."

He shook his head. "You're missing the point. It's likely that her best friend met a very bad end, and the same thing could happen to her."

"I haven't missed your point. But there was no indication of foul play," Chloe said, even though she didn't believe Colleen had run off, not for a second. She had heard all the arguments a million times, and she was certain that something had happened, which was why she had been at the mansion tonight herself. So why was she arguing with him?

*Because I don't like him, and I don't trust him,* she reminded herself.

"Face it," Luke said bluntly. "Colleen Rodriguez was murdered. Quite possibly by someone involved with the Bryson Agency."

# THREE

The *Stirling* was one of five boats berthed at the rickety docks off the Florida Bay side of Key Biscayne.

They would be tearing down the docks soon, along with the old bait-and-beer shop that had been there since the 1920s. Miami had officially been a city then, incorporated in 1896, but to many it had still been nothing but a mosquito-infested swamp, stuck between the Everglades and Biscayne Bay. Technically, the Everglades wasn't a swamp—it was a literal "river of grass," and a slow-moving river at that. It wasn't that the city had been kept secret from the world—Fort Dallas had been erected on the Miami River in the early 1800s as an outpost in the Seminole Wars. After that, the city, and all the smaller municipalities that made up Greater Miami, had grown slowly. Hurricanes, heat, humidity, snakes, gators and other pests had combined to limit its expansion. There had been boom in the 1920s, but the hurricane of 1926 had stopped development in its tracks for a while. The thirties hadn't done much for the area, either, but since the 1940s and the advent of army bases and the industry of war, the city had continually grown. Castro's rise to power had brought a massive Cuban influx, and soon after, Miami had become the haven of choice for people from every country in the Caribbean, and South and Central America.

A lot of what had first brought Luke Cane to the area was part of a dying past. Didn't matter. He liked the diversity of what was going on. He regularly heard Spanish, German, Russian and British accents, all in a normal day, just going out for coffee, stopping for a beer.

He would miss it, though, when the old shops and docks finally went down under the wave of the future.

The old way in the Florida Keys—especially the middle Keys—would perish more slowly. He could always move the *Stirling* farther south.

The causeway led to the luxury residences on Key Biscayne, to the aquarium, the beaches and one of the city's finest magnet schools. There were research laboratories, boat rentals, picnic areas. His own little patch of heaven was behind a forested road that only the natives tended to travel. Boaters knew the bait shop, where you could also buy beer and exactly two menu items: boiled shrimp and burgers.

When he drove back home that night, he immediately recognized the visitor sitting at the end of the dock as Octavio Gonzalez.

He parked his Subaru on the sand spit that was assigned to his slip and got out. Octavio stood right away and approached him. It was almost 3:00 a.m.

He wondered how long the other man had been sitting there. Probably most of the night.

"Did you see her? Did you?" Octavio asked anxiously. "Is she all right?"

"I didn't actually speak with her, but she was there, and I know she's all right," Luke assured him.

Relief flooded Octavio's face, but then he turned anxious once again. "But you went as someone else. Why wouldn't she see you? They have her imprisoned, don't they?" He was about five-ten, stocky, bald on top, mustached. In his youth he had probably displayed the machismo that went with his heritage, but now he only looked broken and desperate. He set his hands on Luke's chest, as if he could force him to make everything all right. "That woman—that Myra woman!" he continued. "She won't let me speak with my daughter. She won't let me on the property. She called the police when I insisted on speaking with my daughter. She even told them that she didn't know where Rene was!"

"She told the police she didn't know where Rene was when they went to see her. If Rene wasn't there when the police arrived, then she wasn't lying. She did tell the police that Rene was all right, and they'll go back to see her again."

"They should camp outside her door!" Octavio said furiously.

"Octavio, I know how you feel," Luke said patiently,

gently grasping the man's hands and forcing them down. "Come aboard, sit, and I'll tell you what I know."

The aft deck led straight into the central cabin. For many years now, the boat had been both his home and his occupational therapy. He'd spent hours on the woodwork and the old chrome. The galley was up-to-date and fully functional; the main cabin offered an elegant teak dining table with a horseshoe-shaped bench that accommodated at least ten. Across from the table, a long, comfortably upholstered sofa invited more guests, and there were two stationary easy chairs, as well. A set of six steps led to the bridge above, while a hallway led to the master cabin at the stern, passing two additional sleeping cabins on the way, one to port and one to starboard. She was a labor of love and the perfect home, at least for the time being. The water here in a canal off the Intracoastal wasn't the clearest he'd ever seen, and there was the noise of small boats of all kinds coming through. Still, the constant movement of the water kept it clean enough, and he liked being able to jump in for a swim whenever the hell he felt like it. People relaxed in tubes and floating chairs outside the neighboring bait-and-beer shop, and on a warm summer's day, there was nothing like the pleasure of being right on the water.

It was a far cry from his native country.

Every once in a while, he still yearned for home, but he figured that was why God had gotten together with the Wright brothers to create airplanes.

Octavio followed him on board, a little more slowly, using the hull rail for support as he carefully crossed over to the deck. Luke led the way into the cabin, helping himself to a beer from the refrigerator as he passed.

"Octavio, beer?" he offered.

"No, no," Octavio replied.

Luke reached into a cabinet above the sink and found a bottle of cognac. He held it up questioningly, and at first the other man looked as if he would refuse, but then he nodded. He accepted the glass Luke poured for him and sank into one of the easy chairs.

"Why?" he asked, running his fingers through what hair he had left. He sounded baffled and lost. "Why won't she just speak to me?" He looked at Luke. "But you say she's there—she's alive and she's well. Somehow we have to reach her. She can't go on that shoot. She will die. I know this."

Luke took the chair across from Octavio, gripping the beer bottle, feeling the sweat. "She's definitely there, and I was able to speak with a friend of hers," he said.

"*Ay, Dios mio.*" Octavio crossed himself in thanksgiving.

"I'll try to get closer and get her to call you," Luke said. "But we're in a tough position. If she was in immediate and imminent danger, I could drag her out of there."

"Yes, yes! Drag her out!"

Luke shook his head. "Octavio, I'm not averse to pulling a few tricks, but not the kind that won't get you anywhere— and *will* get me thrown in jail. What you have to understand is that you can't keep your daughter prisoner. If I forced her to go home, she would just leave again. She could even accuse you and your wife of abduction and imprisonment if she wanted to."

"My daughter could do that?" Octavio said, and he looked like a man about to cry, a man who couldn't begin to understand the stupidity of those around him. "Why doesn't she see the danger?" he demanded passionately. "She loved Colleen. They played together when they were little girls, they knew right from wrong. Rene cried and cried when Colleen disappeared, but then…she believed the story this agency is telling. She believed those lying bastards who said that Colleen had run away. All because she wants to be a model, to be rich and have men lusting after her.

"Yes, we were strict, stern fathers. We cared who our daughters went out with, when they came home. We didn't let our *niñas* get hooked on drugs. We tried to teach them right from wrong. But they watch TV—they see how American woman sleep with so many men with so little thought, how they drink and carry on, all on the giant television screen. I tried to tell my daughter that she mustn't become like a *puta,* a whore, because decent men will not want her, decent men who go to work, love their wives and care for their children and their families. Do you know what she told me? She told me she didn't want a decent man and a decent family. She wanted the American dream. So what is this dream? I ask her. To sleep around like the women on the television set?" He groaned. "So now—now that I don't care who she wants to sleep with as long as she is *alive*—she will not even talk to me. Her mother cries every night. It is agony that she will not speak to us, and it is worse to think about Colleen, to think that Rene will be like Colleen and never come home, never get to live a long and happy life. I know you think I am just a worried father, that my daughter is safe and what happened to Colleen will not happen to her, but I know. I *know*. If she stays there, she will die."

"Octavio, you have to stay calm," Luke told him. "There's no proof so far that anything bad even happened to Colleen."

Octavio stared back at him with wise and tired eyes. "Colleen is dead. Her father knows it, as does her mother. As I do. Her parents went to Islamorada—because those swine at the agency would not allow her mother to go out to the island they own, the island where she…disappeared. They act like her parents are mosquitoes, an annoyance. My wife went, too. They set up crosses, a memorial for Colleen." He winced, then downed his cognac in a swallow.

Luke was silent for a minute, then leaned toward Octavio. "I will do everything in my power, but you have to trust me. As of tonight, we know that your daughter is all right. Her friends told me that Rene wants this modeling career very badly—badly enough that she may be avoiding your calls because she doesn't want you to keep trying to talk her out of it. I can try to get her to talk to you, but no one— not me and not you—can stop her from going on that photo shoot if she makes the decision to go."

"If she goes, then you must go to the island, too. You must find out what is going on," Octavio implored.

"I can do that," Luke agreed.

Octavio stood and pumped Luke's free hand. "Lieutenant Stuckey told me that I could count on you."

"I'll keep you informed," Luke promised. "But, Octavio, if she calls you, no matter how hard it is, no matter how much you feel it goes against tradition, don't try to stop her from pursuing her career or interfere with her life. Be open to her dreams."

Octavio's eyes betrayed his agony. "Even though I fear for her life?" he whispered.

"Especially because you fear for her life. Stay open so she'll know she can turn to you if she needs to, no matter what. Rene is seeing what she wants to see, but even if someone at the agency is dangerous, that doesn't mean the entire operation is corrupt."

"Myra Allen," Octavio said knowingly, his brows furrowing. "That woman is corrupt."

"Everyone involved has been and is still being investigated," Luke said. "They haven't closed the case."

"Officially, no? But in their minds, it is. Another silly girl gone off—that's what they have chosen to believe. Even when they know it is wrong."

The long day was starting to make itself felt. Luke repeated, "I'll do everything in my power to keep your daughter safe, Octavio. And," he promised, thinking of the job Stuckey had asked him to do while he was undercover helping the Gonzalezes, "I'll find out what happened to Colleen Rodriguez."

With that, Octavio nodded and started up the steps, looking older than his years. Luke followed him, jumping to the dock first and offering him a hand. Octavio thanked him, then said good-night and walked down the road toward the bait-and-beer shop, where his car waited beneath a wilting oak.

Luke returned to the *Stirling,* locking the cabin door once he was inside. His windows had security locks, as well, and he had rigged his own alarm system. Despite that, he didn't worry a lot about security. If anyone ever really wanted him dead, they wouldn't worry about gaining entry to the boat. They would just torch it.

In the master cabin he stripped off his suit and stretched out on the bed, staring up at the ceiling. He didn't know why, but Octavio got to him. The man was filled with passion, convinced he knew a truth everyone else was ignoring. Once, long ago, he, too, had known that kind of passion, known what it was like to know the truth, while others refused to see it. That was what had brought him here.

Stuckey had brought Octavio to him, just as Stuckey— and some of his friends—brought him most of his work.

He didn't spy on philandering spouses, schoolgirls who might be smoking pot in the park after school or college kids gambling or stealing exams, and he didn't like corporate intrigue unless it was connected with something more intriguing.

He worked for people who had gone through all the proper channels to find justice but run up against the brick walls that were inevitable in any system.

He didn't have many friends, but those he had were close, and he liked it that way.

He lived alone now, and he liked that, too. He wasn't a decent companion for anyone else.

He felt the slight rocking of the boat while he pondered his next move. The first step would be to get closer to Chloe Marin. She was his ticket to getting to know everyone else, and since her pretense for being there was as false as his own, she could hardly object or else he would blow her cover.

Light from distant street lamps played dimly on his ceiling, and as he watched the shadows stretch and fade, he wondered what would have happened if he'd caught up to Rene. At least he had learned what he needed to know: the girl was alive, and she was living at the mansion. But what he didn't know was what had sent her down from the balcony and running for the beach in the first place.

And then there was Chloe Marin….

He punched his pillow with annoyance. The strawberry blonde certainly knew her moves. Subduing her had been more difficult than if she'd been a man his own size and weight.

It was almost as if he'd been thrown off balance by a supercharged Barbie. Maybe that was what was most annoying.

But she wasn't a living Barbie. She was a woman with entrancing eyes and a suspicious nature. In fact, where he was concerned, she seemed downright hostile. And yet, when he touched her…

Something happened to him when they touched. He was filled with a sudden raw heat unlike anything he'd felt in years.

He'd seen a dozen spectacularly beautiful girls that night. But somehow, she was different.

He punched his pillow again. He had to get to know the woman, whether he liked it or not. She was key to cracking this case, no matter how annoying he found her—and his own attraction to her.

He had a job to do.

He forced himself to watch the shadows, to close down his mind, and finally he slept.

He didn't dream, hadn't in years. Not anything that he remembered, at least.

But that night he dreamed, only it wasn't a fantasy, it was a rerun of the past.

A scene…just that one scene. He was running. Down the streets of Kensington. Up the steps to the beautiful flat they'd kept for three short months. He heard himself calling her name.

And then he saw the blood. The trail on the stairs, drop by drop, as if the killer had collected it and used a paintbrush to arrange it for maximum effect.

And then he heard himself screaming…screaming her name.

He fought the dream. He didn't want to reach the bedroom. But he couldn't stop the replay, couldn't stop himself from running up those stairs and seeing…

Miranda. Her face was still beautiful, her black hair spread out all around her. Her arms, though, had been battered and bloody from the fight she had waged. She looked like a doll, a Sleeping Beauty, except for the band of crimson around her throat.

Luke awoke with a start, screaming her name.

He was sweating as if the cabin were a hundred degrees, even though the air conditioner was humming away.

He stood, shaking his head to clear away the memories. It was all so long ago.

He walked into the head, turned on the shower and let ice-cold water pour over him.

He stood there until he felt himself start to shiver, then turned off the water, whipped his towel off the rack and went back to the cabin to dress for the day.

He liked it better when he didn't dream, didn't feel.


Chloe was jolted awake by the phone ringing and decided to let the answering machine pick up.

But whoever was calling just hung up on the machine, then called again.

She rolled over and picked up the receiver, feeling tired and sluggish, as if it were still the middle of the night. Glancing at the alarm on her bedside table, she saw that it wasn't the middle of the night, but it *was* ridiculously early, given how late she'd been out: 7:00 a.m.

"Chloe, are you there?" someone asked before she could even grunt out a hello.

Stuckey. What the hell was he doing, calling her so early?

"I'm here. What's going on?"

"You shouldn't have been playing detective last night," he said, ignoring her question.

"I was invited. I might even go on that swimsuit shoot," she said.

"Yeah?" he asked. "Why?"

"What do you mean, why? Thanks a lot."

"Well, for one thing, I thought you liked to keep a low profile. You've never even wanted your name in the paper before, much less your picture out there for the world to see."

*Because in my way, I'm still a coward,* she thought.

"Look, my point is, you've been snooping around, and now you're planning to keep snooping out in the middle of nowhere, in the same circumstances where a girl went missing. And that could be dangerous."

"It can be dangerous to fall asleep at night, too," Chloe told him, her grip on the phone growing tight.

"I'm not stupid," she told him. "I won't go anywhere alone, and I'll be rooming with Victoria. In fact, I'd be worried sick if I let Victoria go out there on her own. And if she's there, you know Brad and Jared will be there, too. I could be a big help to you. Just think about it. The case isn't closed, but no one is doing much about it."

"Hey, don't get on my case for that. It wasn't my jurisdiction."

"I'm not getting on you, Stuckey. You know, Uncle Leo pulled a lot of strings to get me something on the case. He doesn't believe she just took off. And I went to court one day last week to pick him up, and her parents were out on the steps of the courthouse, holding a press conference, and they made my heart bleed. They believe she's dead, and they're desperate for someone to figure out what happened, for justice." She was quiet for a moment. "I didn't know her well, but I met her a few times at the mansion. She was nice. She deserves justice. Remember how you told me once that guys like this—like whoever killed her—aren't rocket scientists. They eventually make mistakes."

"But they're still dangerous. Let Luke handle this. He's a licensed professional."

"Yeah, right. He showed me his fishing license."

"You two got off to a bad start, and I'm sorry about that, but I asked him to help out with this because I do want something done about it, and I don't want you in danger."

"But I can help. I can get Rene to talk to him, for one thing." Could she? Maybe. The words had come to her lips without her realizing what she was going to say. All she knew was that something inside her felt it was important for her to be part of this investigation, so she had to get him to calm down before he went to her uncle. She was an adult; she made her own choices. But she loved her uncle, and she didn't know if she could stand up to him if he insisted she get out of there.

"Actually, that's what I called you about, and why I had to call so early, before you got a chance to talk to anyone."

"Oh?" She smiled, sinking back into her pillow. The tables were turning.

"You heard what I said when I dropped you back at the mansion last night, right?" he asked.

"Yes, I heard what you said. Don't tell anyone Luke Cane's real name or his real identity. Whatever I do, don't jeopardize his position. I heard you. You said it three times," she told him.

"Yes, and I meant don't tell anyone. Not even Victoria."

"But I'm going to be asking Victoria to help me—to watch and listen—it's only fair to tell her the truth. I mean, let's get serious, how long is anyone going to believe that 'Jack Smith' is a designer?" Chloe demanded.

Stuckey chuckled. "He's got some help. He'll pull it off.

You'll be surprised. Chloe, I'm asking you this because it's important. Promise me you won't say anything?"

"I promise."

"Good. See ya soon," Stuckey said, and hung up.

Chloe replaced the phone and crawled out of bed, then walked over to the drapes and threw them open so she could look out at the pool. Her bedroom was on the second floor of what had once been a carriage house, and she could see the sparkling water and casual rattan furniture that surrounded it. She could see the main house where Uncle Leo lived as well, with its red-clay tile roof, balconies and two turrets. The house had been built in the 1910s and was one of the oldest in the area. Her great-great-grandfather had purchased the land and drawn up the plans for the house. Once the family had owned twenty acres. Then ten. Now they had one acre remaining, with Bayshore Drive and civilization right around the corner. But the area was still overgrown and wild in old-Florida fashion; oaks dripped moss, and bougainvillea grew everywhere in a riot of color.

Chloe knew she was welcome in the main house anytime; Leo had always told her that it was hers more so than it would ever be his. She had grown up in the main house, and when she had finished college, she had contemplated the idea of getting an apartment with Victoria, but they'd both remained traumatized by the past, no matter how far they had come. Uncle Leo had come up with the solution: refurbishing the old carriage house so Chloe would have her privacy but still feel safe, and Uncle Leo wouldn't spend his life worried about her.

The arrangement had worked out well. She carried emotional scars, a few wounds that might never fully heal, but her uncle had helped her find a purpose and enjoyment in life.

He had always been her rock.

The two of them were the only family they had left. Chloe didn't remember her parents at all; she had been two when they died in a bizarre train explosion that had taken out almost twenty cars and their occupants. She had grown up with Leo, and he had been a good parental figure. He was with the district attorney's office, a position he could afford to hold because he had family money and the insurance from the accident. On top of that, he was brilliant with stocks, no matter what the economy was doing, so they had never needed to worry about paying the bills.

She felt a moment's unease, hoping that Stuckey wasn't already calling him, warning him that Chloe was getting herself too involved with the Colleen Rodriguez disappearance. No, Stuckey wasn't a tattletale. And even while he was telling her to keep her nose out of things, she knew he also realized that she was in a perfect position to obtain information the police might never discover themselves. Like so many Miami-Dade officers, he had been touched by the desperation of Colleen's family, and he had been on a task force assigned to search the area from Florida City to the Broward County line, but all the cops had been reassigned after six weeks. The case wasn't closed, but it wasn't anyone's priority, either.

Her phone rang again, and as she turned to answer it, she let out a little cry of surprise.

And fear.

Someone was there, watching her. A woman, transparent and ethereal.

Oh, God, no! Not again.

She'd fought so hard for her sanity. She'd thought she was finally done seeing people crying out to her for help—dead people—done with longing to help them when she couldn't. After the massacre, she had seen images, dreams, ghosts, ectoplasm—whatever. She had seen them in hospitals; she had seen them on the streets. Strangers who had stared at her beseechingly and, even more terrifyingly, her own dead friends. She'd had therapy, lots and lots of therapy. But now she was regressing, seeing things again, no doubt because her world was changing. No, she told herself. She was stronger than that. She did not see things! Or if she did, then if she was strong, then they would fade away.

Her throat constricted, her muscles tensed, and then she blinked and the image was gone. She laughed nervously at herself; she must have seen the drapes reflected in the mirror.

She had stopped seeing ghosts long ago.

They were nothing but remnants of the fear and trauma.

A decade had passed, and she was fine. She was just imagining things because of Colleen.

She still felt shaken.

She left the window and went to stand over the phone, waiting for the answering machine to pick up. When she heard Victoria's voice, she grabbed the receiver.

"Hey," she said. "What's up?"

"Are you ready?"

"Am I ready for what?"

"Third Sunday of the month. Meeting of the Fighting Pelicans."

"Oh. Yeah, of course. I'd forgotten all about it. You didn't mention a word last night," Chloe told her.

"Last night. Well, last night was just weird," Victoria said.

"I'll say."

"I'll be by for you in twenty," Victoria said.

"All right." Chloe hung up and headed straight for the shower.

They had been meeting Brad and Jared at an old breakfast place out on the Rickenbacker Causeway since forever, when they had all attended a magnet high school for the arts out on Key Biscayne. They called themselves the Fighting Pelicans because even though their school had no sports teams, it had been overrun by pelicans, since it sat right on the water.

Chloe showered and threw on a long casual halter dress, then headed down the stairs. She keyed in the code to open the gate in the fence that surrounded the property, and waited on the sidewalk for Victoria. She thought back to the ghost she'd thought she'd seen and gave herself a shake to banish the memory.

She saw Victoria's little Subaru sweep into the cul-de-sac and hurried out to meet her. As she slid into the front seat, she asked, "Are you sure Brad and Jared are showing up today? I'm not sure I'm ready to be awake, and they were still at the party, last night, when I left."

"What's wrong with you?" Victoria asked her. "You look as if you'd seen a ghost."

It was just an expression, Chloe told herself. And here, in

the bright light of the sun, sitting next to Victoria, the memory seemed absolutely ridiculous.

"I'm fine. So what do you think? Are they going to make it?"

Victoria shrugged. "They were talking to Myra when I left, but it looked like they were getting ready to leave, so I imagine they'll drag themselves out of bed."

"I like Myra," Chloe said. "When you think about her position, it's pretty amazing. She's not cold or snobby or any of that."

"Yeah, but she can be hard as nails, too. You should see her when she's negotiating," Victoria said. "Watch out, that's all I can say."

"Well, I know she was questioned intensely when Colleen Rodriguez disappeared, and the cops were impressed with her."

Victoria glanced over at her. "And you know this because…?"

"Because my uncle's office was involved."

"But Colleen disappeared in the Keys and he's Dade County."

"Doesn't matter. Both counties were involved in the investigation, not to mention that cops talk. My uncle doesn't believe for an instant that she just took off."

Victoria flashed Chloe a glance as she drove. "You're forgetting that I was on that shoot, too."

"I know you were."

Victoria shook her head. "There was nothing, just nothing, to suggest that anyone did anything to her. I do know she'd sort of been seeing one of the bar managers down there, a really nice guy. He's half American, half Bahamian, and he's so gorgeous he should be modeling himself, but he wants to go into hotel management. He wasn't with her that night, though. And even though they seemed to really like each other, they hadn't been together all that long. Who knows? Maybe she did meet someone else. Or maybe—just maybe—she disappeared on purpose. You know, some kind of a publicity stunt."

"I doubt it. From what I know about Colleen, neither scenario sounds like her."

They had reached the restaurant by then, so they stopped talking and turned the car over to the valet. Brad came walking down the steps just as they started up them. "I was afraid you two had forgotten about breakfast. I just sent you a text message, Vick."

"I was driving, and I don't text and drive," Victoria said.

"Sorry," Brad said. "Anyway, come in. Jared is holding down the table."

They walked through the crowded restaurant and found Jared at a table next to the plate-glass window that overlooked the bay—one of the best in the place. It wasn't that they were such big spenders, just that they showed up regularly, in season and out, and had been doing so for years.

"Hey there," Jared said, standing and giving them each a kiss on the cheek as they were seated.

"You're looking good," Victoria told him.

He blushed, and Chloe wondered if Victoria had any notion that Jared was in love with her, that he had been forever. She didn't understand why he tried so hard to hide his feelings. In the beginning, she was certain, he hadn't let on because he was convinced, as they all were in those days, that they were damaged goods, too scarred psychologically to form relationships based on anything other than shared trauma. They had lived through a nightmare, and the aftermath had just been a nightmare of a different sort. They had been hounded by the media, and whenever they met people, whether at school or work, or even casually at parties, they were items of curiosity. Everyone wanted to know the gory details, details the four of them were trying hard to forget.

At least the killers had been found.

Dead.

The sketch Chloe had done of one of them—an image burned into her memory when she and the killer had stared each other in the eye—had allowed the police to identify him when his body was found.

Brad took a seat next to Victoria and picked up the menu. Chloe found herself watching him and feeling a sense of pride. Brad had a trust fund, but he worked hard and had grown his business into a real success, even though one day soon he and Victoria would inherit the entire family fortune. And he never acted like a rich jerk.

He worked out, and he spent time with his friends. He loved women, loved going to the parties Victoria got him into. He'd been deeply religious before the massacre, but he had lost his faith in the aftermath, so now, since he'd never found *the* woman, he played the field and they remained a platonic foursome.

Jared, of course, had no desire to be platonic where Victoria was concerned, but since he wouldn't speak up…

Like Brad, he, too, was extremely good-looking and hardworking. There was no inheritance ahead for him, but he was brilliant with the money markets, and he womanized alongside Brad, while he pined for Victoria.

She wondered if any of them would—or could—get it right in the future.

Brad caught her staring and lifted a brow. "Why the serious look?"

"Just thinking, you two are getting kind of old for a life of nonstop partying and debauchery," Chloe teased.

"Excuse me," Brad said, "but what's so wrong with appreciating beautiful women?" He smiled. "Luckily for us, there will be at least twelve of them on the calendar shoot."

"Speaking of, you *are* doing the shoot with me, right?" Victoria asked Chloe. "Myra told me that she's reserved June for you, so if you're not interested, you need to tell her right away." Victoria smiled. "Myra really loves your look. When you think of all the women who try to get hired by the agency, it's really cool that she's offered you a spot."

Chloe laughed. "Was that a compliment, or are you wondering why she'd choose me?"

Victoria laughed. "It was a compliment. Cross my heart and hope to die. It's just that you don't care, and so many people do. I heard her talking to Harry Lee last night, and she was wishing you'd take a greater interest in a modeling career, and he agreed."

"But you are going to be Miss June, right?" Brad asked.

"Yes," Chloe said. "Yes, I'll do it." She'd been hoping she would be asked. She needed to be a part of things so she could get onto the island and see what was going on. And Stuckey didn't need to be afraid for her; she would be in the company of dozens of other people the whole time.

Of course, Colleen Rodriguez had been in the company of those same people, a little voice nagged. Then again, no one had been suspicious then; there had been no need to be. This time everyone would have their guard up.

"And if anyone comes after you, you can just hit them with that jujitsu stuff you do," Brad said, then grew suddenly pensive. "Not that even that would have helped… then."

For a moment she had no idea what to say. Finally she managed to mumble, "Mixed martial arts. I do mixed-martial arts."

He reached across the table, touching her hand. "Sorry. I didn't mean to bring up the past, not really," he said huskily.

Chloe shrugged and squeezed his hand in return. "You just took me by surprise, that's all. It doesn't bother me to talk about it. In fact, I do talk about it now and then. I still don't believe the finale, though."

"Why not?" Victoria asked, frowning. "They found the guys. They were dead."

"Two guys, dead, and a suicide note taking full blame in the name of the Church of the Real People? I'm sorry—the rest of the world may have bought it. I still don't," Chloe said.

Jared cleared his throat. "Chloe, the experts said it was a ritualistic murder and that it all made sense. And I did a lot of research into cults myself, after that, and I have to agree."

"The church officials were horrified, and of course their membership really dropped," Brad said.

Chloe looked back at Brad. They'd all grown up going to the same beautiful church in the Grove. She had found comfort in returning to that church, but Brad and Jared had gone in the opposite direction. It made her feel sad that Brad, in particular, had lost something that had once meant so much to him.

"Earth to Chloe, you're staring at me," Brad told her.

"Sorry," she said. "But I still don't buy it."

"Chloe, you're the one whose sketch ID'd the one guy," Brad said.

"The dead man was one of the killers, yes. I just don't think it stopped with the two of them."

"Chloe," Jared said, "if there had been someone else—a Charles Manson or whatever—the killing wouldn't have ended when it did."

"I know what you're saying makes sense, but I've just never believed it, that's all." She picked up her menu to end the conversation. "I'm thinking waffles, but the eggs Benedict are really good, too."

She could feel her friends looking at each other and knew they were worried about her.

She looked from one to the other of them. "Honestly, I'm fine. It's just the way I feel."

"It's okay. We still love you. So, how about I get the waffles, you get the eggs Benedict, and we share?" Jared suggested.

★ ★ ★

Luke was surprised by how quickly and easily he had learned so much about Chloe Marin. She had started college late, after going on an extended tour abroad after high school, earning a double major in psychology and art at NYU. She had worked with patients doing art therapy at the Dade County Hospital for three years after graduation, and had been working free-lance, with an office on Brickell, for the last two.

She had survived what they called the Teen Massacre during her senior year of high school. Eight of her friends had been slaughtered. Chloe had survived by being one step ahead of a pair of killers, Michael Donlevy and Abram Garcia, members of the Church of the Real People, a cult with socialist leanings and strict versions of the code of God—their God. To their way of thinking, the teenagers had been sinners, and the killers had saved them from eternal damnation, or so claimed the suicide note found carefully sealed in a Baggie next to the bodies in a wildlife park just off the Tamiami Trail in the Everglades.

Information regarding the massacre had been easy to dig up—the newspapers had carried the story until there was nothing new to carry.

The details were horrifying.

*Death to defilers!* written in blood, on the living-room wall. Eight dead, six wounded, two who had been passed out on the beach, unaware of the tragic events unfolding inside, and four who had miraculously escaped.

Victoria Preston, Brad Angsley, Jared Walker—and Chloe Marin. Victoria claimed that Chloe had saved her life, but

Chloe hadn't wanted to talk about any of it. She had given one interview, and that was that. He'd found a picture of her standing at a news podium, with a tall man at her side. There was a definite family resemblance. He had to be her uncle, the A.D.A., Leo Marin. Chloe had long hair then, falling nearly to her waist. Bangs, and huge eyes. Innocent eyes showing the pain of what she'd been through. She'd been so young, seventeen, and she'd been forced to grow old overnight.

The survivors had spent hours in the police station, giving their individual statements. They hadn't been able to shed much light. The killers had worn black dive suits with hoods, working swiftly and efficiently in the dark.

Only Chloe had been able to give a description that had been any help at all. She had even drawn a picture of the man whose face she'd briefly seen. A picture that had matched one of the bodies that had been discovered later.

*Death to defilers!* And something else. An odd drawing… like a hand.

Everything done in blood. Obviously the work of a cult.

There were also pictures of the two "brothers" who had been found dead in the Everglades. Apparently, Brother Abram Garcia had killed Brother Michael Donlevy, then turned the gun on himself. They had done God's work, saving the teenagers from the greed and gluttony of their parents, the cruelty born of excess, and sent them to God before they could sin beyond redemption.

Brother Abram was tall and looked strong enough to kill. Brother Michael was a smaller, slimmer man. Somehow,

he didn't look like the kind of guy who could overpower
a bunch of high-school jocks—even drunk jocks, and even
in the dead of night.

Luke typed in the name of the sect church and was surprised to find that it still existed, that it even had a welcoming Web page. Those who were lost and seeking the real truth
of God were invited to a potluck supper on Thursday night.

Luke sat back. He'd always found it fascinating to explore
the mind-sets, religions and philosophies of people the
world over. A potluck dinner would be a perfect opportunity to see what made the Church of the Real People tick.

He drummed his fingers on his desk. He wasn't sure why
he had such a fascination with Chloe's ten-year-old horror.
He had a job to do, two cases to work, and he didn't see
how the dinner was going to get him any closer to finding
out the truth behind Colleen Rodriguez's disappearance,
but he had to eat—and he couldn't fight the desire to know
more about Chloe Marin.

He searched until he was able to go back ten years, then
made a list of known members of the cult at the time of
the murders, but nothing he tried got him to a site where
he could find a list of current members. In fact, for the five
years following the massacre, the church hadn't kept any
kind of a Web site at all. Now, however, the Church of the
Real People had been revived.

As he contemplated that, he heard a car coming down the
path. He closed the page and went topside.

He didn't need to go see Stuckey. Stuckey was coming
to see him.

"You busy?" the cop asked.

Shirtless, barefoot and in swim trunks, his hands on his hips, Luke said, "I think I can spare a few minutes."

Stuckey hopped down onto the boat, wiping his hand across his brow. "Hot out here today, huh?"

"The cabin is air-conditioned," Luke said.

"You could just live in a house, like normal people do," Stuckey told him.

"I could. But I like the boat. I can leave without packing whenever I get the urge."

Shaking his head, Stuckey ducked and went down the steps to the cabin, heading straight to the refrigerator, helping himself to a beer before flopping down on the sofa. Officially, Sunday was his day off. Unofficially, he was a workaholic and used the weekends for the cases that weren't technically his to solve.

"I got a present this morning," Stuckey told him.

"Oh?"

"A food basket. Rene Gonzalez's folks sent it. They think you can save Rene, and they wanted to thank me for sending them to you."

"So you got the food basket and I got nothing?" Luke said, then helped himself to a beer as well, and sat down across from Stuckey.

"Can you really do anything?" Stuckey asked him. "Is she even in danger? None of us believe Colleen just disappeared, but we can't prove any differently. So maybe we're wrong. Maybe it's a publicity stunt."

"A six-month publicity stunt?" Luke asked.

"Right. I know. And not that it would change anything where Rene is concerned. She's hell-bent on going out to that island."

"And she's over twenty-one, so if she wants to go, she can."

"And that leads me to my point. She will go on the photo shoot, but so will you."

"So far, so good," Luke said. "As long as Miss Marin doesn't give me away."

"Chloe Marin is as solid as the day is long," Stuckey assured him.

"Yeah, I've been reading up about her. Why the hell didn't you tell me who I was dealing with?" Luke demanded, shaking his head. "That she survived a massacre like that? The kind of work she does? That she's not just some wannabe?"

"You know, in hindsight, I should have told you about her and what she was doing at the mansion for us. She was raised by her uncle—A.D.A. Leo Marin—so she learned a lot from him, and she comes in when we need her to sketch for us. It started the night of the massacre. She drew a likeness that helped us identify one of the cult members found dead in the Everglades.

"She has something that's close to a photographic memory, and an eye for detail." He shook his head. "The night of the massacre… I can only imagine the terror. Chloe got Victoria out of there, and Brad and Jared were there and survived, too. The four of them have been close ever since, but it changed their lives in ways I don't think they'll ever completely get over. Victoria could have done a dozen fashion shoots in Paris, but she didn't accept. You know why?

She works down here because she can be with her friends. Not one of them has ever formed a serious romantic relationship. They pretty much lose themselves in their jobs. Brad has a trust fund and his boat business, and he and his cousin Victoria stand to inherit a fortune when their maternal grandfather dies. Jared trades stocks. And Chloe counsels trauma survivors, in addition to her work for us."

"I should have known all this before I went into that house."

"Other than the fact that Chloe was there to listen in for us, what does the past have to do with a missing girl in the Keys? With a father who worries about his daughter, since it was her best friend who went missing?" Stuckey demanded. "Besides, you said you wanted total anonymity. In my defense, you've been worried that Chloe is going to spill the beans about you. If she didn't know about you, she couldn't have said anything."

"That doesn't mean I shouldn't have known about her. And now that she *does* know about me, how the hell am I going to keep my anonymity if Chloe Marin is as close as you say with the others?"

"I told her not to say anything, and she won't," Stuckey insisted.

"Not even to Victoria—who'll end up telling someone else?"

"No. Believe me. Chloe's rock solid. So what's your next move?" Stuckey asked.

"Let's go back for a minute. You were sure, absolutely sure, that the men who committed that massacre were the two men found in the Everglades?" Luke asked.

"Why are we back on the past? I'm sure. The killers were found, along with a bag holding black, hooded dive suits, one with the mask ripped, and knives covered with dried blood from the victims were found. Not to mention that one of the men matched Chloe's sketch. Yeah, we're sure. Why?"

"Those 'killers' just didn't look the type, that's all," Luke said. "Especially the smaller guy."

Stuckey shrugged. "They were found two days after the murder, with enough evidence to put my grandmother away. And the suicide note—the Church of the Real People denied any involvement, of course. They were devastated, claiming they had never condoned murder, that the killers must have been insane. The church pretty much fell apart after that, though it started rebuilding a few years later."

"What I find interesting, if not out-and-out suspicious," Luke said, "is that the kids were all killed with knives, but Abram Garcia shot Michael Donlevy, then himself."

"What would you rather do? Cut yourself or die clean and neat from a bullet to the head?" Stuckey asked.

"So Garcia shot Donlevy in the head?"

"Yep. Point-blank range. Then himself."

"He didn't put the gun in his mouth?" Luke asked.

"No, shot himself in the temple."

"Hmm."

"Why 'hmm'?" Stuckey sounded annoyed.

"I just find it odd. Suicides have a tendency to eat the gun."

"Maybe he never took lessons on the proper way to com-mit suicide," Stuckey said, sounding exasperated. "Here's another thing. The killers were found, and nothing like the killings happened again."

"Sounds odder still," Luke said. "They weren't caught, so why stop? They could have kept going with their mission and 'saved' more kids from going on to lead lives of sin. Instead, they just killed themselves."

"It was guilt," Stuckey insisted. "You should have seen that place. It was a bloodbath. Those kids died without ever knowing what hit them."

"There's another thing," Luke pointed out.

"What now?"

"Think about it. Mass murders are generally messy. People die trying to get away. This was methodical. Organized. Someone knew enough to wait, and then those kids were killed before they were really awake. And you know as well as I do, as easy as it sounds, it's damn hard to slit a throat. Slice right through. It takes skill and strength, and it's pretty hard to believe no one struggled and alerted the rest, which makes me think there were more than two killers, so it all got done quickly."

Stuckey groaned. "What do you want me to do? Reopen the case? It was closed over ten years ago. And it has nothing to do with whatever happened to the Rodriguez girl. She's what we have to worry about now."

Luke shrugged. "Well, I promise you, I will find out what happened to Colleen Rodriguez, and if need be, I'll keep it from happening to Rene Gonzalez, too. Because until we know what happened to her, every young woman out there could be in danger. Victoria and Chloe are going on that shoot. Something could happen to them, too."

"Don't you think I'd stop them if I could?" Stuckey demanded.

"Is that really why you called me?"

Stuckey shook his head. "No. I called you because one girl's missing and another girl's parents are scared. And I sent you in undercover because there's a strong possibility an insider is involved. And does it bother me that two women I know, women who have already been through more than their share of torment, may be in danger, even when no one can put a finger on what that danger might be...? Of course it does. But I'm a cop—I have to act like a cop. I have to follow the letter of the law, not to mention that this isn't even my investigation. My hands are tied precisely because I'm a cop."

"Stuckey, what exactly do you want from me?"

Stuckey paused for a moment, then said, "I pulled you in because you're not a cop, but you're no-nonsense and you have integrity. I want you to do whatever you have to do to discover the truth. Without warrants. Without reading anyone their rights. Just do me a favor, huh? Don't go getting caught—or shot up or sliced to ribbons—when you're doing whatever illegal thing it is you *need* to do to get to the truth."

# FOUR

She should have been expecting him.

And maybe, in a way, she had been.

When Victoria drove into the cul-de-sac to drop her off at her house, Chloe saw Luke Cane leaning against his car just outside her driveway. She was annoyed to realize that just seeing him made her heart start pounding a little too quickly. She had never seen anyone who appeared to be so relaxed and at ease, and yet ready to spring. She rationalized that it was the tension in the man that made him so sexually attractive, though it didn't hurt that he had the whole rugged-good-looks thing down pat.

"Odd car for a designer, don't you think?" Victoria asked.

It was a Subaru Forester, a few years old, though not in bad shape; in fact, it looked as if he even washed it regularly. Lots of people in south Florida—including herself, on occasion—believed that the rain came just to keep cars clean.

"Maybe he likes driving up mountains," Chloe said.

Victoria stared at her. "Right. The mountains of Miami."

"Okay, so maybe he rides out to the Everglades to spy on the Miccosukees and Seminoles so he can work their traditional designs into his clothing line," Chloe suggested.

Victoria laughed. "I guess he could be a sportsman. He looks like one. Odd for a designer, but I suppose you can be artistic and…masculine. Anyway, he's hot, and he's obviously into you. I mean, you guys already took off for a walk on the beach."

"Oh, yeah. Right. He's into me," Chloe murmured dryly.

Victoria waved to the man she knew as Jack Smith, smiling. He smiled, too, and returned her wave, as she suggested sagely, "Give him a chance. Even Lacy was drooling over him last night."

"Lacy has been known to drool over a correctly proportioned blow-up doll," Chloe pointed out, grinning. She didn't intend the words viciously—Lacy readily admitted that she was interested only in sleek, muscle-bound men. Arm candy, of the male variety.

"Hey, he might be arm candy," Victoria said, as if reading her mind, "but he was polite, and he didn't get sloshed. You're pickier than Lacy. It's like you're looking for a superhero. You're such a do-gooder yourself, it's like you have tunnel vision. If a guy isn't trying to save the world, you're not interested."

"That's not true."

"Then you should go for him. I think he's perfect," Victoria said.

*Except that he's a liar and a sham.*

"Get out, go. He's waiting," Victoria said.

Chloe climbed out of the car, waving goodbye to Victoria, who waved back and drove away.

Chloe stood without speaking and stared at Luke Cane.

"May we talk?" he asked her.

Chloe lifted her hands. "I suppose so. You know where I live, so I can't exactly hide from you. And you're safe enough, according to Stuckey."

"I'm really sorry we got off to a bad start. I'd like to try again," he told her.

She was sure he wasn't actually sorry, that he just thought it was the right thing to say, but she offered him a dry smile and said, "Okay, talk."

"I need your help," he said flatly.

She looked up at him, suddenly wanting to say no, and run into her house and hide, but she knew that wasn't a response to what he'd said but to her own response to him. She tried analyzing her feelings toward him, then gave up. It was chemistry. Just pheromones, aroused by his face, his eyes, the way he moved, the sound of his voice.

"Please. I really need your help," he repeated, and she could tell he meant it.

She forced herself to shrug casually. "All right. Come on in and we'll talk."

"Nice place," he said, looking admiringly at the main house.

"I don't live there—I'm over on the side, in the carriage house. The main house is my uncle Leo's."

"So at least it's all in the family, right?"

"Yes, it's all in the family."

He waited as she keyed in the code for the gate, then followed her along the tile walkway that led to the entrance of the refurbished carriage house. She could feel him behind her all the way.

She opened her door and keyed another code into the alarm pad.

"It's a good setup, after what you've been through," he said, nodding. "All the security, and your uncle living right next door."

He evidently knew a lot about her, she thought, irritated. Either Stuckey had filled him in or he'd been looking her up on Google. Sometimes she hated the Internet. It made way too much information available on people.

"Would you like something to drink?" she asked politely.

"Nothing, thank you. But, please, feel free."

She stretched out a hand, indicating that he was welcome to take a seat in the living room. He seemed to note everything about her place. Bookcases lined one wall, there was a picture window in the front, a pass-through to the kitchen and an entertainment center that held her television, stereo system and game console.

"Nice place," he told her.

"Gee, thanks. So what do you want?" she asked.

"We're on the same side, you know," he said.

"I do know. I'm sorry, but I guess I don't do well with deceit."

He took a seat on the sofa, and she picked up the pillow from the armchair across from him and sat down. "I'm not a spy, if that's what you're thinking," she said.

"I'm not a spy, either."

She laughed. "I know. You're a fisherman. I saw your license, remember?"

"I really do love fishing."

She realized that while he had done his homework on her, she knew almost nothing about him. She would have to rectify that later. "Okay, you need my help to get to Rene. I'll try to work something out."

He leaned forward easily, folding his hands, casually propping his elbows on his knees. "Here's the hard part," he said, and flashed her a rueful smile. "I need you to act as if you actually like me and trust me—especially around the mansion."

She had to admit, that crooked and somehow self-mocking smile changed him. Made him seem human and…touchable. And that wasn't good. The way he looked at her, as if he liked her, as if he found her attractive…that spelled danger. Or maybe she was reading signs that weren't there. She'd already seen a ghost in the mirror earlier today.

She shook off that memory. She had enough to do just dealing with Luke Cane. She could *feel* him again, some kind of vibrant heat that filled a room when he was in it. He had a unique scent, too, a mix of good soap, sea air and a touch of something just a bit musky. He was confident, but not taken with himself. And he was strong and knew how to fight, as she had discovered last night on the beach. Grudgingly, she realized that he would be a good man to have on her side if she was ever in trouble.

"I hadn't actually known there was a problem between Rene and her parents," she said.

He shrugged. "Octavio Gonzalez came to me—referred by Stuckey—because he's convinced that his daughter is in danger, that whatever happened to Colleen Rodriguez is going to happen to her, too."

"Even if something *did* happen to Colleen—" Chloe began.

"Let's face it—we both know something happened to her," Luke said, interrupting.

"Even so, why are they so worried the same thing will happen to Rene? There will be at least twelve girls going on that shoot, and I'm not even sure Rene will be one of them."

"Here's the problem. She cut her parents off because she believes—with reason—that they are trying to control her and keep her from pursuing her dream. She and Colleen were best friends, and her parents, who are already upset because she won't talk to them, feel that she's in special danger because of that fact. If someone did abduct Colleen, if she is dead, maybe it was because she knew something—and the killer may think Rene has the same information. I want to get to the bottom of whatever happened to Colleen and make sure the same thing doesn't happen to Rene."

"Do you really expect people to believe you're a designer?" Chloe asked skeptically.

"If they don't, I'll show them my portfolio."

"You have a portfolio?"

Again that charming grin. "Yes, filled with designs I guarantee people will love."

"So in your spare time you really *are* a designer?" she asked. This time she added amusement to her skepticism.

He laughed. "No, but I have a friend who's good enough to break out, and I'm using her work, with her full agreement. Who knows? Maybe this will help her career. She's been telling me for years that it isn't what you know, it's who you know, and I'll be getting her work in front of some very important people. As for me, all I know comes from the cramming I've been doing."

"Make sure you're up on your handbags and shoes," Chloe warned.

He frowned.

"Shoes?"

"I guess you never watched *Sex and the City.*"

"I'm afraid not."

Chloe stood. "I think we should go shopping."

"Pardon?"

"You need to know something about women's accessories if you're going to pass yourself off much longer. I'll drive. I know where to go."

"You're willing to take me shopping?"

Chloe drew a deep breath. "We're on the trail of the same mystery. Seeing as you've been willing to admit you need me, I'll help you."

"You're going on that shoot, right?" he asked her.

"Yes."

"And you couldn't be convinced to stay home?"

She shook her head.

"Then let's go shopping."

Money wasn't an issue for Luke. He had enough. No matter what he did for the rest of his life, he had enough. Money was useful for what you needed—or whatever game he needed to play to get what he needed. His tastes tended to be simple. A decent beer, preferably on tap, and Jamieson whiskey. Fresh local fish. Good cotton sheets. Dependable dive gear and a car that wouldn't leave him stuck in the swamp. Clothes were fine, but he bought them for comfort and durability, not by label. The same with shoes.

He couldn't believe the price tags on sandals made from about five dollars' worth of materials. This was a foreign world to him. At least a sports car offered a premium engine and high performance.

He saw the point of leather handbags, sort of. At least they were leather and they would last. But the prices—sometimes thousands of dollars just because they dangled a little insignia of some kind, from a metallic sheep to someone's initials? "I don't get it—I really don't," he admitted.

"Frankly? Most of the time, neither do I." Chloe shrugged. "Sometimes something's ridiculous, but I really love it, so I buy it. And sometimes I'm in a thrift store and see something I really love, so I buy *that*. To me, if you love it and it fits well, who cares who made it? Sadly, I have a few very similar suits—I seem to go for the same thing over and over—for my real work, and some fun casual beach stuff, one good coat…though I do like sandals. But you can find supercute sandals in the bargain basements, too. The truth is, I don't like shopping very much."

"Could have fooled me," he assured her with a laugh.

She smiled back at him. "Hey, just because I happen to know what's out there…"

She was so unusual, Luke thought. Maybe it was her eyes. Cat's eyes. She had an amazing mouth, as well, with kissably full lips, and then there were those elegant cheekbones. He was only a man, after all, and she was simply stunning. A dead man would have responded where this woman was concerned. There had been a few moments earlier—bending down to fasten the buckles of a pair of sandals for her, his fingers brushing her flesh—when he'd felt his libido move into truly dangerous territory.

But they were partners in an investigation, he reminded himself. Admittedly, now that they'd spent some time together, he realized that he liked her. Really liked her. But he sure as hell didn't want to get sexually involved with someone he worked with, no matter how much he admired her.

Sex had become something casual for him. Two people playing the game, leading to a hookup that was about having a good time, not commitment.

And yet, there was something about being with her. Something *nice*.

"I would never cast aspersions," he joked, to break the moment.

"Well," Chloe said, looking away, maybe feeling the same

sense of attraction and just as uncomfortable with it, "if you're going to carry off your charade, you need to know all this."

"If I'm going to stay awake, I wouldn't mind some coffee."

"Lincoln Road. Books and Books," she said. "We're not far."

He knew Lincoln Road; he knew a lot of the shops they'd been in, too.

He just hadn't known shoes.

Before they were seated, Chloe found some books she thought he should have. One was several hundred heavily illustrated pages just on shoes.

He'd never imagined that anyone could write an entire book on shoes.

Another was on contemporary fashion, a third on the history of fashion.

"How were you planning to pull off this fashion-designer thing?" she asked curiously once they were seated at a table in the in-store café.

He'd expected her to choose an herbal tea or some frothy coffee concoction, but instead she had opted for plain old coffee and he'd been the one to go with a latte.

"I told you. I have a friend. Her name is Amy Anderson. She doesn't have a lot of faith in her own talent, and she's shy, so this is really helping both of us."

Chloe shook her head. "Aren't you afraid of being found out?"

"Aren't *you?*"

"I can't get found out—I'm not really doing anything," she said.

"If someone did kill Colleen, what do you think he'd do

if he found you do work for the police? That you may be unofficial, but you're looking for him?" he asked.

She shook her head. "The agency knows exactly what I do for a living."

"Art therapy. Right. But these days, everything is available online. Your uncle's position. What happened to you in the past."

She flushed, uneasy, looking away to the shoppers and Sunday strollers on the pedestrian pathway outside. Dog walkers. Old people, young ones. A group so excited about the movie they had just seen that their conversation was loud enough to slip through the doors of the café.

"It's not really fair. You know everything about me," she said, turning back to face him. "But I don't know a damn thing about you, except that you were either born somewhere in England, or you think faking an accent makes you cool."

"Ouch," Luke protested. "Miss Marin, you are jaded. Me mum would be brokenhearted. I was born in York, grew up in London and I lived in Italy for a couple of years during college. I've been in the States for over a decade now."

She smiled, almost laughed. They were casually holding their coffee cups, hands resting on the table. Close. Too close. He moved the barest fraction of an inch, and his fingers brushed hers. Pure electricity seemed to rip through him. God, it was such a little thing. Fingers touching fingers. He had to remember not to touch her.

"And now you live here? In Miami?" she asked.

"I've had what you might call roots in Miami for about seven years, yes."

"Why have I never met you or even heard about you?" she asked. The question was definitely accusatory.

"I like to keep a low profile."

"But you know Stuckey."

"Yes."

"So you've worked with the cops before."

"Yes."

"When? Oh—I get it. You'd have to kill me if you told me, or something like that."

He shook his head. "Nothing that hush-hush. I just prefer my anonymity, and Stuckey knows that. You can trust me, though. I am a licensed P.I., but most of the time the license is just a piece of paper."

"You must be expensive. How do people like the Rodriguezes and the Gonzalezes afford you?"

"I don't charge them."

"Then how do you live?"

He looked away for a moment. "I inherited money. And I have a guy who invests in low-risk opportunities for me."

"You're kidding!"

His look must have given more away than he'd intended, because he saw her blanch slightly. "I am not kidding, but it's not a topic I like to discuss. Trust me. My funds are legal."

She stood and walked over to the counter. He was afraid he might have bitten back so strongly and quickly that she wanted nothing more to do with him, and he gritted down on his teeth, irritated with himself. He had accepted his own past, learned to live with it. Maybe the dream had put him more on edge than he'd realized. Whatever the cause, he was afraid his sharp reply would hurt him.

He got up and followed her, touching her shoulder. Big mistake. Her skin was beautifully sun bronzed and sleek, the texture fascinating. He wanted to run his fingers along her shoulders, down her back.

She whirled around and stared at him.

He took a step back, but spoke sincerely. "I'm sorry. Forgive me."

She nodded, but her expression didn't soften.

"I lost someone, so now I have money. I'd rather have the someone. But it was a long time ago. And I am sorry I snapped at you."

"Of course. And I'm sorry for your loss," she said.

She was going to pay their bill, he realized, and started to reach for his wallet.

"I've got it," she said, and he could tell from her tone that they definitely weren't staying longer.

After a stop at the front register so he could pay for the books she'd picked out, they walked out to the car. As he opened her door, he asked, "You said you don't know anything about me. Want to see where I live?"

She stared at him, brows furrowed suspiciously.

"Totally innocent, I swear," he said. "Seeing as we're going to be working together."

She shrugged. "Is it far?"

"Not at all."

Geographically speaking, Miami Beach comprised several small islands and Key Biscayne, which some considered the beginning of the Florida Keys. As a result, they had to take a causeway back into Miami proper to take a causeway back out. Going via boat, Luke reflected, was definitely easier, especially because, with traffic, something that was relatively close could become, in effect, very far away.

But they had an easy ride that day, even though Sunday afternoons brought sunbathers, Sea-Dooers, boaters, fishermen and more out to Key Biscayne. The aquarium was nearly across the street—albeit a big street—from where the *Stirling* was moored.

Chloe looked at him. "We're going to Jimbo's?" she asked, referring to the legendary south Florida restaurant.

He laughed. "Close."

He guided her along the dirt track that led past a few businesses, the beer-and-bait shop and finally to the dock where the *Stirling* was berthed.

As they parked, Chloe looked at him, laughing. "I never knew this place was here."

"Probably won't be for much longer," he told her. "If they sell out, I'll move on, but in the meantime, I like it."

"I think it's great," she assured him.

He didn't know why, but he was glad that she liked his little corner of heaven. And then he told himself that he was an idiot, because he was glad just to have her on the boat.

Distance, he warned himself. They needed to get along so they could work effectively together, but he needed to keep his distance. She wasn't the kind of woman a man could be casual about, she wasn't a one-night stand or even a two-night stand, and definitely not…a friend with benefits.

He turned away for a moment, grimacing. He really didn't have to worry. She was damn good at keeping her distance, even when they touched suddenly or their eyes met. Chemistry might be a great thing, but it wasn't something they should explore.

She admired his boat, and he had to admit he was surprised that she seemed to know all about the year and model, and that she asked knowledgeable questions about the motor.

"You still need to rent a boat from Brad, if you want to look respectable, or if you want to look the part, I should say," she told him.

"No problem. I don't think the *Stirling* is right for the part, anyway. And I don't want strangers aboard, so…"

"You should get in touch with Brad sometime during the next few days, figure out just what you want. There's a little place down in the Keys off the Overseas Highway—US1— where we usually get together and start out from. You'll really like the island, too. There's a lot of full-time staff, even though it's small. I'm sure you know that—there are hundreds of islands down there. The agency developed this one years ago. It's as much a resort for the execs and the models as it is a full-time locale for photo shoots. There's a staff of five just for the water sports, and the main hotel and the bungalows have something like twenty housekeepers, another twenty in food services, a dozen security guys…five managers…I'll forget someone, I'm sure. Some of the retired managers even have vacation homes of their own down there. The island is small, but it feels large, if that makes any sense."

He nodded. Small but big. Not a bad description.

She moved suddenly. "I—I should get home. I have some things I want to do around the house."

"Sure."

The drive back was slower going, but once they were off the key, they reached her gate in ten minutes.

Just before he got out, he asked her, "So, can you help me get to Rene?"

"I can try, at least. Pick me up at seven tomorrow night. We'll head over to the mansion."

He thanked her, and then there was an awkward moment as they just stared at each another. Damn. It was undeniable. There was something palpable between them.

"Thank you for the help," he said.

She nodded. "You're welcome. See you tomorrow night."

He watched her unlock the gate and drive inside, glad to see that everything seemed to be secure. He had a feeling that A.D.A. Leo Marin was extremely careful—and given his job, that was a smart move

As she stopped to lock the gate behind her, Luke got in his car and drove away, thinking at first that he would just head home, but then he picked up his phone and dialed Stuckey instead.

"Hey. What are you doing?" he asked when the cop answered his phone.

"Enjoying a few hours off," Stuckey said, then groaned. "At least, I was."

"You can still enjoy yourself. I just want you to take a drive with me."

"Where?" Stuckey asked suspiciously.

Luke told him.

Stuckey groaned again, louder this time.

"It's important to me," Luke said.

"Why?"

"I don't know yet."

"It was ten years ago. What do you think you're going to find?" Stuckey demanded.

"I don't know. I just feel as if it's important for me to see it. Come on. Meet me there, and I'll buy you a beer."

"You'd better buy me two," Stuckey warned.

Luke grinned. Stuckey was in.

They agreed on a time to meet—Luke's stomach reminded him that it was well past lunchtime and he needed something to eat first—and he reached the house first. It was farther north than he had been the night before, but not by much.

The place was off the main road, but again, not by much. Other homes stood to either side, but their high walls and lush foliage hid them, so when he drove up, it was almost as if he were at the ends of the earth.

The sun was just beginning its descent when he parked and stood in front of the scene of the crime. There were large iron gates and beyond them a lawn that was seriously overgrown. The paint was peeling, but not ten years' worth of peeling. Apparently, someone did enough maintenance to keep from being fined by the city, but nothing more. A For Sale sign lay haphazardly on its side just inside the gate, as if someone had long ago given up making any real effort to unload the place.

He stared at it and told himself it was just a house. But at the moment, caught in the waning light of afternoon, the windows were like dark eye sockets, looking out at him with brooding menace. He found himself surprised that some filmmaker hadn't picked up the place for a horror movie. However beautiful this mansion might once have been, it carried an aura of evil about it now.

He heard Stuckey's car arrive, saw Stuckey muttering to himself as he parked and stepped out. He was dangling keys and complaining, "I really don't know what you think you're going to find. They had one of those companies come in and clean up the blood. The mansion belongs to the Varacaro family. Their daughter was killed here, and they never stepped foot in the place again after the massacre, just moved with their other kids to their place in Rio de Janeiro. They've had it for sale forever. No one's ever made a bid on the place, but the Varacaros don't really care. They have oil money. Nice people. Sad. They have two younger girls, almost grown up now, I guess. And three sons. Anyway, the taxes are like pocket change to them, so…here." Stuckey handed Luke the keys, separating the one that opened the gate, and a minute later the two of them walked onto the grounds.

"You got a flashlight?" Stuckey asked. "It gets dark fast under all these old trees once the sun starts to go down."

Luke patted his pocket. "Yeah. I got a flashlight."

The driveway was long and expansive. Luke imagined the

night ten years ago when the police had come racing up. "The gate was open that night?"

"Wide open. I guess the kids never locked it. The parents were in Brazil, so it was one big open house as far as those kids were concerned."

With the gate unlocked, anyone could have come in, Luke thought.

"What about the front door?" he asked.

"Open, too, I'm afraid. Along with the back door."

Once upon a time the place had been beautiful. Distinctive architectural elements abounded, like the carved double doors, the use of tile and marble and the giant Chinese lions that apparently hadn't done much good guarding the place.

Luke stepped in. For a moment the house seemed to be bathed in blood, and then he realized it was just the sunset.

He turned on his flashlight and his eyes went immediately to the west wall.

People might have cleaned the house. They might have scrubbed the wall. But he was startled to see that the bloodstains had never been fully erased. The remnants were faint, but the words were still legible.

*Death to defilers!*

And then an image that vaguely resembled a hand.

He closed his eyes. He could almost see the words as they had once been.

Red.

Bloodred.

# FIVE

Monday seemed awfully long.

Chloe was accustomed to changing gears, as Victoria called it. She loved it when she was brought in to sketch for witnesses to or victims of a crime, because as much as it hurt to see someone in pain because of what they'd been through, she got a real sense of satisfaction from helping to see justice done. Art had been her first love, especially drawing. Finding the character in a face, the emotion in a captured movement. Stuckey had brought her in to help the police on a case she had no connection to about a year after the massacre. A witness had seen a suspect running down the street after a stabbing over a purse in downtown Miami. Listening to a description, closing her eyes, trying to make the face real in her mind, had been fascinating. She'd been called in several times after that when the police needed extra help, and she'd done such a good job that she'd even been asked to join the force. But she'd still been in college then, and in college, perhaps because of what had happened to her, she had fallen in love with psychology. Art therapy as an actual vocation had seemed the perfect fit, so she'd turned down the offer.

But today had been long, filled with patients whose troubles really got to her. Mindy Sutton was trying to maintain a normal life with a decent husband and a darling two-year-old, but she had been abused by her stepfather from the age of six until she was sixteen. He had gone to jail, but her mother had never forgiven her, convinced that she had made it all up or, worse, seduced her stepfather. After Mindy, she had worked with her youngest patient of the day, fifteen-year-old Isabel Jacobi, who had been stabbed by a fellow student in the restroom at school. Farley Astin was a gentle thirty-year-old who had been freed a year ago after serving seven years in prison for a rape he hadn't committed.

The day had gone on in that vein, draining her.

She left for home late, thanking Jim Evans, her assistant-slash-secretary-slash-sometimes-very-best-friend, for all he did to keep her patients happy and her schedule in such good shape, and wasn't surprised to see that her uncle had beaten her home.

She was just about to open the door to the carriage house when Leo stepped through the French doors from the main house to the pool area. "Chloe," he called, and his tone was serious.

She groaned inwardly. "Hey, Uncle Leo."

"I hear you've been doing some prowling around," he said. "Want to join me for a minute?"

"Of course," she said, forcing herself to sound cheerful, then walked across the pool area and gave him a hug.

"That's not going to cut it," he told her gruffly.

She rolled her eyes. "Stuckey has been talking to you, I take it?"

"He has."

"Leo," she said firmly, following him into the family room at the rear of the house, "I don't know what he's worried about. I'm telling you the truth. The agency is legitimate, and I haven't seen or heard anything to imply that someone working there is a maniac. And you did tell me to keep my eyes and ears open because of Colleen. So what's the big deal now?"

"I was a fool to suggest that you try to listen for information. I should have known that you'd go a step further and get involved yourself. I know you. And I should have realized you would run into danger if you thought it would help someone, because I remember how you looked that day when you saw Colleen Rodriguez's parents at the courthouse," he said.

"That's neither here nor there. Look, I was already planning on doing that shoot—if they asked me. Leo, I'm a lucky woman."

"None of you girls are lucky—not if you run up against whatever happened to Colleen Rodriguez."

Chloe sighed. These days the parental figure-slash-child conversations between them tended to seem a bit ludicrous.

Her uncle was an impressive man. He was apolitical and had no interest in ever running for office, but he loved the law and he loved a courtroom battle—and won most of the time. He was passionate about his cases. Leo was dark where she was light, but he had the same green eyes, fringed by thick dark lashes, a lean, wiry physique and sculpted features. At fifty-five he was a handsome man and still single, though he'd had relationships over the years. He seemed to run on a five-year cycle. She had liked most of his girlfriends and been sorry to see them leave, and she frequently wished he'd married. She felt sometimes that she really needed to have a good therapy session with him.

She had never known anyone more honest and above-board. Nor could she imagine anyone who could have tried harder to give a normal life to an orphaned niece. She listened to him now because she respected and loved him so much, even though she had no intention of changing her plans.

"I really don't think you should do that shoot," he said flatly.

"I know that, but please, hear me out. First off, I never have to be alone. I'll be extremely careful, but I can—just by sitting around a table and having a cocktail—gather more information on this case than any cop could because I'm an accepted part of the group. Second, it's still possible that nothing happened at all. Maybe Colleen Rodriguez is hoping for major news coverage when she surfaces in Australia or somewhere, looking for sympathy because she cracked under the strain of trying to become a supermodel."

"What a liar you are. You don't believe that in the least," Leo said.

"Okay, I admit I think something happened to her. But that doesn't mean it's going to happen to anyone else, and it doesn't mean that anyone concerned with the agency had anything to do with it. The island is minutes away from a dozen places in the Keys. There's a gazillion boats in the area all the time."

"And endless miles of sea—where someone could easily dispose of a body."

"I know that. I'm just saying that there's no reason to worry about me. Brad and Jared will be there, too. You don't need to be afraid for me. You're the one who taught me to get over the past and not to go through life being paranoid."

"I didn't suggest that you stop being smart."

He had walked over to the wet bar and was surveying the bottles, trying to decide what he wanted. She was making him nervous, she thought.

She walked over and gave him a hug, then kissed his cheek. "Uncle Leo, I'm smart, I promise. I spend my days with people who've faced far worse things than I ever did—abuse victims who were tortured for years. I'll be fine. You don't need to start drinking."

He laughed. "Actually, I was already planning to fix a drink and catch up on the news. So, what are your plans for tonight?"

"I'm going over to the mansion with…with a friend of Tony Stuckey's."

"Luke Cane?"

She stepped away, staring at him. "Don't tell me you know the man, too?"

"Of course. He's been around in the background for a long time," he said.

She stared at him, shaking her head. "Great. Everyone's been in on some kind of secret but me."

"There's no big secret about him. He just doesn't go looking for attention."

"Oh? Want to fill me in? You can save me going online to find out about him."

"You won't find much. He stays under the radar. He does what he does quietly."

"What exactly does he do?" Chloe asked.

"I don't know—exactly. And I don't want to," Leo said. He had found a bottle of brandy that seemed to appeal to him. He poured an inch into a snifter and studied the color.

Chloe decided on whiskey, neat. He eyed her as she measured two fingers into a glass, then turned to stare back at him. "This is making less and less sense. He's legitimate, he has a license. But he's under the radar, and you know what he does, but not exactly."

"All right. Do you remember the Holtzman-Avery case? About three years ago?"

She nodded. "Danny Holtzman was kidnapped, and his body was discovered later in a suitcase in the Everglades. Then one of his friends, Dale Avery, disappeared, too. They suspected the same killer, and it was, except that Dale was found alive in a warehouse out in the Redlands."

"Luke Cane found the boy."

"He did? I never saw his name in the papers."

"That's right. He did whatever he did to hunt down the

perp—a psychotic pedophile named Elia Friar, a Little League coach, the whole bit—and get him to tell him where the boy was. I don't know how he did it, and I don't want to know."

Chloe frowned. "You mean—he…beat the information out of him or something?"

"I didn't say that."

"Then…?"

"He saved a child's life. He didn't kill Elia Friar, he brought him in. Friar didn't go to trial, though. He confessed so he wouldn't have to face the death penalty. He never said a word about Luke Cane."

Chloe hesitated. "And how do you feel about that?"

"I'm an officer of the court. I believe in the law."

"Right. But we're not in court. It's me, your niece. So how do you feel about it?"

"I feel that the law can be slow, and it makes me crazy when a pervert gets off on some technicality. So do I envy guys like Luke Cane? Yes. Could I be him? No. I have my place in the system, and I work within it and fight against it all at the same the time."

"What makes him tick?" Chloe mused aloud.

"Why don't you ask him?"

"What?"

Leo indicated a window that gave a view out to the street. She looked and saw that Luke Cane had driven up just beyond the gate. She swore softly, then turned to her uncle and said, "Sorry—but I lost track of time. Since you know Cane, would you entertain him for a few minutes while I get ready?"

The minute he agreed, she tore out the back door and

ran for the carriage house. She had to take a shower. Had to. It was only April, but it was hot, and she felt sticky from working all day. And she was going to the mansion, so she had to look as if she belonged there.

She shed her clothing in the bathroom and jumped into the shower, scrubbing and rinsing quickly, then stepped out and wrapped herself in a towel.

Steam from the shower filled the bathroom, so she opened the door to let it out…and froze.

It was the steam, she told herself. It had to be the steam. Except that she was undeniably looking at a figure, a woman, standing right where she had stood before, but this time Chloe could see her clearly enough to recognize her.

Colleen Rodriguez.

She was wearing a flowing white gown, but both her hair and the gown were wet, clinging to her.

Fear shot through Chloe like a bolt of lightning.

A ghost. There was a ghost in her house.

And then she could have sworn she heard the ghost speak, except the words weren't actually spoken aloud. They were somehow just there, in her head.

*Help me. I know that you can help me.*

"How? How in God's name can I possibly help you?"

*You can. I know you can. You can see me, and there's so much I need to tell you so you can help me…help…*

Then the steam cleared and the vision was gone.

For a long moment Chloe just stood there in her towel, staring at the spot where the vision had been.

Tears burned her eyes, but she blinked them away.

"Steam. Steam and mist," she said aloud. And then, "This is pathetic. I'm going to have to give *myself* therapy. Or else go back to the real shrink."

She was unnerved, but she didn't have time to think about it now. Luke was there, and she could just imagine telling Mr. Ruggedly Handsome that she had been delayed because she had seen a ghost.

She took a deep breath.

The vision was gone, and she was a psychologist, so she could figure this out. She was probably seeing things because of everything that was going on right now. She was sure that Colleen was dead and wanted to figure out what had happened to her, even though no one else seemed to want her on the case. If Colleen's "ghost" asked her for help, then that gave her a good reason to pursue the truth—alongside Luke Cane.

Ghosts were not real. End of story.

She dressed quickly, slipping into a sheath, grabbing a shawl and hopping on one foot and then the other while she slipped on T-strap sandals.

Then she paused for a moment, looking around her bedroom.

What if ghosts *did* exist? What if they did appear to people, seeking closure? What if...the woman in white really was a remnant of Colleen's soul, and she was looking for help, for justice?

Chloe took several breaths. She believed in God, and if there was a greater power, and if people were essentially energy, and that energy was essentially a soul...

Not now, she warned herself.

She could try to understand what was going on later. This was definitely *not* something to share with others.

Straightening her shoulders, she made herself hurry, but she remembered to lock the carriage house before making her way through the French doors into the rear of the main house.

At which point she completely forgot the ghost.

Because of Luke.

She was surprised to find herself feeling like a teenager going out on a first date with the cutest boy in school, except that Luke Cane looked nothing at all like a teenage boy.

She reminded herself that this wasn't a date. They were headed out to the mansion on business.

"Hey there—I thought you had forgotten," Luke said.

"No, no, I told you I'd take you out there," Chloe said.

Luke offered Leo a hand. The two men shook and said goodbye as Chloe headed toward the door.

"I should go out there with you one of these days," Leo said to her.

"Right. No one will notice an A.D.A. on the premises," Chloe said.

Leo shook his head. "Fine. Don't be late. And, Luke? I'm not even going to ask what you're doing out there, but don't you dare let anything happen to her."

"Count on it," Luke promised.

"I'm not going to pay attention to either one of you," Chloe said as she gave her uncle a kiss on the cheek. "Don't wait up," she teased, then wondered how that sounded and lowered her head quickly to hide a blush. She certainly didn't want Luke Cane thinking that she was imagining a romantic end to the evening. She wondered if he had the slightest clue that she felt a wildfire rush through her whenever they accidentally touched, or that in a secret place in the back of her mind, a place she didn't want to acknowledge, she was imaging him naked beside her, touching her.

She'd noticed things about him that were simply part of who he was. He stood when a woman entered the room; he opened every door. She didn't actually think that much about such things generally. While it was nice to have a door opened for her, she was perfectly capable of opening a door herself and was quick to do so when she saw a woman with a baby carriage or someone on crutches, for instance. But she liked his courtesy, and they did seem to be getting along now that they were partners in the search to find out what had happened to Colleen Rodriguez.

"So, how was your day?" he asked her once they were settled in his car.

"Brutal. How was yours?"

"Interesting."

"Oh?"

He cast her a quick glance before concentrating on the road. "You might not like where I've been," he told her.

"Really? Now I'm intrigued. Where have you been?"

"The Everglades."

Chloe mulled that over for a moment. "I have nothing against the Everglades. People go there every day. Care to elaborate?"

"I went out to the site where they found the two men who tried to kill you and murdered your friends," he said bluntly.

Chloe couldn't have been more stunned. She was silent for several long moments, amazed at his interest in the so-called Teen Massacre.

Ten years was a long time, but in some ways, for her, it could have been yesterday.

"Why?"

"I don't know. The case just…I don't know. There's something about it that doesn't sit right."

"You're looking at something that's over ten years old, just because it doesn't sit right?" she asked, shocked that this man had the same feeling about the case that she'd had ever since the police had officially closed it.

He shrugged but didn't explain further.

Chloe felt at a disadvantage. She still knew almost nothing about him, and even though she agreed with him, she wasn't pleased with this turn of events. She wanted to be wrong. She wanted to think that the men who had killed her friends were dead.

"Don't worry—I don't want to hypnotize you and look for repressed memories," he said.

"Good. Because you're supposed to be working on the Colleen Rodriguez case."

"And you're *not* supposed to be working on it. Not actively, anyway."

Chloe exhaled. "Look—"

"Sorry. Truce.

"But, seriously, if the people who committed those murders are still walking around somewhere, wouldn't you want them stopped?"

"Of course. But they're not," she said wearily, ignoring all her own misgivings. "Didn't you hear? There was a suicide note. And the one guy was definitely one of the killers. I saw him. I'll never forget staring him in the eye, not as long as I live."

"And someone who commits murders like that doesn't just stop, yeah, I know," Luke said. "Forget it. I shouldn't have said anything."

"No. If you did it…I'm glad you told me."

He glanced at her sideways. "Then I guess I should admit I also went out to the house on the beach."

She felt tension streak through her. "I see."

"I'm sorry if that disturbs you."

"I just don't understand why you're doing this."

"I told you, something about the case… Forget it and let's move on."

She sat silently as they drove onto the highway that would bring them to the causeway out to the beach. She was oddly glad, and yet seriously unnerved, that he was taking such an interest. She was afraid, she realized. Afraid that she was right, that there had been more behind what had happened ten years ago.

Ten years ago, when so many of her friends had died.

"Look, I'm really sorry. I didn't mean to upset you."

"You didn't. I'm fine." And she *was* fine at the moment, she realized. It was scary to think that she felt oddly secure at his side. She wanted to have him near her, an ever-confident and assured rock, more often.

Not to mention that she wanted to find out what those hands would feel like touching her flesh.

Somehow they managed to make conversation after that, mostly consisting of her telling him things she thought he needed to know about fashion. Before she knew it, they were moving down the street where the mansion stood. "Just pull up to the gate," she told him, "and I'll hop out. You can't actually reach the call box from the car."

Given how polite he was, Chloe thought, he probably wanted to hop out himself, but it really wasn't practical.

Chloe got out and hit the button, belatedly realizing that maybe she should have checked with Myra to make sure it was okay to just show up. Then again, she was trying to make it look like a casual thing.

Myra's assistant answered the call and told Chloe that their arrival was a pleasant surprise. The gates opened, and they drove in.

Tonight, if there were any guards around, they weren't apparent. They left the car and walked to the door. Myra herself was there, and she kissed Chloe's cheek, then looked over at Luke. "Mr. Smith, how nice to see you. I wasn't really expecting to go over the final details of the shoot with you for a few days."

"We were just going out to dinner and thought we'd stop by. Actually, Jack was hoping for a chance to talk to Rene. Is she here?" Chloe asked.

"Up in her room," Myra said. "I'll call her."

"If it's all right, I'll just run up and get her myself," Chloe said.

"Certainly. Mr. Smith, can I get you something to drink?" Myra asked.

She was leading him to the kitchen as Chloe bounded up the stairs. She tapped on Rene's door, and the girl called, "Yes?"

"Rene, it's Chloe."

"Chloe? Oh, Victoria's friend."

The door opened.

Rene was a stunning young woman. Her eyes were huge and deep brown, adorned by thick lashes. Her lips were beautifully shaped and generous, and the gods of perfection had given her a wasp waist and natural curves, all in a petite package.

She didn't need airbrushing.

"Hi, Chloe. Nice to see you. What's up?" Her eyes narrowed. "You're not with the cops, are you? I actually called them today to assure them I'm not a missing person. My parents were driving me crazy, leaving messages all the time."

Chloe shook her head. "No. I'm with a friend who's going to be doing his own shoot alongside the calendar shoot. Everyone has told him that you're perfect for what he's looking for. He'd like to meet you."

"He's not some weird old guy hoping to cop a feel, is he?"

Chloe laughed. "No. I think you'll like him."

"Oh, my God!" Rene's eyes widened. "I think I know who you're talking about. They were telling me about him. I was sorry I ran away the other night—I thought he was a cop, or someone my father sent after me. I knew he was at the party—and I knew he had followed me upstairs. Later I heard he was a designer and wicked hot."

Wicked hot. Yes, that pretty much described Luke.

Rene was always beautiful, whether she wore an oversize sweatshirt and boxers, or was dressed to the nines. Tonight she was wearing leggings and a silk tunic, comfortable, but more than presentable.

She followed Chloe downstairs and joined Myra and Luke in the kitchen, where they had settled comfortably.

"Rene, this is Jack Smith, Mermaid Designs," Chloe said. "Jack, Rene."

"Hi. Nice to meet you," Rene said, offering a hand. Her almond eyes were alight.

"The pleasure is mine," he assured her.

"We're on our way over to the beach for a casual dinner. Do either of you want to join us?" Chloe asked.

"Thanks for asking, but count me out," Myra said. "I'm still worn-out from the party, and there's a lot coming up that I have to prepare for, and I was in meetings with Harry Lee all day, so I didn't get any of it done."

Chloe hoped Rene would go with them and found herself breathing a sigh of relief when the other woman said, "Actually, I haven't eaten yet. That sounds wonderful."

Luke suggested a few places, but everyone was in favor of something light, so they wound up at a little sushi place on Washington, family owned and operated. Rene ordered sashimi and steamed vegetables, making Chloe feel guilty about the sushi rolls she ordered.

"You're so lucky," Rene told her. "You can eat all that and still look fine, athletic, like you're ready for a game of beach volleyball or something. Not fair."

"Great. Now I feel like a prizefighter," Chloe said, then realized that Luke was grinning appreciatively at her, apparently not obsessed with women being bone thin.

"Well, you kind of are a prizefighter. You do all that tai kwan fu stuff all the time," Rene said.

"Mixed-martial arts."

"I loathe exercise," Rene said. "But I do love living at the mansion, and even though it's a lot harder than anyone ever realizes, I love modeling, too."

"That's great," Luke said. "And from what I've seen, the camera loves *you*."

"So am I going to be in your catalogue?" Rene asked Luke.

"Of course," he told her.

Chloe thought it was too bad there wasn't actually going to be a catalogue. She also wondered how and when Luke was going to convince Rene to phone home.

"Has modeling always been something you've wanted to do?" he asked Rene.

"Since I was a little girl. But I come from one of those old-fashioned families where I was supposed to marry well, raise a pack of children and be a good wife," Rene said. "And I do want to get married one day and have a family. Two children. Manageable. But I don't see anything wrong with having a career, as well. Look at Heidi Klum."

"I'm sure you'll manage everything. And I'm sure your family must be thrilled with your success," Luke said.

"No, trust me, they're not," Rene said. "They want me to quit the agency and come home. All they talk about is how worried they are about me."

"Can you really blame them? After all, Colleen Rodriguez did disappear," Luke said.

A clouded expression filled Rene's beautiful almond eyes. "We've been friends since we were kids. She should have told me what she was up to."

"Aren't you worried that something bad happened to her?" Luke asked.

Rene sighed. "I've been over this so many times with so many authorities. As far as I knew, she was seeing what's-his-face—this cute guy on the island. Mark Johnston. I just can't believe anything bad happened to her. It's making my parents crazy, though. It's just easier not to talk to them."

"I bet they'd be grateful to hear from you," Luke said.

Rene looked uncertain.

"He's right," Chloe said. "Come on, Rene—what can it hurt? If they start to give you a hard time, hang up. But you ought to give them a chance."

"Chloe's right. Hang up if you have to. But…remember what you told me? That you want kids yourself one day. Think how you would feel if your kids stopped talking to you," Luke added.

Rene stared at him suspiciously for a moment, but then, to Chloe's surprise, she pulled out her phone and, still staring at Luke, punched in a number. "Mama?" she said a moment later. "It's me."

They could hear her mother's joyous response. Tears sprang into Rene's eyes, and she looked away quickly.

The rest of the conversation was in Spanish, but they

could tell when her father got on the line because they could hear his gruff voice.

When she hung up, Rene was smiling.

But then she looked at Luke again and asked, "Who are you really?"

"Jack Smith, Mermaid Designs."

Rene still looked suspicious, but she leaned across the table and kissed his cheek. *"Gracias,"* she told him.

Chloe was shocked to feel an immediate surge of jealousy. No, not jealousy, she told herself. That would be ridiculous.

She forced herself to focus on how glad she was that Rene had called her parents.

"My pleasure," Luke was saying to Rene. "Now, be honest, aren't you at least a little bit worried about Colleen?"

Rene sighed. "Yes, of course I am. But I have to believe she's playing some kind of publicity stunt."

"Can you tell me about the day she disappeared?" he asked.

Rene nodded. "We were done shooting for the day, and we went back to my room and talked for a while. Then she was supposed to see Mark, and I was meeting up with some of the others."

"Who were you meeting?"

"Um, let's see. Lacy and Maddy and Lena. We were drinking at the tiki bar down by the dive shack."

"And Colleen said that she was meeting Mark?"

Rene nodded. "But she didn't. He came to the bar looking for her. He was upset because she hadn't shown up."

"Did they fight a lot?" Luke asked her.

"No, not really. They disagreed sometimes, but who doesn't?"

"Was he ever violent?" Luke asked.

"No! Colleen wouldn't have tolerated that."

"Did she have any enemies?" Luke asked.

Rene frowned. "Enemies? Everyone loved Colleen. I mean, I suppose some people might have been jealous of her because she was doing so well, but she was—*is*—so sweet. That's why I think she planned her disappearance—no one on that island would have hurt her. And definitely not Mark."

"Perhaps," Luke agreed. "Still…how much time passed between when she left to meet him and when he showed up at the tiki bar?"

"Maybe ten or fifteen minutes."

"So you were the last one to see her?"

"I suppose. She had her purse with her when she left. And…here's another reason why I think her disappearance was a stunt. We'd been talking about how hard it was to make it to the top. There are so many girls, really young girls, who are so pretty, and some of them are pretty ambitious, too. She was saying how she was afraid she might never make it to the top. Look at all the press she got from this, and think about how much more she'll get when she shows back up. That's why I think it has to be a stunt. But I'll be careful anyway, I told my parents that."

"It's always good to be careful," Luke assured her.

Rene looked at Chloe. "You're going, too, right?"

"I wouldn't miss it," Chloe told her.

"Good. I'll stick to you and Victoria like glue."

"That will be fine," Chloe promised.

"So, tell me about your designs," Rene said to Luke.

Chloe found herself enjoying the next few minutes as Luke played designer. Luckily Rene was excited about swimsuits, and she filled in every gap in the conversation. Eventually they finished their dinner, and Luke drove back to the mansion.

They didn't drive in, but Luke got out of the car at the gate and waited until Rene was safely inside the house. But then, instead of getting back in the car, he still stood staring up at the mansion.

Chloe opened her door and stepped out.

"What's the matter? What is it?"

"Nothing," he told her, turning back to the car.

But by then she was staring at the house herself.

The moon was out, but there was a haze over it, and the color was mixing with the mansion's security lights and the mist drifting along the coast.

The house appeared to be bathed in red.

Bloodred.


He was restless that night. So restless.

He was God's warrior, but he had to be patient. Planning the perfect battle against evil took time.

God wanted his warriors to be skilled and ready. And God had given him what it took to fight the battle and then escape from those who would never understand his cause.

Of course, he had to be honed to the perfect sharpness, like the weapon he was. Honed and ready at all times, so it was only just and right that he kept his edge by killing while he waited for the battle to commence. He was an animal, a predator, and he had come to love the pursuit, the cunning he used, the look in the eyes of those who knew they were about to die. They had sinned, and they were therefore both sacrificed and saved by giving him pleasure in their deaths. He knew that he had a higher calling than others, so he had to kill at other times. A killer couldn't lose his edge.

And he liked it. He had to like it. God knew that. Liking what he did kept him from faltering. It gave him the brilliance to wield the knife and then disappear into the fabric of everyday life. And he played his role well.

He only killed selectively.

Not children. Never children. God did not condone the murder of children.

He chose only those who were going down the wrong path. Only those who were vain and obsessed with material goods. Only those who teased and taunted men with their sexuality. Who drank and fornicated freely. They were his for the taking, and what he did with them, to them, was right.

Tonight…he watched.

Tonight…he waited.

Tonight…

The moon was strange tonight. It bathed the world in red. Red. The color of blood.

He looked at the moon, and he knew that his chance was coming. Another chance to save another soul through death.

As the blood-soaked moon cloaked Miami and the Keys, he knew that his time was coming.

And he was honed, practiced and ready.

# SIX

Chloe had a hard time waking up on Tuesday morning.

She had slept restlessly.

Badly.

She knew that it was all because of the past resurfacing. She and Luke had talked about the massacre, and then they had talked to Rene about Colleen's disappearance.

She shouldn't be surprised that she was having dreams. It would be surprising if she *didn't*.

But it wasn't only the dreams. She was seeing things when she was awake, too.

Last night, Luke had been as proper as ever when they got back to her house. He had gotten out and opened her door, and he had waited not just until she had gone in the gate, but until he saw her go into the carriage house.

She had almost turned around. Almost asked him to come

in. She'd wondered what he would say if she casually mentioned that he was *wickedly hot,* then told him that she didn't trust people easily but she trusted him, and that she had never felt such an overwhelming desire to be with someone. That just knowing he had watched her go inside was incredibly arousing, that his least touch awakened feelings she barely dared to acknowledge.

He would probably have looked at her kindly, before apologizing and turning her down.

She knew almost nothing about his past, and yet...she was sure he was somehow damaged, afraid of intimacy. Just as she was.

Afterward, upstairs in her room, she'd been unable to sleep. All the lights out as she lay in bed, she'd turned on the television for company. The television, that was it. It must have been the reflection from the television that had led her to believe she saw Colleen's ghost sitting in the chair in the corner of her room, watching her.

She had bolted straight up in bed, then forced herself to walk over to the chair to...find...nothing. The image had disappeared.

She had nearly started screaming, ready to race over to the main house, and sleep on the floor at the foot of Uncle Leo's bed. Instead, she had turned on every light and turned up the TV volume.

At least Colleen hadn't spoken to her that time.

With all the lights on and the television blaring, she had managed to sleep off and on, but she had awakened far too many times to look around her room. She hadn't seen the ghost again, but she had been grateful, though still tired, when it was time to get up.

Time to bask in the daylight, anathema to ghosts. Why was Colleen haunting her, even if only in her own mind? She knew all the logical explanations. She was worried about the other woman, certain she was dead, so she was trying to prove her case in the recesses of her mind. Giving herself an excuse to keep on investigating.

Great. She needed help, but there was no time for it now. She was off to try to help others.

She had a decent morning at work.

Chloe worked with a series of children who were destined for special classes unless she could discern the cause of their behavioral problems. It never failed to amaze her how accurate shapes and colors could be in discerning problems. It was easy to deduce that a child who drew himself inside a box or a house with no windows felt trapped. If he chose to color with unrelenting blues, purples and black, he was almost always dealing with a deep sadness. Reds and yellows indicated energy and warmth, but the constant use of red indicated feelings of hostility and anger. The children's art gave Chloe insight into their situations and characters before she spent time in session with them.

She finished with the children by noon and was delighted to discover that she had nothing else scheduled for the day. She needed to review the morning's work and make notes, of course, but she would be able to leave early.

She wasn't sure if she was pleased or dismayed when Jim

buzzed her to say that there was a Jack Smith in the outer office, waiting to see her.

Again she felt that annoying pounding of her heart. She lay her head down on her desk for a moment. What a wreck she was becoming, seeing a ghost in her bedroom and mentally undressing Luke Cane every time she saw him.

The students' drawings were spread across her desk, and she quickly collected them, not wanting to be influenced by anything he had to say, much less to take the chance that he might belittle her chosen methods.

Jim opened the door to her office, ushering Luke in.

"What? Do you have radar?" Chloe asked, gathering the last of the pictures and glancing over at him.

"No," Luke said, grinning. "I have a phone. I called to see if there was a possibility of scheduling lunch with you."

"And you didn't think to ask me first?" she asked Jim, shooting him a frown. Then she relented.

"It's all right, of course," she said. Jim was too valuable for her to stay annoyed with him.

"I told Mr. Smith that you're free all afternoon," Jim admitted. "And I cleared your schedule entirely for the week of the shoot—I just rearranged the last of your consultations."

"Thank you, Jim," Chloe said. "That's wonderful." The rescheduling was wonderful, anyway; she wasn't at all sure about the afternoon. She needed time away from Luke.

Jim smiled and closed the door behind him.

"Art therapy?" Luke asked her, nodding toward the stack of pictures she was still holding.

"Color diagnostics, at the moment," she said. "Want to draw a picture?"

"You wouldn't like what I would draw," he said, striding across her office to look out the window down to the street below. His tone had been gruff, and she found herself thinking again that he was emotionally damaged, just like her.

Who had he lost—and how? she wondered. Was he ever going to tell her?

"Nice place," he told her.

"Thanks." She watched him for a moment. "What do you want?"

He turned around. "How do you feel about taking a drive?"

"Where?" she asked warily.

"First lunch, then the Keys. The agency's private island."

"It's an hour from here just to Key Largo—"

"And another hour down to the island."

"I can't take you out there now," she said.

"Why not? I called Myra and asked her if I could go out and take a look around, choose some of the settings I'd like to use."

"So why do you need me?"

"I'd like an insider's view of the place."

"I'm sure one of the real models would go with you. Like Jeanne or Lacy."

"Jeanne scares the hell out of me."

"You are such a liar."

"Come with me. Please?"

Even before he had shown up, she'd been certain that something bad had happened to Colleen, and she'd been determined to find out if anyone in the agency was behind it. Admittedly, she hadn't turned up a single reason for suspicion, but now he was handing her an opportunity for further investigation on a golden platter. She would be a fool to refuse.

"All right."

He grinned, pleased and, she realized, surprised.

"I want to drop my car off at home, then change. It will take about an hour all told."

"Works for me," he said. "I'll be at your place in an hour."

He left, and she frowned as she noticed that she was trembling slightly. She liked him. She didn't want to, but she did. She was wary of the strength and immediacy of her feelings, but there was something about him that was undeniably compelling. It wasn't just his looks—though there was certainly nothing to complain about on that score—it was something about his manner and the contradictory elements of his character. He was smooth, yet he also had a rugged edge. He was gentle, yet somehow macho. And the sex appeal that emanated from him was so scary it ought to be illegal.

She should have refused to go with him because she just knew she was going to humiliate herself somewhere along the line.

She shuffled her papers into her desk, grabbed her purse and headed out of her office.

Jim was at his desk, and he grinned up at her. "You take your time. But when you land one, he's a prize."

"He's a friend, Jim. A colleague."

"Right."

"I mean it."

"I believe you," he said innocently, but he was still grinning like the Cheshire cat.

"I'm out of here," she said. "And you, Mr. Brilliant, are welcome to take the afternoon, too, since it seems you have everything covered."

"I've got a little bit to finish up, and then I'll take you up on that," he told her. "Have fun with your 'friend.'"

There would be no getting through to him. Chloe gave up, waved and left.

After she had changed into jeans and a tank top, sneakers and a denim jacket, she let herself into the main house to leave her uncle a note, telling him that she was heading down to the Keys with Luke. She noticed that his laptop was open on a desk in the family room, alongside a stack of printouts.

Curious, she walked over to the desk. She never went through her uncle's papers—but then again, he rarely brought files home from the office, and he certainly never left them sitting around out in the open.

The laptop screen had gone into hibernation, but she couldn't miss the top printout.

It was a copy of the front page of a fifteen-year-old British newspaper, and she couldn't miss the headline.

*Murderer Slain by Police Office—Enquiry in Process*

She picked up the page, tension and dread filling her. She knew that she was going to see Luke Cane's name. He was the police officer who had slain the murderer. She knew it.

But she wasn't prepared for the rest of the facts, and she gasped.

*Officer Cane returned to his home in Kensington to discover the slain body of his wife and the murderer, Hugo Lenz, still in his home. He has made no statement to the press, but sources concede that Mr. Lenz met his death at the hands of Officer Cane.*

A horn beeped outside the gate and Chloe jumped, sending the paper fluttering to the floor.

She scrambled to pick it up and put it back, and ended up knocking over the entire stack.

Taking a deep breath, she collected the papers. Her heart was still thundering. She wasn't afraid of Luke, but maybe she was starting to understand him.

How did she feel about what he'd done? If she'd had the power and the opportunity that night, wouldn't she have happily dismembered the men who had so brutally slain her friends?

Then again, she had never been a sworn officer of the law.

She finished straightening the papers, though Leo would probably know that she had seen them. Maybe he had left them there for her to see. Why? Did he wonder how she would feel about Luke once she knew the truth—or did he just think she should be warned.

He had come home to find the murdered body of his wife. No wonder he was damaged.

His wife had been murdered.

And he had slain her killer.

She ran out, fumbling for the right key to lock the door,

then stumbling over the code to unlock the gate, then lock it again behind her.

Luke was out of his car, waiting to open her door. She glanced at him nervously and slid in.

He frowned. "What's wrong?"

"Nothing. I was just hurrying. I stopped to leave my uncle a note, in case he was expecting me to be around for dinner. I don't have to leave notes. I don't like to worry him." She knew she was babbling, but she couldn't stop. "I knocked over some of his papers...I was just hurrying."

"We're not in that big a rush," he told her.

She ought to tell him the truth, she thought. Spit it out.

He wasn't truly violent. Was he?

"You look as if you think you're out with Jack the Ripper," he said. "If you're afraid of me for some reason, you don't have to come."

"I'm not afraid of you."

"Oh?"

She looked over at him. His eyes were an intense gray, like deep smoke, and his brow was furrowed in genuine concern. "Look," he said, "I may not be a psychologist, but something's definitely upsetting you."

She let out a breath. "You were married, and your wife was murdered. And you killed her killer."

He stared back at her. She couldn't tell whether he was surprised or had assumed she would find out sooner or later. "Yes," he said simply, and didn't even try to explain.

"The paper said you killed him."

He turned to stare out the window. "That's true." He was

quiet for a brief moment. "He cut her throat, but she fought him first. Hard. He still had the knife, and he tried to use it against me, but I was stronger than he was. Even so, I had a difficult time wresting it away from him."

"Did he fall on it?"

"No."

"Oh."

He looked at her again. "Did I go a little crazy when I found my wife? Yes. Did I torture him to death—no. I came in, I saw blood on the stairs and I followed it, and then I saw her...on the bed. I went over to her, and he leaped on my back. The paper probably neglected to mention that he stabbed me in the shoulder first. We fought, and I got the knife away from him. When he went for it again, I fought back, not thinking, just reacting. I stabbed him in the stomach. Naturally there was an inquiry. I didn't feel like answering questions, but it was deemed a righteous kill. Even so, I quit. I was furious that the authorities expected me to explain myself when the facts were evident."

"You quit and came to the United States?"

"Something like that. I wasn't running away, but after a few years I just couldn't stay there anymore."

They sat in silence for a minute.

Finally Chloe cleared her throat. "We should go. The traffic will start getting bad soon—and I'm getting hungry."

"I meant it when I said you don't have to go. I don't want to be with anyone who's afraid of me."

"It takes a lot to scare me," she told him.

He didn't smile, but something about his eyes softened. "You probably should get scared more easily. A certain amount of fear can be healthy."

"Fear in a dangerous situation is healthy. But I've driven with you—you're a safe enough driver. Seriously, the traffic gets bad quickly."

He smiled slowly. "Yeah. I even drive on the right side of the road."

They didn't speak as they started out, but the silence wasn't uncomfortable. In fact, Chloe was surprised to find herself feeling more comfortable with him than she'd ever felt with a man before. A man she was attracted to, anyway.

Her life had become insular in a lot of ways. She worked with the police, she had her practice. She talked to Jim at work, she had her uncle and her circle of friends, and she modeled now and then.

But she seldom just enjoyed life or going for a drive—or being with a man.

Especially not a man who called to something inside her, who made her want him, want to be with him in a way that was natural and easy.

Which was ridiculous, because nothing was ever easy.

Certainly not wanting him.

They took the turnpike south to US1 at Florida City. Luke turned and grinned at her, pointing out the window. "There's a Cracker Barrel," he said.

She laughed. "Actually, I love Cracker Barrel, and I *am* hungry. But we're so close to the Keys…and the fish tastes so good on Key Largo."

"Even if it was caught off Miami?"

"*If* it was caught off Miami, which I doubt it was, it still tastes better in Key Largo."

He nodded and kept driving.

There was construction along the eighteen-mile stretch, so it was slow going. They passed a sign that told them they had reached Lake Surprise, and soon after, another that announced, Crocodile Crossing.

"Have you ever actually seen a crocodile cross here?" Luke asked.

"No, but I did see an alligator trying to cross I-95 up in Broward once. Honest," she said.

In another few minutes they finally reached Key Largo, then laughed when they both suggested the same restaurant.

It was mom-and-pop owned, and lovingly operated. The decor was rustic, and prize fish were displayed on the walls. A large deep-sea dive suit was displayed by the front door, and when the menu offered fresh fish, it meant caught that morning. Ordering was an easy affair and an oddly intimate one, considering the fact that they didn't know each other well. She would get the snapper, he would order the grouper, and they would share.

"You never chose to leave the area," Luke said after they had been served iced tea, and the waitress—the mom of the mom-and-pop—left them.

"Uncle Leo was already involved with his career, and there was nowhere I really wanted to go. I love home, crazy as it may be," Chloe told him.

He nodded. "Sounds like staying was the right decision."

"Except that you seem to think that the massacre was never really solved, right?"

He shrugged. Their grilled fish was already arriving. Once the waitress had gone again, he said, "I don't know. It's so difficult to tell now...such a long time has passed. Something just— I don't know. It was too neat. All tied up." He hesitated for a second, then said, "I told you, I made Stuckey meet me at the house the other day."

Chloe said, "What did he think about that?"

"He humored me," Luke said. "I could still read *'Death to defilers!'* on the wall. And that...drawing...like a hand."

Chloe looked down at the table. It was as if someone had snatched her breath away. Even after all this time, the terror of that night could still reach out and touch her.

"You really loved your wife, didn't you?" she asked softly, trying to get way from her own thoughts.

"Sure. We were just kids, really. I met her soon after I graduated from college. If we were going to have problems, there was never time for it to happen," he said gruffly. "Yeah, of course I loved her. What ticked me off so badly was that rather than looking at the five murders it turned out Hugo Lenz had committed, *I* came under scrutiny. While I was still trying to deal with the fact that my wife was dead at the age of twenty-three. I couldn't stop imagining the terror she must have felt, and I couldn't forget that I hadn't been there for her. Anyway, I was young, and I was mad, and I was done with playing by rules that didn't make sense to me anymore. Once upon a time I believed I could change the world. Sometimes now, taking this route, I can

at least change a life for the better. Sometimes I think
Stuckey is like what I might have been if I'd continued along
that road. And I'm the alter ego he needs."

"So how long have you been living on your boat on Key
Biscayne?" she asked.

"Off and on, seven years or so. When I moved to the
States, I headed for New York at first. Big sprawling sea of
humanity where you can get lost in the crowd. I went from
there to Hawaii, from Hawaii to Los Angeles, and then I
came here. I was on the west coast of the state for a bit, then
I more or less settled down in the Miami area. Miami's kind
of big and messy, too. But then you've got the Keys for
diving and fishing and a laid-back life where people still say
please and thank-you, own little restaurants like this and
don't think the world will end if something isn't done in an
instant. It's me, I think. My place. My kind of life."

Back in the car, she thanked him somewhat awkwardly
for lunch, which he had paid for, and offered to pick up
dinner, which earned her one of his charming crooked
grins, along with a thank-you.

A thirty-minute drive took them through Key Largo and
Islamorada and to the turn off to the Coco-lime Resort.

It wasn't really much of a resort—not compared to the
sophisticated places the rich liked to frequent. Coco-lime
was rustic and charming. Like the restaurant they had just
left, it was family owned and operated. Once it had been a
single-story strip motel with fifteen rooms, but a recent
two-story addition offered another thirty. Chloe's favorite
room had always been in the old building—the door opened

out to the pool and the cascading waterfall that constantly recycled the pool water. There was a spit of man-made beach to the left of the pool, with a volleyball net, and, to the right and straight ahead, dockage for ten boats. Farther along, mangroves took over, and there were a few pathways where the trapped sediment had formed soft earth. In the small saltwater pools that bordered the paths, tiny fish whipped around with silvery speed. The Coco-lime Resort was something of a best-kept secret. The island, named Coco-belle by the Bryson Agency years before, was a quick boat ride away, yet somehow no one had ever seemed to notice the models who all gathered there, along with an entourage of technical pros, a dozen times a year or more.

But then, people in the Keys tended to be that way, at least in the middle Keys. Privacy was respected.

"So this is the takeoff point?" Luke said.

Chloe grinned. "Yes. I guess you've never been here."

"Nope."

As they parked the car, Chloe told him, "The place is owned by Ted and Maria Trenton. Ted has a son and two daughters from his first marriage, all in their twenties, and they manage the place and tend bar—when they open the bar, which isn't always. Maria and Ted have two boys, a two-year-old and a three-year-old, and she's younger than Ted's oldest son. She's Brazilian, and she's only been in the States about five years, but she has almost no accent at all, and she's also fluent in Spanish and Italian, as well as her native Portuguese. Myra comes here a lot, actually. She's friends with the Trentons."

"So where do we find the Trentons?"

"The main office, of course."

It was the middle of the week, so there were only a few other cars in the graveled lot. Chloe led him around the pool and over to the new building. The office was on the south side, where Ted and Maria and their toddlers also had an apartment.

Maria answered their knock, and Chloe saw that she was pregnant again. Maria was a petite woman with ink-dark eyes and hair, and a heart-shaped face. "Chloe!" she said, and gave her a hug. "What are you doing here? It's Tuesday. The shoot isn't for another two weeks. Almost two weeks. Anyway, not now."

Chloe gave Maria a hug in return and stepped back. "I drove down with my friend Jack Smith. He's a designer, and this will be his first time out on Coco-belle. I wanted to show him around before the craziness of the shoot. Congratulations! I see there's about to be an addition to the family."

Maria blushed, tousling the heads of the toddlers hiding behind her legs. "A girl, so they say. I'm happy. I love my little boys, and I am fine either way, but...a little girl will be nice. How do you do, Mr. Smith?"

"I'm fine. It's a pleasure to meet you," Luke said smoothly.

"Come in, come in," Maria said. "Are you staying for the night?"

"Unfortunately not. I have to work tomorrow," Chloe told her.

"So?" Maria said. "Two hours—you are back in downtown Miami. You should stay. We have only three couples here tonight. The weekend is fully booked, though, thanks be to God. But tonight…Ted can barbecue out by the pool and we can spend some time catching up."

"We didn't plan to stay, Maria. We didn't bring anything with us," Chloe said.

"You may not know this," Luke said with a grin, "but there's all kinds of shopping in the Keys."

Chloe stared at him, startled, and frowned. What on earth was he thinking? She should insist immediately that they go take a quick look at Coco-belle, then head back to the city, for the sake of her own sanity, if nothing else.

She didn't want to go back, though. She wanted to spend time. Not so much here, or even with the Trentons. She wanted to spend time with Luke. Even if she got hurt in the end.

She groaned inwardly. He wasn't the kind of guy she should want, not even for a night. He wasn't any more capable of a real relationship than she was, and she didn't want to be a casual "call of nature" in his life. She understood why he kept his distance from her. She just didn't know if she could do the same.

"We could stay—Maria is right," Luke told her. "If we leave here at six in the morning, we'll beat all the traffic. I'll have you home by eight, and you can change and be in your office by nine."

He wanted to stay, she thought, and she already knew him well enough to know he never did anything without a reason. Did he think that Maria or Ted would be able to tell them something about the missing Colleen Rodriguez?

Luke hunkered down, facing the toddlers at eye level. "Hello. I'm Jack," he said.

"Sam, Elijah, say hello to Mr. Smith," Maria said. The little boys smiled, then ducked farther behind her legs. "You like children?" she asked him.

"Children are little people—they're just not jaded by the world, that's all. What's not to like?" he said.

Maria nodded approvingly at Luke, then said, "Please, Chloe, stay."

"But Jack really wanted to see Coco-belle," Chloe protested.

"Bill is here—my husband's oldest son," Maria explained to Luke. "He can run you out, and when you get back, I have closets full of toothbrushes and shampoo—we are a resort, after all. I can lend you a bathing suit and a T-shirt to sleep in, and one of the boys will have trunks that Mr. Smith can use."

Maria sounded so hopeful, but Chloe didn't think she had much choice anyway.

"That's wonderful!" Luke said enthusiastically.

"You have your favorite room, Chloe," Maria coaxed. "And Mr. Smith can stay right next door."

Chloe smiled and gave in. She knew when she was beaten. They wouldn't actually have to leave at six, either. She didn't really need to be in the office until ten, and her first appointment wasn't until eleven.

"I'll call Bill and tell him to get a boat ready," Maria said.

She pulled her cell phone out of her pocket, placed the call and explained what he needed to do, then snapped her phone closed. "Go on down to the docks. Bill will run you over. You've got an hour or so of daylight left, if you're scouting for locations, Mr. Smith."

"It's Jack, please," Luke said. "And thank you for your hospitality."

Chloe glanced over at him, amazed at the way he took on his assumed identity as easily as he might slip into a jacket.

"We'll barbecue at about eight," Maria said. Then she hustled the children away, muttering to herself about the evening's menu.

Chloe led the way down to the dock, shaking her head. "I can't believe you want to stay here. You might have mentioned it to me before you started pushing the idea."

"What? It's no big deal. We're two hours away from Miami. We didn't take off in a spaceship or land in a foreign country."

"That's not the point," she said.

He glanced at her, clearly amused. "This is hardly an act of piracy or seduction," he told her.

No, sadly, she thought. And yet, if he did want her, could she handle it? She was afraid she would care too deeply, because it was so hard for her to become involved at all that once she fell, she knew she would fall hard.

She prayed that she wasn't blushing.

"That's not the point, either," she said.

They were nearing the docks when she saw Bill Trenton. He was twenty-nine, just a few years her senior, hardworking, and married, with a three-year-old, so his son and his half brothers were a perfect age to play together. All Ted's older children liked their young stepmother, but then again, their mother had passed away when they were young from a rare form of cancer, and it had taken their father a long time to fall in love again, so they were happy for him.

He gave her a hug, just as Maria had done. "What a surprise!"

"Bill, meet Jack Smith. He designs swimsuits, and he's going to do a catalogue shoot when Bryson does its calendar."

"Cool," Bill said, shaking Jack's hand. "Nice to meet you. So I hear you want to see Coco-belle. It's only a short hop over there. We'll take my little old Donzi down there," he said, pointing to his speedboat. It was old, but it was still a beautiful boat. A classic.

"Thanks," Luke told him as they walked down to the boat. Luke hopped aboard easily, but being Luke—even though he undoubtedly knew she was quite capable of stepping aboard on her own—he turned and offered her a hand.

Chloe accepted, chastising herself for being truly pathetic, but the bottom line was that she liked the feel of his hand. The strength of it. The warmth of his living flesh.

"Hey, would it be too much trouble to circle the island before going ashore?" Luke asked, releasing one of the lines.

"Not at all," Bill assured him. They pushed off from the dock, and Bill thrummed the motor slowly as they maneuvered through the mangroves and out to the open water. Then he opened the throttle, and they shot across the waves.

It was too loud for conversation, so while Luke sat near Bill at the helm, Chloe perched by the railing and drank in the smell of the sea. She loved boats, loved the salt air and the sea spray.

When she turned a few minutes later to look at the two

men, she was stunned by the expression on Luke's face. He
was frowning intently, clearly disturbed by something Bill
had said. That made *her* frown, but when Luke caught her
looking at him, he just shook his head to indicate that he
would explain later.

They circled the island twice, and she saw that he was
paying close attention to the layout—the man-made beach,
the docks, the buildings, the mangrove copses and spit of
highland where the groundskeepers had actually managed
to make flowers grow.

After the second circuit Bill let them off at the docks and
promised, "I'll be waiting."

"We won't be long," Luke assured him.

"No problem. I've got a good book, so take your time,"
he said.

Chloe hopped out before Luke could help her. They
started down the dock together.

"So," Chloe said, staring at Luke. "What was upsetting
you back there?"

"Bill is very protective of his stepmother," Luke said.

"I know that."

"But do you know why?"

"Because she's a sweet woman who really loves his father
and the rest of the family?" Chloe suggested.

"Ted Trenton saved Maria."

"What are you talking about? Saved her from what?"

"She was brought into the United States by a man who
bought her from her father in Brazil."

Chloe was appalled, but she wasn't shocked. Living in

Miami, with its large South American community, she knew all about the easy sale of children in the streets of Brazil.

"I didn't know that. You learned all this in ten minutes with the guy?" she asked. She considered herself friends with Maria—and the entire family, but—

Luke had gotten information she'd never even suspected.

"I ask the right questions in the right way," he said.

"So then what happened?"

"The man who bought her, intending to make her his bride, was a religious fanatic."

"Oh?"

Luke looked at her grimly. "Maria escaped from the man. Ted Trenton found her running down the street, terrified, and he believed her when she said she was trying to get away before she could be forced into marriage. She said the man who had purchased her in Brazil belonged to a cult in Miami. A group known as the Church of the Real People."

# SEVEN

There was a security shed, a little larger than an old phone booth, at the end of the docks. Chloe was still looking shell-shocked as they neared it.

Luke took her hand.

"Smile," he said. "You don't want to look suspicious, do you?"

She smiled as the guard stepped from the air-conditioned shack. His shirt read Dockmaster, Frank Little.

Frank Little was anything but little, however. He was a good six-three and built like a bulldozer.

"Hi, Frank," Chloe said.

"Chloe Marin, great to see you. Rumor has it you're one of the models for the upcoming shoot," Frank said.

Luke noted that Frank was armed. He wondered if that

had always been the case, or whether it was something new since Colleen's disappearance.

Frank looked like a good guy, but looks could be deceiving.

"That's what they tell me, Frank. And this is—"

"Jack Smith." Luke offered Frank a hand.

"Nice to meet you. You're kind of late to see much of anything, but we have some golf carts that will let you take a quick look around the island. You'll want to check out the hotel and bungalows. And you're scouting locations—they've done a lot of work over by the mangroves. The girls stand on the roots, half in the water. Jeanne—have you met her? She got bit by a crab once, and she wasn't happy, I can tell you that, but she was laughing as hard as anyone else that night. Then there's the beach, of course, with lots of palms aplenty and some nice dunes. Anyway, the golf carts are over there. They've all got push-button start, so help yourselves."

"Thanks, Frank," Chloe said.

"Yes, thanks, and nice to meet you," Luke told him.

"Same here," Frank said pleasantly.

Frank went back to sit in his air-conditioning, and Luke and Chloe headed over to the row of golf carts. She barely seemed aware of him. Well, he had just blindsided her with his news.

But once they were far enough away that Frank couldn't possibly overhear them, she spun on him. "Why didn't I know that?" she asked.

"When you're married to a woman who was sold as a

teenage 'bride,' aka prostitute, you don't usually bring it up at the dinner table."

"No, I guess not, but…I've known the whole family for years. They never said a word to me, but Bill just came out and told *you*. A stranger. A guy he'd never met before today." She shook her head, obviously both confused and hurt. "How did Ted get the paperwork to make her legal? I don't get it. This is huge, and Bill told *you!*"

"Chloe, I pretty much asked him point-blank how his father and Maria met, and I commented on how well everyone seems to get along."

Chloe shook her head again. "I'm still stunned that none of them ever said anything to me. I mean, most people know that Victoria and Brad and Jared and I were nearly killed by the Church of the Real People."

"Maybe that's why they kept her past a secret, especially from you. Maybe they didn't want to bring up the past and upset either one of you."

Chloe said, "It's just so bizarre." She stared at him, those incredible lime-green eyes wide with confusion. "After those men were found dead in the Everglades, it seemed like the cult pretty much died, too. The members all quit. They didn't want to be associated with any religious sect that would slaughter children. So how could—"

"Don't kid yourself. The Church of the Real People is alive and well and doing business in Miami," Luke told her. "They are, as a matter of fact, having a potluck dinner on Thursday night."

"You've got to be kidding!" Chloe said in disgust.

"I'm not, I'm sorry to say." He paused for a moment before going on. "Cults like the Real People feed on the pain and weaknesses of others. All they need is a leader who can control people with his smooth words and charisma. You're a psychologist. You know how that works. The Real People might have hidden in the woodwork for a few years, but I don't think they ever went away."

"You know, their elders—priests, whatever!—spoke to the police after the murders. They claimed that the men who were found in the Everglades weren't acting in the name of the church. They tried to whitewash everything. But now you're telling me that someone I know, someone I thought of as a friend, rescued his wife from a member of that same cult that was basically practicing slavery."

Chloe was outraged, but he wondered if her anger wasn't really a cover for her fear. She hadn't believed everything she'd been told over the years, but that didn't mean she wasn't worried to hear that the Church of the Real People was still active—both on and under the radar.

"Poor Maria," Chloe said.

"Maria seems to be a very happy woman right now," Luke pointed out. "But…"

"But what?"

"But it bothers me to know that there's an association between the Church of the Real People and this island."

"Don't be ridiculous," Chloe protested. "The agency has been around for almost fifty years, and they've owned this island for at least thirty. I think the Coco-lime Resort has been around for about thirty years, too, but Ted's only had it about fifteen, and he's only been married to Maria for five. There can't be a connection. It has to be coincidence."

"I'm not a big believer in coincidence," he said as they got in the golf cart and started along the path.

"But if there was some connection, wouldn't someone have tried to hurt Maria by now, or bring her back into the fold or whatever? When Ted found her, didn't they try to go after the man?"

"I don't think so."

"Why not?"

"Because she might have wound up being deported to Brazil, and maybe sold all over again."

Chloe fell silent, and when Luke set his free hand over hers and squeezed, she didn't try to pull away.

"All you all right?" he asked her.

"Of course," she said. "I'm just upset about Maria. And... confused, I guess. Or surprised. Taken aback. Whatever. But I'm fine. And we're here because of Colleen Rodriguez. We should be concentrating on what happened to her."

"We are still concentrating on Colleen," he assured her, then threw out an arm as if to encompass the entire island. "This just isn't a very encouraging scenario for discovering the truth."

It was true. The opportunities for foul play seemed endless. The island wasn't large, just a little over five square miles, but scrub pines and dense foliage were abundant between the hotel and the haphazardly scattered bungalows. If Colleen Rodriguez had been murdered, there were plenty of places where it could have happened without anyone noticing before her body was dumped far out at sea. Depending on how clever her killer had been, her body could still surface, though. The Gulf Stream might cast her back to shore. On the other hand, if she had been weighted down and dumped in deep water, her fate might never be known.

"So they shoot all over the island?" Luke asked Chloe.

"What?"

"Photos. They shoot photos all over the island?"

Chloe nodded. "Waterfalls seem to be a big thing. There's a natural one, and the pool at the hotel has one, too. It's really pretty. There's a bar in the center of the pool, with another bar on top of that, and the water flows down over them. They shoot all over in and around the hotel, actually."

"Let's go see the hotel, then," Luke said.

The path took them all the way around the island on their way to the hotel. He counted eight freestanding bungalows and two bigger buildings that appeared to be apartments, all built on pilings. They were a fair distance from the hotel, hidden by the trees. Most likely staff quarters, he thought as he pulled up in the circular driveway in front of the hotel. A manager in a crisp white uniform came down the steps to greet them.

"Hey, Bert," Chloe said.

"Miss Marin, how nice to see you." He looked more pleased than was strictly necessary, and Luke put him down as something of a sycophant. "Mr. Smith, I presume?" the man said, turning to Luke. "Frank let me know you'd be stopping by. I'm Bert Ackerman," he said, stepping forward to pump Luke's hand. "I understand you've been surveying our humble facility."

"It's quite a place," Luke said.

"Yes, we're very proud of it. But come in, come in… Will you be staying here tonight?"

"No," Chloe answered. "Maria talked us into staying over there."

She seemed to have recovered from her shock at Maria Trenton's background. But then, he'd noticed what a strong woman she was their first meeting. And not just mentally and emotionally strong, either.

She was adept at self-defense, too.

But someone else could always be bigger, stronger, better trained—or carrying a knife or a gun.

Maybe he shouldn't have told her about Maria. No, the time for secrets between them was over. He needed to be truthful, needed to trust her and have her trust him in return.

Right now she was doing an impeccable job of playing the part of a flirty model. She took Luke's hand and spoke almost apologetically. "If you don't mind, I'm going to give Jack a little tour."

"Absolutely," Bert agreed. He was a good-looking man, with sandy-blond hair, bronze skin, lean and fit, about thirty-five. He had probably been hand selected to run a resort intended only for some of the most beautiful people in the world—literally.

Just beyond the entry door, huge freestanding sheets of glass, with water cascading down them like an indoor waterfall, protected the lobby and check-in facilities from the heat and sun of the outdoors. The lobby itself was filled with sofas and daybeds and richly upholstered wingback chairs, low tables and several desks set discreetly against the walls, waiting to serve visitors.

Guests did not stand in line here.

Chloe pointed out the winding stairs that led to the restaurant, and another set that led outside to a patio.

Bert had attached himself to them, proudly listing the available services, ending with homemade ice cream. "Nothing better on a hot summer day. We have the real thing, along with sugar-free and fat-free, and sorbet for the girls. Except," he added, winking at Chloe, "on the last day. Then everyone wants a hot-fudge sundae. Mojito bar right over there. Of course, we serve lots more than mojitos. We've got everything, including mineral water for the girls. Except on the last day—"

"When we all drink whatever we want," Chloe said, and smiled.

It wasn't a genuine smile, though. She disliked this man intensely, Luke thought. Maybe that meant something. Maybe he was just a player who came on constantly to the models. Or maybe he was a murderer.

"Mind if I see a few of the rooms?" Luke asked.

"Sure, this way," Bert said. "The deluxe accommodations are on the south side and have balconies with a view of the water or lanais that lead out to the gardens."

They walked past the ice-cream bar and the pool, and down a winding limestone path, which brought them to an archway that led to a series of doors that opened poolside. Bert opened one, revealing what was really a small apartment. These units, he explained, had living and dining rooms, and kitchenettes, as well as one or two bedrooms apiece. Each also had a sliding glass door at the back that opened out to a tangle of gardens.

He led the way, opening the back door and stepping onto a small patio shaded by the balcony of the room above. A tiled walk led from the patio out to the gardens, wild gardens that fit the tropical setting. Bougainvillea draped over low brick walls, hibiscus bushes grew in abundance, and pines and palms mingled together, providing shade and support for hammocks just made for relaxing.

"Beautiful," Luke said.

"And do you see how perfectly the light falls?" Bert asked.

"I'll let my photographer find the light," Luke said. "I just take a hand in picking the settings I think will show off my designs to their best advantage." He looked around for a moment, then pointed and asked, "If you were to follow that line of trees right here, where would you end up?"

"Eventually? In the mangroves, and then the Atlantic," Bert replied with a look that said he didn't see the point of the question.

"There are no more buildings out that way?" Luke asked. "No docks?"

"No," Bert said, still looking puzzled by the direction the conversation had taken.

Luke hardly noticed, though, too busy considering the fact that the area was overgrown, tangled and led straight to the water. No docks. Still, if Colleen had been killed and left in the mangroves, she should have been found. Stuckey had told him that there'd been an extensive search.

Suddenly realizing that Bert was waiting for him to say something, Luke said, "Sorry. I was just considering the possibilities."

"Not too much back that way, like I told you," Bert said. "The mangroves make a good setting, like I told you, but there's no dock and no beach."

"Lots of mosquitoes, though," Chloe said with a grin.

"Don't worry about getting bitten," Bert said. "We spray— eco-friendly, of course—around the hotel and the bungalows, but you can't really get the mosquitoes out of a swamp."

"Of course not," Luke agreed. "Well, we'll see…"

"Thanks for the tour, Bert. But we should be getting back," Chloe said.

"Yes, we're supposed to get to a barbecue," Luke said. "Thank you for taking the time."

"I'm always delighted to show the place," Bert said.

He locked the door to the patio, and they left by way of the front door, walking back along the tile path and past the pool.

They said goodbye in the lobby, where Bert promised Luke that he couldn't begin to imagine what it was like once more people were here for the season.

"But there are people here now, right?" Luke asked.

"Of course. The staff, and a few residents who've retired from the business," Bert said.

"And the only access is by boat?" Luke asked.

"Actually, there's a spot in the middle of the island where a helicopter can land. In case of emergency, it's good to have," Bert said.

Luke nodded, offered his hand and thanked the man

again, then said, "I think we'll make another loop around the island before we leave. I mean, if that's okay?"

"Um—sure. Absolutely," Bert said.

Luke smiled and urged Chloe out to the golf cart.

"We're taking another loop around the island?" she asked as she got in. "But it's almost dark."

"I'll drive fast."

"Great. You'll kill us both."

"We have one more thing to do while we're out here," he said, setting the cart into motion.

"What's that?"

"Stop in on Mark Johnston."

"Mark?" Chloe said.

"Yes. According to the police records I've read, and from speaking with Rene and some of the other girls, he really cared about Colleen. And she really cared about him."

"Yes," Chloe agreed.

"You weren't on the shoot when she disappeared, though, were you?" he asked.

She shook her head. "No, but I've met Mark, and I think he had real feelings for Colleen."

"So you don't see him as the spurned—and homicidal—lover?"

"He certainly never behaved like one. But then again, I haven't seen a list of identifying behaviors for spurned homicidal lovers. I know that he was questioned over and over, and that witnesses placed him at the tiki hut looking for Colleen—and I know that his bungalow was searched top to bottom, and they went over his boat, too."

"Boat?" Luke echoed, his radar pinging.

"He has a little fishing boat. But they didn't find a trace of anything. By the way, you should slow down. That's his bungalow over there, the one closest to the water. They're all on pilings because this place is really just a big sandbar, so when storms—"

She broke off, frowning at him. He knew why. He had just driven past the bungalow she had indicated.

"What are you doing? I just told you that was his place— the one we've just passed."

Luke nodded. "I know."

"So?"

"Don't look now. We're being followed."

She started to swing around.

He grabbed her arm. "Hey, I said *don't* look! What part of that was confusing?"

She blushed and refrained from looking back. "I don't see any lights."

"Right. There aren't any. But, someone is back there, watching us, following us. Don't you find that interesting?"

"Of course. But how do you know?"

"The side mirror," he told her. "I caught sight of an-other cart."

"Who was driving?"

"I couldn't tell. Too dark. I think someone is trying to see if we're really just taking one last drive around the island."

"So instead of stopping to see Mark we really *are* just taking one last swing around the island?" Chloe said.

"It seems the prudent thing to do."

"But you really do want to talk to Mark."

"Of course."

"Even though the cops talked to him a zillion times?"

"There's a difference in talking to someone yourself."

"Reading the man and not just his answers," Chloe murmured.

"The ultimate psychologist."

He was surprised to see a small smile on her features.

"Why didn't you just call him?" she asked. "Set up a meeting?"

"And say what—I'm not a cop, so I can't make you talk to me, but I'd sure like to talk to you and ask you a bunch of difficult questions you've already answered a hundred times? Oh, and please make sure you don't blow my pretense of being a designer?"

Chloe pulled her phone out of her shoulder bag and started texting.

"What did you do?"

"Just keep driving. Finish making your loop, then head back to Bill and the boat."

"What's going on?" he persisted.

She turned to him, her smile deepening. He was surprised to notice, despite the circumstances, that she had a single small dimple in her right cheek.

"Trust me," she told him.

He had little choice, so he did as she suggested.

They left the cart where they'd found it and said goodnight to Frank, then went down the dock, where Bill was waiting. He was reading, and had obviously been prepared for them to return late, judging by the portable reading light clipped to his book. He greeted them cheerfully, assuring them that he hadn't minded the wait.

"So, think the place is going to work for what you had in mind?" Bill asked.

"Yes, it looks great," Luke said. "Can't wait."

It didn't take them long to make it back to the Coco-lime Resort. Night had truly fallen by then, but the bright lights from the resort joined the moon and stars to show them the way.

Even so, it was evident to Luke that a lot could go on unnoticed in the darkness here. It would be easy to slip someone—alive or dead—into a boat from a dozen different places.

Easy to discard a body out at sea.

As they neared the docks at Coco-lime, Chloe slid closer to Luke.

"I imagine he'll be here soon," she said.

"Who?"

"Mark Johnston."

He looked at her, and she smiled, clearly pleased to have surprised him. "I texted Victoria, who got hold of Mark and said that we were here, and suggested he pop over to Coco-lime to meet you."

"You invited him to the barbecue?"

"Sure. I know Maria, and it will be okay." She was silent for a minute. "I thought I knew Maria, anyway."

"You know who she wants to be," Luke said. "We should

all offer that courtesy to people, accepting one another for who we want to be."

"Hmm," she said, looking at him. "Like a swimsuit designer?"

"All right, barb delivered. Let's say it's *usually* something we should all do," he said.

But she didn't look angry, he noticed, only amused.

"That's my place over there," Bill broke in, pointing. "Come with me, Jack, and I'll get you set with some trunks. Chloe, Maria will take care of you—you know the way."

They walked together toward the new two-story addition where Bill and his family lived, then split up. Bill seemed like an all right guy, Luke thought, and his family was nice, too. He had a toddler, about the size of Maria's oldest son, and his wife, Julia, was welcoming, though he had to fudge when she wanted to know about his designs. He put her off by promising her a suit and a cover-up, assuring her that she would just love them.

They headed out to the pool. He hadn't been able to tell whether Bill and Julia's toddler was a boy or a girl—the child had short curly red hair and was named Alex—but when Julia unwrapped the child's towel to reveal a little bikini, he realized that Alex had to be short for Alexandra.

Chloe was still inside changing, but Bill introduced him to his father, Ted, who was busy at the barbecue. Ted Trenton didn't look old enough to have a son Bill's age; he was well built and bronzed from the sun, and sported a full head of hair, albeit graying. He greeted Luke with the natural friendliness that seemed to be a hallmark of the Keys.

It took very little encouragement to get Luke to jump into the pool, and since he was already in the water and good with kids, he enjoyed some time playing with Maria's two little ones when they arrived.

He came up from playing shark with Alex to see that both Chloe and the man he assumed was Mark Johnston had arrived.

At somewhere around six-three, Johnston was at least his own height, with thick dark hair and bright blue eyes. Everything he'd heard was right: the guy would look perfect gracing the cover of a magazine. He wore cutoff jeans and was obviously on good terms with the Trentons.

And Chloe.

His arm lay easily around her shoulders as they joked about something, and Chloe didn't seem to mind.

Luke wasn't the jealous type, but he felt a streak of envy then. It was odd that, after the way they'd met, now he liked everything about her. Her seriousness, her laughter. The coat of jaded armor she wore, but let slip now and then. But it was more than that. He liked the scent of her. The feel of her skin, the sound of her voice. He liked whatever it was that had formed between them over the last few days, and he would have had to be castrated not to feel downright desire whenever he was around her.

He ducked his head underwater to clear his hair out of his eyes, and clear his mind of a whole lot more. Julia was in the pool, too, watching the kids, so he smiled at her and strode up the steps at the shallow end to greet Mark Johnston.

The man seemed pleased to meet him. He had a good smile, a deep voice and a firm handshake.

Mark explained that he was a bartender, and was in line—or had been—for a management position when Bert was moved up the ladder to one of the agency's other facilities.

Maria snorted, and Mark said, "Let's face it. I'm still a 'person of interest' as far as the police are concerned." He looked at Luke and offered him a shrug that held no apology. "I've never hidden anything from my friends."

"And we love it that you're honest about everything, Mark," Chloe said.

The look Mark gave her was warm with gratitude.

Luke's gut was telling him that that the guy was legit. But even so, he didn't believe in coincidences, and it was just too odd that the Church of the Real People had come up again—among this group of *friends*.

"At least no one's talking about firing me," Mark said. "Hey, Chef Trenton—that burger is getting an edge to it, and you know I like my meat screaming rare. Oh, sorry— I hope you're not a vegan, Luke."

Sam, the oldest of the children, was out of the pool and asked, "What's a weegan, Uncle Mark?"

"It's someone who doesn't eat burgers," Mark said, and everybody laughed.

The evening kept going in the same casual manner. The food was good, the company better. It wasn't until Maria and Julia had taken the kids to bed and the rest of them were sitting around, drinking their last beers of the evening that

Mark turned to Luke and said, "So let's get the issue of who you really are out in the open."

Chloe, sitting in a lawn chair next to Luke, spoke quickly. "I told you. He's Jack Smith, a designer who—"

But Mark was staring at Luke intently now. "No, you're not. I'm from New York, and I know who you really are. I was living there when you disarmed that guy in the bank who was holding a dozen hostages. I was out on the street when it all went down. Your name is Luke Cane, and you're a private detective or security guy or something. And I'm damn glad you're here, because we all know something on that island isn't right. And we all know damn well that Colleen is dead, and that someone associated with that island and the agency is her killer."

# EIGHT

Chloe looked from Luke's frozen expression to Mark Johnston, and then to the other two men.

Ted and Bill looked from Mark to Luke, and it was suddenly obvious to her that the three of them had discussed Luke before Mark brought up the issue of his identity.

She sat frozen, but Luke seemed unfazed. "I would appreciate it if you didn't share this information with anyone else."

"Are you kidding me?" Mark demanded dryly. "I sure as hell have no intention of doing anything that would prevent you from discovering the truth."

"Ditto," Bill said, and his father nodded.

"You do know it was someone involved with the agency who made Colleen disappear, right?" Mark said.

"Let's just say I strongly suspect it," Luke said.

"Good. So if you want to grill me," Mark told him, "grill away."

"All right," Luke said. "Did you and Colleen have any kind of an argument? Even a minor disagreement? What were the last words you exchanged?"

"No, we didn't have a fight, and I didn't say anything at all, other than, 'Okay, so you're on your way over here? Can't wait to see you.' We had a good relationship. I wasn't jealous of her modeling career—something the police suggested. I was proud of her, and something more—I trusted her. I trusted the way she felt about me. I don't mean to sound like a cocky asshole, but I've never had trouble with women. My life was filled with beautiful women even before I started working here or met Colleen, some of them wilder than the jungle and, frankly, horny as cats in heat. Sorry, Chloe, but you know some of those girls."

"No offense taken," she told him.

Mark smiled at her and went on. "Colleen was supposed to get in one of those little golf carts and come to my bungalow. It's not a big island! She told Lacy that was where she was going, so when she didn't show, I started getting worried. I went to the tiki bar, but she wasn't there, so then I went to her room, but she didn't answer. I went back to my place, then back to the hotel, but I still couldn't find her. I got really worried then, and I told people something was wrong, something had happened. At first no one paid any attention to me. Jerks like Bert thought it was funny, that she had found a photographer or someone important to mess around with. But they didn't know Colleen. She would never do that to me, and especially not to her family. I'm telling you, she walked out of her room at the hotel and disappeared. Like into thin air. Except no one really disappears into thin air."

"No, they don't," Luke assured him, frowning. He turned to Ted Trenton then. "Ted, this is important. I'm sorry to bring up something so painful, but this is really disturbing me. Bill told me about Maria's connection to the Church of the Real People, and I need to know. Who else knows about your wife?"

Ted was startled and looked at his son, who had the grace to look embarrassed.

"I'm sorry," Luke said, "but, like I just said, this is important. We've been speaking frankly here, and we're going to have to trust each other all the way. Who else knows about Maria?"

"I didn't," Chloe said, looking at Ted.

He looked abashed and uncomfortable. "Well, Chloe, I knew about what had happened to you, and…I didn't want to bring up such a painful memory for you," he said. "And…frankly, it's something I almost forget sometime. Maria's so happy now that it's as if none of this ever happened. As far as people knowing…we never talk about it. Do people know? Yes, sure…Alice Copeland at Immigration knows, of course. She helped us. Maria didn't have any papers, but Alice understood. She's seen it before, children stolen or bought, then smuggled into the U.S. She knew what to do to make things legal."

"So, was Maria smuggled out of the country by this man?" Luke asked.

"She told me that she came in a small plane, so I assume it was someone's private jet," Ted explained.

"I don't mean to downplay what happened to Maria, but what does this have to do with Colleen?" Mark asked.

"I'm not sure," Luke admitted. "My question is, do the people on the island—people with the agency—know about Maria?"

"It wasn't a deep dark secret," Ted said. "But did I specifically tell anyone about it? No."

"So…Maria just appeared here one day, and no one ever asked you about her?" Luke asked.

"Sure, when you're with someone new…people say, hey, cool, where did you meet, how's it going, that kind of thing," Ted said. "But no one gives you the third degree on who you're dating, unless it's your father or mother—and my folks have been dead for years. I had to explain to my children, and that was all. I didn't owe an explanation to anyone else."

"And nothing about Maria was in the papers? Were you ever afraid someone would come after her?" Luke asked.

"Nothing was written in the papers. We handled everything very quietly. Maria didn't know enough about the man she'd escaped—or where she'd been kept—for us to find him or bring charges, and Maria was afraid he'd come after her again, besides. So, I believe that, as far as that man knows, she just disappeared on the streets of Miami."

"But you don't really know that, do you?" Luke asked.

"Well, no," Ted said uncertainly.

"But as friendly as we look," Bill said firmly, "we're not

stupid. Dad and I both keep legally registered Smith & Wesson revolvers and you may not have met her yet, but Maria has a Belgian shepherd up there named Amanda who was trained as a police dog. And we're kind of on the isolated side of life down here anyway."

"And you should know, I have a registered Colt .45," Mark said. "The thing is, having a gun doesn't do a damn thing for you when you can't see the enemy. I've taken a boat around that island every day since Colleen disappeared. I've beaten my way through the undergrowth and been in every single room. I can't find anything—anything at all. There's no answer to where she is."

"The answer is that she's no longer on the island," Luke said. "Someone got her off the island in a boat. Someone who knew what he—or she—was doing. Either she was kidnapped or she's dead. I'm not trying to be harsh, just truthful."

"I pray she's alive—I just don't *believe* she is," Mark said. "I need to know the truth, and so do her parents. Whatever it is."

"Her body hasn't washed up, but I'm afraid that doesn't mean a lot. A killer who was familiar with the area would know how far to go out so he could sink a body for good. And to make sure he kept the body far away from any dive spots," Luke said.

"That's not actually an easy task around here, you know," Chloe pointed out.

Luke nodded his agreement. "That's why I think we need to look not only for someone with ties to the agency, but to the area, as well. We're looking for a Florida native, or someone who has lived here long enough to really know the waters surrounding the Keys."

"I take a dive boat out several times a weekend and sometimes during the week," Bill said. "I've never gone out without thinking about Colleen, without looking for her."

"Well, here's a fact—if the ocean has her, we may never find her. But that doesn't mean we can't find out the truth. And we will," Luke said.

"How?" Mark asked bleakly. "When?"

"I think the killer will strike again during the shoot. The same photographers will be here, the same staff. Most of the models will be the same, too. And once the shoot starts, I have a legitimate reason to spend time on the island and explore. And then I can find out exactly where everyone was at the time Colleen disappeared. As long as no one else knows that I'm not Jack Smith, designer."

"Believe me, I'm the last man to do anything to prevent you from learning the truth," Mark assured him.

"We'll keep it quiet, I swear. I won't say a word to anyone else, not even Maria," Ted swore.

"Me, neither," Bill promised.

"In the meantime...?" Mark asked.

"Keep working and keep looking. The sea can hide terrible secrets—but sometimes she'll cast them back with the tide," Luke said.

Silence fell. Chloe realized she had barely said a word, but she was both afraid and grateful. She had meant to pry, to investigate, to learn all she could. Maybe she hadn't realized the danger she was putting herself in until now. She was glad to be among this company, and knew that nothing would keep her away from the shoot, but she felt better being forewarned to be extremely careful.

And then she glanced toward the docks.

It was dark, and the lights from the pool area didn't reach that far, but the moon and stars shone down, casting just enough light to show her the woman in white.

*Colleen Rodriguez.*

She was standing there, staring at Chloe, and she seemed to be more clearly defined this time. She was wearing what looked to be a floaty silk dress, and she was barefoot, and wet. Her long hair was very dark, almost blue-black in the night. The look she turned on Chloe was imploring. Then she turned to look toward Mark, and there was a sadness about her that was so real, it seemed to reach across the distance between them and physically touch Chloe with its power.

Her mouth went dry.

Mark rose, drawing her eye. "All right. I'm heading back."

Chloe opened her mouth to speak, to point out Colleen's presence. But then she looked back and saw that Colleen was gone.

The others rose, as well, but when Chloe tried to follow suit, she found she could barely stand.

Luke took her arm, frowning at her. "Are you all right?" he asked.

"Fine," she managed to say. But she knew she wasn't.

Inside, she was a mess.

Was she going crazy, or was there more in the world than

met the eye, something she was fighting and denying, but that might be…

Necessary?

"Too much beer?" Mark asked jokingly, then gave her a kiss on the cheek.

She gave herself a mental shake, smiled and kissed his cheek in turn.

"Good night, then," Ted said. The men shook hands, as if sealing some kind of pact. Then Ted and Bill followed Mark's lead and kissed Chloe on the cheek, and started home. Chloe's and Luke's rooms were just behind the pool, down by the waterfall.

"I'll see you inside…and make sure you keep your door locked," Luke told her.

*I don't think you can lock a door against a ghost,* she thought.

But she wasn't afraid of the ghost anymore. She was sure Colleen intended her no harm.

"Thank you," was all she said.

He walked her to her door, waiting while she got out her key.

He didn't kiss her cheek, or even offer her a handshake.

"Good night," she told him.

"Lock the door," he said.

She went into her room. And she locked the door.

Luke had just showered off the chlorine when he heard the knock at his door. He quickly wrapped a towel around his waist and hurried out to answer it, concerned that someone was there now, when everyone should have been in bed.

It was Chloe. Her hair was damp and roughly towel dried, and she was wearing one of the white cotton robes provided in the rooms.

Fear streamed through him, but split-second logic took over and assured him that she was fine—she was standing right in front of him, for heaven's sake.

"What are you doing here?" he asked, sounding colder than he'd intended.

"I didn't realize I was a caged beast," she replied, clearly surprised by his tone. "I couldn't sleep. My mind is racing."

"I see. So you thought you'd keep me awake?" he asked.

"Am I bothering you?"

Bothering him? Hell, yes, he thought, disturbing his compartmentalized mind. No, he admitted, the way she was bothering him had nothing to do with his mind. But all he said was, "No. Come in."

He stepped aside, and she headed straight for the minibar. "Can I get you something?" she asked him. "We could have rum and Coke. Or in my case, since I'm the heavy one, rum and Diet Coke."

"You? Heavy?" he asked. She was at least five-nine and couldn't have possibly have weighed more than a hundred and thirty-five.

"In the Bryson crowd, I'm an Amazon," she told him, sounding completely unconcerned.

"In the Bryson crowd, a string bean would look heavy," he replied.

She grinned. "So what will it be?"

"All right. I'll have a rum and Coke," he said, eyeing her

closely. She seemed restless. With her green eyes and fluid way of moving, she looked catlike to the extreme.

He sat on the bed, still watching her carefully.

Chloe took out the tiny rum bottles and the soda, shrugged, drank a bit from each can, then added the rum.

She handed him his can and toasted, "Cheers!" Then she took a long sip.

"Cheers," he murmured.

She sat across from him on the second bed, staring at him, and he found himself staring back, fascinated by the planes and angles of her face, her defined brows, deep auburn lashes and full lips.

He lifted his drink. "So?"

She shook her head, watching him with those cool, assessing eyes.

"Is there something you don't like about me?" she finally asked.

"No," he told her. "I like you. I more than like you."

She offered him a crooked smile. "You've never come on to me."

"It's not because I don't like you," he assured her. "Are you coming on to me?"

"Aren't you sharp, Mr. Smith," she teased.

He hesitated. "It's a tempting offer," he said. Tempting… and agonizing. His drumming libido was battling ferociously with his mind.

"But not tempting enough?"

"It's not you, it's—"

She laughed. "Oh, good God, surely you can come up with a better line than that!"

"I sincerely doubt you've been turned down often—if ever," he said, "so I'm not sure how you can be familiar with any lines."

She looked away for a moment, then started to rise, her knees just a little wobbly. He half stood himself, catching her hand.

"It's not a line, Chloe. I'm…damaged, I guess."

She met his eyes. "And you don't consider me—with all you know about me—to be completely broken?" she asked softly.

He smiled, shaking his head. "I think you're incredibly strong. You took everything that went horribly wrong in your life and turned it around. You have a great relationship with your uncle, you have friends, good friends, you've kept most of your life. You've already been through hell, but you're still determined to help out in a potentially dangerous situation because you're convinced a girl didn't just disappear. I'm not sure how bright that is—" he grinned to take the sting out of the words "—but I don't like delicate string beans. I like a woman who can kick some ass. I like that very much."

A soft flush darkened her features, the contrast turning her eyes greener. But she didn't speak, only turned to leave.

He should have let her. But he couldn't.

"Don't you see, Chloe, I wasn't as strong as you were. When things got tough, I left. Stuckey and Jimbo are the closest I have to real friends, and I usually talk blood and guts and murder to Stuckey, and bait and beer to Jimbo. I can put on a facade, convincingly be someone else when I need to be for a case, but I'm not really sure anymore of who I really am, who I want to be or where I'm going. I drift through life, waiting for the next interesting case, and if I'm not in the mood, I sail away somewhere."

She stared at his hand, which still lay on her arm, then met his eyes again. "I came looking for sex, Luke," she said bluntly. "I didn't offer you a marriage proposal."

"I do like you, Chloe," he said.

"I like you, too. I see someone who refused to compromise, and who has dealt with way more in the past than I ever imagined. That's not running away. And it doesn't sound like a death wish, either. I guess I just thought that having sex with someone you like wasn't a bad thing."

He had to laugh. She sounded so earnest.

"I don't do it often. In fact, I can't even remember the last time—" She broke off, embarrassed. "Sorry. I didn't mean to share that much."

Later, he would blame it on her eyes.

At that moment, he blamed it on the fact that he was touching her, that she smelled so clean and sweet, fresh from the shower, that her skin beneath his hand was soft, and her very presence seemed to scream of heat and sensuality.

Maybe it was simply because somewhere along the way he lost the towel.

In his mind, the voice of reason was muted by the sudden smoke of desire, and he pulled her into his arms. He found her mouth, the lips he had admired, and found that they parted beneath his with liquid sexuality. When he kissed her, it was as if he breathed her vitality into himself. When he held her, he felt her fire and strength, everything that was vibrant and alive about her, flow into him. He cradled her face between his hands as he lingered over that first kiss, savoring it, but then the fusion between them turned hot and wet. He slid his hands inside her robe and down her torso, feeling the silk of her skin, the curve of her hip. Their lips never parted as she pressed her body flush against his. He gripped her harder, his hand running down the length of her back to the base of her spine and around her buttocks, pulling her still closer. Conscious thought fled. They fell onto his bed together, limbs tangling, their embrace urgent, frenzied. Her breasts were full, her body so perfect that he gasped in sheer amazement. Somehow he forced his now-aching erection to be patient as he bathed her throat and collarbone with his kisses, savoring the hollows and rises, while he cupped her breast and felt a new surge of desire sweep through his body, leaving him shuddering in its wake. His mouth replaced his hand on her breast, then moved on to her ribs, her hip. He savored the sensation of her moving beneath him, with him. He felt her palms on his back, the whisper of her breath against his ear, and he groaned, moving lower against her, as if in this one night he was driven to know her completely. Her hands were a sweet torment against him, fingertips teasing with featherlight caresses, then stroking more boldly.

He feathered his own fingertips down over her abdomen and between her thighs, and he followed each caress with his lips and tongue. He felt her lips against his shoulder, the miraculous undulations of her body, and was aware of a thunder that was the beating of his heart. They rolled together, and then he was above her, thrusting into her at last, sinking into a tight and burning velvet heaven. He didn't know how long the world rocked, aware only of the pulsating need between them, as beautiful as soaring above the world and as basic as the grinding of flesh against flesh. Bathed in a sheen of perspiration, he felt the explosion of his climax and was momentarily embarrassed, but was then gratified instead as he felt her buck beneath him, then shudder as her own orgasm carried her over the edge. They remained locked together as they came down from the pinnacle, until finally the thrumming of the air conditioner drowned out the thundering of his heart, and he eased off her, one arm still holding her close. For what seemed like a very long time they simply lay there together, and he was gratified that she, too, didn't feel the need to speak right away.

At last she shifted against him and looked up to meet his eyes, a teasing, still-sexy look in her own. "I don't usually have to work harder to win a guy's interest than to turn him down, but you were definitely worth it."

"Thanks—I think," he joked back, grinning.

He kissed her again then, because he had to. She kissed him back, but finally they broke apart and she started to rise.

He pulled her back, shaking his head. "Where are you going?"

"I don't want to impose and take up your entire night."

"Get back here."

"You want me to stay?" she whispered.

"All night. I mean, we've gotten past the awkward pre-liminaries." He spoke lightly, even as he found himself smoothing back a lock of her hair. "Seriously, what do you take me for? Someone you can just use, then walk away from? Excuse me."

"No, I just thought that you might like…sleeping alone. *Actually* sleeping, I mean."

"Not tonight," he told her. "So…my turn to beg. Yes, please stay. I confess I'm fascinated by the prospect of waking up beside you."

"Is that all?" she murmured.

"Of course not." She smiled

Maybe it was her smile that did it, that and the little dimple that formed in her right cheek. Or maybe it was the feel of her body against his.

He never wanted to move.

He never wanted *her* to move.

They were quiet for a while after that, almost dozing. But then she moved, just an adjustment of her body against his, but that adjustment hit him like instant lightning. He pulled her into his embrace, and they made love again.

Impossibly, it was even better the second time. He realized, as he fell asleep, that it could never be just sex with this woman.

They overslept, filling the morning with swearwords when they finally awoke.

They took separate two-second showers, and then Luke

insisted on watching Chloe until she was safely back in her own room, so she could dress. That took five minutes, and then they were back in the car, heading north.

They were lucky. The traffic was light.

At one point, Chloe's phone rang. It was Leo, upset that she hadn't called him to say that they weren't coming home. Luke could only hear half of what Leo was saying, but he watched Chloe's face as she first defended herself —"But, Leo, I didn't say we were coming back last night!"—and then apologized up and down.

Luke found himself liking the fact that though she was twenty-seven, she still felt responsible to the man who had raised her.

She blushed as she closed the phone. "I don't think I'll forget to call him again," she said ruefully.

"It's good to be responsible to someone," he said.

She nodded, watching the road. "Luke, seriously, what could Maria's situation have to do with anything on the island?"

"I don't know, but I think I'm going to start doing my own searches—more thorough than what the police were able to do—on the people involved with the agency. I think it's more apparent than ever that Colleen didn't just run away, but it's still an island, and the only way off is by boat. That's the trick—finding out how she was spirited away, and by whom."

"Can it really have anything to do with the Church of the Real People?"

"I don't know. I think it's possible that someone knows

Maria is here. Maybe they came for her and realized they weren't going to get her back, but they spotted Colleen and targeted her instead, for some sick reason of their own. Whoever they are, they must have an in with the agency to have access to the island. All I know is that for the time being, I don't want you going anywhere alone. Any woman associated with the agency and the island could be in danger. Unless…"

"Unless it really was a publicity stunt. Colleen could have arranged to slip away—but she still would have needed someone with a boat to get her off the island without being seen."

"But there's always a guard on the docks. The guy with the boat could have come in through the mangroves, though he would have needed to know the area well to make it without bottoming out. Anyway, it's a possibility, but to be honest, I don't think it's probable. So *you*—" he smiled warmly at her "—need to be careful. Very, very careful."

"I've spent my life being careful, trust me," Chloe told him.

He laughed. "Oh, yeah, that was real careful, following me over that balcony and chasing me down in the sand when I was following Rene."

She flushed. "I thought you were going to hurt her."

"So you call security, or the cops. That's what you do from now on, right?"

"Absolutely."

"I shudder to think what you might have been up to in years past."

"Nothing dangerous, I promise you."

He got her to her gate by nine forty-five, giving her a shot at making it to work more or less on time. Despite her worry about being late, she didn't get out of the car right away. He was afraid she was thinking that she had made a mistake, being with him. But when she spoke, she startled him.

"Colleen is dead, isn't she?"

"I believe she is, yes."

Chloe hesitated for a moment, then said, "Luke, I keep seeing her."

"Remembering her, you mean?"

She shook her head. "No. *Seeing* her. Her…ghost."

She was serious, he realized.

"Chloe, you're involved in trying to find out what happened to her, you believe she's dead, it's only natural that your imagination is working overtime."

She shook her head. "I know it sounds…as if I'm crazy— but I'm seeing her. For real."

He hesitated. If there was one thing he'd developed in the time he'd spent with her, it was complete respect for her honesty and intelligence.

"Just when and where have you seen this ghost?"

She closed her eyes, looking miserable but unable to deny what she believed. "Twice in my room. And last night, at the docks. She's all wet, as if she's been in the water. But not as if she'd been swimming, because she's wearing a dress, a white dress."

She was simply under too much stress. One too many terrible things had happened in her life.

He didn't want to mock her, but he did want to lighten her mind.

"So you came to me for sex because you were afraid of a ghost?"

She looked at him, eyes wide and clear and beautiful. "I came to you for sex because I've been dying to touch you ever since I met you."

He didn't know what to say to that, so he didn't say anything.

"It terrified me at first, seeing her, but I'm not afraid now. I think she's asking me for help," Chloe went on, as if determined to ignore his silence in the face of her last admission. She inhaled deeply, still looking at him. "I wanted to give you an out. I mean, if you think I'm a nutcase, I don't want you to think you have to see me again."

He cupped her cheek in one hand. "If I thought that I'd never see you again, never sleep with you again, I'd probably implode here and now."

She smiled. "Thank you."

"But, Chloe…"

"What?"

"Ghosts don't exist. I believe that *you* believe you're seeing one. But what's haunting you now is fear, and sadness for a young woman you knew, even if only casually, and your desire to find justice for her."

She was suddenly all business. "Sure. Right. Well…I have to get to work."

He hopped out and quickly opened the passenger door. She stood and kissed him by the car. Slowly, sensually. Too sensually for comfort. He stepped back.

"I don't think we have time to make love again right now. Not to mention that I think we'd be arrested if I suddenly ravished you on the road in broad daylight."

She grinned, broke away and hurried toward the house.

He waited until the gate was safely closed behind her before driving away.

Feeling both touched and disturbed, he headed straight back to the *Stirling*.

Despite his best efforts, he was involved with her now. And he was worried about her. Every word she had spoken, she believed.

His boat was just as he had left it.

And yet it was different somehow. He searched the boat carefully, but everything was where it should have been, just how he had left it.

He realized then that no one had been aboard his boat. *It* hadn't changed. *He* had. He'd liked being alone here, but now he wanted her here with him. He wanted to keep her from being haunted by ghosts, from being torn apart by both the past and the present.

Impatiently, he put on a pot of coffee and logged on to his computer.

He was willing to admit that he was worried about her, and he didn't even mind. In fact, it was exhilarating to care for someone so much, to remember the scent of her perfume, the silken texture of her skin, the memories so real that he felt as if he could reach out and touch her.

But right now he had to put those tempting memories aside and get on with the search for the truth.

Because he couldn't—wouldn't—give her up, and that meant he had to learn to function normally with her in his life.

He set his mind on the task, and for an hour and a half, he surfed from site to site, looking for information on the Bryson Agency and everyone associated with it, though pretty much all he got was press drivel.

He went onto Facebook and MySpace, and read the pages of everyone he could think of.

A link to Myra led to an article about her accident, which mentioned that she hadn't been with the agency long when it occurred, and that she was a very religious woman, whose faith in God had gotten her through her trials. She went to St. John's every Sunday then, as she did now. In an interview, she mentioned that she had converted to Catholicism as an adult. "As converts, we believe exactly what we have sworn we believe. Those born or raised in a religion aren't always as devout."

She was a convert, he thought. But a convert from what?

He picked up his phone and put a call through to Stuckey.

"Hey, what's up?" the lieutenant asked.

"I'm looking for the police reports on the Church of the Real People."

"From the Teen Massacre? You sure do have a burr up your butt, Luke."

"I'd like to see everything you've got. Membership rosters, whatever else you have."

Stuckey groaned.

"It will take me some time. Faxed or e-mailed?"

"E-mailed. I don't want papers lying around."

"You got it, but go to lunch or something. This will take a while."

Stuckey hung up, and Luke realized that he was in fact hungry, having skipped breakfast as he hurried to get back to the city. He prowled around the kitchen, irritated to see that he hadn't been shopping and his one option was peanut butter on stale bread.

He left the *Stirling* and headed over to the bait shop, where he would at least be able to get a burger.

The usual afternoon group of retirees was sitting around the picnic tables. He waved and called out his hellos, then went straight to the shack for a burger. When he reemerged forty-five minutes later, a bunch of the men were at the end of the dock, exclaiming over something someone had just reeled in.

Curious, he walked over to see what was going on.

"Don't that just beat all?" Milton Beca demanded, offering him a near-toothless grin.

"What's that?"

"Granger just pulled up an old waterproof canvas bag I lost overboard about a year ago! It's chewed up some, but I got my Swiss Army Knife back. It's sure a funny thing, huh? The bag must have floated in with the weather."

"That can happen," Luke said. "Well, see you. Have a good day."

"I make all my days good now, Luke."

"That's the way."

As he headed to the *Stirling,* Luke wondered again about Colleen Rodriguez. Even if her body had been dumped, that didn't mean it wouldn't come back. It might be tangled in seaweed or stuck under pilings somewhere, but the current was a powerful force and could wash her to shore a day from now or a year. Or never, he reflected glumly.

He decided to make a point of doing a lot of diving off the island. He could take one of Brad's boats and blend in with the crowd from the resort, maybe even have Bill come with him, since it was safer to dive with a dive partner even when there wasn't a killer on the loose.

He paused for a moment, remembering Chloe's description of the ghost of Colleen Rodriguez.

She was wet, and wearing a white dress.

Back aboard the boat, he went online again and found that Stuckey had been as good as his word and e-mailed the promised information.

He studied page after page, then stopped, stunned, at a picture of a woman. She was noted as having left the Church of the Real People years before the Teen Massacre.

Her name was Myrna.

Myrna Rae Edwards.

She had been young, and extremely beautiful. Shy and wide-eyed—the innocent type cults were so good at preying on.

It didn't matter that she had been so much younger when the picture was taken.

And it didn't matter what she called herself.

The woman in the picture was Myra Allen, head of the Bryson Agency's Miami Beach operation.

# NINE

---

Chloe had just finished a patient session when Victoria called. "Hey," she said, recognizing the caller ID.

"Hey," Victoria echoed. "What's up?"

"I don't know. You called me."

Victoria laughed. "Were you able to talk to Mark last night?"

"Yes. He's a really nice guy, and he's still really broken up over Colleen."

"Yeah." Victoria was quiet for a moment. "He's convinced that…something happened to her."

"I know."

"Okay, now tell me about the stud."

*"What?"* Chloe demanded.

"Oh, please. I'm talking about Jack Smith. I know you're not blind. Half the girls at the mansion were coming on to him the other night," Victoria said.

"He—he seems like a decent guy."

Chloe heard Victoria's snort over the phone. "So you drove down to the Keys, you showed him the island—and you texted me to have Mark show up. But after that…it was a nice night?"

"Yes, it was a lovely night," Chloe said.

"*How* nice?"

"Um…nice."

"You're not going to share the details, huh? But you like him?"

"Yes. I like him." She wasn't ready yet to admit just how much. Plus, she couldn't even tell Victoria yet that his real name was Luke Cane. "I like him a lot."

"I'll make you spill the good stuff later," Victoria teased. "Anyway, I really called to remind you that you need to go over to the mansion tonight."

"Oh?"

"I signed you up for some fittings. Is it okay?"

"Sure, but I probably won't even get home till around six-thirty or seven, and then I'll need to change and stuff. Is that all right?"

"I'm sure it will be fine," Victoria assured her. "I'll call Myra and tell her we'll be there around eight or eight-thirty. I'm so thrilled they wanted you to be June—and that you agreed to do it. Call me as soon as you get home, and I'll come pick you up. I thought I could get the guys to go with us, too, but Brad is busy with paperwork, and you know Jared. If Brad doesn't go with me, it seems like Jared doesn't, either." She sighed. "Why do you think that is?"

Chloe hesitated, then decided just to say what she was thinking. "Because Jared is in love with you. If we're all around, it's kind of okay. He feels safe. I think he's afraid if it's just him and you, he'll say or do something and you'll figure out how he feels. And he's afraid you don't feel that way about him, so he doesn't want to take a chance on wrecking the friendship."

"I should know better than to ask a psychologist!" Victoria said. "But you have to be wrong. We've all been friends forever. If he felt that way about me, I'm sure he would have said something by now."

Chloe was bemused. Victoria really hadn't noticed the way Jared looked at her.

"Trust me. I'm right about this."

"Well, it's ridiculous. Anyway, I adore Jared."

"But do you adore him the way he wants to be adored?" Chloe asked, then was surprised by her friend's answer.

"I—I don't know, but…I don't know. Maybe."

"Well, I think that's why he keeps his distance when it's not going to be a group."

"But—you'll be there tonight."

"Maybe he's actually busy," Chloe suggested.

"Maybe. He *is* a great guy. He's smart, he's charming, he's easy to be with. He's sexy. He's…oh, my God, Chloe!"

"Slow down, this has been going on forever."

"But—he really loves me. Really cares about me."

"Vickie, bear in mind, there's a world of men out there who think you're hotter than a July barbecue."

"That's my point. I'm just an object to most people. All

they see are my looks. Don't get me wrong, I appreciate the fact that I was genetically blessed, but I don't fool myself—ever—that people are in love with *me,* or even that they know me or really want to. But Jared really does know me, and I've known, even as friends, that he really cares about me. Thank you, Chloe. You've really opened my eyes."

Maybe she should have spoken up before, Chloe thought. So much for her professional evaluation of the situation.

"I'm glad, but I still say, take it slow. He's been like a drooling puppy for at least a decade. Make sure you treat him kindly."

"Of course I will! And why didn't you tell me this before?"

"I guess I thought it wasn't really my place."

"Really? Well, I'm happy you said something now. Anyway, I'll let you go now and see you later. As soon as you call me, I'll leave my place."

"Perfect."

Luke stopped staring at the image of Myra on his monitor and called Chloe's cell, but he was sent straight to voice mail. He immediately called her work number, but he only got a machine saying it was lunchtime and the office was closed. Frustrated, Luke told himself that he would just have to call back later, so he called Stuckey, instead, and told him what he'd discovered.

"Myra Allen, model and now surrogate mother to some of the future's biggest models—*she* belonged to the Church of the Real People?" the lieutenant said, incredulous.

"Didn't you see the picture and notice the name?"

"Hey, big shot. I've never actually met Myra Allen. I've never been to a party out at that mansion," Stuckey told him.

"Well, now that you know, don't you find it pretty strange that she has ties to the Church of the Real People and Chloe's working for her?"

"Years ago. Looks like she got smart and left."

"Don't be so quick to dismiss this. I think we could be looking at a connection between the Real People and the Colleen Rodriguez case. Let me tell you what I discovered in the Keys," Luke said, and went on to tell Stuckey about Maria Trenton.

"Those *are* some strange coincidences," Stuckey admitted. "You don't think that Myra is a murderer, do you?" he asked, his voice skeptical.

"No, I don't. But I do think this makes her a 'person of interest.' Don't you?"

Stuckey said, "No. I think it makes her smart. She got suckered in when she was young, but she was bright enough to get the hell out. Sometimes people find God in all the wrong places, just a part of the human need to believe."

"Stuckey, trust me. I believe in God. I just don't believe God wants people to go out killing in his name, and I don't believe he—if God has a sex—thinks the way to get to heaven is to hand over everything you've worked for, leave your family and join a cult."

"Hey, I'm on your side," Stuckey said. "Want me to question Myra?"

"You'll put her on the defensive. I'll do it."

"Keep me informed."

"Will do."

Luke hung up and then put a call through to Myra's office, asking for an appointment. Her mousy secretary penciled him in for 3:00 p.m. He thought he had heard that her name was Alana, but he wasn't positive, as neither he nor anyone around him had been introduced to the woman. He hung up and showered quickly. It was a hot day, so he took a few minutes to ponder what to wear for the meeting, something he wasn't accustomed to doing. He eventually chose chinos and a short-sleeved tailored shirt. Miami chic, he hoped.

He headed out and pulled up in front of the mansion a few minutes before three. He parked on the street in front of the house and walked over to the gates, where he hit the buzzer and waited for a reply. A disembodied voice asked him his name, and as soon as he gave it, the gates opened.

Alana met him and led him back to the patio, where Myra sat at an umbrella table, a pile of sketches in front of her. She was studying them, and he saw that she was putting names on the different sheets.

"Mr. Smith, good afternoon. Please excuse me, but we're down to the wire here," she said. "I'm making my last choices for the shoot. So—did you enjoy seeing the island?"

"Very much. It's a beautiful place," Luke said, joining her at the table.

"Have you decided which models you'd like to use for your catalogue?" she asked. "That will be important in our final negotiations. Naturally, the established models demand higher salaries."

"Naturally," he said. "Rene, Victoria, Jeanne and Chloe," he said.

She smiled. "You're not going to use Lacy?"

"I don't think I can afford Lacy."

"Jeanne is almost as pricey as Lacy."

"Yes, but I think I have the combination I'm looking for with those four."

"Then I'll finalize agreements with them for you," Myra told him. "Now, have you made arrangements for bringing whatever you need to the island?" She looked up as she spoke, waving a hand to summon Alana to the table. "Alana, dear, will you ask Viv to brew some coffee for Mr. Smith and me, please?" She turned to Luke and said, "Unless you'd prefer iced tea—or something stronger? It is hot today."

"Coffee is fine, thank you." He watched as Alana, ever so slightly hunched over, went to arrange the coffee. The poor girl was thin enough to be a model, that was certain, but her posture was a deal breaker. "I'll follow Chloe Marin's recommendation," he said to Myra. "I'll rent a boat from Brad."

She nodded. "Perfect. And of course, you'll have a lovely room at the hotel. Now, as to your photographers. Are you bringing your own, or are you using ours?"

"Yours, please. This is my first catalogue, so I'm grateful for all the help I can get."

"Well, from what I've seen, you have an absolutely beautiful line. You should do well. Would you like my suggestions for which girls should wear which suits?"

"I'm all for suggestions," he said. "But I have a few ideas, too."

"Tell me what you're thinking," Myra said, sitting back.

He was grateful when just then a middle-aged woman with a friendly smile brought out a tray of coffee, which bought him time while he tried to remember what was in "his line" and how to segue into the conversation he wanted. "I'm seeing Victoria as a blond, ethereal type, showing the gauzy cover-ups. Jeanne's the bold, in-your-face type, perfect for the rhinestone pieces. Rene will look perfect in the animal prints, and Chloe in the red white and blue one-piece suits, ready for a dive off the high board."

"Sporty," Myra agreed.

"There's something special about her. She's got confidence," Luke said, then leaned forward to speak confidentially. "Frankly, I was surprised. I mean, I gather no one talks about it, but weren't she and Victoria and some of their friends involved in that terrible mass murder about ten years ago?"

Myra had been looking down, making notes. Now her hand went still, and he saw color flood her face.

"Yes," she finally said, but she didn't elaborate.

"But they're all right now? I like both of them very much. Victoria's worked for Bryson forever, right? And Chloe, too, on a part-time basis? Without any problems?" He did his best to sound sincerely worried about his models, as if making sure he wasn't going to stress them into breaking down.

Myra looked up at him at last. "Both Victoria and Chloe are completely stable and professional. Victoria has been with Bryson for nine years, and Chloe's been working with us on and off for almost as long. Victoria teaches and does local theater on the side, and Chloe has a private psychology practice and helps the local police on occasion, and both of them could do double the modeling work if they wanted to. Neither of them even needs to work for a living, but they enjoy what they do and don't want to stop."

"Oh, right. I think I heard that Victoria is an heiress…?"

"She and her cousin Brad stand to inherit Preston Enterprises, and they both have trust funds in the meantime."

"And Chloe?"

"Her parents were killed when she was very young. There was a settlement, and her uncle managed her assets for her quite successfully. She's quite an amazing young woman, to have overcome what she has."

He liked the way Myra defended her flock, with dignity. She gave information without turning it gossipy.

"The Church of the Real People," he murmured reflectively, shaking his head.

Myra's pencil snapped, and she didn't look up for several long seconds. When she did, she was pale, but she tried to speak casually. "I don't think they exist anymore."

"Yeah, they do. I don't remember what I was looking at— the newspaper, maybe? Or one of those local flyers? Anyway, they're having some kind of a potluck supper tomorrow night," he said.

He watched her carefully, trying to decide whether she was surprised by his proof that the cult was still around or if she was just covering her reactions better.

"Really?" she said. "I thought they'd disbanded. The church elders were horrified when the bodies of two members were discovered—with a note taking responsibility for the killings. I once knew something about them, actually. They didn't preach violence of any kind. And though they did ask for a percentage of the members' incomes, so does the Roman Catholic Church."

"Were you a member?" he asked, keeping his tone curious but light.

She hesitated. "Briefly. That's why I was astounded by what happened."

"Why did you leave?" he asked her.

She shrugged. "I was uncomfortable with everyone knowing all my business, with turning my whole life over to the church. I actually felt bad when it all exploded—some of the members were good people. If you ask me, it was the kind of thing that could happen anywhere. A couple of crazies ruining it for everyone."

"You mean the way fanatics in any religion will take the group's beliefs and twist them to their own ends?"

"Exactly. I think those two, the ones who killed the teenagers and then themselves, were totally insane. They acted on their own, based on some crazy belief that they were saving the souls of those kids. That's what I thought then, anyway. I don't really think about it at all anymore. I was young when I joined the church, lost… I'd had a lot of bad relationships…I needed guidance. That's why I joined. That's why most young people join cults. They need friends. Anyway…" She paused, looking at her watch. "I have another appointment, and it's going to be a busy night. You're always welcome here, of course."

He was always welcome, he thought—but she wanted him to leave *now.*

He stood. "Thanks, Myra. I think I'm all set. I really appreciate your help."

She laughed, the color returning to her cheeks. "I'm always happy to help you spend your promotional dollars, Mr. Smith."

Alana was there to see him out—and lock the door behind him.

He called Chloe soon after he left the mansion, thinking that she should just about be out of work, heading home. But she was still busy, doing paperwork. "I have to go out to the mansion with Victoria tonight for fittings."

His fingers tightened around his cell phone. "I'll go with you."

He winced, realizing how curtly he had spoken, hoping she wouldn't just tell him no.

She didn't. He let out a breath as she said, "All right. We were supposed to be there at seven, but we're going to be late. I can't get home in time today. I'm writing up reports for the school board, and they have to go in tonight. Victoria is going to pick me up at my house about seven-thirty— she's sure that Myra will be all right as long as we're there by eight, eight-thirty."

"I'll be at your place by seven-thirty, too," he said. "Victoria won't mind me tagging along?"

"Would it matter to you if she did?" Chloe asked. "You sounded...pretty harsh a minute ago."

"I'm sorry, but no, not really. I learned something about Myra today, and I'd really like to be around anytime you're at the mansion."

"What did you learn?"

He hesitated, remembering how she had reacted to the information about Maria Trenton.

*Remembering that she had admitted to seeing ghosts.*

"How about I show up at seven-fifteen and fill you in then?" he said.

"Very mysterious," she said. "Tell me now."

"Not over the phone."

"Even more mysterious."

He grinned. "Good. That means you'll be happy to see me."

"I'm happy to see you anyway," she said.

Sitting in his car, he smiled. That was another thing he liked about her. She wasn't a game player. She didn't fish for compliments, she didn't act aloof—she just said what she felt and meant what she said.

He grimaced. Maybe thinking about that wasn't such a good thing. It reminded him of the night gone by.

"I'll get to your place early, so I'll be there whenever you make it home."

"Leo gets in around six."

"Then I'll say hello to Leo."

"Sounds good. Okay, bye. No, wait. You do know I'm going to be going crazy wondering what you're planning to tell me, don't you? Myra isn't a prison escapee or anything, right?"

"No."

"A transsexual?"

"Certainly not that I know about."

"A foreign spy?"

"I very much doubt it. Now stop. I'll tell you as soon as I see you, I promise." She was silent for so long that he thought she might have hung up on him.

"I hope everything is okay with her. I like Myra. She's always been nice to me."

"I think I like her, too."

"You *think?*"

"You're not getting any more out of me for now. I'll see you soon."

They hung up, and he used his phone to access the Internet and look up the Church of the Real People. The address was in an area near downtown Miami.

He pulled out onto the street, and started driving toward downtown.

He exited at Biscayne Boulevard, and fifteen minutes brought him to the church. He found street parking about a block away.

The building had clearly been designed for a Russian Orthodox congregation and sat in a mixed neighborhood of old houses and a few freshly painted and repaired commercial buildings near the city's Design District. It was small but pristine—either the members could afford to pay for upkeep or they took care of the labor themselves. There was a small grassy area in front of it, and an actual yard on the eastern side, with picnic tables set up there under the shade of old oaks. There was a little iron gate at the front, and a decorative wall surrounding the property. A sign on the gate read, All Are Welcome Here. He had to admit, there was certainly nothing menacing about the place's appearance.

He pushed open the gate and started up the concrete walk. The front door was painted red. He tried the knob, and the door opened.

There were no statues of saints, no crosses, and there wasn't actually an altar, just a slightly raised stage and a podium. The room was plain, almost barren. As he stood there surveying the area, a man rose from a front pew and turned to meet him. "Hello. Welcome. May I help you?" he asked.

The man was about fifty and balding. He was wearing jeans and a T-shirt that read, Church of the Real People, Living in the Real World.

"Hi," Luke said, stepping forward. He offered his hand and introduced himself as Jack Smith. "I saw something about a potluck supper tomorrow night, and since I was passing by, I thought I'd come check it out."

"Please, come in. I'm Brother Mario Sanz, an elder here. We're all about welcoming people, about finding friends through God's way. Peace, giving, helping one another. Despite the sun and the crowds, Miami can be a cold and lonely place. People come here following their dreams and too often find everyone else is in a hurry, busy worshipping money and searching for a perfect tan out on the beach. We're here to welcome those who need friends, or just need a hand. We are about the human need for relationships, and learning to do unto others with warmth and kindness."

And buying young girls from Brazil, Luke thought.

He nodded gravely, though, as if approving of such lofty principles. "I have to be honest with you, Brother Sanz. I want to come to the church. I want to come to the potluck supper. But I'm concerned. I've read some things…"

Brother Sanz lifted a hand. "Say no more. We are well aware of how we have been depicted, how evil and frightening we're supposed to be. Two of our members were self-confessed murderers who committed heinous crimes ten years ago. Since then we've tried very hard to prove the truth, that those men were working entirely on their own. We have never spoken against others, never wanted to harm anyone. We feel only pity for those who put money and worldly goods above friendship and love."

"But those men who were found dead in the Everglades—they *were* members of the church, right?" Luke said.

"We bar no man from seeking to find God here. I can only tell you—and the police know this as well, because they tore our church apart after the murders—that we cannot understand the insanity of the men who carried out such horror. Brother Michael was here at the time—he will tell you the same thing, too," Brother Sanz said, pointing down the aisle.

A second man had come into the church from a side door. He looked close to sixty, but had all his hair. It was long and white. He wore a brown cotton robe, but it looked more like a bedouin's dress than a monk's.

"Brother Michael, this is Mr. Smith. He is hoping to join us, but he is concerned about the church's past history."

"Ah," Brother Michael said, taking Luke's hand. "There is real tragedy in how the world sees us, for we barely knew those men. No one regrets more than we do that they used us to justify their own delusions. Can I give you a brochure? It's about our work in the community, and the tenets of our church."

"I'd be delighted," Luke said. "I understand what you're saying—an entire group can't be held responsible for the actions of a few. You must have lost a lot of members because of it, though."

"Some come into the church to stay, while others do not. This is a free country, and we are not God. We don't see ourselves as his chosen, merely as his students. When we do not provide what our members need, they must move on. I do hope you'll come to our supper Thursday night."

"I'll certainly try," Luke said as he accepted the pamphlet Brother Michael handed him from a stack on the front pew.

He started away down the aisle, and then turned back. "Excuse me, I'm sorry, but one more quick question. Where does the church stand on relationships? You know, like marriage and homosexuality?"

"We obey the laws of the country and state," Brother Michael said. "We don't encourage divorce, but we don't condemn it. We do believe that God created man for his role in life and women for their roles, as well. But we're not a backward society here—we believe in education, and in a woman seeking achievement."

"Family is everything," Brother Sanz added.

"And if a member decides to leave the church, there is no problem if he stays friends with others who are still in the church?" Luke asked.

"Of course not."

Luke hesitated one more minute, the personification of a man in doubt and trying to make his way past it. "You were both here—when the murders occurred?"

They nodded in unison.

"And you've stayed true to your beliefs and brought the church back," Luke said.

"One day our church will be among the most thriving in the world," Brother Michael assured him. "We are patient, and we will stay the course."

"Well, thank you very much for answering all my questions. I'll read this, and I'll be seeing you," Luke told them, then left, feeling as if the pamphlet were burning in his hands.

He didn't have time to read it right away, but he would keep it for later. Right now he was anxious to get to Chloe's house, to be there when she arrived. He realized he was eager just to see her face again. To be near her. And for much more. He cursed himself softly as he drove for getting so involved on an intimate level. He was only human, though, and having tasted her, now he wanted more. In fact, he wanted to forget everything about this case, and drown in the fragrance of her flesh and her warmth....

But he couldn't forget the case. He didn't know why he was so convinced that the Church of the Real People had something to do with Colleen Rodriguez's disappearance and the possible danger facing others. But the strange facts were piling up—and they were definitely facts, not coincidences. Maria Trenton—who had been saved from being sold to a member of the church. And now Myra Allen—a past member.

Could Myra still be connected to the church? Was it possible she was somehow providing the members with… the occasional…what? Sacrifice?

He didn't want to believe it or even think about the possibility. But far too often a killer turned out to be someone who was known, liked and trusted.

Even loved.

He gave his attention to the road then, making his way through the after-work traffic that clogged the streets.

When he reached Chloe's house, he saw that Leo's car was in the driveway inside the gate. He was all set to go in and see Leo when he picked up the pamphlet and started to leaf through.

The first picture was of Brother Michael, with a caption that read, "Helping children in poverty-stricken areas."

Luke recognized the location.

The picture had been taken in the slums of Rio de Janeiro, Brazil.

# TEN

Chloe managed to finish up by six-thirty. She was touched that Jim Evans had stayed late, too, so he could finish the mailing duties.

"Thanks. You're a doll," she told him.

"You look so tired, I thought you could use the help," he told her.

"Tired—or old?" she asked.

He waved a hand in the air dismissively. "Tired. You're a baby, Chloe. Twenty-seven. Are you trying to wheedle a compliment out of me?"

She laughed. "No, honestly. I'm just thinking about doing the shoot, that's all. Vickie and I are actually pretty old when it comes to modeling."

"Personally? I like models who look like adults," Jim said. "Male or female. I may be gay—"

"No!" she teased.

He arched a brow, grinning. "The point I'm making is that most people like to look at pictures of pretty people, but male or female, gay or straight, I think we're uneasy when we find out we're perving over a kid. So my point is, you and Vickie are just the right age."

"I knew I loved you for more than your phone skills," she said, grinning and picking up her purse to go.

"Wait! Work is over, so spill," he said.

"Spill?"

"I have never seen you look as good as you did when you walked in today. You were glowing. I think you've actually had sex."

Chloe blushed. "Jim!"

"Don't go getting all panicky. The only reason I can tell is because I know you. I'm pretty sure the doorman hasn't figured it out."

She groaned, completely at a loss for a coherent response.

"If it's who I think it is, I like him. I hope you're planning on having lots more sex with him," Jim said. "He's just the right kind of guy for you."

"I'm only in it for the sex—and the photo shoot, of course," she said.

"Oh, come on. I'm sure there's a lot more going on."

"No, there's not, and there can't be."

"Why not?"

"He's made it plain that he's not looking for commitment. Which is cool, because I don't want a commitment, either."

"And why aren't *you* looking for commitment? You should have a home and a family—you're fabulous with kids."

"I'm not ready, I guess. I don't know. Maybe I'm afraid of getting too close to anyone."

"Really? I kept thinking that you and Brad would hook up one day. He's cute, employed, and one day he'll split the family fortune with Victoria."

"I love Brad, but we're friends," she said. "I could never take it any further than that."

She realized that she had expected Victoria to feel the same way about Jared. But she'd been wrong. Victoria had been more than interested when she found out that Jared cared about her.

"Whatever. I don't want to analyze my own problems at the moment. Just don't go telling anyone that I'm having sex, okay?"

"I should put it on the Internet," Jim said.

She groaned and waved, leaving the office at last.

Rush hour usually lasted much more than an hour— more like two or three—but she actually had a smooth ride home. She found her curiosity growing the closer she got to her house, so she was pleased to see Luke was already there, just as he had said he would be.

She waited impatiently for the gate to open fully, then pulled her car into the driveway and waited for the gate to close behind her.

Leo had taught her long ago never to get out of the car until the gate had closed—even if she knew she hadn't been followed. It wasn't that it would be impossible for someone to break in, even with the alarms that protected the gate and the house, but Leo meant to make it hard. If anyone were to come after her, all she had to do was hit a button on her key chain and alarms as loud as radar sirens would go off.

She knew how loud they were, too, because once she had hit the button by mistake.

As soon as the gate was safely shut, she hopped out of her car and hurried up to the main house, fumbling to find the right key.

As she stood there, the door opened.

Uncle Leo was still in his work suit, though he'd gotten as far as loosening his tie and unbuttoning the top button of his shirt.

"I don't like the way this is going," he said as he stood aside to let her in.

She frowned. "The way what is going?" She looked past him and saw that Luke was standing in the family room, just past the archway that separated it from the entry hall. A little thrill of intimacy swept through her, but she told herself that it was just a result of how long it had been since she'd made love with anyone. Not to mention that he was by far the best lover she'd ever known, and it was impossible not to remember their lovemaking when she saw him. He was just so…touchable. And he touched so damn well in return.

Had Leo been talking about Luke?

She didn't get a chance to ask him, because he headed straight back to the family room, clearly expecting her to follow.

He walked to the bar and poured himself a Scotch, without asking her if she wanted anything.

"What's going on?" she asked.

Luke smoothed a stray lock of hair from his forehead. "I told Leo what I found out—and Stuckey, too, of course."

She let out a sound of exasperation. "And what was that?" she demanded. "Seeing as I'm apparently the last to know."

"Myra was once a member of the Church of the Real People," Leo said flatly. "She's changed her name since, and it was before—before the events at your friend's house. But she *was* one of them."

She looked at Luke curiously, wondering if he had also told her uncle about Maria.

Luke was watching her in turn, and she realized that he was concerned about how she would take the news. It was a startling discovery, certainly. But last night she'd been so shaken that maybe she just couldn't be shaken any more. And she couldn't fault someone who had been part of the church but then realized that there was something wrong with it and gotten out.

She was pleasantly surprised to see that Luke looked as if he wanted to rush over and hold her, protect her from danger—and disturbing news. But she really was all right now, she realized. She was stronger than anyone—herself included—had realized.

She lowered her head to hide her smile at how nice it was to see his concern, even if it wasn't entirely necessary.

"I don't think we can hold the past against Myra,"

Chloe said slowly. "You said that she'd left the church before the massacre."

At the bar, Leo shuddered and swallowed his whiskey. "I'll never forget. Never." Then he met her eyes and added, "I'm sorry, Chloe. I didn't have the right to say that. You were the one who was there."

She nodded, walking over to join him by the bar, where she slipped an arm around his waist and smiled as he looked down at her. "I'm okay, honestly. So, Luke, what else did you find out?"

"Not much. I found her picture in some old records Stuckey got for me, and then I went to the mansion and managed to slip the information into the conversation. She told me there were lots of nice, normal people involved with the church, but she was uncomfortable with some of its tenets. She had joined for the same reason most young people join a cult, she needed something to fill an empty place in her life, and the church promised love and friendship and a place to belong."

"The church denied any involvement in the murders— they swore the dead men acted on their own," Chloe said. "Maybe the church itself *was* innocent, maybe those two men really did go off on that killing spree themselves, maybe they even believed in what they were doing."

"I don't know, Chloe," Luke said. "I really don't know. There was nothing the police could do to close the church down—not even while they were actively investigating— but I still find their message to be very mixed. I went by there today."

"What?" she asked, startled.

"After I talked to you, I visited the church. It's downtown, not far from the Design District. I met two of the elders…brothers…whatever. And I took one of their pamphlets."

"Are you going to show it to me?" she asked.

He nodded. "They advertise their work in Brazil. There's a picture of one of the men I met right on the first page, feeding kids in Rio."

"And kidnapping young women—like your friend down in the Keys," Leo said, answering Chloe's earlier question as to how much Luke had told him.

"Technically, she wasn't kidnapped. She was purchased," she said.

"Sold into slavery," Leo said. "The point is, I want to find out if Maria recognizes anyone in the pictures. If she sees someone she knows, I want to make certain that he's prosecuted."

"Uncle Leo, how can you help make sure that anyone is prosecuted *here*—for something that happened in *Brazil?*" she asked.

"If this man forced Maria to stay with him in the United States, I can see that a federal prosecutor brings charges."

"But—"

"Maybe Maria can help us, Chloe. Maybe Colleen isn't dead. Maybe she was taken by someone in the cult and is a prisoner now, just as Maria was a prisoner," Luke explained.

"They didn't do anything when Ted rescued her because he wanted her to stay safe and be able to stay in the States," Chloe said.

"But she has her papers now," Leo said impatiently. "She's a legal resident, right?"

"A naturalized citizen, I think," Chloe said. "But...re-opening the case, bringing all that back up, would be awfully traumatic for her."

She desperately wanted to find out what had happened to Colleen, though she was certain the girl was dead, but she was also afraid of shattering Maria's existence.

A horn beeped outside, and Chloe swore.

"Chloe Elise Marin," Leo said.

"Will you let Victoria in, please?" she asked him. "I'm running really late, and I have *got* to take a shower. It will only take me two seconds," she promised.

She burst out the back way, fumbling with her keys once again, finally finding the right one and letting herself into her house. She started to race up the stairs, then raced back down and locked the door. Upstairs at last, she left her clothes wherever they fell, jumped into the shower and quickly scrubbed off the day's grime. All the while, her mind kept spinning.

It was all so bizarre. She hadn't heard anything about the Church of the Real People in almost a decade. And now...

Now it seemed to be everywhere. But what did it all mean?

She chose a simple knit strapless dress—easy on and easy off for her fittings—and a pair of sandals, and went racing back downstairs again.

When she returned to the main house, Victoria was in the family room with the two men, talking about a play she

had been asked to do in Coral Gables, with rehearsals con-
veniently starting the week after the shoot ended.

"I'm sorry," Chloe said breathlessly as she joined them.
"I'm really late, even though I managed to get out earlier
than I'd expected."

"No, no, it's fine. I told Myra we'd probably be there
around eight-thirty," Victoria told her. "And I didn't know
that Jack was joining us. That's great." She fought to maintain a totally innocent expression as she looked at Chloe, but
she was clearly delighted that Chloe might actually be
getting involved—with a man.

"I'm glad it's not a problem for you," Luke said.

"Not at all. And after we finish, a late dinner would be
great, don't you think? Something light, since I think we
need to be living on fish and lettuce for the next few weeks."

"Speak for yourself," Chloe assured her as she glanced at
Luke and Leo, impressed with their ability to switch gears
so easily. She still felt horrible, hiding the truth about Luke
from Victoria. "I intend to order a steak."

"You burn the calories," Victoria said with a sigh.
"Sadly, I don't."

Chloe laughed. "Okay, we'll put you on nothing but
alfalfa sprouts. Come on, let's get going, or we won't even
make eight-thirty."

"I can drive," Luke offered.

"No, that's okay," Victoria said. "I have a gizmo that
opens the gate so we can park right by the house."

"Keep an eye on the girls," Leo said firmly to Luke.

"Well, he can't very well come in the dressing room,"

Victoria said lightly. But then she frowned, as if suddenly aware that Leo seemed tense. "Is something wrong?"

He shook his head. "To tell you the truth, I'm not exactly happy about either of you working with that agency, and I won't be until Colleen Rodriguez is found."

"We'll be okay," Victoria assured him. "Tonight we're only going to the mansion. And Brad and Jared—*and* Mr. Smith—will be with us on the island, and we'll all watch out for each other, just like we always have."

"Good night, Uncle Leo," Chloe said, giving him a kiss on the cheek to put an end to the uncomfortable conversation.

He took her by the shoulders, looking down into her eyes. "Stick with Luke, please?" he asked in a low voice for her ears only.

"I will," she promised.

They went out to the car, where Chloe insisted that Luke take the passenger seat next to Victoria, since his legs were longer.

As Victoria drove, she asked Luke how things were going. "Did you like the island? Oh, how rude of me. I forgot to say thank-you. I hear you chose me to model your line, too."

"You're absolutely perfect for the Ethereal Collection," he said.

In the backseat, Chloe noticed that he was getting awfully glib with his lies. He had to, she supposed, but it bothered her anyway.

She leaned back in the seat, watching the lights of the city as they drove. It was a quiet night. Even when they reached Miami Beach, the streets were oddly deserted.

"That's strange," Victoria said as they drove up to the gate.

"What's strange?" Luke asked.

"The gate's already open. They must have left it that way for the seamstress. She doesn't have a clicker because they don't use the same people all the time—depends on whether they're fitting gowns or swimsuits and cover-ups. I doubt that we're going to have many cover-ups for this shoot, though. They like to focus on the fact that we're Florida girls and the beaches are sunny all year round. Though, frankly, not many natives are in the water in January."

Chloe realized that Luke wasn't listening to Victoria ramble; he was staring at the house as Victoria stepped on the gas, heading up the driveway.

When the car came to a halt, Luke quickly opened his door. "Stay here, in the car—and get the hell out if anything happens."

"What? What's wrong?" Victoria asked.

But Luke didn't hear her. He was already striding up to the house. As Chloe strained to see what he was doing, she noticed that the door was slightly ajar. Luke approached it carefully, then slowly pushed it the rest of the way open and stepped into the mansion.

"What is he doing?" Victoria demanded, opening her door.

Something cold had slipped over Chloe the instant they arrived, holding her in its grip. "Vickie, don't!" she said.

But Victoria was already out of the car, staring at the house, puzzled.

"Vickie, wait!" Chloe implored.

But Victoria ignored her and started moving toward the house.

Chloe got out herself and stood by the side of the car. "Victoria!"

Too late. Victoria had followed Luke into the house.

A second later, a bloodcurdling scream sliced the air.

Chloe rushed in after her friend, then froze, the chill that had descended over her turning to solid ice.

Blood.

Everywhere.

So much blood…

It dripped down the wall of the elegant entry hall by the base of the stairway.

And there, head on the third-lowest step, feet sprawled five or six steps higher, lay Myra Allen. Her throat had been slit, but her sightless eyes remained open, staring.

A few feet above her, at an angle like a broken doll, was the mousy little secretary, Alana. Alana—whose last name Chloe didn't even know.

The scent of death was strong in her nostrils.

The color of murder seemed almost garish in the glow of the artificial light, like crimson paint tossed about by a maddened toddler.

Déjà vu.

It had been pathetically easy.

All those ridiculous crime-scene shows on television…

They just helped train those who wanted—needed—to kill.

But he was angry, and his fingers twitched on the knife. He had thought he'd gotten it right this time for certain.

Still, it hadn't been a complete failure.

Myra Allen had needed to die. The others…well, they were there, so they died, too. None of them had been the one he needed, but he couldn't take the chance that they would recognize him, even with the mask….

It really had been easy, though. So damn easy. Be the darkness, be the night, disappear in the shadows. Then walk out and become one with the elements. Bless the water, bless the darkness.

And still, his fingers were twitching.

He'd been close. So close.

If only the girls had come alone, he could have stayed, could have…

He had briefly considered it. He was brilliant, a warrior, a killing machine, trained in his craft, able to move like a wraith. For a split second he had weighed the pros and cons in his mind. But in the end he'd opted for caution, because the man…might be dangerous, and it was better to wait for the perfect moment than risk failure now, when he was so close.

No, the mission hadn't been complete. But God's warrior must have patience. It was better to win the battles one by one than to lose the war. And in between…

There were others who deserved to die. To fulfill his needs, and have their filthy souls cleansed and saved.

Best to disappear…into the night and the infinite darkness.

The time for real killing was coming closer and closer.

# ELEVEN

Luke had heard Victoria coming, but he hadn't been fast enough to stop her.

Her scream was deafening as he turned, hoping to push her out of the house. It was imperative that neither of them touch anything. But he didn't move fast enough. He should have known that Chloe would race after Victoria.

She didn't scream, though. She only stared in horror, stared at Myra and Alana, and at the wall, as her eyes narrowed with fury.

She was horrified—and furious, but she wasn't scared, though she should have been terrified, should have fallen apart, as Victoria was doing now.

"Take Victoria. Get her out—just to the steps." He managed to push Victoria into Chloe's arms, and urge the two of them back out the door. Then he took out his cell phone and dialed 9-1-1, speaking as clearly and succinctly as he could, giving the address and the situation, and asking that Lieutenant Stuckey be informed immediately.

He knew the drill, and he held his temper when he was asked to repeat the address twice.

He didn't want to go back in; he didn't want to take a chance that the killer or killers might still be around. But the police would arrive shortly, and he couldn't take the chance that the killer had left someone alive upstairs or in the back, someone who might die while waiting for help.

He reached under the back of his jacket and pulled out the small custom Smith & Wesson he carried; the gun was compact, light and snub-nosed, and held seven rounds rather than the usual six. He handed it to Chloe. "You know how to use this, right?"

She nodded.

"The safety—"

"I know how to use it. Go."

"I'll be right back. I'm checking for—"

"Go."

He left her and prayed the rest of the house would be empty. The stench of blood was overwhelming this time.

He didn't go near the dead women; there was no point. No hope. He avoided touching anything, and checked out the kitchen first.

The kitchen offered up more horror. He found an older woman—he suspected she might be the seamstress—also dead. She was prone on the floor, but her head was twisted toward Luke. Her eyes were open. They didn't register horror, just surprise. There was no need to go closer and destroy evidence. The woman was long past help.

He hurried upstairs. Every door was open, as if the killer had been thorough in his search for victims. Luke entered each room and each bath, moving swiftly, touching nothing.

Thankfully, there were no more bodies. He hadn't looked under the beds or out on the balconies, but he was sure that the balconies would have been far too visible from the nearby high-rises, and that if there were bodies under the beds, pools of blood would give them away.

He hurried back outside. Chloe and Victoria were right where he had left them. He took his gun back from Chloe and slid it into the narrow holster behind his back.

Victoria sat on the steps, crying and speaking incoherently. Chloe was sitting by her side, holding her quietly, apparently unable to think of anything to say, and smoothing her hair.

Luke hunkered down by Chloe.

"Are you all right?" he asked her.

She nodded, looking at him over Victoria's bowed head. "But I don't think Vickie is doing very well," she said. "What did you find in the rest of the house?" she whispered.

"The seamstress."

Chloe winced. "What about the girls?"

"They must not have been home," he told her.

He stood. A cruiser was arriving, its siren blaring.

Two uniformed policemen came running up the walkway to the steps. They stopped and stared at Luke.

"There are three female victims that I can see so far," he said. "I didn't touch anything, so the scene is the way I found it."

"Right," said the taller of the two. His badge identified him as Brian Marley; his partner, three inches shorter, was Ivan Slovenski.

"I'll tape off the walk," Slovenski said.

"You told the dispatcher to send Stuckey from Metro?" Marley asked Luke.

Luke nodded.

"Any reason?"

"He handled the last massacre on the beach, didn't he?"

"The last massacre—oh, my God, you mean the Teen Massacre?" Marley asked. He pushed past Luke to the door, looked inside and made the sign of the cross.

Then he looked back at Luke with a ghastly expression his face, before pulling himself together and taking out a notebook.

Luke gave him his real name—wondering if Victoria would even notice, she was sobbing so hard—Chloe's name, Victoria's name and their reason for being at the mansion.

Then he heard more sirens screaming through the night, and Stuckey's car—flashing lights the only sign that his car wasn't an ordinary sedan—pulled up on the curb just beyond the gates. He stepped over the crime-scene tape that Slovenski had stretched out in front of the house and hurried toward Luke. He flashed his badge to Marley, and stared at Luke disbelievingly. "Marley, gloves and booties, please—quickly. And keep the area clear of gawkers, you got it?"

Marley jumped to obey. Stuckey looked down at Victoria and Chloe, who looked back up at him. He took a minute to touch Chloe's head, and pat Victoria's shoulder. But the only thing he could manage to say was, "There, there."

Finally Stuckey looked back at Luke. "How many?"

"Three."

"You certain?"

"I looked for survivors."

Marley produced latex gloves and booties just as the crime-scene unit arrived, producing more.

An emergency vehicle made it then, and Stuckey brusquely ordered one of the officers to see that Victoria was given some help.

He pointed at Chloe. "You, don't move away from Victoria and the EMTs. And you," he said to Luke. "Ah, hell, get your hands and feet covered, and come with me."

Luke was surprised that Stuckey was allowing him entrance when others had already arrived at the scene, but Stuckey was powerful, and he could call a lot of shots.

Luke just hoped he could get the hell out of the way before any cameras showed up, and that he could keep his name out of the papers.

He stepped back into the house with Stuckey.

"Hell," Stuckey said. "Hell and damn. Well, I can see why you didn't need to check for a pulse. Do you know the house?"

"Somewhat."

Stuckey walked over and hunkered down by Myra. "Left-to-right slash. Looks like he caught her on the stairs…then tossed her down, and that's the way she landed."

"I don't think so. I think she was posed," Luke said. He pointed to several blood smudges higher on the banister.

"I think you're right. Upside down, eyes open. The pose must mean something to him." Stuckey quickly moved past Myra to Alana. "Different M.O. One stab wound straight into the back of the neck. Fast, sure. Twisted the knife, just to make certain. Looks like he was upstairs and caught these two coming down." He stood and looked at Luke.

"Where's the third?"

"Kitchen," Luke told him, pointing.

"Jesus," Stuckey said, shaking his head and leading the way to the second crime scene. He bent down by the victim, moving her hair aside to study the back of her neck, then rose.

"The doors to the patio are open," Luke said.

"So I noted. In by the front, out by the back?" He looked around the room once more, then asked, "You went upstairs?"

"Cursory inspection," Luke assured him. "Looking to see if anyone was still alive."

Stuckey turned and they walked back to the foyer and on up the stairs, careful to avoid the blood. They walked down the hallway, repeating Luke's journey, going room to room, though Stuckey paused to look under the beds and pull back the drapes. None of the balcony doors appeared to have been opened.

"Clear so far," Stuckey said. "And no one escaped from up here."

They were in the room where Luke had once followed Rene Rodriguez off the balcony.

By the time they headed back downstairs, two homicide detectives had arrived, along with the medical examiner.

Grim introductions were made, but everyone deferred to Stuckey, who clearly had the leeway to run with this one.

"I need a time of death, as exact as you can get it," Stuckey told the M.E.

"Body temps are just about normal. These two couldn't have been dead more than thirty minutes to an hour," the M.E., an efficient woman of Hispanic heritage, told him. "I'm headed into the kitchen to check the third woman."

"It'll be about the same," Stuckey said wearily. "This was fast. Well planned, and fast."

"He—or she or they—was looking for something," Luke said.

"Why do you say that? Nothing looks out of order."

"The doors upstairs. They were all open. Last time I was here, they were closed."

"I thought some of the girls lived here."

"They do. Luckily, they don't appear to have been home. The three of us are only here because Chloe and Victoria had fittings."

A man in a crime-scene jumpsuit was taking pictures. "Doug," Stuckey said. "Get someone to find Myra's address book or cell or PalmPilot—whatever the hell she used to keep track of her life. We have to start calling the girls who lived here. We need to make sure they're all safe and accounted for.

"Who lived here? Who should I be worried about?" Stuckey asked.

"Rene Gonzalez and Jeanne LaRue, for certain. You'd have to ask Victoria or Chloe about anyone else," Luke said.

Stuckey groaned. "Rene? Sweet Jesus, I hope to God we

can find that girl fast. I can't believe Chloe and Victoria had to walk in on this."

They were supposed to have been here when it happened, Luke realized. Only Chloe's work schedule had kept them from coming at seven. He would have been with them, and he might have been able to stop it. Or he might not have suspected the killer until it was too late, because the killer might have been a regular at the mansion.

He kept his thoughts to himself for the moment; any ideas he had, he would share with Stuckey when they weren't surrounded by other people.

"I'm going to go and give my statement, and then get Chloe and Victoria out of here. You're not going to need them anymore tonight, right? They barely stepped inside. I'm not sure what they can tell you, and I don't think they can take much more."

"Chloe seems to have it together," Stuckey said. "But don't worry. I'm sure one of the officers has already taken down whatever they saw. So yes, go finish up, yourself, then get those two out of here. If we find out anything, I'll let you know."

"I'd say Chloe was right, and the real killers weren't discovered ten years ago," Luke said.

Stuckey frowned. "This isn't the same. It can't be the same. There's no writing on the wall."

"Maybe the killer heard us coming," Luke suggested.

"Hey, found the PalmPilot," a crime-scene tech called over.

"Get on the phone. Call all the women who are listed as living here," Stuckey ordered. "We need to find them fast!"

Luke left the house and headed for the ambulance, where Chloe was sitting with Victoria.

She looked up at him. "Tell Stuckey—I got hold of Rene and Jeanne. They were together. They finished their fittings early and went to a new club down on Washington. One of the beach security guys is going to go and get them."

He nodded, and after checking to make sure she was okay for the moment, turned to go back and give Stuckey the information. He couldn't recall ever seeing the hardened cop look so relieved.

Luke was certain he would soon be receiving another visit from Octavio, begging him to hog-tie his daughter and keep her away from the agency and the shoot. Although he doubted the shoot would even take place now.

He looked up and noticed that the press was arriving and the street was getting crowded, despite the uniformed officers' efforts to keep control. Gruesome news traveled fast, apparently. He dialed Chloe's number. "Hey."

"You're calling me?" she said. "When you're twenty feet away?"

"How's Victoria?" he asked, ignoring her question.

"They gave her a sedative. Can we go?"

"See if you can get her to her car. Will you be able to drive? I'll meet you there, but I don't want to be seen, especially now."

She was silent for a moment. "Luke, every cop here tonight has your name."

"And the cops won't be giving it out."

"Do you need this charade any longer?"

"Maybe."

"Okay. We'll be right there. I'll have one of the EMTs help me with Vickie."

"Thanks."

A minute later, Chloe and Victoria, helped along by Marley, met him at the car. As soon as Victoria was settled in the passenger seat, Marley briefly saluted Luke. "Thanks for...thanks. And don't worry. We're all under a gag order on tonight," he assured him.

Luke nodded. "Thanks. Can you get someone to clear curiosity seekers so we can get out of here?"

"Will do."

Chloe dug through Victoria's purse for her keys and slid them into the ignition without trembling, then edged the car out onto the street. Marley was as good as his word, and they were able to get past the crowd and make their getaway. More police vehicles were descending on the house as they left. Luke stayed down in back, out of sight until they were on the Rickenbacker Causeway and headed back to Miami, when he finally sat up straight.

Victoria wasn't making a sound. She wasn't asleep, though, simply leaning back in the seat, staring straight ahead.

"Victoria, hang in there, okay?" Luke said, patting her shoulder.

"She's going to be fine," Chloe said.

"Myra was...my friend. Even poor Alana," Victoria said, then started to sob softly again.

Chloe met his eyes in the rearview mirror. "I'll keep her at my house tonight," she said.

"Actually, you're going to keep *me* at your house tonight, too," Luke said.

She frowned.

"I'll be on your couch," he said firmly. "I'm not leaving you alone tonight."

She smiled at him. It was a sad smile, a serious smile, but still a smile. "That will be fine. I'm sure Leo will be glad that there's a man sleeping in my cottage, as odd as that sounds."

He offered her a smile in return.

In another twenty minutes they reached her house. Leo was waiting at the door for them.

"I called him," Chloe explained.

"Good thought," Luke told her.

Victoria stumbled, getting out of the car, so Luke picked her up and walked straight for the main house.

Leo took in Vickie's state and apparently decided there would be no discussion about their working for the agency, being alone, or leaving at all. "Chloe, I know you like having your own place, but this house is huge and everyone's staying here tonight. Just pick rooms upstairs."

For a second Chloe looked as if she was about to argue with him, but she said, "Vickie and I will sleep in my old room. Luke can take one of the guest rooms."

"Point me in the right direction," Luke said. Chloe led him up the stairs, where he laid Victoria down on the king-size bed, then turned to meet Chloe's eyes. "I'm going to head back down and talk to your uncle for a few minutes."

She started to go with him, but Victoria called out and reached for her hand.

"I'd better stay with her," Chloe said.

He nodded. "I'll be back up soon, see if you two need anything."

He turned to leave.

"Luke."

He looked back.

"Thank you."

He nodded and left. Downstairs, he found Leo pacing the kitchen.

"What the hell is going on?" the older man demanded, raking a hand through his hair. "Did you actually see the— the bodies?"

"Yes."

"Was there writing on the wall?"

"No. But our arrival might have interrupted the killer— or killers."

"And the victims…?"

"Myra's throat had been slit. The two other women were stabbed in the back of the head. The killer knew what he— or she or they—was doing. This was someone with experience. I'm thinking someone who has been in the military, someone who has studied the art of death."

"I can't imagine what it was like for Chloe and Vickie, walking into that house—after what they've already been through," Leo said. "They have to catch this maniac, fast. People are going to go crazy over the similarities to ten years ago, but it can't be the same killers. They're dead."

"Maybe. But there's something off about this. I wasn't around for the Teen Massacre, but something about *that* doesn't feel right, either. Doesn't feel closed. I'm not sure they did get the right guys for that."

"I *was* here," Leo said. "I remember every horrific minute of it. I remember shaking with gratitude that Chloe made it out alive, and feeling guilty at the same time, that I could be so grateful and relieved when other families... I saw the dead men. I went to the morgue. I saw the confession and the writing on the wall. Those men were murderers. I believe it with my whole heart. Chloe sketched one of them to a T."

"What if there was a third killer?" Luke asked.

Leo stared back at him stonily. "You had to have been around at the time, trust me. In a way, it was like trying to restrain a mob bent on vengeance, and that was just the police. Every single member of that church was brought in. Held as long as the law allowed. They were questioned, and they were furious, demanding to know if the other eleven apostles were guilty because Judas betrayed Christ. Every single member provided an alibi, and the church itself was searched top to bottom, and so were the members' homes. The church fell apart, the lawsuit they filed against the city disintegrated, and there was simply no solid evidence of a third killer. Not to mention the fact that nothing resembling the murders occurred again."

"Until tonight," Luke said.

"But there was no writing on the wall," Leo said flatly.

"No."

"No message of any kind?" Leo asked.

"Not one that was discernible, no," Luke told him.

"There's always another maniac out there," Leo said. "And this one wouldn't be the first to copycat an earlier crime." He shook his head as if to clear it.

"Hey, I could be wrong. Maybe the Church of the Real People really was totally innocent and those two 'brothers' just went off the deep end. All I know is, they were dead, the case was dead, nothing else like it ever happened."

A sound at the foot of the steps alerted them that Chloe had come down. They turned toward her in unison. "Actually, I feel rather sorry for the members of the Church of the Real People," she said. "I don't think they're all fanatics—just people searching for something, maybe desperately, maybe pathetically."

Leo walked over to her and put his arms around her. "I know this had to be really hard on you. You can't let it get to you. You have to be good to yourself, maybe take something so you can get a good night's rest—I'm assuming Victoria is passed out?"

She nodded. "The EMTs gave her a shot to calm her down. They wanted to take her to the hospital, but I wouldn't let them. I wanted her here with us, where she'll be safe."

"Of course," Leo said, then frowned. "Wait. Why would Victoria be in danger?"

"She should have been there when it happened. Me, too. We both had fittings tonight. If I hadn't had to work late, we would have been there when the killer came," Chloe told him.

"That's it. There will be no more modeling going on," Leo said. "Don't you agree?" Leo asked Luke.

"Let's not get ahead of ourselves," Luke said. "Logically

speaking, Myra might have been the target tonight. It was her house, after all. She was the one person the killer could expect to be there."

"But," Leo argued, "you're only involved yourself because a girl is missing and—let's face it—presumed dead, and the parents of a second girl were afraid for their child's life. Now—this."

"Uncle Leo, let's see what the police come up with, okay?" Chloe said. She glanced at Luke, and something in her expression seemed to be speaking to him alone.

*Please don't say anything to make him worse.*

They were eloquent eyes. But then again, she had been the one to suggest that Victoria might be in danger. Oddly, she didn't seem particularly worried about the other girls— and at least two of them had lived at the mansion.

Luke had his own thoughts on the matter, but he wanted to investigate before speaking.

"I do think a good night's sleep might help everyone think more clearly," he said.

"Sleep would be good," Chloe agreed. "After a drink. I don't have any sleeping pills around—I'll have to go straight for the alcohol."

She walked over to the bar and poured herself a large Jack Black, and she didn't add soda. She tossed it down in one long swallow, then winced. Both Leo and Luke stared at her. "Oh, sorry. I should have offered you two drinks, too."

"What the hell," Leo muttered, and strode over to join her at the bar.

Luke joined him, but he sipped his Scotch slowly. He didn't need to be knocked out—didn't *want* to be knocked out.

No one was coming to this house, he thought. The killer would know the odds were against him here.

"Good night, then," Chloe said. "I'll be in my room. I think Vickie's out for the count, but in case she wakes up frightened...I'll be there."

"You should be afraid, too, you know," Leo pointed out.

Chloe put a hand on his shoulder. "Uncle Leo, I'm always careful—I learned that lesson ten years ago. But if we become terrified of living, then life is wasted on us. I had a major close call then, and it would be a disservice to my friends if I were to waste the life I was granted. But I love you for worrying, now good night."

She kissed Leo on the cheek. After that, to Luke's surprise, she came straight over to him, stood on her toes and kissed his lips.

It wasn't a passionate kiss.

But it spoke of something between them.

As she turned and headed for the stairs, Leo stared at Luke.

"I thought she didn't like you," he said.

Luke shrugged. "I guess I've grown on her." He cleared his throat. "I'd better try to get some sleep, too."

"A lot," Leo said, eyeing him like a protective father. "You've grown on her a lot."

Luke lowered his head, aware that he was trying not to smile, and amazed to realize that he was blushing.

"I, uh, like her, too. A lot," he added.

"Hmm. Well, at the moment, I'm glad. If you two are sleeping together…"

Luke looked up at him calmly, hoping the color had faded from his face and that his expression betrayed nothing. It was up to Chloe to share whatever she wished with her uncle.

Apparently, Leo realized he wasn't going to get anything out of him.

"If you are," he said gruffly, "don't let me stop you. God knows, she never gets out and even if she's hell-bent on a relationship that could easily be a train wreck, right now I feel safer with her sleeping with you."

Luke still didn't reply—unless his silence was a reply in itself.

"Good night, Leo," he said after a long moment. "And thanks for the hospitality."

"Thanks for the guard duty."

Luke headed up the stairs and found a comfortable-looking guest room. He set his gun on the table next to the bed, removed his jacket and lay down. He kicked off his shoes but stopped there. In the morning, he would head back to his own place for a shower.

Tonight, even as certain as he was that the killer was basically a coward who waited until his victims were vulnerable, he intended to sleep lightly.

When she finally woke up late the next morning, Victoria was much better. If anything, she was angry, though still very sad for Myra.

"Why would anyone hurt her?" she demanded.

Chloe had decided that the best thing she could do for

her friend that day was keep her at the house, away from prying eyes, even though she was amazed to see that neither of their names—nor Luke's—had wound up in the paper or on the news.

Stuckey really had issued a gag order, and it seemed it was being obeyed. None of the details had leaked out, and in a press conference, Stuckey stated flatly that none of them *would* be released. Police had arrived at the mansion at approximately eight-fifteen after being called by three visitors. Two models had departed the property at approximately 7:30 p.m., which meant the murders had taken place in a span of less than forty-five minutes. As it was an active investigation, that was all he was willing to reveal. He wouldn't even say how the victims had been killed, but given that the families had been notified, he did release their names.

Given the surface similarities—multiple murders at a beachside mansion—the press naturally brought up the Teen Massacre, but Stuckey calmly deflected the question, pointing out that these were not the first murders in a mansion or on the beach in the past ten years.

The Church of the Real People also came under scrutiny again, but a pastor or elder or whatever he called himself made a brief statement to the media, and, like the press conference with Stuckey, it played on TV over and over again as the day went on.

Though Chloe didn't know much about the church's tenets, it was obvious that Brother Mario Sanz believed in them wholeheartedly. His speech was passionate. He was, he said, horrified, as all good men must be, at the terrible events of the previous night, but he was equally horrified that people were instantly looking at the church, ready to lay blame at the feet of a fine congregation. The Church of the Real People, he pointed out, was no less vulnerable to those who might interpret religious texts according to their own misguided views than any other religion. The Koran specifically stated that no woman or child should be harmed, ever. Christ would have never condoned the terror of the Inquisition. There was nothing to indicate that the murders had been committed by someone with ties to any church whatsoever, much less to the Church of the Real People. He invited the authorities into the church to search for evidence, and every member of the congregation was willing to be questioned, and to open their own homes to be searched.

Chloe was sitting out by the pool, watching yet another repeat of Brother Sanz's speech on her cell phone, when Victoria came up behind her, startling her.

"It's a crock," Victoria said.

"The Church of the Real People?" Chloe asked.

Victoria shook her head. "Blaming them."

"You don't think it's a repeat of what happened when we were kids?"

Victoria drew her finger through the sweat on the glass of iced tea she was carrying and shook her head. "I don't believe the church was guilty back then. Oh, yeah, those two guys were guilty. But I don't think the church made them do it. They're pretty weird, but...I don't know. I think those two men were disturbed to begin with, and then they decided to start killing kids who they thought had too much and might go to hell. Someone taught them that—but not the church." She looked at Chloe and smiled. "And you don't have to coddle me. I fell apart last night, but I'm okay now. I'm going to go home."

"No, Vickie, not yet, please!" Chloe said, sounding more desperate than she'd intended. She took a calming breath and went on. "Not this soon. The police may have something by tonight." *Luke* might have something by tonight.

Victoria smiled. Chloe knew that she hadn't spoken out loud, but Victoria said, "Or 'Jack' might. Jack Smith, my ass. So his real name is Luke? Luke Cane? That's right, isn't it? Is he an undercover cop or something?"

Chloe shook her head. "P.I."

"Don't worry, I won't say anything to anyone. He was going to the island to find out what happened to Colleen Rodriguez, wasn't he?"

"Yes."

"Where is he now?"

"Investigating, I guess," Chloe said. The truth was, Luke had been gone by the time she woke up and she had no idea where he'd gone.

Victoria looked at Chloe. "I think we should go."

"Go where?"

"Potluck supper."

"What?"

"I heard it earlier. The Church of the Real People announced that they're still having a potluck supper tomorrow night, and that everyone is welcome."

"Victoria, we can't go. You're too recognizable, for one thing. And it might be just plain dangerous, for another."

Victoria shrugged. "I'm over twenty-one. I can do what I please. Besides, you're forgetting, I'm an actress. I know makeup and costuming."

"But, Vic—"

"I'm going. With or without you."

"Any sane person would try to stop us," Chloe told her.

"Then," Victoria said, "we shouldn't tell anyone sane that we're going. Come on. Cops will be all over the place like ants, with everything going on."

She was right about that, Chloe had to admit. They would just have to keep quiet about what they were doing, because Luke would definitely try to stop them if he knew. And so would Uncle Leo.

But fate seemed to be intervening on their behalf, because just then her cell phone rang, and she knew from the caller ID that it was Luke. "Hello?"

"Hey, are you still at the house?" he asked her.

"Yes, of course. Where are you?"

"On my way to you, but I don't have long. Meet me at the gate and we'll go back to the carriage house, all right?"

"All right," she said.

She told Victoria that Luke wanted to see her for a little while alone, and Victoria smiled and nodded. "I'm fine, so don't rush because of me. In fact, if you come anywhere near me in the next few hours, I'll hit you, I swear."

"I don't think he has that much time," Chloe said, grinning despite herself.

★ ★ ★

Luke must have been close when he called, because it was just a matter of minutes before he appeared at the gate. She let him in, and was startled by the intensity in the way he looked at her, and touched by the strength in his arms when he wrapped them around her, and then looked into her eyes again, as if assuring himself that not a hair on her head had been harmed in any way.

"Where have you been?" she asked him.

"Up at the Broward sheriff's office. I'll explain. Let's go in."

She led him into the carriage house. They had barely gotten through the front door before he pulled her into his arms again, and once again it was as if he simply had to feel the beating of her heart, the heat of her existence.

He drew away finally and found her eyes again, and then her lips. His kiss was passionate and charged, but finally he broke the contact and said, "I'm sorry. I know you're in a traumatic tangle at the moment and that—"

She rose on her toes and shut his mouth with her own, threading her fingers through his hair and darting her tongue into his mouth, pulling him closer and closer, then letting her fingers slide down his back to force him even more tightly against her. She was definitely eliciting a reaction; she could feel the rise of his erection against her abdomen, and her own arousal and need increased as if swept along by a tidal wave.

And yet he still tried to step back. "Chloe, I know—"

"No, you don't know. Right now I want the…the reaffirmation of life. Something wild and wicked and beautiful, but why do I always have to be the aggressor?" she asked softly.

His slow smile was devastating. But the way he picked her up, as if she weighed nothing, and headed straight up the stairs, was even more devastating. He was talking, she realized, erotically, but not with the words she might have expected. "Sofa…no, we're too tall…kitchen table, looks sexy in films but kills the back…how about the bed? What a concept."

He all but dropped her on the bed when they got there, then practically fell on top of her, clearly having decided to take the role of sexual aggressor to heart. Then he had her breathlessly laughing as they struggled to remove their clothing while still kissing, stroking, fighting not to lose touch with each other.

Even so, she could barely move against his onslaught. His lips, his tongue, his hands, were everywhere, his touch so tender and light and elusive, followed by the pressure of his lips and teeth and tongue in a way that seemed to demand everything. She trailed her fingers down the length of his spine, cradled the tight muscles of his buttocks, teased a finger back up his spine and then down again, all the while losing herself in the fever of his kisses and caresses.

He was an amazing lover. A man unafraid to show tenderness, adept at teasing, he could be gentle, and then, when he moved, it was with a force and passion that left her breathless and fulfilled, and yet somehow longing for more.

His mouth grazed the whole of her length, first avoiding her most erogenous zones, then focusing on them in a way that sent waves of lava and electricity shooting through her. She teased and taunted in return, relishing each word that escaped his lips as she stroked, caressed, licked and teased, until the world was fire and so were they.

And then his eyes met hers and he moved inside her, and all her cares and fears were gone as they transcended heaven and earth, joined together in the most raw and physical way known to man, tangled in the sheets, dampened with sweat. Finally, wrapped around one another, rigid and alive, they climaxed nearly simultaneously, gasping and moaning as their hearts thundered, then slowed, and their breathing once again hit normal.

Chloe lay with her head on his chest, wondering if it would be possible to explain to anyone that despite being in the middle of an emotional nightmare, for the first time in her life, she had realized just what love could be.

She couldn't explain how, but she knew that he cared about her. Just as she cared about him. But she could never force him. They were both damaged, both still learning to move past the damage.

She didn't speak about what had just passed between them, not physically and not what came from the heart and soul. Instead, she ran a finger over his chest and asked him, "So…what's going on? Why did you say you don't have much time?"

"I was up in Fort Lauderdale this morning, and now I'm going to New Orleans."

"Why? What's going on?"

He had an arm crooked behind his head, and he looked at the ceiling for a moment before turning to look at her. "Stay in tonight, huh, just to indulge me and your uncle," he said.

"Why are you going to New Orleans?" she asked again.

"Remember how I told you before that something just didn't sit right with me about the past? Well, I decided to put out a call for information on the disappearance or murder of young women that had a religious aspect. I found a girl who'd been part of a strict religious sect for a while, then disappeared from one of the casinos in Broward about a year and a half ago, so I went up to investigate. That led me nowhere, but then I heard from the police in New Orleans. They had a young female murder victim with strange, possibly cult-related, carvings on her back and forehead. I have a flight this afternoon, and I may not be back until tomorrow sometime, so, please…don't go out. Stuckey has a car watching the house. You'll be safest here at home."

He wasn't telling her, she realized; he was asking her. "I won't go out tonight," she promised, meaning it.

She looked away from him for a moment, knowing she needed to tell him about Victoria's determination to go to the potluck supper. In the end, she kept silent. The potluck was still a day away, and she'd only promised not to go out tonight.

Besides, she wouldn't go to the Church of the Real People unarmed.

But she *would* go.

She laid her head against his chest again, and he wrapped an arm around her. "How much time do you have before your plane?" she asked huskily.

"A few hours," he said.

"Well…"

She drew patterns on his chest, then crawled on top of

him, teasing his flesh with her hair, moving against the length of his body. In a few minutes they were making love again, and when they were spent, she fell against his side, glad just to be held by him.

In that comfortable state, and perhaps because she was still exhausted, she must have dozed.

When she opened her eyes, the room was filled with people.

She was paralyzed with terror for a moment, unable to move or scream, not even able to open her mouth.

Dead people were arranged all around her. Friends from long ago. No blood dripped from their necks, and they were dressed as they had been in their coffins all those years ago. David Grant, football hero, in his handsome, go-to-church suit, and Kit, his girlfriend, at his side, in the navy dress her mother had chosen for her funeral. And there was Jen, wearing the beige suit *her* mother had picked out… And Vince Mahaffey, Sue Whalen, Jack Axelrod…

They stood around her, looking at her sadly, both there and not there, as if they were made of the mist that accompanied a hot shower, except that she hadn't been in the shower.

And there were others….

Girls she didn't know, had never seen. Some of them…

Decomposed. Wet, or covered with earth, only scraps of clothing remaining.

Even mistier than the others, barely visible at all, were Myra…and Alana…and the seamstress.

Frozen, she couldn't move. Did Luke see them? No, he was breathing evenly, asleep; she could feel his chest moving beneath her head. Bizarrely, she found herself thinking that she was glad they had pulled the sheet up somewhere along the line.

Someone stepped from the crowd, moving closer.

Colleen Rodriguez.

She wore the same dripping white dress, and her hair was wet, as well. She looked worse than she had before. More desperate. Her lips were moving, but Chloe couldn't catch her words. Yet at the same time, a single whisper seemed to fill her head.

*Help us. Help us…and those who will come.*

Chloe rediscovered the ability to move at last. She bolted up, but she didn't scream, just snapped up to a sitting position. Beside her, Luke awoke, stretching, sitting up, too, and staring at her before swiftly taking her into his arms. "Chloe, what's wrong?"

She was shaking, trembling. She tried to speak, couldn't.

"You had a nightmare, didn't you? I can't leave you. The police can't protect you from your dreams, and I know how bad they can be."

She managed to pull away from him, to stop shaking. She kept her voice level and calm as she told him, "No. Luke, you have to go. There are more of them. Lots more of them."

"What?" His hair was tousled, and she could see him struggling to understand what must have sounded crazy.

"Luke, I'm not dreaming. I'm not having nightmares. I— I'm really seeing ghosts."

She could read it in his eyes. He cared about her, so he wasn't going to call the men in the white coats to take her away. He answered slowly and carefully. "Chloe, you're amazing. You survived one massacre, and you just witnessed a second. It's natural that you're having a hard time accepting what's happened. I'm going to cancel my flight and—"

She pulled away from him. "No, you are not. Luke, I'm a psychologist, remember? I know all the symptoms of every kind of crazy. But I'm not crazy, and I'm telling you, they're trying to help me, help us. This isn't in my mind, and it's not a dream. I've been right all this time. I know it. Two of the killers are dead, but there was a third. And you know how they say serial killers don't stop? Well, he hasn't stopped. He's been clever. He's been moving around the country, covering his tracks and practicing his craft. I think he's got some kind of agenda with the murders at the mansions, but…he likes killing, he needs to kill. You have to go to New Orleans and find out everything you can. I'm not afraid, and don't go telling me that I should be. I'm not afraid of the ghosts. They're trying to speak to me, to help us. You have to go and do what you do best— investigate. And I have to see what *I* can learn—here."

She could see how concerned he was and gripped both his hands. "Luke, I'm all right. I feel that we're on the right track, and that we have to keep moving forward. The dead deserve the truth—and a lot of living people may stay that way if we can discover what's going on. Please, go. I'll be waiting for you when you come back, and we'll find Colleen. I'm certain she's in the water somewhere. I told you, when I see her, she's…wet. Hair and dress dripping."

He ran his fingers through his hair. "Chloe—"

"I'll sleep in the main house while you're gone. And you said Stuckey has a patrol car guarding the place."

"Let's shower. Then I'll decide what I'm doing," he told her.

He got out of bed and started walking toward the bath-room, then paused suddenly, staring at her. He hunkered down then, frowning.

"What is it?" she asked, rising, as well.

He looked at her. "The carpet. It's…wet."

# TWELVE

The flight to New Orleans was less than two hours, but it seemed like forever to Luke. He still wondered if he should have left or not.

Ghosts. He didn't believe in them. He wasn't an atheist, exactly; he just hadn't decided yet if there really was a God, and if there was, what he expected out of people. He'd heard about the soul being energy, and energy never actually disappeared, had heard a dozen different takes on life and death, but in his experience, dead was dead—and it was for the living to find justice.

He was worried about Chloe. Yet he had never seen her more certain or more confident. Or more determined.

And then there had been the damp spot on the rug.

Easily explained. A leak in the roof—except that there was

an attic above the bedroom and no wetness there. Or someone had trailed water coming from the bathroom—except that no one had been in the bathroom.

It was baffling.

As the plane landed and taxied to the terminal, he told himself that he had to forget the possibility of ghosts and concentrate on what he could discover here in New Orleans.

As he walked down the concourse, he thought that it was good to have friends. Knowing and working with the right cops often got him where he wanted to go.

Making his way past baggage claim and toward the exit, he spotted the man in the jeans, T-shirt and baseball cap who was waiting for him. Detective Joseph Mulligan was somewhere around thirty-five. The cap kept his sandy hair off his forehead, and his eyes were a clear blue that was steady and sure. He was of medium height and medium build, maybe five inches shorter than Luke, but similarly strong.

It was apparent that Detective Mulligan worked out and took it seriously. But then, he was a cop. It was part of his work and nothing to do with vanity.

"Luke Cane, as I live and breathe," Mulligan said, stepping forward, grinning, and offering his hand.

Luke offered his own in return. "Thanks so much for helping me out."

"I'm thrilled as hell to see you. Sad to say, my case isn't going anywhere. I'll be glad to have you hustle up some more interest. Can I take your bag?"

"I look like a girl to you?" Luke cracked, smiling. "It's

fifteen pounds, tops, and I've got it, thanks. Where are we heading?"

"My place. I pulled the files after you called. I'll show you what I've got, then take you around to a couple of the sites."

Joe Mulligan lived in an old Victorian a block off Esplanade with his wife, Clancy, and their two children, Ashley and Aislinn. Clancy and the kids greeted Luke, and Clancy offered the men a plate of sandwiches, along with coffee, while Joe handed over a stack of printouts and started pulling up Web pages.

Seated in his swivel chair, Joe turned to Luke and explained, "Some of this is official, and some is stuff I've come up with but haven't gotten very far with. It's no secret that we've had our problems here, that we're still struggling to establish law and order after Katrina, but the pity is, so many folks here are just good, hardworking citizens, and they're getting tarred along with the rotten apples." He sighed.

"Here's the thing, we're talking a few years back now, but after Katrina, our missing persons list was longer than Santa's." He passed Luke a photo. "Like everywhere, when someone's killed around here, we generally find the body. A lot of our violence is drug or gang related, and they don't even bother to try to hide their victims. Too high, or sending a message. In the beginning, it looked like this girl just disappeared."

"Girls disappear every day," Luke said quietly. "Thing is, most killers are careless, or even want their victims to be found. When people disappear into thin air, there's a clever, organized killer at work. I think we're dealing with a psychopath back in Miami, someone—probably a man—who knows that what he's doing is against the law but, for whatever reason, doesn't, in his own mind, think it's wrong. He feels no regret, no empathy, and sees himself as above everyone else, so special that he deserves his needs to be met, even if that means somebody else has to die. And I think some of those people have been dying in other places."

"You asked about disappearances and unsolved murders that might have a religious aspect. Like I said, for a long time, we had a missing-persons case. Her name was Jill Montague, a local girl. She was coming into the Quarter to meet friends at a bar. She left her residence in the Garden District, planning on taking the streetcar down, and never showed up. We gave her picture to every driver, ran it in the paper. No one saw her. Or no one admitted to seeing her, anyway. She left her house and that was it. Gone, zero, vanished."

"But you found her eventually?"

"Beside the Mississippi. With carvings in her flesh that could be religious stuff. Where I'm lost is, I don't understand what all this has to do with a cult massacre," Joe told him. "Or the murders that just occurred in Miami. I know that the old case had a cult connection, but from what I've heard, there was nothing like that with the murders that just occurred."

"Ten years ago, two men were found dead in the Everglades alongside a written confession. But some people thought someone else had to be involved in the massacre. The big argument against that was that nothing even remotely similar ever happened again, or not around Miami, anyway. And you know as well as I do that most profilers agree that a killer like that doesn't just quit," Luke said. "Either he dies—like the two killers they found in the Everglades—or he goes to prison on some other unrelated charge, or he moves on to someplace else. I think there was a third killer and he went somewhere else—until last night. What interests me about your case is the design carved into your dead girl's back and forehead."

"Did the killers write on their victims ten years ago?" Joe asked, puzzled. "Or just on the wall."

"Just on the wall. In blood."

"I forget. What did they write?"

"'Death to defilers!'," Luke said. "And they drew a design." He leaned forward. "What was on your victim?"

"I don't know. The body was in pretty bad shape when we found it, so there's no way to tell for sure. All I can say for sure is that something was cut into her back and something else into her forehead. Maybe you can figure it out." He looked at his watch. "I'll take you out now and show you the lay of the land, Uptown, the Garden District, the French Quarter. Show you where the body was found, down by the river. Tomorrow we'll head into the office and you can talk to some of the detectives. Your friend Stuckey sure knows the right people."

He hesitated. "Have you ever heard of a man named Adam Harrison, or a group called Harrison Investigations?"

"No," Luke said.

"Do you believe in…psychic help in solving cases?"

"No," Luke said flatly. He knew that a lot of law-enforcement agencies had called in psychic investigators over the years, and that they claimed sometimes it helped. Personally, he doubted it. Looking at Joe, he frowned. "Do you?"

"Yes, actually. This is New Orleans, home of Marie Laveau, remember? Well, later on that. Anyway, the super-intendent sent word down the ladder—you can come in and see the autopsy photos. I don't bring things like that here. Kids, you know." Joe picked up his coffee cup, drained it and set it back down. "*Laissez les bon temps roulez,* my friend. I'll show you what I can."

"Oh, my God!" Brad said to Victoria. "I had no idea you guys had anything to do with finding Myra!" He shuddered and gave his cousin a massive hug. "Poor Myra. And poor Alana, too. She was so young." He and Jared had come over as soon as they'd heard what had happened.

"She wasn't, actually. Don't you read the papers? She was thirty," Chloe told him, setting a tray of iced tea and sand-wiches on the patio table.

"It's so horrible, and so sad," Jared said. "But here's the point. There's no reason for you two to hide out. Jeanne sure isn't. Have you seen that interview she gave? She's milking this for all it's worth. She cries, she trembles, she looks so sad and scared. But it's sure getting her a lot of press." He shook his head, as if disgusted that anyone would use such a horror story for her own advancement.

"Smart of her," Chloe commented, taking a seat. "She'll get what she wants—fame."

Brad looked at Victoria. "She's out there turning herself into a major-league overnight sensation, and you're hiding at Chloe's. Chloe—you could be cashing in on this, too."

"Brad, after everything we've been through, how can you even suggest that?" she protested, appalled.

"Don't get me wrong, I think it's horrible, too. And God knows, it could backfire on her. There's a killer out there—and he might just decide she's ripe for killing, as well."

"Don't even say that!" Victoria said with a shiver.

"I'm sorry—I'm just trying to make the two of you feel better, but I'm doing a terrible job of it," Brad said apologetically.

"No, what *Jeanne's* doing is terrible," Jared said, then sighed. "But she *is* a sensation. If you two were the sensation, we could get into any club—on the beach." His eyes were teasing, though, and he took Victoria's hand.

"I don't want that kind of fame," Victoria told him. "Sure, it would be nice to be a well-known model, but I'd rather be recognized for my acting. Anyway, let's face it. Which one of us is ever really hurting for money? We've been lucky. Jeanne didn't have such a great life. If she's an instant celebrity, good for her."

"I think we're forgetting something here," Chloe pointed out.

"What?" Brad asked.

"Three women were brutally murdered," Chloe said.

"You're right, and I'm ashamed," Jared said. "It's just that you can't turn on the news without seeing Jeanne—or Lacy or one of the others. Not to mention the head of the agency. He flew in this morning, apparently. I forget his name."

"Harry Lee," Victoria said. "The head of Bryson Worldwide."

"Yes, him," Jared agreed. "He's all over the news with the rest of them."

"We just feel like lying low for a bit," Chloe said.

"Well, it's going to be interesting to see how long you can stay off the radar," Jared said.

"What are you talking about?" Victoria asked.

"Harry Lee announced that no psychopath is going to get the better of him. He promised a reward of a hundred thousand dollars to anyone who helped find the killer. And he said that the calendar shoot on Coco-belle Island will take place as planned."

"I can't believe it," Victoria said.

Brad smoothed her hair comfortingly. "I don't know what to feel, myself. In a way, it's in incredibly poor taste to capitalize on a murder spree to sell calendars. But maybe Harry Lee's right. Bowing down to a killer, letting him call the shots…That's wrong, too."

Jared said, "I think he's right. The shoot needs to happen. With all kinds of security in place, of course."

"Well, one way or another, Harry Lee means to make it happen," Brad said. "He said he owed it to Myra, who had worked so hard for her girls."

"I don't suppose he mentioned Alana?" Chloe murmured.

"Or the poor seamstress," Victoria said. "Do we even know her name yet?"

★ ★ ★

The mule-drawn carriages clip-clopped down the street.

Last night, crossing Bourbon Street had been an act of derring-do, dodging frat boys, tourists and happy drunks, all moving to a sound track made up of country-western competing with pop competing with heavy metal competing with some decent jazz, thanks to the many clubs lining the street.

But now it was daylight. The tourists who wanted to know the history of the city and admire its remarkable architecture were out in force, and the carriage drivers were talking loudly about the Louisiana Purchase, the reign of Marie Laveau, the voodoo queen, or the making of Anne Rice's *Interview with a Vampire*.

Luke had seen the home in the Garden District where Jill Montague had once lived. The street wasn't busy; the house wasn't hidden.

Canal Street was big and broad, to accommodate the streetcar that ran along it. The sidewalks were teeming with locals and tourists alike, and traffic was constant. There was nothing secretive about Canal Street—unless it took place in havens of vice that were hidden from the daily flow, which was certainly possible.

What seemed impossible to Luke was that a girl could have been attacked on Canal Street without being noticed.

They entered Joe Mulligan's district office. They passed cops going about their business, streetwalkers, junkies and the occasional person who had apparently never been arrested before and looked as stunned as a doe in the headlights.

Luke met Mulligan's superior, and then they went into his friend's office. There, Mulligan took out the full file on Jill Montague. The police work had been thorough. Any and every lead had been followed. After she was found, she had been given a painstakingly exact autopsy, and when the medical examiner had exhausted any possible clues the body might give him, she had been returned to her family to be buried in Lafayette Cemetery in the Garden District.

Joe gave Luke a magnifying glass, and he studied the pictures slowly and carefully. It didn't matter how long you worked with death—this kind of picture made your heart ache and your insides turn over. She had been a beautiful young girl. In life, she'd had a smile a mile wide. In death, her flesh was shrunken on her bones, her color had darkened and she looked both far too real and like a prop out of a horror movie.

Luke let himself acclimate to the appearance of the body, then began studying the carvings on the girl's back and forehead.

At last he looked up and found Joe studying him.

"It looks like a—a hamza hand," Luke said, for the first time realizing what the handlike drawing on the wall had been.

And that it was the same as this.

"What?"

"You can find it in jewelry or Judaica shops—it's an ancient symbol."

"Oh, great, don't let that get out or—"

"No, it isn't just a symbol in Judaism. Arab cultures—"

Joe groaned aloud.

"—and many others around the world use the same symbol. For a lot of them, it represents protection against the evil eye," Luke finished.

"You're sure that's what it is?" Joe asked.

"Pretty sure. But I need some transparent paper," Luke said. "And is it all right if I mark up these copies of the autopsy photos?"

"Photos we got. Go for it," Joe said.

Luke traced the drawings on the dead girl's forehead and back, connecting what lines and grooves he could where the flesh was gone. In both cases he was able to form the hamza hand, with an eye in the middle of the palm and circles on the extended fingers.

Joe sank into his chair and stared at Luke. "Well, I'll be damned...."

"Supposedly those kids were killed a decade ago because they were living lives of sloth and sin, and the killer thought they would be better off in the hands of whatever god he worshipped. 'Death to defilers!,' he wrote. They were unclean. And he drew this—a symbol to ward off evil, the same symbol he carved into your dead girl, who was on her way to a club, as if she needed to be protected from her own proclivity to sin. Partying, drinking, meeting up with friends, probably having boyfriends. I can't say for sure, but I have a feeling if we searched hard enough, we'd find similar cases in a number of other places. I'm sure the FBI would step in if we could prove similarities in different states. Then..."

"Then we'd have to trace the movements of who knows how many people," Joe said with a groan.

"This killer—or these killers—may have some kind of religious agenda. Or he may be using what looks like a religious agenda as a means to his own end. Or maybe he wants certain people to die, but likes to kill in between, which, if discovered, would certainly deflect suspicion from his real intent, and he travels to make the himself harder to find. But I don't think all the killers died after that massacre, though I suspect that anyone who could name the mastermind behind the killings—like those two men in the Glades—is dead. So now it's going to be a lot of footwork, computer searching and piecing together a puzzle."

"I'm telling you, I know some folks who can help you," Joe said.

"Psychics?" Luke wanted to be polite, because Joe obviously believed, but he couldn't keep the skepticism out of his voice.

"How do you think we found Jill's body?" Joe asked.

Luke frowned. "Joe, I'm really sorry, but I just don't believe in dial-a-ghost."

"Neither do these people. I asked you if you'd heard about a man named Adam Harrison. He's more under the radar than you are, but he's totally legitimate. Not only the FBI, but a number of other agencies, have called him in, or consulted one of the people who work for him, and we happen to have a few of those who live right here in New Orleans. They're not mediums or even psychics, at least not in the customary vein. The Native Americans refer to them as nightwalkers. Those who see through the darkness of man's night—death."

He knew Joe really was trying to help him, so he bit

his tongue to keep from saying something that would offend the man.

But it already bothered him that Chloe was seeing ghosts—and now he was being offered psychic help. He had dealt with worse, and he could deal with this, too.

"I'll be happy to meet your friends," he said, pasting a smile on his face.

Joe stood. "But first, in search of your hamza hands, we should go down and talk to Mama Thornton."

"Who is Mama Thornton?" Luke asked cautiously. "A voodoo priestess?"

Joe grinned. "A shopkeeper. She may be a voodoo priestess, but I see her a lot at church in Jackson Square. Half of voodoo comes from Catholicism, you know. But she runs a shop that sells everything—rosaries, crosses, Stars of David, chicken feet, alligator heads, you name it—probably including those hamza hand talismans you drew."

"I would like to talk to her, but I've got to make a phone call, and if possible, I need to get a flight back tonight, too."

"I'll get you on the 5:52 into Miami, will that work?"

"Yeah, perfect," Luke told him. "But if you'll give me a second…"

"Take your time," Joe told him, and headed out to wait by the car.

Luke dialed Chloe, who picked up on the second ring and sounded pleased to hear his voice. "So it's going well up there?" she asked.

"Interestingly, let's say. I think we'll get a lot more help on this case once I show people what I've found out. But at the moment, I'm worried about you."

"Don't be. Everything is great. Brad and Jared are here, Uncle Leo somehow managed to get out of work after only a few hours and Victoria is doing really well. Oh!"

"Oh, what?"

"Harry Lee, the head of Bryson Worldwide, said in a news conference that we're still doing the calendar shoot." She was silent, no doubt waiting for him to object to her taking part in it. When he didn't say anything, she went on. "Victoria is very determined. But here's the thing—I think it's important for us to do it. We'll stick together, so nothing can happen. And you know I'm good with a gun. I don't usually carry one, but I do have a little lady's Smith & Wesson five shot. And Brad and Jared will stick with us, too, and with everything that's happened, we'll have you, and I know Harry Lee will hire extra security. Oh, Victoria knows who you are—she must have overheard you talking to the police at the…the other night—but she's not saying anything to anyone, not even Jared and Brad." She was silent again. "Say something, Luke."

"I'll be home tonight," he told her. "I probably won't make it to your house until nine-thirty or ten."

"I'll be here," she told him.

He hesitated. "And how about you? Any more…experiences?"

"You mean ghosts?" she asked dryly.

"Yes."

"No, but I'm not afraid of them, and yes, I really do believe I saw them. I wish I could see more."

He still felt uneasy, but Chloe did sound fine, and entirely rational.

Feeling relieved, he hung up and rejoined Joe. They took the unmarked car down Orleans Street, to Mama Thornton's shop, aptly named Believe in What You Will.

Looking at herself in the mirror, Chloe had to laugh.

Victoria was every bit as good as she claimed. She had said that they would keep to the basics, so they looked as natural as possible for their appearance at the potluck.

She had made use of neutral shades to give them both a pale appearance. Not dramatic, just a look that signified they didn't see the sun much, even if they lived in Miami. She had produced two wigs in blah shades of brown, and used pencils and eye shadow to play down their eyes rather than play them up, and she'd given Chloe brown contacts that turned her immediately recognizable lime-green eyes to a more normal hazel. Amazingly, such minimal effort had left them looking so different that even their friends wouldn't have been able to recognize them unless they were close-up and personal. To finish, they wore serviceable shoes and dowdy flowered cotton dresses.

"See?" Victoria said proudly. "I rest my case."

"You've worked wonders," Chloe agreed. "But what I don't understand is…what do you think we're going to find out tonight? It's a potluck supper. No one is going to set down a plate of meat loaf and suddenly declare that he's a murderer."

"Stop trying to talk me out of it. We both know that you really want to go, and that you know what to watch for and what questions to ask," Victoria said. "Don't look away. It's the truth, and you know it."

"All right, so…I guess we should get going. Luckily, Uncle Leo got called back to work, but we've got to be out of here before he gets back or we're doomed never to leave. Okay, here's the plan. We'll walk out—we won't take the cars—and call a cab. And we'll get there at seven and leave at eight, agreed?"

"Yes, I promise," Victoria said. "Are you sure we shouldn't wear buckteeth?"

"Yes, I'm sure. We don't want to be noticed. You make us look any worse, and they'll remember us for certain. Let's walk down to Main Street and get a drink at Mister Moe's or Greenstreet's, then call a cab from there."

"Sounds like a plan," Victoria agreed, and together they left the house.

Chloe was reassured when she passed a neighbor who had known her most of her life, and he just nodded politely and kept walking.

"See?" Victoria said.

"Yeah, yeah. Walk faster. It's hot out here. I need air-conditioning or this makeup will melt right off my face."

"You have your gun, right?" Victoria asked nervously.

"Yes, but I'm not happy about it. I have a permit to own it, but not a permit to carry a concealed weapon."

"Hopefully, no one will ever know," Victoria said, then laughed suddenly. "Did you see that car?"

"What car?"

"The one that just passed us. The driver took one look

at us and hit the gas pedal. We're really all right, Chloe. We're really all right."

Chloe wasn't sure, and she didn't like the feeling. She had spent her life since the massacre doing everything she could to learn how to defend herself if necessary, and how *not* to ever put herself in a compromising position where defending herself was necessary, and now she was doing just that. In addition, she felt like a kid who had not lied, exactly, but she had certainly avoided telling Luke or Uncle Leo the truth. A truth that had to do with life and death and murder.

But just because Victoria and she had been due at the mansion, it didn't mean they were in particular danger. Other girls actually lived at the mansion, and they didn't seem unduly afraid. There really wasn't anything to connect the murders now and the massacre in the past.

As for the Church of the Real People, it was bound to be crawling with cops. And no one would know who they were, anyway.

Maybe it was the situation with Luke that had her so on edge. She cared too much about him, and he certainly cared about her, but he'd also made it clear that he wasn't a man who stayed around, who sought anything real, lasting or stable. And now, of course, he probably thought she was crazy.

Maybe she had shared a few too many of her thoughts with him, she decided wryly. At least she hadn't mentioned that she was seeing ghosts to anyone else. And she didn't intend to, either. She trusted Luke more than anyone else she knew, she realized, even if she had him worried about her mental state.

They chose a restaurant they knew, and sat down at the bar, deciding on sodas. It wouldn't do for anyone at the church to smell alcohol on their breath. The bartender, a guy their own age who they'd known casually for years, came over and took their orders, then walked away without a glimmer of recognition.

The minute he was gone, Victoria whispered, "See? I told you. We're going to be fine."

"Yeah—so long as you quit laughing," Chloe told her with a laugh of her own.

Mama Thornton's shop was one of a kind—even by New Orleans standards. Crystal balls, chicken's feet, rosaries, crosses, Stars of David, alligator heads and more all fought for space. Pictures of Christ, Buddha, Mohammed and Greek and Roman and Indian gods crowded the walls. There was a shelf of Wiccan herbal powders, and to top it all off, customers could buy vampire wine and witches' beer, and something called Doc Holliday's Extra Special Tennessee Bourbon.

Mama herself was in the back, but Joe knew the clerk, who led them behind a beaded curtain to an office in the rear.

Mama herself was a beautiful middle-aged woman with deep-set dark eyes and café-au-lait skin. She was dressed casually in jeans and a white cotton shirt, and her hair was tied back in a neat queue. She smiled when she saw Joe, rose to greet him and cordially welcomed Luke to her shop.

"Sit down, sit down. Would you like coffee or tea? There's nothing like our New Orleans coffee, and I have a special blend with just a touch of chicory. Or would you gentlemen like something stronger?" she asked.

"Nothing for me, thanks," Luke said, and Joe agreed.

"Then you've come for information," she said, leaning back. "And I'm happy to help you, if I can."

"We're looking for anyone who might have come in here a few years back who struck you as being strange, even for a religious fanatic," Joe said.

She stared at the two of them, then burst into laughter.

"A religious fanatic—in here?" she demanded. "Darlins, you *are* jokin', right?"

Luke shook his head. "I'm afraid not. And I've already got the impression you're a pretty good judge of people, so I'm thinking you might remember someone out of the ordinary."

"You're not looking for the kooks who think they're vampires, or my run-of-the- mill voodoo folk, are you?" she asked.

He shook his head. "I'm looking for someone who worships a god who condemns everything, someone who believes in the Old Testament God of wrath, the kind who would destroy a city to prevent sin, who believes that the body is a temple. He walks and talks like any normal man, and he may even be charming on the surface, but there's something underneath that, when he gets going on the subject of religion, makes your skin crawl."

"Interesting," Mama Thornton said, and gnawed on the end of a pencil, watching him, thinking. "I may have to ask some of my staff."

"Are most of your sales by credit card?" Joe asked her.

She nodded. "Most, these days. Not all. I have so many folks come in here, and you're asking about a lot of time gone by. I'll tell you what, I can't help you this second because I'll have to go through a lot of records to see if something jogs my memory and about ten different people who've worked for me, but…can you tell me anything else about who you are looking for?"

"Someone from Miami," Luke said. "And also, anyone who might have bought a charm or necklace of hamza hands."

"Miami and hamza hands."

She let out a sigh. "We're a hop, skip and not even a jump from Miami by plane. But Miami and hamza hands… maybe that will help. I'll check my records and see if anything comes up."

They stood, and Luke gave her his card. "I'd sure appreciate any help."

She nodded to him gravely, not rising. Despite her modern garb, there was something of the wise priestess about her.

"You're looking for someone who has caused a lot of terror and death, aren't you," she said, and it wasn't a question. "I will do my best to help you."

He thanked her again, and they started to leave.

"Wait!" she called suddenly.

She reached into a drawer and took out a necklace. It was a beautiful piece, and a strange one, hung with a wide variety of symbols: a cross, a star, a hamza hand, a four-leaf clover, a crescent moon and a pentagram. In the center was a delicate gold circle with the words Believe in Love and Goodness.

"Take this," she told him.

"No, no, I couldn't. Thank you so much," Luke said. "But it's—"

"It's not for you. Give it to the one you love."

"I don't—"

"You don't believe in talismans, and maybe you don't believe in love. Give it to a special friend, then. But take it, please. It will mean a great deal to me."

He realized that it would be churlish of him to refuse, but he felt bad—the piece was gold, and obviously not a cheap trinket.

He thanked her sincerely, reminding her that any help she could give him would be vastly appreciated, and he and Joe left.

"You've got about an hour before I have to get you to the airport," Joe told him. "And I've arranged another meeting for you."

Luke knew what was coming and tried to come up with an excuse to get to the airport early. No luck.

"We're going to the carousel bar at the Monteleone, just around the corner and down the street. I know you think it's going to be a waste of time," Joe told him. "But at least you'll get a farewell drink out of it."

Sure. A drink before he headed home. That would be fine.

He wasn't sure how he knew, but when they entered the bar, he saw the couple and knew they were the ones Joe wanted him to meet. He was a distinguished-looking older man, slender, with white hair, sitting at one of the window tables with a beautiful teal-eyed blonde who was perhaps Chloe's age or a year or two older. They stood, and Joe was greeted with a kiss from the woman, and a warm hand-shake and a pat on the back from the man, who was almost Luke's height.

Joe introduced them as Nikki Blackhawk and Adam Harrison, and they both shook Luke's hand.

"A pleasure," Adam Harrison said as they all sat. "I've heard about you, so it's nice to actually get to meet you."

"You've heard about me?" Luke said, surprised. "I can't say the same."

"I don't advertise."

"I don't, either."

"But I'm always aware of people who work a little dif-ferently from everyone else," Adam said.

"I'm not a psychic, you know," Luke said.

"No, you're not," the woman told him.

He looked at her, regretting the fact that he had come. The whole thing seemed ridiculous. "Do you read minds?" he asked politely.

She smiled, glancing over at Adam Harrison. "No, I don't." She leaned toward him. "But I do read corpses."

He didn't have a chance to decide just how she meant that, when a fifth person joined them.

He was definitely a Native American, tall and muscular, with light-colored eyes betraying European blood some-where in the past. "Brent Blackhawk," he said, introducing himself. "Nikki's other half."

"Mr. Cane isn't happy about being here, Brent. He thinks we're a bunch of frauds," Nikki said.

"I never said that," Luke protested.

"But he doesn't believe in ghosts," Joe said unhelpfully.

"Look," Luke said. "I'm sorry, but in my experience, knowledge comes from following physical clues, determining a criminal's mind-set, studying the victims…from what we can see, feel, touch."

Joe was shaking his head. "Nikki found Jill for us, Luke."

Luke looked over at the woman. He had a feeling that her husband would be fiercely unforgiving if he mocked her in any way, though the man had a pleasant enough manner. And he honestly didn't mean to mock anyone; he just thought there were too many corpses piling up for playing games. "How?" he asked her.

She glanced over at her husband.

"You seem like a decent sort, Luke, and Adam said that you're the real deal when it comes to solving murders," Brent told him. "So we're all here to help if we can, especially because the corpse Nikki helped find might be a victim of the same killer you're seeking."

"How did you find her?" Luke asked Nikki again. "Did you hold something she owned and try to sense her?"

Nikki smiled politely. "No. I run one of the local ghost tours."

"I don't understand," Luke said.

"I was giving a lecture when I saw her. She wasn't an accomplished ghost—you're laughing at me, Mr. Cane," she said.

"I just didn't know that ghosts could be accomplished or unaccomplished," he said, but he couldn't help remembering how serious Chloe had been about seeing ghosts.

Nor could he forget the dampness on the rug in her room.

Brent spoke up. "There are actually all kinds of hauntings. Residual hauntings, for instance—happen a lot on bat-
tlefields. Ghosts stay to relive the last traumatic moments of
their lives—over and over again. Sometimes they become
very strong, what we call accomplished. There are areas at
Gettysburg where even people without a hint of a sixth
sense can feel the dead around them. New ghosts are seldom
as talented as those who've been hanging around a long time,
but the longer they're around—and the harder they work at
it—the better they get at appearing to others, and even
creating physical manifestations."

"Like rattling chains," Luke murmured.

"Yes," Adam said pleasantly. "Like rattling chains."

"Jill appeared on the corner where she had been ab-
ducted," Nikki said.

"She didn't happen to mention her killer's name, did
she?" Luke asked.

"This is a waste of time," Brent said, but Nikki ignored
him and went on.

"He wore a mask, so she never saw his features. But she
felt she'd met him a day or so earlier at a bar. She would
have told me more if she could have, Mr. Cane. He raped
and tortured her before he killed her. He kept telling her
that he was saving her soul. That he was a warrior for God.
Does that help you at all?"

Luke was startled. Maybe Nikki Blackhawk was playing
up the religious angle because Joe had told her about his own
interest in the religious angle, but there was something
sincere about her. About all three of them.

And he couldn't forget Chloe's insistence that she'd been seeing ghosts. Or her belief that they were trying to help.

He sighed softly, then grinned ruefully at the others. "It does. Thank you. I believe that the killer is a religious fanatic. I don't mean to have a closed mind, but I have never believed in ghosts. Dead is dead—and gone. I lost my wife. For a while I actually prayed she'd come back as a ghost so I could beg her forgiveness."

"Perhaps you always had her forgiveness, or there was nothing for which she felt she needed to forgive you," Nikki said. She was studying him intensely with her aqua-colored eyes. "She was murdered, wasn't she? But her killer is dead." She leaned back. "By your hand."

He was startled. And defensive. Then he remembered that Adam Harrison had said he knew about him.

Joe suddenly cleared his throat. A waiter was standing there, ready to take their drink order. Luke opted for a beer, then looked at his watch while the others ordered. He had about fifteen minutes left. Looking from Nikki to Brent, and then to the soft-spoken Adam Harrison—who hadn't ordered a drink, he realized—he wondered if he wasn't a fool to refuse to accept any help, no matter what the source.

"To be honest," he said, "I have a friend who would love to talk to you. She was one of the survivors of the first massacre, a friend of the currently missing girl, and involved with the agency where the latest murders took place—and now she believes she can see ghosts."

"Then she probably can," Brent said with a shrug.

Luke wanted to say that was impossible, but he refrained.

Joe pitched in then. "We've just been to see Mama Thornton. Luke believes that the symbol on Jill's back was a hamza hand, and he believes that the killers a decade ago painted a hamza hand on the wall in blood. Mama Thornton is going to ask her staff and go through her records to see if she can come up with the name of someone from the Miami area who might have been up here and shown an interest in hamza hands and been a religious fanatic."

"I'll give her a call and mention the importance of the project," Nikki said.

She had a soft drawl and, unlike her husband, was obviously a native of the area.

Adam rose suddenly. "I have a car outside—five-thirty flight to D.C., I'm afraid." He glanced at Luke, amused. "Appointment at Quantico. But if we can be of any help…" He offered Luke a card.

Luke accepted and thanked him, then rose, as well. "I'd better skip that beer, because I have a flight, too. I'm afraid to be away from Miami too long."

"Ride with me, then," Adam said. "Save Joe the trip."

"Thank you," Luke told him, though he privately wondered if he was going to be lectured about the paranormal all the way to the airport.

The others rose to say goodbye. Nikki shook Luke's hand, then hesitated, before smiling suddenly. "For what it's worth, I thought I had lost my mind the first time I saw a ghost," she told him. "If it hadn't been for Brent and Adam…" She shrugged. "If I can help you or your friend, please let me know."

"Thank you," he said, and he meant it.

He left with Adam Harrison. Not only did the car taking him to the airport have federal government plates, it wasn't a car at all. It was a stretch limo. Someone certainly thought Harrison was the real deal.

As they drove, the older man kept the conversation casual but still focused on the paranormal. "I envy them so much. People who have the gift."

"You don't have it?" Luke asked, surprised.

Adam shook his head. "My son did. He knew I would lose him. And when I did, I discovered that he'd passed his gift on."

"To Nikki? Or Brent?"

"No," Adam said, smiling and shaking his head. "I have many agents. That's my talent. Finding them. It's only recently that I've been able to see Josh."

"Your son," Luke said politely.

Harrison nodded, still smiling. "He's here in the car, sitting right across from us."

Luke didn't know how to react. There was no point in telling the other man that there was no one sitting across from them.

"Does he know anything?" he finally asked politely. "Can he help me?"

Harrison laughed and looked over at Luke. "He said that you're a skeptic with a closed mind, and that you should listen to those around you."

Luke looked at the empty seat across from him. "Nice to meet you, too, Josh."

Harrison merely smiled.

Luke debated as he stared at Harrison. Every government agency in the country seemed to respect the man, even though he was obviously crazy.

*What if he wasn't?*

Luke let out a breath. "All right. Maybe Josh is there, but I don't see ghosts. I only see what's real and tangible." One more hesitation. "But someone I care about very much believes that *she's* seeing ghosts, and *I* believe in *her*. What would you say to that? What would Josh say?"

Harrison lowered his head for a moment, then looked up at Luke. He didn't look insane. He looked confident, like a man who didn't need to prove anything to anyone.

"Josh says that it's a start, and he also points out the fact that you're deep in a quagmire and wants to know what the hell you have to lose? I'm willing to send Nikki and Brent down to Miami, and they'd be happy to help you. If nothing else, trust me when I tell you that Brent is as solid as the day is long. He's a brilliant investigator whether seeing ghosts or—and I know you'll find this hard to believe—proving that they don't exist. Since you have nothing to lose and only help to gain, why not say yes?"

Luke was surprised to find himself laughing.

He still didn't see Josh. But Brent was flesh and bone, and it would be good to have someone around who wasn't involved, who was rock solid—and another few bodies to keep watch wouldn't hurt.

Josh—or the ghost in Harrison's mind—was right.

"I *am* in a quagmire. And I *can* use all the help I can get," Luke said.

Harrison nodded. "Good."

Luke smiled ruefully. "Mind if I ask Josh a question?"

"Not at all," Harrison said.

"If ghosts exist, why have I never seen my wife?" Luke asked, and he was surprised by the huskiness in his voice.

"Because," Harrison said after a moment, "she loved you, and she knew you loved her in return. Because her murderer was stopped—by your hand. She's moved on, and that means it's time for you to move on, as well. She's gone, Luke. She's happy and at peace, and she would want the same for you."

Luke was surprised by how deeply the answer seemed to affect him, surprised by the tension inside him.

Surprised at how much he wanted to believe.

He decided it didn't matter what he believed. Having outside help from a crack agency would be great.

At the airport, they parted ways, but he couldn't stop thinking about everything Adam Harrison and his agents had said, and he had plenty of time for thinking, because his plane was scheduled to take off almost forty-five minutes late. He wasn't sure why, but after his meeting with the Harrison Investigations team, he was more anxious than ever to get back.

He was worried. No, he was more than worried, he was afraid. Afraid for people he was coming to care about. Afraid for Chloe.

He chafed, looking at his watch.

This was the night that the Church of the Real People had been planning to host its potluck supper. At least that wouldn't be happening, not after everything that had gone on.

He called Stuckey from the plane, while they were still at the gate, just to check in, and discovered it hadn't been canceled after all.

Stuckey was well past annoyed. "Oh yes, the righteous indignation of Brother Mario Sanz has been all over the airwaves. And get this—they've been so cooperative that it's almost ridiculous. An entire list of past and present members arrived on my desk this morning. Not one of the current members would object to any questioning, and we were invited to search any and all premises. Since we're all afraid of what might happen tonight, we have more officers than we can spare guarding the church. It's a zoo, and that's exactly what I don't need."

"Do you still have someone outside the Marin house?" Luke asked.

"You bet. Leo has come and gone, but the girls have stayed in. I got a report from my patrolman just a few minutes ago—both cars are there and the girls are inside."

Luke thanked him and said that he'd be in the following morning to report on what he had seen, what he thought, and compare notes.

He hung up and dialed Chloe's number. It went straight to message.

He was concerned and about to try again, but the flight attendant came by, asking him to please turn off his phone. She waited for him, watching with knowing eyes.

He turned off his phone.

The flight was barely an hour and a half, but it seemed to stretch for an eternity.

★ ★ ★

Before they left the restaurant, Chloe and Victoria remembered that it was a *potluck* supper, so they ordered a large salad and bread to go. The streets were crazy when they neared the church, with the police stopping anyone who looked even slightly suspicious.

Victoria's makeup and costuming passed muster, because the officers let them right through, along with their contribution to the meal, and they walked up to the church. Neither of them had ever seen the building before, and they were both surprised by the onion domes, but then again, as Victoria mentioned, at least one nightclub in New York City had once been a church.

At first, they might have been at any church gathering. People greeted them, thanked them for the food and told them to help themselves, and offered them punch.

Neither of them drank it, though they accepted the paper cups.

After a while a bell rang, and everyone put down their plates and moved into the sanctuary. Brother Sanz, the man who had appeared on television, welcomed the congregation and their guests, and explained that despite what they might have heard, the church never preached violence of any sort, because human life was always sacred. "What we teach is tolerance for others, accompanied by our belief that we know the true way to reach heaven. And that way is through goodness to others and a knowledge that we are blessed, and that our bodies are our temples. Our members eschew the poisons that are so easily available everywhere you turn. We don't imbibe alcohol, we don't smoke—legal or illegal substances," he said, bringing a laugh from his audience. "We promote a community in which all of us care for the welfare of children. We are friends to one another. Yes, we ask for a portion of our parishioners' earnings, but all to fund the church and her outreach programs. We help those who are stricken with illness, and we are there to support our members who find themselves without jobs. Giving of oneself is everything, and it earns one everything in return. Tonight, we are here to tell you who we are. No one is ever compelled to join a church or stay in a church, but we hope you will join us and stay with us. We hope to provide the hope, faith, love and charity that we are all seeking in life."

His rhetoric went on for a while longer. Chloe looked nervously at her watch and saw that it was almost nine, nearly an hour later than they had planned to stay. She was relieved when Brother Sanz blessed those present, and people rose to leave.

Afterward there was coffee in the garden area beside the church. Chloe was impatient and ready to leave, but she went stock-still when she saw a man streak past the police barricade, shouting, "Whore of Satan! Killer—murderess!"

He hurled the tomato at a woman of about forty who was standing very near Chloe.

The woman ducked, slipped and fell. The police went after the man, who raced away down the sidewalk.

Chloe bent instinctively to help the woman who had fallen. Others nearby also stepped forward, but as the woman stood up, glancing at Chloe gratefully for her support, she said, "Please, please, I'm fine. Don't hover, my friends. I'm all right."

Chloe dusted off the woman's shirt, where bits of grass had clung. "Thank you," the woman said. She was bone thin, and had a sadness about her that was haunting. She was pretending that the attack had meant nothing, but there were tears in her eyes.

"I'm sorry," Chloe said. "I don't mean to pry, but…why?"

"It's because of what happened in that house on the beach," the woman said. She met Chloe's eyes and said, "You're a kind soul, I can feel it. Would you get me some coffee?"

"I've got it," Victoria said. "You two sit down. There's a table over there."

Chloe led the woman to the nearby picnic table and sat next to her.

"Luckily most people have no idea—" The woman broke off and offered her hand. "I'm Sister Lucy. I don't use my last name, but it's Garcia."

Chloe stared at her blankly for a minute, then realized that Garcia was the name of one of the men who had been found in the Everglades, not the man she had identified but the man who had been with him.

"You know about my brother, don't you?" Sister Lucy asked.

Evidently her face had given her away, Chloe thought.

She nodded. "Yes. He was one of the dead men found in the Everglades ten years ago, wasn't he?"

Sister Lucy nodded. "He didn't do it," she whispered.

"Everyone thought I was crazy, because there was a note… he was dead. But he didn't do it. I know he didn't."

Victoria came over with the coffee, sitting down next to Lucy and saying, "It's all right. We believe you."

"Shh!" Sister Lucy said. "He's coming."

They looked around to see who she was talking about and saw Brother Sanz heading their way.

Lucy stood immediately. "Brother Sanz. I was welcoming these ladies to the church and thanking them for helping me up."

Brother Sanz offered his hand to Victoria and then Chloe. His handshake was firm and warm, and his smile was warmer. "I commend you ladies for your courage, not just in helping Sister Lucy but in coming here tonight. We're being blamed once more, and once more we are innocent. But I will not let our church fall apart again. We do too much good. Thank you for coming, and for helping Lucy against those who would condemn without trial and take what they think of as justice into their own hands. I hope to see you here again."

"I'm sure we'll be back," Victoria said. "But it's quite late for us. We have to go to work in the morning, so we'd better say good-night."

"Thank you so much for a very informative and enjoyable evening. And good night," Chloe said, then turned.

And crashed straight into Luke Cane, who caught her, steadied her and looked into her eyes.

And knew exactly who she was.

# THIRTEEN

Seated next to Victoria in the living room of her carriage house, Chloe appeared aloof and indignant, but he knew it was a ruse. Just like the ridiculous dresses, wigs and makeup they had been wearing. Now the wigs were gone, their faces had been washed, and they were down to the dowdy dresses.

Now it was just himself versus Chloe and Victoria, who was staying absolutely silent. She had started off by trying to take the blame, but Chloe, in a burst of temper, had told her that she was an adult and absolutely free to make her own choices, and she had chosen to go along to the church.

That was now.

But he had seen her expression when she and Victoria had first run into him, and he knew that she was also being an-

tagonistic because she realized she had done something foolish and potentially dangerous. And yes, she had allowed
Victoria to urge her into it.

He was trying hard to tread carefully here. She was over
twenty-one and *usually* of sound mind, and if she chose to,
she could demand that he get out of her house and he
would have no choice but to go. And yet it was difficult not
to betray his anger and incredulity that they had pulled such
a stunt when they had just seen their friend's blood congeal-
ing in a pool of solid crimson.

He was pacing back and forth, and he told himself to stop,
and managed to at least stride into the kitchen and find a
beer. A long, slow swallow helped him get a grip.

He went back to the living room and looked at the two
of them. "What didn't you see when we went into that
house the other night?" he asked. "You know—you *know*—
what people, and quite possibly *those people,* are capable of.
You've seen it twice now. What were you thinking?"

"We were never in any danger," Chloe insisted. "Whoever
killed Myra and the others doesn't go after his victims in
public places. I'd be in more danger here, if he were after
me. But he's not. Think about it—fanatics killed our friends
ten years ago. If someone had specifically wanted either of
us dead, they wouldn't be waiting around ten years. And the
crime scenes weren't the same, so there's no reason to think
the two crimes are even related."

"Maybe the killer didn't have time to write on the wall
this time," Luke said, finally taking a seat across from the
two women.

"Why did you go looking for us at the church, anyway?" Chloe asked suspiciously.

"I called you, but you didn't answer. Then I came here—and you were gone. Why did you turn your phone off, anyway?"

"Because we were in the meeting," Chloe said. She turned away, looking guilty for a moment, but her mask of regal independence was quickly back in place.

"Well, when you didn't answer, and then I saw that the cars were still here, I figured you were up to something, and I figured it had to be the potluck supper."

"You mentioned that you were thinking about going, but that was…before," Chloe murmured.

"We learned something tonight," Victoria said. "Well, Chloe did. She managed to be in the right place at the right time."

Luke stared at Chloe. "You might have mentioned this."

"You might have given me a chance."

He waited silently for her to go on.

"There's a woman there named Sister Lucy. Sister Lucy Garcia. She was the sister—the biological sister, I mean—of Abram Garcia, the man who supposedly shot and killed Michael Donlevy and then himself in the Everglades. The guy who supposedly put his murder-suicide note in a plastic bag so that it could be found with the bodies out on the trail. And here's the interesting part—"

"A guy tried to throw a tomato at her," Victoria interjected.

"He missed her, but she slipped, and I helped her up, and she told us that her brother didn't do it—that the church got the blame, but it wasn't responsible. The thing is, Abram Garcia wasn't the man I saw. So I know Michael Donlevy was there, but I can't guarantee that Abram Garcia was, so maybe his sister is right and he really was innocent. No one believed her, of course. There was the note, and there was my sketch of Michael Donlevy. I don't know. It's confusing, that's for sure."

He shook his head. "I'll go down there and find a way to speak with her."

"Right. It's fine for *you* to go there," Chloe murmured.

"Please. I never thought of you as stupid, Chloe. I'm an investigator. I was a cop. I know what I'm doing."

"Excuse me, but I got information you might not have gotten. And don't go telling me that you're so big and strong." Chloe's eyes narrowed suddenly. "I saw some of the biggest macho jocks in town die in a pool of blood, just like the girls."

"I know that," he said quietly. "But it's my job to deal with the killers of the world. Those guys were still just kids, and they were taken by surprise."

"She had her gun with her," Victoria volunteered.

"Victoria," Chloe said flatly, unhappily, before turning her attention back to Luke. "It wasn't a bad idea, going there. Vickie is good at what she does. You knew it was us, but only because you were expecting to find us there. And we did find out about Lucy Garcia. That gives you a lead. Right?"

He nodded. "A good lead. And thank you. But please, I don't want to die."

"What?" Victoria said, puzzled.

"You two almost gave me a heart attack."

"Oh, be serious," Victoria said, smiling.

"I *am* serious," Luke said.

They didn't get a chance to speak further then, because there was a soft tap at the door, and Chloe leaped up to answer it.

Leo came in and frowned when he saw her dress. "What? Did you sneak out and hold up a flea market?" he asked.

"Vickie and I were just fooling around," Chloe said.

Well, Luke thought, he couldn't really call her a liar for that.

Leo looked distracted when he turned to Luke. "Welcome back. I'm glad you're here."

"Thanks."

"Was it a worthwhile trip?"

"I think so."

"I hope so," Leo said. "The police have nothing, from what I've gotten from Stuckey. No footprints, no fingerprints. There was no forced entry. They're figuring the murderer left by the back, but sand doesn't hold prints, and there was no blood trail, nothing. It's like a phantom committed the murders and then disappeared."

"How are they doing with their investigation into the Church of the Real People?" Luke asked. "I see Stuckey tomorrow morning," he added. "So if you feel uncomfortable talking about it, it's fine."

"No, I don't mind. The church is being open and seemingly helpful, but everyone still has to tread carefully. You can't rip a place apart because of something that happened a decade ago."

"No," Luke agreed.

"All right, then I'll see you tomorrow, since it looks like you've all decided to stay over here," Leo said. "I just wanted to be sure Luke was back safe."

He left. But before the door closed, Victoria called to him to wait. "I'm going to sleep in the main house," she told Luke and Chloe. "And no offense, Chloe, but please, don't follow me and worry about me. I'm fine on my own, and frankly, I like to stretch out. The two of us in that bed did not work."

She was out the door before either of them could say anything.

Silence fell.

Chloe looked at Luke. "I didn't do anything wrong," she finally said.

"Wrong? No."

"Oh, God, I hate that! I like it better when you're yelling."

"You scared me. It wasn't wrong, exactly, but it wasn't the right thing to do, either," he said.

"I wouldn't have lied to you. But I don't have to ask for your permission to do what I think I should," she said.

"No," he admitted grudgingly.

"Oh, God," she groaned. "I'm sorry. Really. Do you believe me?"

"Of course."

"But?"

He shrugged. "You'll do whatever you want again, Chloe. You're a wild card."

She stood up. "I'm sorry, then. I wouldn't have done it if I hadn't known there would be police everywhere."

"All right."

"I'm going up. To bed."

He nodded.

"Are you staying here?" she asked.

"Yeah. I'll be here."

She hesitated for another second. Then she was gone, up the stairs.

He sat, staring at the emptiness of the couch for a long time. He didn't know what had him so paralyzed. It wasn't his time in New Orleans; it wasn't even realizing that the government called on psychics for help.

He closed his eyes and remembered Miranda.

Remembered getting home.

Seeing her.

He didn't dwell on the memory, but sometimes it came back unbidden. At least tonight he knew why.

After a while, he dozed in the chair. And he stayed there all that night. He didn't want to sleep well, didn't want to dream.


She dreamed, and she was sure it was a dream because things weren't exactly right. Things were too big, out of proportion, and melting, dripping, like in a Dali painting.

And Colleen Rodriguez was in her room again, wet and staring at her. And she was dripping, too. The white dress dripped. Her hair dripped.

And tears dripped down her cheeks.

*Help me, please. Find me. Catch him.*

When Chloe woke the next morning, she was exhausted. She didn't know whether or not to mention her dream to Luke, especially since he had never come up to join her last night.

It hurt, but she still felt that going to the church had been important.

It wasn't even nine yet when she went downstairs, but Luke was already gone.

She wasn't alone, though. There was something on the couch. A mound, covered with a towel. She walked over to it—cautiously, because something under there was making little whining noises.

She moved the towel and saw that it was a pet carrier with a note taped to it.

*Hi. My name is Theodore Roosevelt, Theo for short. I'm a Belgian shepherd, and I'll grow up to be a very big boy. I'm not much good as a watchdog right now, but my father is coming by to stay with you for a while. He's good at guarding yards and houses. Of course, a dog can't go everywhere, but my dad is a cool dude and will behave anyplace dogs are allowed.*

Chloe had been feeling particularly depressed, not because she was being haunted, but because Luke had chosen to stay away from her.

But the letter and the puppy made her smile. She took the little creature out of the carrier, and he immediately started licking her half to death. "Hey, hey, calm down," she told him. Then, to herself, "Okay, this is great, I have an untrained puppy. How on earth did he manage that at such an early hour?" She turned back to the puppy. "I don't even have food for you. What do I do with you now? Take you to work?"

There was a tap at her door, and she opened it. Leo, dressed for work, his briefcase in his hand, was standing there.

"Well?" he asked.

"Well what?"

"I wasn't sure I should let him leave you a puppy, but…he was so damn cute," Leo said. "The puppy, I mean."

"He's adorable," she agreed.

"His dad is out here. Want to come meet him?"

"I guess so," Chloe said, and stepped out, hoping that the bigger version of Theo wouldn't jump on her.

"Dad's name is George," Leo told her.

"Don't tell me—let me guess. George—Washington?" she asked.

"You got it. He actually belongs to a police trainer—George, not the puppy. The puppy is yours. I guess Luke is friends with the guy and knew he had a litter of puppies ready to go. George is on loan. He's supposed to be one of the handler's best dogs. Nice as can be—unless someone threatens whoever he's guarding. But I'm supposed to introduce you right away, so he'll know you're not threatening."

"What about Victoria?"

"She met him on the way out," Leo told her.

"Oh," she said. She could see Theo's father already. The dog had to weigh close to two hundred pounds. He was a giant, but he was beautiful.

"Hi, George," she said.

George trotted over to her as sweetly as a kitten and nuzzled her hand, and she stroked his back.

"George stays in the yard while we're gone. He'll sleep with you at night, wherever you are," Leo said.

"I see."

"Oh, Luke left something else for you, as well," Leo told her. "It's on the counter. I've got to go. See you tonight. If you're not coming home for any reason, call me."

"Will do. And you do the same, okay?"

"Absolutely."

Leo left, and Chloe walked back inside to check out the counter, where she saw an exquisite and unique piece of jewelry lying on the counter. "Guess he was covering all the bases, huh, Theo?" she murmured as she picked up the necklace and examined it. The center circle, with the blessing, or whatever it was, was large and dangled lower than the other, smaller, charms. The necklace was beautiful, but she didn't think it was the kind of thing Luke Cane would have picked out. Was it really intended for her?

She slipped it on anyway, picked up the puppy and headed out. She was careful with all the locks.

When she reached her office, Jim Evans was at his desk in the waiting room. He looked up in surprise, and she wasn't sure if it was because she was there, or because of the puppy in her arms.

"Don't ask," she told him.

"He's adorable. A therapy dog?" Jim asked.

"Um, no. A present."

"Ooh. Cute. I suppose I get to walk him now?" Jim said.

"We'll both walk him, I guess. I don't know. I haven't had a puppy before."

"What's that on your neck?"

"Oh, another present."

"Double ooh," Jim teased. Then he grew sober. "You shouldn't be here. I didn't expect you, so I cleared your calendar."

"Make a few calls. Some people may want to come in."

"If you insist," Jim said. "But…are you sure?"

"Absolutely."

"Okay, I'll get you going in the next hour. But a lot of people know you worked with Myra and the Bryson Agency. They'll be thinking you're the one who needs the help."

"I'll let them help me. That's always good therapy," she said, and started into her office.

"Oh, wait!" Jim said, and stood, then brought her a piece of paper. "This is from Harry Lee, the big honcho at Bryson. He's been trying to get you—even came by, but I refused to hand out your home number. The man is still planning the calendar shoot. In Myra's memory, no less." Jim was indignant. He obviously didn't believe it was to honor anyone's memory. He was certain it was for the big bucks.

And it probably was.

"When does he intend to start?"

"Same days—you need to be on the island by Friday morning, a week from now."

"All right, thanks."

"Are you going to do it?" Jim asked her.

"Actually, yes," she said, and escaped into her office at last.

She'd walked the puppy right before she'd come up, but he piddled a few seconds after she put him on the floor. At least he'd avoided the Persian rug and gone on the tile. She cleaned up the mess and told him that he was going to have to learn better control of his bladder, pronto, if he was going to come to work with her. He just wagged his tail.

She started on paperwork, and in a few minutes, the intercom buzzed.

"Farley Astin is on his way in, and Mindy Sutton has an appointment just after lunch."

"Super, thanks."

Farley arrived in less than half an hour. He gave her a sympathetic hug, then stepped back, as if he was afraid he had overstepped his bounds. "I'm sorry. I heard about the murders, and I knew that you worked for the Bryson people sometimes. But I shouldn't have hugged you. I'm so sorry."

"Thank you, Farley, and the hug was very nice. Now, how about coffee or a soda or something?"

He didn't want a soda. He did want to talk, and to hear her talk. He played with the puppy for a while first, then wandered around the room. He picked up one of the sketch pads and looked over at her. "I wish I could draw the way you do."

"Actually, you're pretty good."

He smiled, pleased with the compliment, sat down at the far end of the couch and started drawing.

"What are you sketching?" she asked him.

"Oh, the strangest thing. I was heading home last night when I got detoured all over the place. Parts of Biscayne Boulevard were closed off. Anyway, I wound up stopped in traffic in front of that weird cult place. I was just sketching what I saw."

"Oh?" Chloe rose and went over to see his sketch.

He had done a caricature, showing the police every-where, the media held back behind barricades, and the church itself, with all the carefree "picnickers" in the garden. The biggest face belonged to Brother Mario Sanz, and Farley had drawn dollar signs for his eyes.

"Do you think they were involved the other night?" Farley asked her. "Oh, man, I'm sorry. I forgot that you…you know. Survived that massacre ten years ago.…"

"Don't be afraid to talk about it, Farley. I'm not. As far as the Church of the Real People goes, well, I don't think we know enough to make a judgment. Lots of religious sects asked for tithes from their practitioners."

"But these guys—they're scary," Farley said.

"It's a free country—including freedom of religion," she reminded him.

After that, they finally talked about his problems rebuild-ing his life after a false accusation of rape.

At last, he left, scratching Theo's fuzzy ears before he went.

Jim came in a minute later. "I ordered sushi," he told her. "It should arrive shortly. Since Mindy Sutton is due in so soon, I thought it would be what you wanted."

"You are the eighth wonder of the world," she assured him.

"I do try. Anyway, after Mindy and a session for the school board—which I managed to get in this afternoon at three—you're patient-free until after the shoot."

"You're amazing."

"Yeah, I deserve a raise. In fact, you'll make a few bucks on that shoot, so I think I *will* pencil myself in for a raise."

She laughed. "I guess you're due."

A little while later, over sushi, the conversation turned to Luke Cane—or Jack Smith, as Jim knew him.

"That…designer will still be going to the shoot, right?" Jim asked her.

"Yes."

"Good. Though I don't think he's a designer."

Her eyes widened, but she didn't reply, only stood, throwing the sushi container in the wastebasket. "I'm going to go call Harry Lee and let him know that I'm still participating."

"All right. Let me know when to send Mindy Sutton in."

As she waited for Harry to pick up, she studied Farley's picture of the church potluck. The dollar signs in the eyes of Mario Sanz were particularly intriguing.

Harry came on the phone at last. "You're a hard woman to reach," he told her; then his tone softened as he said, "How are you? I understand you were there when the bodies were discovered."

"I'm all right," she said.

"And you're still game to go on the shoot?"

"Yes."

"That's what Victoria told me this morning, but I'm glad you called. I'll be handling everything personally, of course. Myra will be all but impossible to replace, so for now I'll be taking the helm."

"That's good to hear." Was it? Her answer had been entirely rote.

"Victoria said your friends Brad and Jared are still planning to be there. And Jack Smith is still going to be shooting his catalogue."

There was really nowhere for the conversation to go after that, and he was about to hang up, when she said, "Harry, wait. What about the—the funerals?"

"They'll have to take place after the shoot. The police haven't released the bodies yet."

She thanked him and hung up. A minute later Jim buzzed her to say that Mindy was there.

"Send her in."

As Mindy talked, she played with the puppy, and Chloe found herself thinking that maybe Theo would make a good therapy dog one day.

But while Mindy continued talking, Chloe found her thoughts wandering to Coco-lime—and Maria.

After Mindy came the members of the school board, but as soon as they left she scooped up Theo and went out to the waiting room, where she was uncertain whether to feel pleased or cranky at being caught off guard.

Luke was there.

She might not know exactly what their relationship was—other than awkward, at the moment—but he was a great guardian, that was for certain.

"Hey there," she said.

He stood and walked over to her, taking Theo from her arms. "So you like the pup, huh?" he asked.

"He's—adorable."

"You should always start with a dog," Jim offered from

behind his desk. "If you can't handle a dog, you're never going to be able to handle children."

"Thank you for that bit of wisdom, Jim," Chloe said, grinning to take the sting out of the words. Then she turned back to Luke.

"Are you parked?" she asked him. "I mean, in the building? I can stamp your ticket."

He laughed. "No, I'm not parked in the building. I was dropped off."

"Oh."

"By a police cruiser."

"I see. No, wait. I don't see at all. What have you been doing all day?"

"Going through a lot of public records. And now I'm famished. Where can we go where they'll allow dogs?"

"Outside in the Grove," she told him. "Or the beach."

"I vote for the Grove. It's closer to your…place."

He wasn't angry with her, she realized. Or if he was, at least it wasn't keeping him away. She understood his point of view, but didn't he realize she never would have gone to the potluck supper if she hadn't been sure she and Victoria would be safe?

He held the dog while she drove. "I'm thinking," he told her, "that I'd like to pull things together tonight and tomorrow morning, then head down to the Keys."

"This soon? Officially, I don't think anything's happening until Thursday night, and then it's just people coming down and getting settled."

"I want time to talk to Maria. Somehow everything's

connected through the Church of the Real People, I'm sure of it. We just have to find out how," Luke said. "Maria isn't going to volunteer anything. She's afraid—and so is Ted— that she'll get in trouble somehow, even be in danger again. I need to spend some time with them, get them to trust me. I want to show her that pamphlet the group gives out, see if she recognizes Brother Michael. Besides, I want a little time to explore the island. I want to get a head start," he told her. "And I talked to Jim, so I know your schedule is clear for the week."

"I thought you'd be more involved here, working on the murders," she said. "And…I still don't know what you found out in New Orleans."

"A lot, I think." He looked at her intently. "Chloe, right now all I have are pieces of the bigger puzzle. I'm still trying to put them together. But I'm afraid for you and Victoria, so trust me for now. Please? Don't make any moves I don't know about. Harry Lee has managed to get five guys from Miami-Dade and Monroe Counties to take some vacation time—for a substantial financial incentive, of course—and come along for the entire shoot. This is not a stupid killer. I think it's someone who stays out of sight, who watches people coming and going, and strikes only when his targets will be vulnerable. And he may be religiously motivated, but not necessarily, if that makes any sense. I think you're right and that someone involved with the Teen Massacre is still alive. He hasn't been an angel for the last decade, either. He's moved around and found victims in other places, so no one here would get onto him. What we did today was try to trace the movements of every member of that church and align them with missing-persons cases and murders in other states." He hesitated for a long time, then said, "I believe that our killer murdered a woman in New Orleans. Her name was Jill Montague. She was missing for a long time, and then they found her body with the help of a—nightwalker."

Chloe glanced over at him curiously.

"What's a nightwalker?"

"Someone who sees ghosts."

She almost veered off the road, but she quickly brought the vehicle back under control.

"You—*you*—met with a psychic?"

"I met with a cop. He took me to a…a faith shop, I guess you could call it, where I met a woman named Mama Thornton. And then he took me to meet some people from an agency run by a man named Adam Harrison. They're psychics."

"I see," she said.

He grinned. "No, you don't. But you will. I've invited two of them down here. They're a couple, Brent and Nikki Black-hawk. She's the one who showed the police where to find the body after the dead girl's ghost appeared in front of her."

"The ghost didn't mention who killed her?" Chloe asked.

His grin deepened. "My first reaction, too. No, she never saw his face, so all she could do was ask for help. Like when you see your ghosts."

She jerked the wheel again.

"That's it," he said. "No more conversation while we're driving."

"But—you didn't believe *me* when I told you that...*I* see ghosts."

"I'm still not sure what I believe. But these people seem legitimate. They've even done a lot of work for the government. And at this point...I'll take any help I can get."

"But if you've invited people down, how can you leave?"

"The wonder of computer technology," he told her dryly. "And I'm concerned about Maria, with the weekend coming up. It's better for me to be down there. Besides, I made Brent and Nikki a reservation at Coco-lime, so they'll join us soon enough."

"Maybe we should wait. I mean, why are you suddenly so worried about Maria?"

"Why was Myra suddenly murdered now?" he asked. "Maybe it was because someone knew that she had been found out as a onetime cult member. So someone could be figuring out the truth about Maria and her connection to the cult, too. And with so many people coming and going for the shoot, it would be easy for our killer to blend in and get close to her."

"Oh. I never thought..."

"Don't worry. She'll be all right. The cops are on alert—and so is her family. But I still want to get down there."

They reached the Grove and decided to go on to Greenstreet's. Theo was allowed out on the patio where he sat in her lap, exhaustion making him angelic, while they ordered. Surrounded by so many people, Luke kept the conversation to the weather, boats and designer swimwear.

When they reached the house, she thought she would

question him further, but then George bounded out to give them a hearty welcome, followed by Leo, who accompanied them into the carriage house, where he made himself a drink.

She realized that her uncle had talked to Luke at some point during the day, when he asked, "So you still intend to leave tomorrow?"

"Yes, but don't worry. Chloe will promise that she'll never be alone. She'll stick with me, and if I can't be there, Victoria and Brad and Jared," Luke assured him. "Or Brent and Nikki."

"When are they arriving?" Leo asked.

Luke looked at his watch. "Any moment."

"I can't believe you'd never heard of Adam Harrison," Leo said.

Luke shrugged. "It's not really my...field of interest."

"Wait. Uncle Leo, you've heard of Adam Harrison?"

Leo nodded. "A year or so ago, someone was trying to pull a murder off by pretending one of the old houses in the Grove was haunted."

"And those psychics proved that it was haunted?" Chloe asked.

"No—they proved it wasn't. The murderer had been doing the haunting so the neighbors would believe the guy who lived there had been pushed out a second-story window by a ghost, or that he'd jumped to get away from a ghost."

Chloe heard the gate bell chime, and George started to bark furiously. "That must be them now," Luke said.

He rose and left to let them in. Chloe stared curiously at her uncle, who ignored her and followed Luke out. She hurried in their wake and found Luke calming the dog while he opened the gate.

She stood back as an extremely attractive couple—the man obviously Native American, the woman blonde and elegant—paid their taxi driver and walked onto the property. They smiled and met George, petting him while Luke announced that they were okay.

Then it was Chloe's turn to meet them.

They certainly *looked* normal.

"Brent and Nikki Blackhawk, Chloe Marin. And this is Leo Marin, her uncle, and a local A.D.A."

After that everyone filed into the house, the Blackhawks explaining that no, they weren't hungry, they'd eaten at the airport before leaving New Orleans. They did accept drinks, so Chloe and Leo led them to the family room, while Luke took their bags up to a guest room.

When he returned, he grabbed a beer and took a seat on the sofa near Chloe.

"Luke says you see ghosts? How do you know what you're seeing and what they want?" Leo asked Nikki, his tone intrigued, without a hint of judgment or skepticism.

"Brent is actually the expert," Nikki said.

"Things are always different—ghosts retain elements of who they were when they were alive, and they're still driven by emotion," Brent said. "They like some people better than others, trust someone more than someone else. I'm Lakota Sioux. My culture is far more attuned to the spirit world than most Western cultures. I fought my... ability when I was a kid, but I learned to appreciate it later in life. Now I consider it a privilege to help when science is a dead end."

Chloe glanced at Luke. He was listening closely, though she couldn't tell from his expression whether he was starting to believe or not. She wondered if he had invited them down just because of her, and she was gratified.

"Can you—can you make a ghost appear? You know, invite them?" Chloe asked. "Should we have a séance or something?"

"Ghosts usually appear when they choose to—not because we ask them to show themselves. And not everyone comes back after death. Most of the time, someone only remains behind because of unfinished business," Nikki said.

"Like murder," Chloe suggested.

"Like murder," Nikki agreed, and smiled at Chloe, a knowing smile, as if they shared some private knowledge.

They did.

Ghosts.

Chloe still wasn't sure how she felt about seeing ghosts herself now. She certainly wasn't going to admit it in public. Yet these people made it sound so normal. As if some people were color blind, and others were ghost blind.

They talked about the girl who had been killed in New Orleans, Jill Montague, and Chloe almost felt as if she knew her, Nikki drew such a clear picture of her, and she said so.

"It's a gift, and it's our responsibility to share it," Brent said, and looked intently at her. "And we also try to help others accept it as a gift."

Uncle Leo suddenly turned to her. "So I understand you're

seeing ghosts, too. Was it something you were going to share with me? Or were you afraid I'd send you off to therapy?"

Chloe flushed and stared at Luke.

"Sorry. It slipped out when I was explaining why Brent and Nikki were coming down here."

Leo shook his head in amazement. "So it's true? I wish I could see ghosts." He turned back to Nikki. "Do they ever tell you where to find evidence?"

"Sometimes they lead you right to it." She looked at Chloe again, smiling. "I nearly jumped out of my skin the first time I saw a ghost. It was one of my best friends, a girl I worked with. I thought she was really there, in my house. Then I found out she had died hours before I saw her. But I got used to it, and now I have Adam and Brent and the rest of Harrison Investigations to tell me I'm not a madwoman. I've learned to let the dead help me, and I'm hoping they'll help us now, too. Chloe, what do you see?"

"I see Colleen Rodriguez, and she's dripping wet."

"But…individuals, mass killings—I'm not seeing anything that points to either a motive or an M.O.," Leo said.

"I think three killers perpetrated the Teen Massacre," Luke said. "And I think one of them is still alive. He may not have been the mastermind, or maybe he's just a puppet and a fourth person is pulling the strings. And I think that when he's not killing in service to some bigger agenda, his appetite still has to be fed, so he goes after single girls like Jill in New Orleans—and Colleen down here. And God only knows how many more," he finished bleakly.

Leo sighed. "And now you're all going down to the Keys,

where it will be a lot easier for him to get to you than here in the city."

"But if he travels to find his victims, he could be in Kansas for all we know," Chloe pointed out.

Luke shook his head. "He's not. He's here, and he's close. And I pray to God he doesn't figure out just how close we are to discovering exactly what's going on before we get a chance to grab him."

Leo had gone up to bed, Nikki and Brent were settled in their room, George was on guard outside, and little Theo was happily curled up on the carriage house sofa.

And at last Chloe and Luke were alone.

"What you did...bringing them down...it was for me, wasn't it?" she asked, curled up next to him on the couch.

"Not exactly. I'd take a lot of gambles to solve this case."

"But—"

He pressed a finger to her lips. "Trust me, I'm too tired to think any more about this tonight." He smoothed back a lock of her hair. "No more discussions, recriminations or puzzle pieces tonight, okay? Please?"

She smiled and wrapped her arms around him. It hadn't been that long, but she kissed him as if he'd been away for a year. She reveled in the force of his lips, the deep passion of his tongue, the wetness and heat of the kiss. She was ready when he lifted her, carrying her up the stairs. They laughed together when she bumped a knee against the banister, and when they reached her bedroom, they fell onto the bed together, laughing and breathless.

She loved his eyes, loved the way he looked at her.

For a moment they just lay there together, looking at one another. And then the world disappeared and they were tangled together, struggling with their clothing and the paraphernalia of his trade, his holster and gun.

After that, laughter became urgency, as their bodies moved together, hot, slick and wet. He was beautiful, hard-muscled and lean, and she loved touching him, loved kissing him. There was something about the way he moved, the way he knew where to touch her when, the way his lips slid provocatively over her, avoiding the most sensitive regions as if his sole intent was to drive her mad. He knew how to tease and when to stop, and she reveled in being able to arouse him in turn, taking him in her mouth, then inviting him fully into her body. At first their movements were excruciatingly slow, then they built to the wild rhythm of a windstorm, before slowing again. He swept her along, taking her up and up, almost to the precipice, then stopping, until she was frantic with need. He was everything that a lover should be, gentle and then passionate, by turns tender, then wild and forceful, exploring every cadence of lovemaking, every magical movement and breath….

She climaxed wildly again, and then again, and he was with her every time. And then they lay exhausted, until they turned into one another's arms and, completely spent, lay entwined, just breathing, listening to the music of the night.

Finally they slept.

In the middle of the night, Chloe was startled awake. Luke was twisting and turning, fighting the covers as he battled unseen demons.

She reached out to touch him, and he woke instantly, jackknifing into a sitting position, staring into the darkness.

"Luke?" she said softly.

He turned to stare at her in the darkness. For a moment she was afraid he didn't see her, but then he groaned, reached out and cradled her against him.

"I'm…worried about you, Chloe. Worried about you going on this shoot. I know I can't stop you," he said, drawing away, holding her head between his palms and staring into her eyes, "but…swear to me that you won't wander off, that you'll stay close to me or the others, and always in plain sight."

"I swear," she promised. "I swear," she whispered again.

He eased back down, drawing her with him.

"Luke," she asked hesitantly, "you're not…seeing ghosts?"

"No. I'm only having nightmares. Though maybe they're just ghosts of a different kind. I didn't mean to wake you."

She leaned against his chest, and he moved his hand over her hair.

He didn't speak again, and she didn't question him further.

She knew all too well what it was to fight the ghosts of a tortured past.

# FOURTEEN

Luke and Brent were up very early; when Chloe woke, she heard noise, and saw that they were already dressed and outside on the patio.

When she got down herself, she found that everyone was back in the main house. Leo was sitting in the dining room with Brent, and Nikki was in the kitchen, setting out fruit and cereal and bagels. Luke was there, too, on the phone.

Chloe walked into the kitchen to pour herself coffee.

"Good morning," Nikki said. "Your uncle asked if I wouldn't mind helping.... I hope you don't think I'm being pushy."

"Good God, I'm never offended when someone pitches in to get things moving," Chloe assured her, smiling.

"Who's Luke talking to?"

"Your friend Brad. Apparently he, Vickie, Jared and a few

others—I can't remember all the names—are bringing the boats down to the Keys in a few days, so he's arranging for Brent and me to go with them."

"Oh?" Chloe said, surprised that Luke hadn't asked his friends to keep a low profile.

Nikki nodded. "You'll be going with him, he said. Brent and I will be watching over Vickie."

"She's promised to stick with our friends, too," Chloe said. "Neither one of us is going anywhere alone, and Brad, Jared, Vickie and I have known each other forever."

"How about you?" Nikki asked. "Did you see the ghost again? It's remarkable that she's coming to you right in your house. Did you know each other well?"

"No. I just worked with her a few times."

Nikki studied her for a moment, then smiled. "She must have sensed that you…have the sixth sense, or whatever you feel comfortable calling it, and she knew somehow that you would help her. The thing is, once you've seen a ghost, they won't stop visiting until things are settled for them. It's a tough road. I know. So, had you seen ghosts before?"

Chloe hesitated, then told her, "After the massacre. They would drift past me, and I didn't even know if what I was seeing was real or not. I had a lot of therapy back then, though, and they managed to knock the belief right out of me."

"Were you scared?"

"Yes. Then."

"But not now?"

"No. I can honestly say I'm not scared anymore," Chloe said. "I didn't know her well, but I liked her a lot. She was a nice person. I wish she would talk to me. I think she knows who killed her."

"She's not strong enough to figure that out yet," Nikki said. "Let her come to you when she's ready. She'll get more and more comfortable, and she'll learn to speak. But you have to be prepared for the fact that she may not know who killed her. Or she may know but never have the power to tell you."

Brent and Leo walked in just as Luke hung up the phone, drawing their attention. "Okay, here's the plan. Nikki and Brent, you'll go down with the others. Rene has insisted on going with you guys, as well." He looked at Brent. It was clear from his expression that he respected the man—and liked him. "Rene Gonzalez was best friends with Colleen, and I'm much happier knowing that you two will be along to keep an eye on her along with Vickie."

"It'll be fine," Chloe said. "Vickie knows boats almost as well as Brad. Their great-grandfather made the family fortune in boats. And if you're really worried about someone going after them, I think Brad even has a permit for a little Colt revolver. They'll stay close. I'm not worried as long as people stick together. Honestly, I wouldn't be leaving them alone and going with Luke if I didn't know that Brad and Jared would never let anything happen to Vickie."

"I can't believe I have to stay here," Leo said, aggravated.

"Leo, I'll talk to Maria as soon as we get there and convince her to talk to you," Luke promised. "I don't want to spring the authorities on her without warning, that's all."

"I'll be there by the time the shoot starts whether you've talked to Maria or not," Leo said.

"I doubt I could keep you away," Luke told him.

"Oh, you can bet on that," Leo said.


The time was coming. The very special time. His hands itched, his palms growing sweaty, as a state of excitement seized him.

The police were fools. They thought they were ready, that they could stop him from striking, but they were wrong.

Once again, God would protect him. And he would prove that he knew more than any of them.

It was all coming to fruition.

The need would always be there, of course. But God had fed his hunger while he waited, and God would continue to do so, even after he'd carried out his plan at last. He had to have those kills. Had to feel the blood…

Still, he had to be smart, had to be careful. This was a time to be cunning, exceptionally clever.

They had no idea about Myra. No idea how close he had come to being caught in the act. Then again, even if he had been…

He would have survived. Those who had stumbled upon him would have died, too.

Including…

The one.

But they hadn't interrupted him, because time was on his side, even though, for others, time was running out.


As soon as breakfast was over, Chloe and Luke headed out to Coco-lime ahead of the others. They drove for a while before she reached over and set her hand on his knee. "So, while you weren't arranging for a different kind of investigative help yesterday, what else were you doing?"

He glanced over and grinned at her.

"I spent a big chunk of the day on the phone, then hopped over to Immigration and talked to an official there about Maria, stopped by the Church of the Real People for a bit, and then I went over to Stuckey's office and holed up with a computer expert who looked like the Hulk on a very bad day but knew his stuff backward and forward. Some of the things we couldn't trace, but this guy—they call him 'Bear' because he's so big, though his name is Lyle MacDonald—is a wizard. You can't access credit-card records without a legal reason, but he can trace employment histories, travel records, automobile registrations and even the Pony Express, I'm pretty sure."

"And?"

"We spent most of the day tracing the current whereabouts and past histories of people who were involved with the Church of the Real People before and after the Teen Massacre, and people who are still involved now. The only consistent name was Brother Michael, whose photo is in the pamphlet the church gives out. But the cops took some pictures the night of the potluck, so I have a few other photos for Maria to take a look at, too. I think the key to figuring out what's happening lies with Maria Trenton."

"But even if Brother Michael was the one who 'bought' Maria in Brazil, that doesn't mean he had anything to do with the murders, ten years ago or now," Chloe pointed out.

"That's true. But I still think we're missing something that will tie everything together. It can't be a coincidence that the cult was involved in the Teen Massacre, whether the killers were renegades or not, that Myra was once a member, and that Maria—who lives so close to the island where Colleen disappeared—also has a connection with the church," Luke said.

"But I don't think Myra knew about Maria, or that Maria knows about Myra," Chloe told him.

"But someone *does* know everything."

"You think?" Chloe asked.

He nodded. "Of course. The killer. Well, and your ghost."

"You believe she's there, that it's Colleen, and that she really is trying to contact me?"

He let out a long breath. "I still don't know what I believe. I do know that there are demons that live in our minds."

"I'm not imagining things," Chloe insisted.

"I'm not saying you are. I checked out Brent and Nikki, and they are the real deal. I found records of a dozen cases they've helped out on, and I'm sure there are more no one's talking about. They're the perfect pair to pretend to be old friends of mine—friends of Jack Smith's, that is—and that means they can hang around undercover with no one being the wiser."

"This whole thing—I mean the Blackhawks coming here, the shoot, all the time everyone's putting in—could be an exercise in pure frustration," Chloe told him. "Say that Brother Michael *was* involved in kidnapping Maria. That doesn't mean he killed anyone. I mean, after the murders the other night, the police went in—at the church's invitation—and searched the church and every member's house for evidence, clues…anything. I guess they're still investigating, but still—no blood, no bloody clothing, no murder weapon. So maybe Brother Michael is guilty on one count but not the other."

"If he brought Maria to the United States to sell her to some bastard in search of a 'wife,' he's scum and deserves to be punished to the fullest extent of the law. If he's going off to Brazil or any other country where much of the population is living below the poverty line and buying children, he needs to be locked up," Luke said. "Forever."

"Yes, if she can—or *will*—identify him. You're sure her residency status won't be affected—here in the States, I mean?"

"She'll be fine," Luke assured her. "She's a naturalized American citizen, and any help she provides in tracking down someone involved in human trafficking would in no way affect that. Believe me, I would never jeopardize her happiness. She's found a good husband in Ted Trenton and a good home in the Keys. And I'm sure they never knew that her kidnapper was part of a cult, much less that someone they knew and probably considered a friend had been involved with that same cult."

"I just wish I could make sense of it all," Chloe said.

"I think all these things we're learning are like pieces in a puzzle. Once the puzzle is completed, the full image will be so obvious we'll wonder how we ever missed it, but while we're still putting it together…it's nothing but pieces."

"I hope the missing pieces come to light soon, then."

"They will," he assured her. But would they? he privately wondered. In the next few days, he intended to get a lot of diving in, hoping to find Colleen or at least a clue to what had happened to her. But that could turn out to be wasted effort, too.

Everything he was doing was based on the assumption that he was right, that there was a killer out there with an agenda. Someone who killed in the name of his own personal and very strange god—or wanted the world to think so, anyway. Someone who was psychotic, feeling no remorse and no guilt whatsoever for his deeds. If his own suppositions were right, the murderer's purpose was to kill certain people not only because his god had told him to, but because he was also, in his own mind, a killer by nature. And his other victims had simply been put into his path to die at his pleasure, to fulfill his need. This person had a plan, he was bright and smart, never appeared to be a fanatic and moved through the world with the charm of a Ted Bundy. *If* his assumptions were right.

"The man everyone loves, the charmer," he murmured.

"What?" Chloe asked.

He shook his head. "Sorry. I'm just thinking out loud."

"Want to share? And what's Stuckey saying?"

He glanced over at her. "There are over three hundred million people in the States, and a lot of them travel. So far, the cops haven't found so much as a footprint at the last crime scene, and they didn't get much of anything at the Teen Massacre scene, either. I'm guessing the killers left by water back then. I'm guessing the killer used the same escape route this time, too. At night, who in hell is likely to notice a shadowy figure disappearing into the water?"

"So…local," Chloe said. She was fingering the locket he had brought her from New Orleans. She seemed to really like it. Was it protective in any way? He doubted it, but he was grateful for the thought. And it certainly looked lovely on her, and she seemed to like it.

Luke cleared his throat.

"I'm sorry?"

"Say you're right. Then the person has to be local, has to know the area. He either has a boat waiting somewhere just offshore, or an accomplice."

"I agree." He looked thoughtful for a moment, then said, "You know, I talked to Lucy Garcia yesterday."

"The woman I met? Abram Garcia's sister?" she asked.

He nodded. "She's very convincing. She swears up and down that her brother had nothing to do with the Teen Massacre. She's convinced that he was a scapegoat, that he was lured to the Everglades to be killed so it would look as if the case had been solved. She thinks that Michael Donlevy—the man you sketched—lured him out there. She says Donlevy believed in what he had been doing, that he was nuts, and that someone else had to be involved, but it wasn't her brother. She thinks someone lured Donlevy out there, as well, not that it would have been hard, since he thought he had done the right thing. In the end, they both died, because whoever was behind the massacre needed to put an end to the police investigation, so he convinced Garcia that murder-suicide was the only course. So, just like

Donlevy, Garcia became another victim of the real killer."
He fell silent for a long moment. "I've worked with profilers, done some profiling myself, and the kind of killer
behind the Teen Massacre *needs* to kill. So whoever was
behind those killings, he moved around so he wouldn't get
caught, and he kept killing, even if not on the same scale."

"I know you think Colleen Rodriguez is dead," she
said. "Even if you're not a hundred percent sure I'm seeing
her ghost."

"Yes, I believe she's dead." She had fallen into the killer's
sights, and fallen prey to his dark needs. What he needed to
figure out was who had been around at the time of the Teen
Massacre, then moved from state to state, keeping a low
profile all this time, only to come back and murder Myra
and the other two women at the mansion. And why.
Because he was certain those hadn't been random killings.
They had been part of the agenda.

He was beginning to think that while it had looked like there
were two possibilities—an almost random killer, or a psychopath who had a clear-cut purpose—there might actually be just
one possibility: a psychopath with a mind so warped that even
as he pursued his agenda, he couldn't keep himself from killing
on the side, because he *needed* to kill, even when it didn't serve
his ultimate goal. The murders that had taken place in Miami
could not be coincidental. And neither could the all-too-
similar murders that had taken place elsewhere.

But in his experience, every murderer eventually made a
mistake. So if he could follow this murderer closely enough,
he would catch him.

And he wanted—*needed*—to catch this killer before another life was lost.

She nodded. "Meanwhile, we're getting to Coco-lime ahead of everyone else so we can have a chance to talk with the Trentons, especially Maria, alone and see if we can find out anything helpful, and also convince Maria to talk to Uncle Leo about bringing charges against Brother Michael."

"Yes. The other models will start arriving midweek, but Jared and Brad are bringing the boats down sooner, probably tomorrow or Monday. And the photographers and lighting techs have to show up ahead of time, too. Harry Lee arrives Tuesday."

They were just exiting the turnpike onto US1. Chloe turned to him, grinning. "Let's act like tourists for a change and stop at Cracker Barrel. I want to buy presents for the kids."

They stopped and had brunch, and Chloe took a few minutes to buy presents for Maria and the children. Then they started off along the eighteen-mile stretch to Key Largo and on to the chain of islands where Luke prayed they would discover the truth—and catch a killer—at last.

Leaving everyone still alive when it was over.

He turned off soon after they reached Key Largo. Chloe looked at him expectantly but waited for him to speak.

"Dive gear," he told her. "I'm renting ours from here." He didn't bother to add "the better to make sure no one's had a chance to tamper with it." Why spook Chloe if he didn't have to?

He knew the dive shop and had for years. Apparently

Chloe knew it, too—his friends greeted her by name before he had a chance to introduce her.

"You're all set. I've got two bags all ready for you," the owner said to him. "You brought your own regulator though, right?"

"Yeah," Luke said, stuffing it in the bag along with everything else.

After that, they were back on the road. Next stop: Coco-lime.


Stepping out of the car, Chloe was struck by the beauty and peace of Coco-lime. Despite everything, that sense of having reached Eden hadn't changed.

Late spring. The days were warm but not hot, and the nights cooled off, unlike the dead heat that paralyzed the area in the heart of summer. In winter, the water was cold, and only the snowbirds went swimming. The natives waited until summer, when the sun and the Gulf Stream warmed the ocean.

It was a perfect day. A mellow breeze played through the palms, and she could hear the tinkle of the waterfall.

Maria had evidently been waiting for them, because she approached the car immediately, Elijah holding her hand, Sam in her arms.

"I'm so glad you came down early," she said, clearly pleased to see them.

While Luke got their things out of the car, Chloe took Sam from Maria's arms and gave her a kiss.

Maria's eyes were wide, and she looked almost as if she was about to burst into tears. "I wanted you to come so badly. We all did. But after what happened…I'm not sure they should be going through with this. It's so soon. But I'm still glad you're here. I'll be happy to see the others, too, but I'm especially happy that the two of you are here."

"Maria, that's so sweet. Thank you very much," Chloe told her.

"You have your favorite room, right by the pool and the waterfall, and Mr. Jack is next to you, just like before," Maria said.

*Mr. Jack.*

Either Maria was playing her role very well, or her husband had kept silent about Luke's real identity, figuring that even though Mark Johnston had revealed it, it still wasn't common knowledge.

Maria looked anxiously toward the car, where Luke was still busy unloading their gear. "I am worried after Myra's murder, I admit. Do they think the Church of the Real People was involved?"

"I don't think the police really know anything yet, Maria. But I…well, just let me get settled, and we'll talk, all right?"

Maria nodded. "I'm going to get the kids a snack. Here are your keys. Just give me a call when you have a few minutes."

Chloe thanked her, noting that Maria had given her two keys for each room.

Ah, Maria. The heart of discretion.

Maria walked over to Luke for a quick hug, then took the boys and left. Chloe joined Luke, and they carried their bags to their rooms. Luke arched a brow when she handed him his key and nodded toward his door, then shrugged and headed into his own room. He was only there about five minutes before he joined Chloe in hers—dressed in swim trunks.

He took an appreciative look around.

"I can see that you rate," he told her with a smile.

She grinned. She loved this room; it was big and had a kitchenette, along with that wonderful door leading straight out to the sparkling pool.

"So what are we doing next?" she asked him.

"Something important, especially for inquiring minds."

"And that would be?"

"Relaxing."

"Oh? And just what do you propose?"

"Some energetic physical activity, followed by lounging around the pool with the Trentons, talking Maria into helping us. But activity first."

"And the activity would be?"

He closed the short distance between them and pulled her into his arms. His voice was husky as he said, "Something that's supposed to be one of the best forms of exercise ever." His lips brushed hers. "Something that seems to come quite naturally."

She laughed and leaned into him, returning the kiss. It did, indeed, come naturally. The air conditioner hummed, they could hear the splashing melody of the waterfall beyond the door, but then everything went silent as she slipped from her clothing and into his arms, and even in the coolness of the room, she felt as if she were melting.

The exercise was beyond excellent.

★ ★ ★

Luke knew he had to gain Maria's trust and help her see not only her own situation but the bigger picture. She was safe, but he had to start by making her believe that. Then, and only then, would he ask her to look at the pictures he had, the one in the pamphlet and those the cops had taken at the church.

By two in the afternoon they were lounging out at the pool. Bill had taken his boat out, but Ted and Maria and the children were all there. Maria had put together a huge tray of sandwiches, beer and soda were chilling in the cooler, and the conversation was casual.

Luke let Maria ease back on a lounge chair and chat with Chloe, while he and Ted played with the kids in the pool. Eventually the kids would need to go up for a nap, and then he would be able to turn the conversation in the direction he needed it to go.

But they didn't get a chance to reach that point. He was letting Elijah dive off his shoulders when Chloe called to him from the side of the pool.

Elijah swam off to join his father, and Luke headed over to her.

"What is it?" he asked.

"Stuckey," she said quietly so as not to be overheard, handing him his cell phone. "I saw the caller ID and answered. He says it's important."

He took the phone, thanking her.

"Stuckey?" he asked. "What's going on?"

"You're on land, right?"

Luke looked over at the pool. "More or less. What's up?"

"Body parts."

Luke's heart missed a beat.

Stuckey went on. "We've got two bodies, I think."

"Where?"

"Get your ass back up to Florida City. I'm in the Everglades. Just got the call myself about an hour ago. I'll meet you here."

"You need to give me better directions than that," Luke said.

Stuckey told him all he had to do was follow the trail of law enforcement vehicles west from Florida City.

"What good am I going to be in the Glades?" Luke asked. "I need to be where I am. With Chloe."

"The Trentons are good people. Chloe will be fine. Just get up here," Stuckey said, and added, "Damn it! You need to see this."

"Maybe you should have gone with him," Maria said, shaking her head as she set a cup of tea down in front of Chloe. "It could be fun, scouting locations."

They were no longer by the pool.

Chloe and Luke had just had their first full-fledged—and public—argument.

He'd wanted her to go with him.

She'd been determined to stay.

What had infuriated her was that obviously, no matter what he said or claimed to think, he didn't trust the Trentons.

She did.

The Trentons, she was pretty sure, hadn't realized that he didn't trust them, possibly because she'd taken the fight inside. They had brought the argument down to a low level. Only a few times had their voices even risen.

Luke, she knew, was really angry that she wasn't willing to blindly do whatever he said she needed to do.

"You want information from Maria," she told him. "You want Maria's help. And Ted's, because Maria will never go against Ted. But now you want to drag me away from them, as if you're suspicious they might be involved in what's going on. I don't think you trust anyone anymore, and I understand that, but in this case I think you're just being paranoid. As far as my being safe here goes, their kids are here. Ted's grandkids are here. And they protect this place for all they're worth, no matter that it seems so open. I'll be safe here," she'd told him. He had simply stared at her until she'd exploded with, "I'm not stupid!"

"Not stupid, too nice. And too trusting."

"But *you* trust the Trentons."

"Yes—and no. You can never really trust anyone."

"So how can I really trust *you?*"

The glare Luke had given her then had just about frozen her in place.

Just then his phone had rung again. He had answered it, staring at her all the while. It was Stuckey, she could tell, but Luke didn't share the conversation with her. She hadn't expected him to. Even so, it hurt.

Then he had left. As soon as he had gone, she started worrying that she might have closed a door between them, which she had never meant to do. Immediately she had decided that the best way to open it was to talk to Maria and pave the way for what they wanted—needed—from her.

"No, I'm fine where I am," Chloe assured Maria. She leaned closer to her friend and spoke softly, though the boys were sleeping. "Maria, I have to tell you, we're going to need your help."

"My help?" Maria edged back, alarmed.

"Colleen Rodriguez has disappeared and is most likely dead. Myra and two other women were killed. We think that the same people who kidnapped you from Brazil, or at least associates of those people, are guilty in those murders, as well. When he comes back, Jack Smith is going to have some pictures from the police and show them to you. We need to know if you can recognize the man who bought you and brought you to the United States."

Maria shook her head. "They're dangerous. Those people are very dangerous."

"Yes, I know. That's why we have to stop them."

Maria wasn't happy. She pushed her chair away from the table, distancing herself from Chloe and her words. "They don't know where I am. I made no stink. I disappeared. That's why I'm safe."

"Maria, listen to me. Once upon a time, Myra was a member of the Church of the Real People. They might know all about the island—whoever took Colleen Rodriguez took her from the island. And if they know about the island and the agency, they know about Coco-lime."

Maria opened her mouth in a large O, but she wasn't

looking at Chloe, she was looking past her at the door to the apartment, which was creaking open.

Chloe swung around to see who had caused Maria to ice up in fear.


"Hell," Luke said to Stuckey. He pointed to the display— there was no other word for it—that had been discovered a few hours previously by two park rangers. "Was this supposed to be a murder-suicide, too?"

They were staring at two barrels that had been filled with oil—and body parts. Both had been tipped over, and spilled their gory contents.

Stuckey snorted. "Hardly.

The M.E. was on the scene. Luckily, it was a man Luke knew, Pete White. Small glasses, sparse hair, intriguing man. Pete specialized in anthropological forensics, and Luke was sure that he'd been called out specifically, since all they had were body parts covered in oil.

Pete, gloved and booted and looking like something out of a biological-warfare horror movie, was carefully examining the remaining contents of the barrels. "I'd like to get them back to my place before we lose much more—may be evidence in those barrels we're not expecting," he said. He looked over at Stuckey and Luke, and grimaced. "To answer your question, Luke, this is obviously murder. Two people can't dismember each other and put each other into barrels. I don't think you need a degree to know that."

Apparently the rangers had been the ones to spill over the barrels, thinking at first that someone was still alive, since they'd seen hands sticking out of both barrels. The first ranger had reached out to help—only to have the hand come free as he grabbed it, with half an arm attached. He'd screamed, knocking over the barrel, and that had sent the second ranger jumping back, knocking over the second one. So now oil was seeping into the water table, and Pete White's assistants were trying to protect the crime scene as best they could without losing any body parts or any more oil.

It was so macabre that it didn't seem real.

Pete dived forward suddenly, almost slipping into a swampy section of the "river of grass." But he steadied himself and grabbed something before it could slide into the muck. "A missing piece," he said.

A head.

Luke let out a gasp, his eyes widening in recognition.

"What? You know who that is?" Stuckey demanded.

He wasn't sure. He couldn't be sure. The hair was matted, the eyes closed. Diesel oil dripped down the face, turning it an extremely odd color. …

The head had been cleanly severed, clearly by someone who knew how to wield a knife.

"Well?" Stuckey demanded. "Who the hell is it?"

# FIFTEEN

"Surprise," Ted Trenton said.

Chloe and Maria stared at him, and he looked suddenly confused. Clearly this wasn't the reception he'd expected. "Uh…your friends are here—to surprise you," he said.

"What friends?" Chloe asked, glancing at Maria. The look of alarm the other woman had worn was gone; had she been afraid that Ted would find out what they'd been talking about?

"Brad, Victoria, Jared and…I'm not sure about the other girls. I've met them, I think. The pretty one who's kind of famous? Lacy Taylor, that's her name! And…oh, I'm not sure. Anyway, they're here. And the other two people Luke said were coming." He lowered his voice. "Investigators," he whispered. "They're docking the boats now."

Startled, Chloe rose. "I didn't know they were coming today."

"Yeah, they told me Monday, too," Ted said. "Like I said, it's a surprise. Anyway, they're out there now. They're lucky none of the other guests came by boat, or the berths would be full."

Maria smiled indulgently. "Ted, you never accept other guests for this week."

"That's not the point," he told her. "Besides, I do sometimes take other reservations, so long as they're out by Monday."

"I'll go down and greet them," Chloe said. Then, suiting action to words, she hurried down the stairs and outside, then made her way over the scrub grass toward the docks. Victoria, bright and perky, waved at the sight of her. Lacy looked as pretty as ever, but Jeanne was wearing an irritated look, and Maddy, Rene and Lena were mainly just windblown.

Jared and Brad both looked tired—though whether physically or because of the company, she couldn't tell—while Brent and Nikki appeared to be slightly amused. As Chloe started down the dock, Jared looked up at her and rolled his eyes toward Jeanne.

"That was the ride from hell," Jeanne proclaimed. "From hell, do you understand me? Hell!"

"The seas were a lousy three feet, and we hugged the flipping Intracoastal most of the way," Brad said.

"Oh, Jeanne, it was fine," Lacy said. She strode over to Chloe and told her excitedly, "We saw dolphins. A puddle of dolphins!"

"A pod of dolphins?" Chloe suggested quietly, and smiled.

"Yes, a pod, thank you."

Lacy really was beautiful, Chloe thought. She was destined

for runway stardom, and though she might never take the grand prize playing *Jeopardy,* she was intrinsically sweet.

"I need a room. Now," Jeanne said flatly.

"I didn't know you all were coming down today—I would have gotten your keys for you if I had," Chloe said.

"It was a surprise for us, too," Brent said.

"Jared and I figured there was no point wasting time at home, and the girls decided they'd like a little extra R & R, too." Brad grinned teasingly at Chloe. "Sorry to intrude on your...private time. Looks like you're getting to know our new designer pretty well, huh?"

She made a face at him.

"We decided to come along, too, and we certainly enjoyed the ride," Brent said.

Jared groaned. "That's because Jeanne wasn't on your boat."

"Hey, we're all safely here now," Nikki said easily. "I'm sure she'll calm down."

Brad rolled *his* eyes at Jeanne, too, as she strutted self-righteously away. "Four hours, twenty knots an hour. It was a good trip. No rain. No wind. She's just being a princess. Anyway..." He nodded toward the second boat. "That's the *JimJam*—she's for Jack Smith. As soon as the girls get their stuff off her."

"I thought it was a lovely trip," Rene told Chloe, smiling. "And I was very careful. I have promised my parents I'll stay locked in my room or with Vickie at all times. And they know exactly where I am. They keep calling me—I think I may scream."

"I'm glad you're being careful," Chloe said. She couldn't help it; she was still worried about Rene.

Brad put his hands on his hips and looked around curiously. "Hey—where is Jack, anyway?"

"He had to run back to town for something. I'm not sure what," Chloe lied quickly. "Now, come on. We need to get you guys into your rooms."

Brad gave her a quick hug and said, "And after that? I'm having a drink. A big-ass drink."

Vickie came up behind him, her eyes sparkling.

Chloe gave her a hug. "I'm glad you're here safe and sound."

"Of course I'm safe and sound. I'll never be the coward I used to be. Never," Victoria assured her. She grinned at Brent and Nikki. "It was a pleasure traveling with you."

"Well, thank you," Brent said.

"No incidents at all?" Chloe asked, looking at Brent.

He shook his head.

Vickie slipped an arm around Chloe's shoulders. "Come on—I need a room. Can I be next to you?"

"Um…Luke is next to me," Chloe whispered.

Victoria looked at her, then laughed. "Great. I'll take his room."

"No! Everyone will know—"

"That you're sleeping with the hot new designer? They know already. Just give me the key. I'm getting into a bathing suit, and I'm going swimming," Victoria said cheerfully.

"All right. I'll hang around the pool with you," Chloe told her.

"Chloe?" Brent called to her.

"Yes?"

"Where's…Jack?" he asked.

"Oh, he…he had to run back to the city to pick up something. He'll be back soon," she said.

She couldn't tell him the truth, not with the others there.

He knew she was lying, and why. He would wait. She was suddenly glad that he and Nikki were with her.

"If I'm not mistaken," Luke said, "that's Lucy Garcia."

"Lucy Garcia," Stuckey repeated, frowning. "Sister of Abram Garcia?"

"Yes."

Stuckey groaned. "So…this really is all…the same case."

"So it appears."

"Didn't you say you'd talked to Lucy Garcia yesterday? And didn't you ask me to check out her whereabouts over the last ten years?"

He *had* talked to Lucy Garcia yesterday, which meant this had all happened between last night and the early hours of this morning.

"These bodies weren't meant to be found," Stuckey said.

"Apparently not. Or not so soon, anyway."

It was still spring; the heat and mosquitoes weren't half as bad as they would be when summer came around, but Stuckey swabbed at his face with a handkerchief and swatted at something buzzing by.

"Damn swamp," he muttered.

"Technically, it's a river."

"Screw technically," Stuckey said. "This damn case just gets weirder and weirder. Ten years ago, a massacre and two bodies in the Everglades. This time, another massacre and two more bodies in the Everglades. Only this time, no note."

"Yeah, well, we all agreed that they couldn't murder one another then chop up their own bodies and put them in those barrels," Luke said.

Stuckey shook his head stubbornly. "This is too much like last time. You weren't around then, Luke, so don't go getting all superior on me."

"Sorry. I'm not trying to be superior, I promise you," Luke said. "Any idea who the second set of body parts belongs to?"

Stuckey smacked his neck as something landed there, and swore. He was dripping sweat. "Damn Everglades," he said, shaking his head. "No, I don't recognize the other body. It's male, we know that much, but we haven't found a head yet."

"Hey!" someone shouted.

Luke turned to see that one of the local uniformed cops was hunkered down, using a stick to move some of the oil and muck around.

He'd turned up another head.

Despite the mud and oil, the features were surprisingly recognizable.

"Hell," Stuckey swore. "Even I know who that is."

"Mario Sanz, head of the Church of the Real People," Luke said.

Everyone had checked in, and some of the girls were lazing in their air-conditioned rooms. From her window, Chloe could see that Jared, Brad and Victoria were already out at the pool. They were boaters. A four-hour ride down to Coco-lime was nothing for them, and now that they were here, they meant to enjoy the sun and the water. Nervously, Chloe called to Victoria, asking her about Rene.

Rene turned out to be locked in the room she was sharing with Vickie, sleeping.

Since everything seemed to be under control, Chloe tried calling Luke. He didn't answer, but he called her back seconds later. "I'm assuming this is going to hit on the news any minute," he said. "It's like damn déjà vu."

She sat down hard on the bed. The sheets were cool, she noticed dispassionately, afraid that she knew what he was going to say next.

"You found...cult members? Dead?"

"Lucy Garcia—and Mario Sanz."

"What?" Chloe gasped. "Lucy? And—*Sanz?*"

"Yes."

"How...?"

"I don't know. But someone cut them up and stuck them in a couple of barrels of oil. Stuckey thinks someone was convinced they were part of the killings at the Bryson mansion and took matters into their own hands."

"But that's not what you think." It wasn't a question.

"No, I think someone just wanted the two of them out of the way."

"Makes sense," Chloe agreed, feeling ill. Lucy had been afraid when they had spoken, but it had seemed to be because Mario Sanz had been nearby. "I...it's odd...one of my patients yesterday drew Mario Sanz—with dollar signs for eyes. But that's what I thought myself, that he wanted money. Lots of money for his church, and probably for himself, too, so he could be like one of those big-deal televangelists. I wouldn't have thought that…that he'd be a victim. And poor Lucy. All she wanted was for people to know the truth about her brother, but maybe someone didn't want the truth to get out."

"Maybe," he agreed. Then, "Dollar signs for eyes, huh? Your patient sounds pretty smart. Money is a powerful motive, and some evangelists become multimillionaires. A couple of them out there now can fill venues that most singers can't fill. One of them was just convicted in Kentucky for kidnapping and rape. He'd been taking nine-year-old girls over state lines and marrying them. Look, I'm still in the muck out here, so sit tight. Stuckey is convinced things are all but wrapped up."

"Why? You said Lucy and Sanz were murdered."

"Like I said, Stuckey's theory is that someone thought these two killed Myra and the others at the mansion, then killed them, maybe to keep them from killing again. It sounds too simplistic to me, and even he admits that it's only one scenario. Stay where you are, please. Stay safe."

"Everything's fine here. Don't worry. I'm never alone except in my room. Brad, Jared and Victoria showed up, along with Lacy, Maddy, Jeanne and Lena—and the Blackhawks."

"I'd be annoyed," Luke said, "except that I didn't want you there alone, and now you're not, although there goes any alone time with Maria."

She smiled. "They came down early to surprise us. And I was definitely surprised."

"Me, too. Though I missed a call from Blackhawk. I bet he was trying to keep us from being surprised."

"Victoria is all proud of herself for pulling it off, so just be nice, huh?"

"I'm always nice," Luke insisted. There was a pause, and then he said, "Uh-oh, looks like the press have found us. I'm going to say goodbye to Stuckey, then get back down there as fast as I can, so sit tight, all right? Hold on a second, will you?"

"Sure." She heard him telling Stuckey goodbye, heard Stuckey complaining about the Everglades, muck on his shoes, mosquitoes and damn alligators. She smiled, listening.

"Sorry," he said.

"Stuckey doesn't sound happy," she said.

"He hates the Glades. He's not much of a nature man," Luke said. "Okay, I'll be back in an hour, hour and a half."

She waited, sure he was going to say something more. Something emotional.

He didn't. He only muttered a quick goodbye, and then he was gone. She snapped her phone closed and stood, ready to join the others out at the pool, when her door suddenly burst open. It was Maria, and she was obviously distraught.

"Did you see it?" Maria demanded.

"I— See what?"

"The television. The news. It's the church again. That Church of the Real People," Maria said. "Two members have been found dead in the Everglades."

"I heard," Chloe agreed, hoping Maria wouldn't notice

that her TV was off. "Maria, did they show pictures of the victims? Did you see the man who brought you to the U.S.?"

Maria shook her head as she sank onto Chloe's bed. Then she looked up with hopeful eyes. "Can they shut the church down now? Can they make those people stop?"

"I don't know, Maria. The members they just found were victims. Someone killed them, and unless the murderer turns out to be someone from the church, there's no excuse for shutting it down." She took a deep breath. "Maria, Jack and I…we're helping the police, trying to find the man who brought you here and stop him, so he can never do it again. I—"

She broke off. Once again, Ted Trenton had appeared, for all the world as if he had some sixth sense that told him when the subject was turning to something he wouldn't like.

Luke was headed back toward Florida City and the juncture with US1 that would lead him to the Keys when his phone rang.

He picked it up, expecting it to be Chloe. He couldn't get over the tension that had gripped him the moment they'd identified the bodies.

Someone hadn't wanted those bodies to be found. Did that mean that something was unraveling?

"I'm on my way," he said without even offering a hello.

"You're on your way where?" Leo Marin asked sharply.

"Leo?"

"Yeah, Leo. Where the hell are you?" Leo demanded.

"Heading toward US1. Why?"

"I've been doing what you asked, pushing the cops to check out absolutely everyone who might be involved."

"Yeah?"

"Wait. Is Chloe with you?"

"No, I— Stuckey called me to come and see the—"

"Oh, my God, you're not with Chloe?"

"Leo, I'm heading back as fast as the law allows. What the hell is going on?"

Leo swore. "I've finally gotten some information back from my police sources. You need to get to Coco-lime."

Ted said, "Hey, Chloe. I'm just wondering if I should plan something special for your friends tonight?"

"I...wow, I'm sorry, Ted. I didn't know they were all showing today. I guess a barbecue would be great, but don't put yourselves out. What can they expect when they didn't give you any warning?"

"I guess not," Ted said, visibly relaxing. "I just...want to make people happy. That's what running a resort is all about." He frowned suddenly. "Maria, are you all right?"

"Of course," Maria said quickly. Too quickly?

But if there was tension in her voice, Ted didn't hear it. He was still thinking about the evening's activities. "We can barbecue by the pool." He was still for a minute, then looked at his wife. "Maria, I saw what happened on TV, and I know that you're scared, that it brought back memories for you. But I have always protected you, and I always will. I love you."

It was beautiful, Chloe thought, the way he looked at his wife.

And her smile in return was just as beautiful.

The moment was so intimate that Chloe felt as if she was intruding.

She cleared her throat. "Ted, I should warn you that Jack and I need Maria's help to try to identify one of the church members, but we'll keep her safe. I promise."

"I'm ready to do whatever is needed," Maria said, cutting Ted off when he would have spoken. She turned to Chloe and hugged her fiercely.

"Thank you," Chloe said. "You're…amazing." She stood up and headed for the door. It might be her room, but she was leaving it to them. They deserved a moment alone.

She walked down the hall to number 7, where the Blackhawks were staying.

Brent opened the door for her. Nikki was at the computer, but she pushed her chair back and said, "Everything all right? Besides the bodies in the barrels," she added dryly.

"So you know already," Chloe said.

"The media air everything in minutes these days," Nikki said.

"I'll be out front," Brent said, kissing his wife on the top of her head.

"Out front?" Chloe asked.

"I just got a call from Luke. He asked me to keep an eye out for Stuckey," Brent explained. "Stick with Stuckey—those were his words."

"Why is Stuckey coming here?" Chloe asked.

"Beats me. I only swore to watch for him, then stick to him like glue. Call me, if anything comes up," he said to Nikki.

Nikki nodded, staring at her computer screen again. "I just called Mama Thornton and asked her to put a rush on things." She looked at Chloe and explained, "Voodoo-shop owner in New Orleans. So, have you seen Colleen Rodriguez again?" she asked.

Chloe shook her head.

"I'm sure she'll be back. Just be as open to her and any others as you can. Anyway, what's up? Did you come by with a question?"

"Some of the others are out at the pool, and I just wondered if you wanted to join me."

"I want to do some more research into the symbol—it's called a hamza hand—they found at the original crime scene, and then I'll be out."

Chloe left Nikki to it and headed out. When she reached the pool, Jared, Brad and Victoria were still the only ones there, all three of them bent over Jared's iPhone, watching the news.

They looked up at her, wide-eyed, as she arrived.

"You've got to see this!" Victoria said.

"I know all about it," Chloe said, sinking onto a chaise.

Jared walked over to stare down at her. "Chloe, this is fantastic news. The police think someone from the church killed these two because *they* killed Myra and the others. Probably Colleen, too. That means we don't have to be afraid anymore."

"What makes you think they were the killers?" Chloe demanded.

"I thought you said you knew all about it? It's what the cops are saying," Jared said.

"They're dead," Chloe said. "But they didn't kill themselves, then chop themselves up and stick the pieces in a barrel. Come on, think about this. There's still a killer out there somewhere."

The others stared at her.

"They were chopped up and stuffed in a barrel?" Victoria asked.

Chloe froze, wondering if that information had been withheld from the press. "I don't know which channel I was watching, but I thought one of the reporters said something about the bodies being dismembered and hidden in barrels," she lied. "It doesn't matter—"

"It matters if you're the one in the barrel!" Victoria said. "It's horrible."

"But maybe justice in a way," Jared said. "They did something horrible, and they came to a horrible end. Besides, I'm sure they were dead before they were dismembered. I mean, you could only cut someone up so much and then they'd die from loss of blood."

Chloe stared at him, appalled. "Jared, that's awful."

"Let's face it—we've all seen worse," he told her.

"Hey!" Brad said suddenly. "It's that Brother Michael again. He says his church is filled with good people, that they cooperated fully with the police, and now they've been victimized, and that proves the church isn't involved. Who knows? Maybe he's right. Maybe his church is a perfectly nice place, and they just—"

"A perfectly nice place that just happens to attract every homicidal nut out there?" Victoria demanded. "I don't think so. I think it should be shut down completely."

"On what grounds?" Jared asked, shaking his head.

"The FBI has raided other compounds," Victoria pointed out.

"Yeah, because they were stockpiling arms, sleeping with children, that kind of thing," Jared said. "But…the Church of the Real People is just a building on a Miami street. Its members don't live there. They don't practice polygamy. They don't promote drug use."

"They just kill," Victoria said.

"There's something wrong with this whole picture. I mean, Lucy Garcia? I just can't believe she killed anyone," Chloe said.

"Why? Because she's a woman?" Jared asked skeptically.

"I'm not saying that women can't kill—just not Lucy Garcia, that's all," Chloe said.

"Oh? And you knew her how?" Brad asked.

Chloe looked out at the pool, realizing that only she and Victoria—and Luke—knew about their excursion to the potluck supper.

"I…I think I saw her on a newscast just after the…after Myra died. She was scared, and…like a little mouse," Chloe said.

"Oh, just tell them," Victoria said. "It's just Brad and Jared. Chloe and I went to a potluck supper at the church."

"You what?" Brad exploded.

"Vickie!" Jared stared at her in dismay. "That could have been dangerous." He glared at Chloe. "What were you thinking! After everything that happened when we were kids, how could you drag Victoria to that awful church?"

"Hey!" Chloe protested.

She didn't get a chance to say more—Victoria wasn't going to let her take the blame.

"She didn't drag me, I dragged her," she said. "And it was perfectly safe. We met Lucy Garcia, and all she cared about was convincing us that her brother had been framed for the Teen Massacre."

Chloe was dimly aware that she could hear a motor. She looked down toward the docks. There were only two slips left, and a boat was maneuvering its way into one of them.

Victoria raised a hand to shield her eyes. "Hey, it's Mark. Mark Johnston."

"Yeah?" Brad said. "Creep."

"Why is he a creep?" Victoria demanded.

"He was dating Colleen and now she's missing, so you tell me. He's a creep," Brad said.

"I'll bet someone from the church got hold of her," Victoria said.

"Oh, come on," Jared said. "What the hell would people from the Church of the Real People be doing at a photo shoot on a private island? Get real. Brad's right. That...creep did something to Colleen."

"I don't think so," Chloe said.

"Of course he did," Jared argued. "He claims he cared about her so much, but when she disappeared, he spent all his time defending himself."

"He had to defend himself," Victoria said. "People kept asking him questions."

Jared stretched out a hand, caught her fingers and squeezed. "If you disappeared, I'd die before I stopped looking for you."

Victoria smiled warmly in return.

So, the romance was heating up, Chloe thought.

Chloe looked across the pool, toward Mark's boat. It was berthed, but she didn't see Mark.

She saw someone else instead.

Colleen Rodriguez was standing on the dock in her white dress, hair dripping, arms outstretched, as if entreating Chloe to come to her.

Then she saw Mark. He was half-hidden by the branches of a huge mangrove next to the dock, and he was beckoning to her wildly.

She frowned, wondering if it would be crazy to join him, as close to the water as he was.

But the ghost was calling to her, too, and Colleen wouldn't call her over if it would put her in danger. Mark couldn't be evil—or Colleen wouldn't be urging her closer.

She'd brought her gun, but it was in her purse, and her purse was in her room. So was her phone, and she chastised herself for not keeping both of them on her.

Why?

There were plenty of people here, and she was safe so long as she stuck with the crowd. Because this wasn't over, no matter what Stuckey thought.

Sad, skinny little Lucy Garcia hadn't killed anyone. Chloe would bet on it. She and Sanz hadn't been killed for their crimes; they had been killed for what they knew, for what they might say. She was absolutely certain of that.

Someone had butchered two people.

And there was Mark Johnston, waving madly at her.

---

Only a fool would walk away from a crowd, given the situation.

She needed her phone and her gun.

Armed, she would go see what Mark wanted.

Even as she thought it, she felt foolish, because the truth was, for some odd reason, she just believed in him.

And in Colleen.

"I need my phone," she murmured as she rose and stretched casually, then tried to motion to Mark that she'd be there in a minute. Was she crazy to trust him? No, there was just something about him. She couldn't forget how he had known who Luke was and sworn to keep silent.

When she got to her door, she found it locked. She knocked softly, but no one answered. Apparently Ted and Maria had left—and locked the door behind them. She was going to have to get another key.

She turned back to the pool. Victoria and Brad were gone, and Jared had gone back to watching the news as it unfolded on his iPhone.

"Jared, where's Victoria?" she called, suddenly panicked.

Jared looked around. "Here. Somewhere."

"Where's Brad?"

"Probably with Victoria." He looked at her, frowning. "Hey, Chloe, lighten up. You're too tense. It's us. The Fighting Pelicans."

She nodded. "Right."

She walked down to the end of the pool and looked toward the docks, still anxious about Victoria. Had she seen Mark and gone to find out what he wanted? Her friend was nowhere in sight, but Colleen was still there, nearer the mangoves now, and looking distressed.

The ghost hadn't evaporated, hadn't disappeared into the air. She was still there, and now she was waving madly at Chloe.

Chloe started running toward the docks. She raced along the wood planks, past one of the Coco-lime dive boats and on to the place where she had seen Mark.

She reached the ghost of Colleen Rodriguez, who had now fallen down on one knee and appeared to be sobbing.

"It's all right," Chloe said. "I'm here." She tried to touch the ghost, but she felt chill air and nothing more.

She stared at Mark's boat, which appeared to be empty. She saw eight air tanks in their slots in the rear of the boat, the ice chest clamped down, towels neatly folded…but no sign of anyone.

Then she felt a hand on her shoulder, light as air, cool, and somehow urgent.

She jumped and turned. No one was there. But before she had time to be afraid, she heard a groan and spun around again. The sound had come from the mangroves. "Mark?" she called tentatively.

She felt like an idiot. Even her fear for Victoria should not have driven her to come down here like this, alone and unarmed.

But Mark could be hurt, and Colleen had loved Mark. She had gotten Chloe to come to her, and she had remained visible because she was desperate. Mark needed help.

"Help." The call was faint, but it was real.

She followed Colleen into the mangroves. There were

roots rising from the water, and occasional patches of dry land. She carefully wound her way through the roots, her heart pounding as she saw a body.

"Mark!"

She rushed over to him and hunkered down. He had fallen like a rag doll between the gnarled roots, boneless on the sand, lying half in a seawater puddle. She was afraid to touch him and afraid not to. She gingerly reached for his arm and felt for the pulse in his wrist, then slid a hand under his neck, trying to cradle his head.

That was when she felt the blood.

His eyes opened, huge and blue against the copper of his skin. "Chloe. Get away. I tried to warn you, tried to tell you…went through her things…"

"Mark, stop talking. I'm going to get help, all right?" she said.

His grip around her wrist when she tried to move was surprisingly strong. "No, had to talk, you wouldn't believe… I found it…here, in Myra's office…I found…"

He wasn't making any sense, and he was losing strength.

"Mark, let go. I'm going to go find Ted and Bill. We have to get you to a hospital. You have a head wound."

A voice sounded in her head. Not aloud, but undeniably there.

*Chloe, run! Get out of here now!*

Colleen's voice.

Then Mark stared at her, his eyes widening in sudden alarm.

Had he seen Colleen's ghost, too? Had he heard her?

Chloe started to turn.

But the old piece of dock planking caught her right in the temple.

The world was there, and then the world was gone.

She crashed straight down on top of Mark and felt no more.

# SIXTEEN

For the fifth time, Luke tried Chloe's number.

For the fifth time, his call went straight to voice mail.

He cursed as he drove. Naturally there was a Suburban pulling a boat going ten miles below the speed limit, and the next passing zone was miles ahead.

He still didn't know if Leo's findings actually meant anything, but Leo was concerned enough that he was heading south, as well.

There had been no way to keep Leo away, and it didn't really matter anymore, anyway. All the dice would be on the table from this point on.

Fact—the island could be dangerous.

Fact—they could take all the pictures they damn well wanted, but more than extra security would be on Coco-belle.

Fact—the shoot might not even happen.

Fact—three people involved in one way or another with the Church of the Real People and/or the Bryson Agency had been in or near New Orleans at the time when Jill Montague had been murdered and thrown into the Mississippi, with a hamza hand carved into her back.

Three.

And they were all down in the Keys right now.

He put through a call to Brent Blackhawk.

"Brent, is everything still all right?" he asked.

"Still waiting, but there's no way Stuckey can come up the driveway without me seeing him. But, Luke, isn't he your old friend? A decorated cop?" Brent asked, puzzled.

"All I know right now is that he's one of the three people involved in this case who happened to take a trip to New Orleans at the time Jill Montague disappeared," Luke said. "Don't confront him, just hang with him—and don't leave him alone with the girls. I'm almost there."

"Are you certain he's coming this way?"

"No, he left ahead of me, and I thought he was headed back to his office, and for all I know, he is. But after I heard from Leo, who's had his contacts tracking people's movements over the last decade, I got worried that maybe he was heading down to the Keys instead. But what I called to say was, don't worry about Stuckey for now. I keep calling Chloe's cell, and she's not answering. I need you to attach yourself like glue to her, and Victoria, too, if you can," Luke said.

"All right. They're at the pool—maybe she forgot her cell phone," Brent said. "And Nikki called Mama Thornton. I know they've been trying to find the receipts."

"Okay, go."

Luke hung up, gritting his teeth, knowing it would be senseless to beep at the Suburban towing the boat. Not even the cops could get by right now.

He thought about calling Stuckey, but decided against it.

Stuckey was one of the three who had been in New Orleans when Jill Montague went missing. Stuckey had been in Miami a decade ago, when the Teen Massacre had occurred. Stuckey had been at the mansion after the slayings there. Stuckey had access to the Church of the Real People. He could control reports and records.

No, he refused to believe it. Brent was right. Stuckey was a good cop. A friend.

He called the Monroe County Sheriff's Department instead. Stuckey couldn't do anything that he couldn't do. He asked them to send a car to Coco-lime. He might not know exactly what, if anything, was going on there, but his gut told him that backup could be useful.

He couldn't think of anything but Chloe. If he couldn't reach her directly, maybe he could reach her through the hotel. He tried the main number and was relieved when Maria answered. "Maria! Thank God. It's Jack."

"Is something wrong?" she asked.

"You're all right? Everyone there is all right?" he asked, breathing a sigh of relief that at long last he was coming to the passing zone. He pulled out and hit the gas.

"Everything is fine."

"Chloe hasn't been answering her phone."

"She's at the pool with Vickie and Brad and Jared."

"Maria, where is Ted? Is he with you?"

"He went out to get supplies for a last-minute barbecue."

Ted was the number-two name on the list.

"All right. Maria, do me a favor. Go down to the pool and make an excuse for Victoria and Chloe to go to your room with you. I want the three of you to lock yourselves in somewhere together."

"I'll call Ted. He'll come back."

"No, no, don't call Ted. Just get Chloe and Victoria. In fact, I sent Brent Blackhawk out to the pool, too, so take him with you. The three of you should go to his room and wait for me to get back. And get Chloe to call me right away. All right? Is Bill around?"

"Bill was working on one of the dive boats. Do you need him? If you want to hold, I can get him for you first."

"No, no, listen, Maria. I'm worried. I think people might still be in danger. The sheriff's department is sending people out. Ask them to wait until I get there, okay? And do exactly what I've asked you, please. It's very important."

"You're scaring me," Maria said.

"You don't need to be scared. Just do as I asked you."

He hung up and kept driving.

No one called him.

He wound up behind a delivery truck that poked along and looked as if it would incinerate if anything so much as tapped it.

He stared at his phone, willing it to ring. Seconds seemed to last forever. He wanted to call Stuckey. He didn't dare.

Nikki Blackhawk was Mama Thornton's friend, and she

had Mama doing her best, he was certain. But that wasn't good enough. He dialed Joe.

"Hey, how're you?" Joe asked cheerfully. "Nikki has been hounding us all to death, you know. And to think—I introduced you."

"Joe, time is ticking."

"I know. I saw the news."

"So, any luck finding what we need at Mama's place?"

"I'm there now, going through receipts with her staff. We're doing our best, Luke. Honest to God."

"Thank you, Joe."

"You bet. Be patient."

Patient? Fat chance.

He called Coco-lime again.

The phone rang.

And rang.

Someone was trying to wake her up. She felt someone tenderly stroking the side of her head. But when she looked, no one was there.

She became gradually aware of the slap of the water against the boat and the staggering pain in her head. But at least her instincts had been right about Mark. He was innocent. He had been trying to warn her, even though she still didn't understand what he'd been trying to say.

Mark was lying just inches away from her. They'd been tossed on the bottom of the dive boat as if they were fish that had been reeled in.

Then she realized who'd been trying to wake her up.

Colleen Rodriguez was there, looking extremely agitated. She was so easy to see now, as if she were made of mist, her eyes…haunted and in agony. She looked at Chloe, and Chloe could hear her again.

*I'm so sorry! I wanted you to help Mark. I didn't know, I didn't see…*

Chloe's heart sank as she realized that Victoria was just a few feet away, as well. Her alabaster forehead was marred by a streak of blood. Chloe's heart began to thunder as she feared that her delicately built friend might already be dead.

And if she wasn't? Maybe it would be more merciful if she was….

No. While there was life, there was hope.

She tried to twist around, to see who was manning the boat. It was Mark's boat, she realized, but she couldn't tell who was at the wheel.

She tried to shift position so she could see what was going on, but when she couldn't move she realized that her wrists and ankles were tied by white nylon bands, the kind used to secure diving tanks. She blinked and tried to focus. Mark and Victoria were neatly bound as well, their wrists and ankles secured like hers.

Feet. She saw feet. And legs. But she had no idea whose feet she was seeing.

She got a glimpse of scenery and realized they were approaching Coco-belle, cruising around to the tangle of mangrove roots and vines just past the manicured patios of the hotel. She had spent dozens of hours there, laughing with friends, sharing drinks and secrets.

Suddenly she knew.

This was where Colleen Rodriguez had died. How easy. The hotel and the manicured lawns led straight to the mangroves. Maybe there were old pilings below the surface. Not that it really mattered what was down there. There was *something* below, hidden by seaweed…something that could hold a body down.

She would soon discover what.

The motor stopped, leaving only the slap of the water against the hull.

Then the killer turned.

Colleen tried to stop him, tried to keep him from touching Chloe, and he frowned, as if he felt something, but Colleen was only mist. She couldn't stop him.

Then he hunkered down next to her and smoothed back her hair, as he had so many times before.

Brad. Brad Angsley. The friend she had turned to for safety, time and time again.

"Oh, Chloe. I wish there were more time," he said. "I'd really like to explain it all to you. You would understand."

Her mouth was like cotton, but she tried to speak. She needed to buy time.

There couldn't possibly be enough time. No one knew where they were, and no one was close enough to help them even if they knew where to go. Still, she had to try.

"I would love to understand," she managed to say, her voice thick.

What fools they'd been, spending so much time worrying about Rene Gonzalez because she'd been Colleen's friend.

But Colleen, like so many others, had died only because she'd been in the wrong place at the wrong time, a convenient victim to satisfy his need to kill.

Colleen had never been the target.

"This is all for the glory of God," he said, his voice ringing with passion. "I am the instrument of God. I must...I must keep my talents honed, and so I release those who are laden with sin. That's what it is, you know. Death. It's a release. I am his machine, and I must keep myself fit, so...I practice my craft. But I'm careful, choosing only those who need to die before they're eaten alive by sin. Please, Chloe. You have to understand." He rose.

Colleen jumped up as well, panicked, looking from the killer to his three victims, but she could do nothing. She was a ghost. Vapor. Insubstantial.

Panic filled Chloe. The three of them were trussed like hogs for slaughter. He was going to kill them, then dispose of their bodies in the water, where they would decompose quickly, where evidence would be lost.

"Wait!" she cried. "I'm just beginning to grasp—"

"Very clever. But then, you always were the smart one. But I'm even smarter, because you didn't know, not until this moment, did you? It's because I'm God's instrument, and he shields and guards me. Actually, I wanted to go after you so many times, but I had to wait until the time was right, until I received a sign. You're the one who ruined the whole thing that very first night. You have the luck of the devil, Chloe. If I hadn't seen that you were getting Victoria out, and that you were too far ahead of me, I could have stuck with the plan. But I saw you, and then I hit my head, and I was dizzy…had to get rid of my knife and skin, but that idiot Abram—who never should have been there—was there to pick up the pieces. He knew I was God's warrior, but he was a thin-blooded pansy, and he screwed it all up. And then Brother Michael said Garcia and Donlevy had to die, so no one would catch the two of us. But it wrecked the church. It was all for the church, but it *wrecked* the church. Brother Michael said that we had to save ourselves because we were God's warriors, and that the church could be built again."

He paused, thoughtful for a moment. "Come to think of it, other than the fact that it set us back, it was a glorious moment. I had killed those decadent fornicating sinners— and had done so like a true warrior of God, smoothly, quickly…and then I ditched my stuff, followed you, and the emergency crews doted on me. Everyone cried over me and tried to help. Pretty great, really." He shook his head and stared at her, his laughter gone, anger in his eyes. "Now you think you've wrecked the church again. Well, think again. The idiot police may have their theories, but they'll never figure out who butchered poor Brother Sanz and simpering Lucy, who was about to go to the press with 'proof' her brother was innocent. He wasn't innocent, he was stupid. And they'll think that Mark killed you and Vickie. He killed Colleen—I'll make sure they discover her at last—and he'll have killed you all, too. They'll find his body, too, a suicide, too filled with guilt over what he'd done to live. And I'll be in tears, desperately searching for you and Vickie. I'll also be rich, with no cousin to share my inheritance with. I'll have enough money to make the church everything I've always dreamed it could be. Chloe, I really am sorry, but maybe we'll meet again one day in heaven, and I'll tell you more." He paused to laugh for a moment, and his laugh was childish, and more chilling than any of the words he had spoken.

"Brad, you're so full of it. You meant to hide those bodies in the Everglades, but the police found them anyway. You think you're so smart, but you're not. Everything's unraveling all around you," she said.

"Don't worry about me. Brother Michael knows all the right things to do."

"Colleen is going to tell everyone the truth," Chloe said.

"Colleen? Haven't you been listening to me? Colleen is dead and gone."

"No, she's not. She's here, right here with us now. Maybe you can't see her, but you felt her. You felt her when you came over to me, because she tried to stop you. I know you did."

He stared at her, stunned. "*You're* the one who's full of it, Chloe."

"You can believe whatever you want, but she's come back, and she's going to see that you get arrested, go to trial—and face the death penalty," Chloe said. She wasn't sure if angering him was the right thing to do, but at least she was buying time.

"You're going to shut up. And do you want to know how I know that? I know it because I'm going to shut you up," he said. "And I need to hurry. You've wasted too much of my time. Now all that's left is for the three of you to die."

He picked up Mark Johnston's body with ease and tossed it over the side of the boat.

Then he reached for Chloe. And he threw her over the side, too.

Luke's phone rang. He snatched it up, praying that it would be someone from Coco-lime. It was Leo.

"Where the hell are you?" Leo demanded.

"Reaching Key Largo."

"I can't get anyone to answer at the resort."

"Where are you?"

"Behind a fucking Suburban towing a boat."

Luke would have laughed if the situation hadn't been so serious. "I've got cops heading to Coco-lime, but everyone's probably just out by the pool, enjoying the sun."

"What about Stuckey? Is he heading there, too?"

"I don't know," Luke admitted.

"And Ted Trenton…he's there somewhere," Leo said.

"Don't forget Brad," Luke said.

"Brad survived the Teen Massacre. He couldn't…. No, they're friends," Leo said weakly. "Why on earth would Brad hurt anyone?"

Luke had a sudden image of the picture Chloe had described, the one her patient had drawn. Brother Mario Sanz, with dollar signs in his eyes. But Sanz was dead. The only one left to control the church was Brother Michael. Did he have it in him to be a Rasputin type, a Svengali, and manipulate others?

Would he lust after the fame and power that could be his
if the church came into a fortune?

"Money," Luke said suddenly.

"Money? Brad has tons of money, and he stands to
inherit more. If Victoria were dead, he'd be worth fifty
million, at least."

*If Victoria were dead…*

The phone rang again seconds after he and Leo hung up.
It was Nikki. "Brent can't find Chloe or Vickie or Brad,
just Jared, who says he doesn't know where the others are.
Luke, I was on the phone with Mama Thornton when they
finally found the right records. I know who bought the
hamza hands."

Chloe held her breath as she hit the water. It was warm,
the sea calm. If she hadn't been bound, making shore would
have been a breeze.

But she was trussed and helpless, and she was sinking behind the boat.

Suddenly she stopped, snagged on something.

The necklace—the lovely necklace Luke had brought home
for her from New Orleans—had snagged on the propeller.

The delicate chain broke, and she drifted downward, but
it had given her an idea. She kicked her bound legs awkwardly, sending her slamming back against the boat, and
began to work her wrists against one of the propeller blades,
praying Brad wouldn't suddenly turn the motor back on. The
nylon cord was stronger than it looked. If she hadn't been

dying, she might have smiled, because Colleen was there with her, helping her work at the cords.

She heard a splash.

Victoria.

*You can do it. You have to do it. Don't let him get away with this.*

Vickie and Mark were both unconscious. The propeller was her only hope to save all of them, and she had to hurry. Not only was she running out of air, but any second Brad would be diving in to make sure their bodies were anchored somewhere at the bottom. There was a drop-off here; just beyond the twisting shoreline and the mangroves.

*Yes!*

Her wrists were bleeding and raw, but she'd snapped the cord.

She surfaced, desperate for a gasp of air.

She caught a glimpse of Brad. He was getting his diving gear on. She was down to seconds.

She plunged beneath the surface, knowing that somehow she had to drag the others up and find a way to stop Brad.

Luke barely stopped the car before he was leaping out, the door open behind him as he raced toward the pool.

No one was there.

As Luke stood, staring, he heard more cars crunching up the stone driveway, and he turned to see two officers from the sheriff's department arriving, followed by Ted Trenton, whose arms were laden with grocery bags as he got out of his car.

Jeanne LaRue, in heeled sandals and a delicate lace cover-up over a bikini, came out of the hotel, yawning. "Oh, thank God. Food at last."

The two officers approached Luke, their expressions puzzled. He identified himself and spoke quickly. "I need you to secure the property—and keep your eyes open. We're looking to arrest a man named Brad Angsley for murder."

Nikki came running out then. "Brent and I have combed the place—they aren't here. Jared said Mark Johnston arrived, but his boat is gone and so is he. Brent just called the Coast Guard."

He grabbed Nikki by the shoulders. "Get Brent, and get out on the water. There's no time to wait for the Coast Guard. Oh God, there's no time!"

He took off toward the docks, his heart sinking.

Brad had taken them out on a boat, probably Mark's boat.

Logic said they were already dead.

Screw logic.

Bill Trenton's dive boat was ready and waiting. Luke vaulted aboard, thanked God that Ted kept the key in the ignition and gunned the motor.

"Hey!" Bill came running down toward the docks. "Hey, you may need my help!" he cried.

"Hop on," Luke told him.

"What can I do?"

"Make her go as fast as she can."

"Where?"

"Back side of Coco-belle Island." It was the only place that made sense.

\* \* \*

Chloe freed her feet, untying the cords as she pitched down into the deep water. She saw that Mark, who had been down the longest, was struggling to reach the surface. She shot toward him, catching his hands, breathing air from her lungs into his mouth. She worked at the bonds around his wrists as she propelled them upward. They broke the surface, and she saw that the boat had drifted and Brad was no longer on board. She kicked, treading water, and told Mark, "Free your feet and get out of here. I'm going back down for Victoria."

The salt water slapped against her as she tried for a deep breath, her head was still ringing, and she had inhaled what felt like a gallon of seawater already, but she had no choice.

She pitched downward. Time was everything now.

She could see Victoria, but she couldn't tell if she was alive or not.

Chloe caught Victoria around the chest in a lifeguard's hold, then shot back to the surface.

Mark was still there, and he reached out to help. "Let's get to shore," Chloe said, choking on sea water as she spoke.

She kicked.

And went nowhere.

She felt the vise of a gloved hand around her ankle, and then she was jerked below.

"How do you know where we're going?" Bill demanded.

"I don't. Not for sure. But it's where Colleen disappeared, so it makes sense." Luke broke off then, shielding his eyes.

There was something on the water. Something shimmering and white.

"That way!" he told Bill. "See?"

"See what?"

The shining white figure on the water. The woman beckoning to them. But he realized that Bill didn't see what he saw. Couldn't see it.

It didn't matter. Bill revved the motor and aimed in the direction Luke was pointing, and in a minute, they could see it.

Mark's boat.

With no one aboard.

In seconds they had reached the boat and Luke donned a tank and slipped a regulator into his mouth, adjusted and held his mask, then toppled into the water below.

At first, he saw nothing, but then his eyes adjusted and he saw broken bits of dock and pilings, rusting iron rods reaching toward the surface.

And there was…something else. A shimmer of white… ahead of him in the water.

He realized that he had found Colleen Rodriguez at last. Not her ghost.

Her mortal remains.

There was nothing that he could do for Colleen. She was hardly recognizable as human anymore. She had been hog-tied and the rope looped to one of the twisted metal rods. In a little while, her body would have begun to disarticulate. Parts of her would have risen and she would have been found, but…by then any evidence would have been virtually destroyed.

Luke felt his heart thundering. At least Brad hadn't brought the others to this watery tomb. Or not yet, anyway.

But that didn't mean they were still alive.

No. They *had* to be alive.

Something touched him, and he jerked around. She was there, like white mist in the water, but somehow very human, very sad....

And very desperate. She pulled at him, and he followed.

And then he saw them, a hundred feet ahead.

He was big and strong, and he had a knife.

And she knew he had learned to kill like a pro.

Brad jerked Chloe downward and took aim. She saw that he had on huge flippers, wonderful for surging powerfully through the water, but big, inhibiting certain movements.

She was free, and she twisted hard, then kicked with all her strength.

The maneuver bought her a few seconds, but she knew that in a race, he would win.

For a moment, sheer despair filled her, as she realized she didn't have a prayer of winning this fight.

But she couldn't just give up. She stroked hard for the surface and caught a deep breath of air, sure that he was close behind.

He was.

He grabbed her leg again and jerked her back down, and this time he was ready for her to fight back.

To her amazement, he paused, just for a second. She saw him blink as something floated between them. Something white and shimmering... Colleen, taking form.

Rage filled his eyes, and denial. He bent the arm that held the knife.

But when he drew his arm back, ready to strike blindly, wanting only to draw blood and weaken her, it didn't come forward again.

She blinked and realized there was another diver in the water, carrying a knife of his own. And he and Brad were entangled in battle, muscles taut, twisting and jerking in the water, like sharks thrashing in a feeding frenzy.

She shot up to the surface again, caught a gulp of air and pitched downward.

She wanted to help, but she couldn't tell what limb went to which body, or which knife was catching the bits of sunlight that penetrated the water.

Then one of the knives fell, pitching in a silver streak toward the bottom.

Chloe kicked hard, surging down to catch the knife. She turned, and Brad was there, ready to wrench the knife from her grasp.

She saw his eyes. Eyes she had seen virtually all her life.

And never really known.

There was something in them as they looked out at her, framed by the dive mask.

Rage, righteousness, insanity.

Then her attention was caught by his hand on her wrist, his grasp so tight that she was afraid she would feel her bones snap any second.

His eyes widened suddenly and he looked past her. She turned, and there was that shimmering white vision again.

Brad had denied it before, but she knew that he could see Colleen, and she was filling his soul with a terror unlike anything he had ever known before.

Brad's grip tensed, and Chloe realized that ghost or no ghost, he was going to kill her.

But suddenly he jerked back as something slammed into his back. He gasped, screamed, losing his air hose, then shuddered, and released her.

Luke! The second diver was Luke, and he was on Brad like an enraged octopus, drawing him away from her.

Her hand, released from the pressure of Brad's grasp, slammed forward, plunging the knife into his stomach.

Blood.

Red against the turquoise of the water.

Red, like the color of the coming sunset.

She stared at the color, at the man, staring back at her with eyes that were filled with recrimination now. Sorrow. Hurt.

She felt someone behind her. Helping her. She turned and saw that it was Brent Blackhawk. He thrust a regulator into her mouth, and she desperately breathed in oxygen. She saw that Brad's body was floating away. No, it was being dragged. Luke was still there, and finally she had a chance to wonder how he had found her, how he had made it back in time and somehow known to take a boat and where to look.

She broke the surface with Brent.

"There, Bill's boat…go on," he urged her gently.

It was over. Really over. A decade in the coming. She felt numb. Cold.

They reached the boat, where Bill was already hauling Brad's body up as Luke pushed. Then Luke waited for her, taking off his mask before pulling her into his arms and staring into her eyes as the salt water rocked them gently.

She was vaguely aware of Coast Guard cutters pulling in to help, but she didn't really care.

They were safe; it was over. And Luke was there.

She smiled slowly, seeing his face. She was alive, and she wanted him in her life. He didn't know how to say certain words anymore, and it might be a long time until he did. But he'd been frantic. For her. And she knew what that meant.

He loved her.

He wove his fingers through her wet and tangled hair, and he kissed her, heedless of the fact that they had an audience.

Then Bill reached down to help her up, and Luke followed. She turned and saw Brad. She didn't need to ask if he was dead. Blood was still seeping from him and mixing with salt water to pool on the deck beneath him.

But it wasn't the blood that told her he was gone.

It was his eyes.

They were staring toward the heavens and the dying light.

And they were glazed, seeing nothing, betraying nothing.

"Hey!"

She turned.

Victoria, alive and well, was standing next to Mark on the deck of one of the Coast Guard cutters, both of them waving madly.

Chloe waved back.

And for a moment she saw the shimmer of Colleen Rodriguez, who, in the end, had helped save her life.

She was there, a shimmering beauty, and then…

The sun seemed to glow a little brighter, and she was gone.

# SEVENTEEN

Silver.

It was the color of the morning sky as Chloe stood by the drapes, looking out at the new day. Night was falling away, but not in pastels. The sun would rise fast today, and so, as the darkness broke, it was as if the whole world turned to crystal and silver. She felt the gentle rocking of Luke's boat, in its little area of forgotten Florida. She could dimly hear shouts from the bait shop as fishermen stocked up for the day.

Silver. A beautiful silver.

The color didn't stay long. The summer sun was powerful, and it quickly changed the world to gold.

Chloe fingered the delicate gold chain around her neck. She was amazed to think that the necklace, with its many symbols of faith, had saved her life. It had broken, of course. They had spent a day finding all the pieces, but it meant a lot to her and she was glad they'd made the effort. She cherished it first because it had made her realize that she had the power to free herself. And then, when she had learned how Luke had known Brad was the killer, because of a trip to New Orleans and the purchase of hamza hands, she had known she wanted her necklace back, just as it had been.

With Brad dead, the story had been easy to piece together but not to prove. Brother Michael had thought at first that he would come out of everything untouched, but Maria had identified him, and pressed charges for kidnapping, unlawful imprisonment and rape. And since he had never gotten hold of the supreme riches he had expected Brad to inherit, he didn't have the wherewithal to post the kind of bail that the judge had set or hire a pricey attorney.

Leo was a top-notch prosecutor; he knew what questions to throw out and what deals to offer. Eventually, they had gotten the truth.

Victoria had been Brad's intended victim ten years ago. Or, rather, Brother Michael's intended victim. Brad had stumbled onto the church, and once Brother Michael had discovered who Brad was and what he stood to inherit, he had made Brad his chosen one—teaching him everything he knew about killing from years spent as a "missionary" and then a mercenary in the Asian jungles. He had engineered the whole thing, down to the fact that Brad and the others would slip away—to the water, where dive tanks awaited them, so they could reach the boat moored offshore, once the massacre was complete. But Chloe had foiled him then, and Brad had realized that his wisest course was to pose as a victim himself, letting his accomplices disappear with his gear.

Brad, Brother Michael assured them chillingly, had taken exceptionally well to the art of murder. He'd recognized in Brad the signs of a psychopath, and though he'd indoctrinated Brad into the church's beliefs, he'd never allowed him to officially join, making the link between the killers and their crimes almost impossible to uncover. When they had failed the first time, they had engineered the murder-suicide in the Everglades. And then they had waited.

Chloe hadn't understood why Brad hadn't tried again to kill Victoria. But Brother Michael explained that there had been no reason for Victoria to die then, not until the church rose again, a sign from God that the time was right. Besides, if she had been killed too soon after the Teen Massacre, someone might have suspected that she had been the intended victim at the center of the murders, and suspicion might have fallen on Brad.

But Brother Michael had known that Brad would need to kill while they waited, so he'd taught him how to hunt his victims elsewhere. He'd been angry when Brad had murdered Colleen Rodriguez—that had been far too close to home—but Brad was what he was. A psychopath and a killer. A charming boy gone horribly wrong.

Together, Brother Michael and Brad had killed Lucy Garcia and Brother Sanz. Lucy had been about to go to the press or the police in her quest to vindicate her brother, and Brother Sanz had begun to think that he really was running the church. As to the second massacre, Brad had known that

Victoria was supposed to be there for a fitting. Instead, she'd been late, and Myra and the others had just gotten in the way.

Mark had been in Myra's office on Coco-belle, looking for some documents Harry Lee had requested, and he'd found a file of old pictures Myra had kept from her time in the Church of the Real People. He'd recognized Brad in several of them, sitting in the background or talking to Brother Michael, and he'd realized there had to be a connection to the murders and it couldn't be good. When he'd seen them with Brad by the pool, he'd tried to get their attention, so he could warn them.

Colleen had tried to get her attention, too. Meanwhile, Brad had seen Mark and been forced to act.

It was terrifying to think of all the time they had spent with him over the years. Terrifying to realize that he'd wanted Victoria dead the whole time, and yet he'd been able to smile and laugh with her while his plan was on hold.

Red.

It was the color of the rose that was suddenly placed before her. She turned. Luke had gotten up early, and gone out for coffee and pastries—and the rose he handed her now. She stepped into his arms, smoothed back his hair and looked into his eyes, smiling.

"How beautiful, thank you."

"You'll see a lot of them soon, England is famous for its roses." He smiled at her, but then his smile faded for a moment as he studied her eyes. "I owe you so much."

"You saved my life. I think I'm the one who owes you."

"You were doing pretty well on your own."

"Yes, I'm tough," she agreed, and then her tone grew serious. "I know you're not a believer, but Colleen was there. She scared Brad. Enough so that he paused for a split second. A split second—and then you were there. And you saved my life."

"I'm selfish. Didn't know what I'd do without you."

He was silent for a moment.

"What?" she asked.

He turned away from her. "I still don't know what I believe, exactly. But...I saw her, too."

"Colleen?" she asked.

"I knew more or less where we had to go, near the mangroves, but finding the exact spot could have taken a while. Then I saw her, a shimmer on the water, telling me where to go. And then I found her—her body—and she led me to you."

Chloe gasped. "You never said anything!"

"I wasn't sure it would be good for my image."

"Your image will survive," she said, laughing.

"I'm going to see them again—Brent and Nikki. And I'm going to take you to meet Adam Harrison when we get back. I want to know more. I *need* to know more."

"I'm glad." She kissed him again. "But in the end, *you* saved my life."

"What can I say? I need you. Of course, you don't listen and you can be a pain in the ass sometimes, but..." He paused, touching her hair. "But you always face everything head-on, while I...I left. Now it's time for me to go back, and then I can move forward again."

"That's lovely," she told him. "Thank you. What time do we leave?"

"The plane isn't until two this afternoon."

"Then we have lots of time left here. What shall we do with it all?"

He drew her closer, and his hands slipped beneath the silk of her wrap, warm against the cool naked flesh of her hips. She moved against him until they were flush, and his mouth was hot and vibrant, wet and arousing, against hers.

Soon they were a tangle of limbs, their mouths and hands roaming everywhere.

Crimson.

It was the explosive color of the world when they climaxed together, then turned to make love again.

Never before had life seemed so precious, she thought then, and she thought the same thing again hours later, as their 777 lifted off.

Luke murmured something as he looked out the window.

"Pardon?"

"Nothing."

He was holding her hand, and she squeezed his fingers. "That wasn't nothing. I think you said, 'I love you.'"

He shrugged, looking embarrassed. "Maybe I did. Look, I mean…well, it's obvious, isn't it? I'm just not good with words."

"So that is what you said?"

"Yeah. Are you all right with that?"

She smiled and met his eyes. "Oh, I think I can manage to live with it."

Then she settled back comfortably. It was going to be a long flight.

And, with…any luck, a long and very happy life.

★ ★ ★ ★ ★